# THE HEALER'S DAUGHTERS

# THE
# Healer's
# Daughters

## JAY AMBERG

ILLUSTRATIONS BY
JONATHAN SMITH

AMIKA PRESS

END PIECE: ELIF'S FIGURINE

First Edition    ISBN 13: 978-1-937484-69-9
AMIKA PRESS    466 Central AVE #23 Northfield IL 60093    847 920 8084
info@amikapress.com    Available for purchase on amikapress.com
Edited by John Manos and Ann Wambach. Cover photography by Yakira_photo, Shutterstock. Illustrations by Jonathan Smith. Designed and typeset by Sarah Koz. Body in Dante MT, designed by Giovanni Mardersteig and Charles Malin in 1957, digitized by Ron Carpenter in 1993. Titles in Marathon, designed by Rudolf Koch in 1931, digitized by Ute Harder and Jovica Veljovic in 2006. Thanks to Nathan Matteson.

For the Turkish people and their dear children.

Thank you to all of those who helped bring *The Healer's Daughters* into being. In Turkey, the administrators and teachers at Çakabey School welcomed me to the country and, through their focus and diligence, demonstrated the deep truth of Atatürk's adage, *Teachers are the one and only people who save nations.* Jonathan Smith and his mates also provided a perspective I very much needed. In Bergama, Fatih Kurunaz and his colleagues introduced me to the glory that was ancient Pergamon's. In İzmir, Dr. Özlem Özyapici and her husband Tigin taught me a great deal and shared with me the amicability and hospitality that is the nature of Turkish people. On various day-trips, Özge Kömürlüoğlu and Çağdaş Baş took me to Bergama, introduced me to people in the neighboring villages, and tended to me when I fell off Molla Mustafa Tepesi. Our rambling conversations continue to this day.

Thanks also to Leah Manos, Debbie Larson, and Mark Larson for their careful reading and thoughtful advice. Ann Wambach was again wonderfully exact—and exacting—with the manuscript. As always, John Manos provided astute editorial input, support, and friendship. Sarah Koz shared the story's entire journey from its inception and early research through its final design, layout, and publication. My gratitude is absolute.

# ORACLE

False gods, all—though all be real.

We dwell on this hill, now scarred and overrun. We reside by the once whispering river, now dammed. We inhabit the sacred grove—or what is left of it. Consecrated stray dogs lie among us with the once worshipped snakes and goats, cats and cocks. Above us, the debased remnants of that wondrous Altar of Zeus. And not far off, the Aesklepion's blessed, still flowing fountain.

We live in time and without. All is present to us, past and future. We speak through time. Listen. The earth quakes at our words.

What now? Chaos yet again, plunder and massacres. Newborns wail, and the mortally wounded howl. We taste dust and ash. We smell smoke in the olive branches—and blood and dung. Devastation. Greed and lust. Folly and hubris. Evil rolls this way.

There are other ways, of course, but you only ask for help when you are already lost.

# 1

PERGAMON, ASIA MINOR; 148 CE

Galen brushes his dying father's lips with a damp cloth. Nicon, who has been wasting away for most of a year, can no longer swallow. Though his muscles sometimes twitch, he cannot voluntarily move his limbs at all. His eyes don't blink, and his breathing is shallow and sporadic, as though his spirit is slipping away as his body withers.

Nicon lies on a couch in the atrium of the peristyle villa he designed. He is one of Pergamon's leading citizens, a philosopher, an avid collector of art and antiquities, and the architect of both the Temple of Trajan on the acropolis and the Serapeam, Emperor Hadrian's grand red-brick sanctuary for Egyptian gods. He was also Galen's first teacher, personally instructing him in mathematics, geometry, science, logic, philosophy, politics, and the proper Greek of the classical Athenian orators and dramatists.

Three years ago Aesklepios, the god of healing and medicine, appeared to Nicon in a dream, telling him to have his only son study medicine. Galen, now nineteen, is the most promising medical student in Asia Minor. He studies at the Aesklepion, which Nicon himself renovated and expanded into the finest health spa in the world. But Galen can do absolutely nothing to save his father. He can only offer palliative care and filial devotion and infinite love to the man who has provided him with every advantage and set him on his life's course.

Galen's mother breaks through the ring of Nicon's friends and the household slaves that stand in the atrium at a respectable distance from the couch. Shrieking, she tears her stola and under tunic. Her screams, high-pitched and hysterical, echo through the atrium. She pulls out clumps of her long black hair and throws herself on her husband, almost knocking his emaciated body from the couch. Burying her face in his chest, she calls to Athena, pleading for intervention.

"Stop it!" Galen shouts as he grabs her shoulders and tries to pull her away.

She turns on him, raking his cheek with her long nails.

He raises his hand but does not strike her. "Get her out of here!" he yells at two of Nicon's slaves. "Take her away! Now! Immediately!"

She writhes, clawing at his face again while the two men lift her off her feet. As they drag her away past Nicon's favorite statue, a bronze rendering of a naked warrior with a bleeding sword wound in his chest, she kicks and snarls and bites at the slaves' arms.

Galen leans over and presses his ear to his father's heart. For a moment, he can neither hear nor feel any sign of life. Then, Nicon's chest heaves and an agonized breath escapes. Silence follows and then, finally, uneven gasping. As Galen shifts his father's body, straightening his legs and resettling his head and shoulders, blood drips from his cheek onto his father's toga. Only then does he become aware of his own heavy breathing and of his mother's continued wailing.

Those gathered to pay their last respects move closer, surrounding father and son. Without looking up at them, Galen says, "Go! It is not yet time." His voice is composed, stronger than he actually feels—almost, but not quite, imperious. "I will call for you."

Although the men are older and aristocratic, they step back and slowly turn away. Galen takes his father's hand, which lacks the warmth he has felt throughout his life. It may not yet be time, but it is close. Very close. He gazes across the atrium at the bronze statue of a Galatian plunging a sword into his chest as he supports his dying wife with his other hand. Galen then looks into his father's eyes which stare blankly into the clear Aegean sky. He may not even be able to see the light that he has taught his son to love so much.

Galen bows his head but does not waste prayers on gods, household or Olympian, that he does not believe in. He feels gratitude for having had a father who was learned and just and moderate and good. But above all and far more deeply, he feels loss—an immense void that, to honor his father, he must somehow fill.

As soon as the funeral rites are performed and his father's vast affairs are settled and the household put in order, he will leave this villa and his mother's interminable, incurable mental illness. Her repulsive display of emotion in this hour is, despite what others might think, merely the culmination of the domestic strife she has sown. Throughout Galen's life she has demonstrated a penchant for harping and hectoring and berating his father, who did nothing to deserve her irrational eruptions.

He will depart from this city that, thanks to Nicon, he will always feel is home. He will go first to Smyrna and then wherever the learning of medicine and the search for truth take him. The enormous material wealth he is inheriting will not bind him but rather provide the freedom to discover medications and procedures that will alter the world of medicine. Nicon taught him to avoid following any particular sect or tradition—Empiricist, Dogmatist, or Methodist—but instead to take the best techniques and curatives from each and to discard the ignorant, the useless, and especially the harmful.

And yet in this moment, he cannot even help himself. He has been taught that mourning is weak and irrational. He knows he should not grieve, but his sorrow runs so deeply that he clings to his father's cold hand. Tears mix with the blood running from his cheek. For an hour, his head remains bowed to the sheer weight of loss. His breath is erratic, and his shoulders shudder intermittently. As the brilliant Aegean light traverses the atrium's statuary, he is so consumed by grief that he misses the exact moment of his father's last breath.

## 2

BERGAMA, TURKEY; 2017

Osama Flynn's scarred left hand squeezes the steering wheel as he drives along the main street. His phone is on the seat between his legs, and the gnarled fingers of his right hand fondle the detonator at his side. He is cramped in the white pickup truck's cab, but his mission is holy and his discomfort unimportant. His black headband is hidden beneath a blue and white service cap. The sweat trickling from his temples and running down his neck is nothing. He brushes his right hand through his long beard gone to gray since he turned forty-five.

Traffic is moving slowly this morning, a snake in the sun. Flynn's blue eyes dart at the pedestrians. The men smoke as they walk. Some of the women have on colorful scarves, but none wears a niqab. They may all be Sunni, but no one is entirely devout. And in the caliphate, none will be spared but those who obey Sharia law. These people might as well be kuffar as he himself once was.

But now he is on his journey to Paradise, on his mission of Glory, a mission for which he alone was selected. Allah is his Commander, and all is clear. God's mercy and righteousness fill him. He has moved from darkness into light. This is his moment to liberate the world from the control of Jews and the United States. To strike a death blow against the globalists, the United Nations and its Coalition of Devils.

When he passes Bergama's central police station, he pulls his cap lower and slouches in his seat. Despite his conversion to Islam, old habits die hard. He raises his right hand and stares at the scars. At fifteen, Terrence Patrick Flynn, who he once was, dropped out of Catholic school to work in Dublin's pubs. But what he did best, even then, was fight—over football or politics or anything at all. "Fightin' Flynn!" He went back to school twice, but the pub life was far more compelling than any classroom. By the time he was twenty-six, he had three children by two women.

The construction job in Saudi Arabia provided an escape from the pressures of fatherhood, and a couple of times he sent a little money back to the mothers. Selling illicit liquor on the side enabled him to live large in the desert until the three stills he set up in his apartment caught the attention of the Salafist authorities—and saved his life. He converted to Islam early in his prison term, before he had ever read the Quran. He saw Allah's mercy and truth in all things and emerged ready to fight for something worth believing in. And he has brought jihad to Ireland and Pakistan and England and Syria and Iraq and now Turkey.

The Bergama Archeology Museum, clean and solid, seemingly permanent behind its wrought iron gate, is a target worth obliterating, but its destruction would not garner the international attention that his glorious mission will. As his right hand slides again to the detonator, adrenaline pops. But no. It's too soon. He's got to stay in control. When the Haci Hekim Turkish bath comes into view on his right, exactly where his operational tactics video pointed out it would be, he slows the truck—and himself. At a mosque also on the right, a new ablutions fountain is being built. His breathing quiets.

The massive brick Red Hall looms to his right. Though the Romans built it two thousand years ago to honor false gods, it is not the target either. And one of its two circular outer buildings is now a mosque. When he turns left onto the steep road leading to the acropolis, sheep are grazing on stubby ground cover in an empty lot. He is transported for a moment to the fields of his grandfather's farm in County Kilkenny, but he banishes the thought. His is a jihadist mission to eradicate the memory of Western Devils.

The truck's wheels rattle on the paving stones as the street narrows between stucco houses. A dog runs along barking at the truck's wheels. A girl on a side street to the left feeds a goat. A little light-headed, he rolls down his window to relieve the cab's stifling heat and fumes. Five bent old crones in long, multicolored dresses and bright headscarves file down along the walls of the buildings. A rooster crows in the distance, and another, much closer, answers.

When he sees a beardless younger man in a white shirt standing in front of a blue door talking on his cell phone, he stops the truck, leans out of the cab, and asks in English, "The acropolis? Is the gate ahead?"

The man's eyes meet Flynn's. "Take the right fork." When the man steps forward, Flynn hands over his cell phone, his last contact with corrupt society, the final evidence of his worldly existence. The man pockets the phone, nods, and says, "Allahu Akbar."

"Allahu Akbar!" Flynn proclaims.

# 3
## BERGAMA'S ACROPOLIS

When his grandfather taps his shoulder for the third time, nine-year-old Mehmet Suner logs out of *League of Legends*. He stows his new phone in his pants pocket with the special gift from his grandfather. They ride up in the elevator from the cable cars' ticket office to the cable car platform; the four other people in the elevator are Asians, chattering in high-pitched voices. His grandfather ruffles his hair and smiles down at him. Mehmet is excited, not just about the visit to the acropolis and its piles of old stone on which he'll get to leap and run, but even more for the cable car ride and the bird's-eye view of Bergama that his grandfather promised.

The elevator door opens to the platform where more Asians are standing in a knot. The cable cars' cogs and wheels are whirring. A woman with red-blonde hair lines up the first six Asian men for the shiny cable car swinging down toward the enclosed platform. Her speech is just as rapid as theirs but less singsongy. The car's doors slide open, and the first six bustle in. As the doors shut and the car slides away, she is already lining up the next six. Mehmet takes his grandfather's hand and grins up at him. When a mother and father with twin girls about his age exit one of the elevators and line up behind him, he avoids eye contact with any of them.

He and his grandfather follow the Turkish woman and the last two Asian men onto the fourth car, number nine. In perfect, musical Turkish, the woman offers him a seat on the bench to the left so that he can watch the acropolis come into view as the car rises, but he shakes his head and tells her he *wants* to look *down* the hill, back toward the town, and out into the sky over the valley. His words are halting because the woman's bright gray-green eyes astonish him. The car clicks over and swings up and away from beneath the station's roof.

When the wind buffets the cable car, startling him, Mehmet hooks his arm around his grandfather's and slides close. The two Asian men, even older than his grandfather, are already taking photographs with large cameras that have lenses that turn. He pulls out his phone and takes a shot down through the plexiglass at the olive grove to the left of the station. When the wind rattles the car again, he slides back to his grandfather's side. The bus and cars parked on the bluff beyond the station are already starting to shrink.

As they float into the sky, his grandfather asks the woman who these people are. She explains that they are Hui, Muslims from China who visited Islam's holiest shrines and now want to see the ruins of older civilizations.

Mehmet glances back and forth between the valley spreading below and the woman's face. "And who are you?" he blurts. It is the boldest question he has ever asked anyone, but she is so beautiful he can't help himself. When he realizes how rude he is being, he blushes.

Both his grandfather and the woman laugh—but not *at* him. She cocks her head and smiles. "I am Uighur," she answers. "I am Chinese, too, and Muslim, but from a western province." She reaches over and pats his hand. "Uighurs are the oldest of the Turkish tribes." She takes his hand for just a second. "You come from my people." Her smile envelopes him. "I've been living in Istanbul for... How old are you?"

"Uhh...ten tomorrow..."

"Happy birthday! Since just before you were born."

*Forever!* he thinks. He has never been to Istanbul, and he would love to go, but he can't find the words to say anything at all. His face burns.

The cable car jiggles as its taut aerial cables run over the first towering stanchion's wheels. He is higher than he has ever been before in his entire life. The two men glance at the car's roof, nod, and whisper. The car rises at a steeper angle so that the world opens even wider.

"Look at that!" his grandfather says, breaking the embarrassing silence. He points back down the hill at a spot near the cable car station. Mehmet presses his nose to the plexiglass. At a sharp turn in the road, two black cows, now the size of cats, are blocking the way of a shrunken white truck.

ACROPOLIS CABLE CAR

 # 4
BERGAMA

$O$sama Flynn does not look back at the beardless man. He rolls up the window and shifts into four-wheel drive. His mouth goes dry, but it doesn't matter. As adrenaline erupts, surging and spiking, he sucks in his breath. *It's a go! The mission's a fuckin' go! Beyond the final checkpoint! Beyond the point of no return! Allahu Akbar!*

He drums the steering wheel with both hands. The air is bright, swirling, the day itself aflame with vengeance and righteousness. *All for the greater glory of God!* His hands shake, but it's not the fuckin' jitters. Not at all! He's ready. All in! Spoiling for the fight!

All of his thoughts should be, must be, prayers. He's devout, a devout jihadist, but Fightin' Flynn is tearing his way to the surface, too. He'll show his father, that drunken, shit-ass bum who beat his mother and him. And the Jesuits who drummed him out of school. He'll show all those bastards who mocked him and his religion when he returned from Saudi Arabia to preach the Quran. And the mothers of his children who wouldn't even let him see his sons, much less convert them. And his daughter who shunned him completely. He'll get all those arseholes that called him a traitor and worse, far fuckin' worse. Those fuckers that jailed him twice but couldn't make anything stick. Now he'll stick it up theirs big time! Yes, his mission is holy, the holiest, but he's also going to go out with a massive bang!

He'll be honored in the caliphate—and famous all over the world. Legendary! *Allahu fuckin' Akbar!*

But he's got to slow things down again. Can't draw attention *yet*. The acropolis cable car station is coming up on his left. It's monumental, five or six stories of tinted glass and green steel and brown trim. Struts and supports like buttresses. They've built a fuckin' cable car cathedral! A fuckin' St. Patrick's dedicated to Western decadence! He rolls down the window and starts to flip off the faggots milling outside the four elevator doors. Stops himself just in time. He needs a cigarette! No, a shot and a chaser! No, the call to prayer. That's what he needs. But there's no call to prayer, just heavy metal drumming in his head.

A tour bus is parked on the bluff to the right, a delivery truck and a couple of cars on the left. He shakes out his left hand, grabs the wheel again, and shakes out his right. He's real close now, coming up to that last blind hairpin turn the operational tactics video showed him. As he swings into the turn, two huge cows lumber at him. Black and white dairy cows, even bigger than his grandfather's Friesians, utterly bovine, slow, stupid, and blocking the road.

Screaming, "Geezus fuck!" he slams on the brakes. The truck stalls. He rips off the service cap and thrashes the wheel with it. He's panting. Can't stop. That could've done it! Could've done him! He could be fuckin' smithereens, and he didn't come all this way, sacrifice everything, to blow up a couple of cows. No fuckin' way!

As the cows file past his cab, close enough that he can smell them, a little girl follows. She's got a stick like a staff and a brown dog at her side. She smiles at him and says, *"Teşekkür!"*

He bangs his forehead on the steering wheel. His hand shaking, he restarts the engine and shifts back into first. He rolls his neck and slouches his shoulders, but his muscles are never going to loosen up. Never. His sweat, gone cold, stinks. He looks down, realizes he's shit his pants. That's the stench—but who gives a flyin' fuck! He clutches the steering wheel to stop the shaking.

The truck takes the hairpin curve. The gate is locked but only with a chain and padlock. And somebody's painted *"Açık"* in red letters on the white sign. He stops the truck again, flings the service cap out the window, adjusts his black headband, revs the engine, and pops the clutch. When he busts through, the gate swings over and clanks against the stone wall that lines the road. Whooping, he roars up the road until he's beyond the wall.

He shifts and then veers right up the hill into an olive grove. Branches whip against the windshield and scratch along the roof; olives ping like black hail. He finds a line up and through, the grove rushing past. He's bouncing, riding the light-blasted moment, rocks striking the truck's undercarriage. He's wrestling the wheel with his left hand, grabbing the detonator with his right.

The video warned him to be careful, but he's rocketing way the fuck beyond caring now, he and the truck a missile. Free of the grove. The perimeter fence coming at him—the slit in the barbed wire right where the video said it would be. Wheels are spinning and rocks flying. The fence's chain links bursting. The truck plowing up the hill. He and the engine roaring. At the top of his lungs! "Allah!" The stanchion dead ahead! The cable cars high above. His right thumb is twitching. "Allah!" The world itself is screaming for him. The greatest fuckin' rush ever!

 5

BERGAMA

Tears run down Özlem Boroğlu's face. Standing on a grassy promontory jutting from Bergama's great hill, she drags on a cigarette, shakes her head, and exhales through her nose. She is only a few meters from where twenty-three hundred years before the renowned Altar of Zeus stood on Pergamon's acropolis. The carnage that scars the steep slope below her is, however, wholly modern —and instantly infamous.

The last of the ambulances and fire trucks left at dusk, but the lights of the police cars still flash. The klieg lights set up by the investigators glare, making the blast site ghostly and surreal in the night. The wind has blown the truck bomb's smoke away, but the smell of smoldering grass and plastic remains. She can't keep her eyes from the fallen cable cars, whipped and crushed, the steel and plexiglass flattened by the impact on the ground. The wrenched and twisted stanchion the terrorist's bomb blew up is only partially visible; nothing identifiable remains of the truck itself. The tangled cables strewn down the hill present a cursive warning in the language of terror, violence, and death.

Boroğlu takes another drag, coughs up the smoke, glares at the butt, drops it, and grinds it into the ground. Twenty-two tourists are dead, two of them children. Nine more are critically injured, including a boy barely alive in intensive care. No one has claimed responsibility yet, but this is the work of Daesh. Criminals! Worse—radical Islamic thugs that defame God to further their evil ambitions. This destruction, this murder of innocents, this spread of terror—Allah has nothing to do with any of it. This horror is only about the worst in humans: greed and hatred and prejudice and the lust for power.

Boroğlu paces the promontory. She is so deeply heartsick and bitterly angry that she cannot stand still. And there is nothing else she can do. None of the officials or investigators here will even speak to her because she has no authority, having been so recently forced out of her job. But she knows better than anybody else what this carnage is really about. The town of Bergama is built upon ancient Pergamon, once the greatest city in Asia Minor and the cultural rival of Athens. Bergama is a UNESCO World Heritage site, and she was until last fall the municipality's director of Archeology and Antiquities.

Bombing this place, which she herself considers sanctified, not only debases shared human heritage and strikes terror locally and internationally, but it also draws attention away from the fact that what ISIL's leaders are really doing is looting ancient archeological sites and selling off unique, irreplaceable treasures to line their own pockets and fill their war chests. Their buyers are the world's rich, insatiable collectors from Russia, Europe, and the United States— exactly the people who ISIL's propaganda declaims as Satan's agents. For their part, the superrich collectors are knowingly funding the radical Islamists they say they abhor. She is not naive to the ways of the world, but she still loathes the fact that some of her country-men, well organized and absolutely cynical, act as brokers for these utterly immoral deals.

A shadow passes under the branches of the trees at the site of the Altar of Zeus. Boroğlu turns as her daughter approaches. They throw their arms around each other, clinging and weeping.

"Oh, Elif!" Boroğlu whispers through her tears. "Elif..." Her daughter is twenty-nine, taller than Boroğlu and thinner, but they share the same strong jawline and high cheekbones. Elif's black hair is long, almost to her waist, and tied back in a loose braid.

Looking over her mother's shoulder at the disaster, Elif weeps harder, her breath coming in gasps. She, like her mother, has lived on this hill for the last nineteen years. It is in ways simple and complex her home. And now it is, literally and metaphorically, ravaged.

"Mom, I can't...," Elif says.

"No, I can't believe it either." Boroğlu brushes tears from her daughter's cheek.

"How could any...anybody...?" Elif tries to catch her breath but cannot. "Why...would...?"

Boroğlu has no answer for her daughter. There are reasons, of course, but they aren't rational, aren't sensible to someone like Elif who would never hurt anybody to gain fame or wealth or power.

"It's...it's...evil!" Elif chokes. "They've got to be..."

When a siren blares, the two women clasp each other more tightly. Boroğlu cups her hand on the back of her daughter's head and draws her close as she did when Elif was a girl. Gradually, Elif's breathing becomes more regular as she rests her head on her mother's shoulder. She is not at all calm, but she returns from the edge of hysteria.

Boroğlu steps back, clasps her daughter's wrists, and asks, "Have you talked to your brother?"

Elif shakes her head.

Boroğlu's hands clutch her daughter as she looks into Elif's large, dark eyes. "Have you heard from him? Anything?"

Elif buries her face in her mother's hair. "No," she murmurs. "Nothing at all."

## 6

### ANKARA, TURKEY

Shortly before midnight, Tuğçe Iskan stares at her computer in the windowless Ankara Ministry of Culture office that she shares with seven others. Despite the horrific news from Bergama, she is the only one still here working. Her colleagues left several hours ago, but she has stayed, culling through the media coverage, the official reports, and scores of files, old and new. Her memory is pretty much photographic, and she is already noticing patterns in the information, *some* of which she will share with her boss.

Iskan, a large woman, tall and solidly built, sits back and runs her fingers through her short blonde hair, scratching her scalp. At the office, she wears long-sleeved blouses buttoned to the collar partly to discourage her colleagues, *all men*, who seem obsessed with her figure, and partly to cover her tattoos, which she has chosen not to share with them. Now, though, both sleeves are rolled up. On her left forearm, in bold letters, is Ataturk's dictum, "My people are going to learn the principles of democracy, the dictates of truth, and the teachings of science. Superstition must go." On her right is, "The greatest war is the war against ignorance."

Just before her boss left at 18:45 to attend a formal, official Ministry dinner, he assigned her to fly to Bergama in the morning. Although the department is an investigative unit, he instructed her not to run her own inquiry but simply to find out if there is anything about the attack that could embroil him or his domain in the investigation. He chose her because she has had previous business in Bergama, and, most likely, he wanted to get her the hell out of the office.

Iskan's official Ministry cell phone pings, but she doesn't immediately check it. She logs out and shuts down her computer, then takes a deep breath and exhales. Her group—she would not call them a *team*—is supposed to be investigating criminals involved in the smuggling of antiquities out of Turkey, but most of the leads she has generated since she joined the unit eleven months ago have simply vanished into the Ministry's bowels. Only one of her reports on a lesser target has led to an arrest. And her colleagues in the office have shunned her because she gets so much work done.

When Iskan was a child, she was ostracized within her family because she was left-handed and, therefore, unclean—the child of the Devil. Her mother never allowed her to cook or even enter the kitchen when food was being prepared. Still, she obstinately refused, even when very young, to do tasks right-handed. She retreated to her room, taught herself to read, and devoured books. Only over time did she become aware that others could not, as she could, read a text once and then always picture it later. This gift, if it really was a gift, was something she did not share even with her parents and her older sister and brother. Nor has she shared it with the men in this office. She does not at all mind missing out on the office's rumors and gossip, but there must at *some point* have been *something* relevant to her investigations that *someone* should have proffered.

When Iskan checks her Ministry phone, there is a single text message confirming her flight from Ankara to İzmir at 7:15 in the morning. On her private iPhone, which she always keeps silent, there is an e-mail from her anonymous source. In the past four months, she has received numerous photos of and documents about Hamit Antique Emporium, the most venerable of the licensed, established dealers of Hellenistic and Roman antiquities in Istanbul. Turkish regulations concerning the sale and export of antiquities have become exponentially more byzantine, but the Hamit family still releases an annual catalog of stunning jewelry, artifacts, and statuary for which it has legal provenance. There have, of course, been stories that the family moved into the lucrative illegal markets long ago and, worse, has established recent ties to the Daesh terrorists who are plundering ancient cultural treasures in Iraq and Syria. Antiquities now comprise a minor part of the family's extensive financial holdings. And as long as the legitimate family business makes a few astronomical sales each year and the family continues to make lavish donations to certain public entities, no one in the government is going to question the integrity of the firm. In fact, her initial investigation into the family's operations was quashed within two weeks of her opening it last year. This source has, however, recently gotten her again intrigued enough to follow up on her own time. She has kept all of her relevant files on a private server outside the office.

As usual, the e-mail has no message, just an attachment. When Iskan clicks on the icon, she finds a single photograph, a long shot of two men sitting on a stone bench in a park. She is not one who startles easily, but as she zooms in on their faces, her breath catches. The well-dressed, silver-haired man on the right is Mustafa Hamit, the family's patriarch, but she also recognizes the older portly man on the left—a Russian diplomat stationed at the consulate in Istanbul who is widely recognized both as a spy and a member of the Russian president's inner circle. It can't be. The two men might well do business together but would never be seen together in public. It doesn't make any sense. Or, does it? A pattern forms in her mind, a possible fit within a sequence of other images.

Iskan unfastens the top three buttons of her blouse, revealing two more Ataturk quotes, each curved below a collarbone. Her subdued demeanor during office hours belies a deeper, vibrant, and, at times, more fierce energy that, since her childhood, has often emerged at night when she is alone and imagery and information are forming and reforming into something akin to understanding. Still holding the iPhone, she pumps her arms in the air and then dances among the desks, exulting—strutting, high-stepping, bobbing and weaving, but not smiling. The phone held high in her left hand, she whirls and whirls.

She stops abruptly. Lowers the phone. Stares at the image on the phone. It's real, not Photoshopped. She's sure. What, other than the obvious one about collusion, are the implications? Who is setting up whom? Which one of the men was being followed? Who was the follower? Why? And, who is her source? *What's in it for him?* Her visual memory is spectacular, but she has at times in her life jumped to conclusions. She has got to slow herself down. Do her due diligence. Scour her electronic sources. Utilize her methodology. Make the case, not merely break it.

# 7

BERGAMA

At seven thirty in the morning, Recep Ateş carries two cups of Starbucks coffee toward the bench on which Özlem Boroğlu sits. Without saying anything, he hands her a cup as he joins her. Nodding her thanks but not looking at him, she draws deeply on her cigarette. Once each week for seven years, they have met here on the second level of this tiered park cut into the hill overlooking Bergama's main street. The park lies near his Ministry of Culture office on the Bergama Museum grounds and not far from the office she had at the town's municipal building. Their meetings most often began with remarks about the weather and questions about her children and his sixteen-year-old twin girls, but pleasantries aren't possible today.

"Three more died during the night," she says as she exhales. Her hand holding the coffee shakes. A heavy truck shifts gears as it rumbles by, but, given the hour, the road isn't yet congested.

He takes a slow, deep breath and then sips his coffee. When she turns her head toward him, he sees her bloodshot eyes. He has not slept either.

"The two dead children are twin eight-year-old girls."

He nods. "Yes," he says. "Both Sirma and Ferida told me that, too. How is Elif taking it?"

"Hard. She's very sad. Distraught." She sighs. "Angry…"

"Like the rest of us," Ateş says.

"But even worse. Taking it all so personally…like she has to…do something… "

"You mean, like her mother."

Boroğlu glares at him for a moment but does not contradict him. Then, shaking her head, she says, "Serkan hasn't even called."

Ateş, knowing better than to pursue that topic, takes another sip of coffee. He is an exceptionally large man, even sitting down a full head taller than she is. An ex-basketballer good enough to play at university but not professionally, he has grown thick and heavy; his hair is short, gray at the temples and thin on top.

"You've visited the site?" she asks.

"Yes. Scorched earth. Crushed cable cars. Blood. It's even more horrifying than the media is showing." He sniffs his coffee. "The stench of the burnt…" He looks away at something she cannot see, then stares at the steam from his coffee. "I saw you on the acropolis…" He tries to force a smile but cannot. "Or at least the glow of your cigarette." She has, for as long as he has known her, climbed in the evenings from her house to the site of the Altar of Zeus, where she can best think—and brood and scheme.

"Any news on the killer?" she asks.

"An outsider. Foreign. My age or older. A witness, a little girl from the neighborhood, saw him just before the explosion. Apparently said he was mean looking. Scary blue eyes. And a long black and white beard."

"And?" she asks. They have for years briefed each other on what is happening at the area's archeological sites, in town, and at their respective, sometimes contentious, offices. But she is no longer connected to, much less the titular head of, her office. She has nothing to trade, but she needs the information. And nothing even remotely like this has ever occurred.

He takes a deep breath. "And there are fingerprints, perhaps even DNA. The girl said he was wearing a cap. Investigators found a cap on the road near the grove. They'll probably release a name by this afternoon."

"He couldn't have acted alone."

Ateş doesn't answer right away. He scratches his chin, the whiskers dark even after he has just shaved. "That's true."

"Someone must've provided the truck…the bomb." She drops her cigarette butt onto the cement and grinds it with the heel of her shoe. "But who would…?"

"Somebody connected to Daesh. Nobody from town."

She sucks in her breath, gazes up at the pale morning sky, and exhales slowly. "Where does that leave us?"

He leans out, his forearms on his thighs, like a coach looking over at his player. "It leaves you entirely out of it—and out of harm's way."

She purses her lips. Like her daughter, she can't leave any of this be. It's too close to home, both her family's and her work's, too horrific, *too evil*. "And what about you?" she asks.

"I don't know. Wait, I guess. See if there's anything I can help with."

She puts her cup on the cement next to the bench and then lights another cigarette. "But you know what this is about."

He looks into her bleary eyes. "Another terrorist attack on a Middle Eastern UNESCO World Heritage site."

"But why *this* site, Recep?"

He shrugs and drinks his coffee. "Why not this site?"

"You know what I mean." Her tone is for the first time sharp. "We're close. We've got to be."

"I know what you're thinking." He shakes his head. "But, Özlem, not everything has to be connected."

She stares at him, holding his gaze. "This is."

# 8

GÖREME, TURKEY

In late afternoon, three people sit around a table on the cave hotel's veranda in the heart of Cappadocia. They look out at scores of the valley's fairy chimneys, huge cone-shaped tufa pillars capped with basalt. Wind and water have eroded them for ages, and people have been hollowing out caves for homes and churches for longer than two millennia.

"It has nothing to do with you," Jack, the elderly Californian, says as he raises his Glenlivet on the rocks with a twist. "You've been terrific." His skin is leathery, but the glint in his eyes is youthful, both, perhaps, the by-products of his having accumulated vast wealth in oil and natural gas. "Given the situation, we need to change our itinerary."

Serkan Boroğlu nods, but his mind is screaming. He has spent the last five days with this couple, providing them with an upscale, elite personal tour of Pergamon, Ephesus, and Cappadocia, topped off by this morning's hot-air-balloon excursion. He is supposed to take them on his special private tour of Istanbul the next five days, but the Bergama bombing has spooked them.

"A couple of days earlier," Clare says, "and we would've been on that cable car."

Serkan nods again. He knows all too well that she's right. He would have been there with them. He has been a high-end Turkish tour guide for almost five years, and yesterday's atrocity is a crippling blow to an already hobbled industry. And, personally, it's a knife to his throat. He can't put out of his head the fact that he grew up only a short walk from Bergama's funicular that carries passengers up to ancient Pergamon's acropolis. His mother and sister still live in Bergama. Neither would, each for her own reasons, ever ride the cable cars, but still. He has been meaning to call to check on them, but he's been too busy.

Clare reaches across the table and brushes her fingers across the back of Serkan's hand. "And we will, of course, pay your full fee," she says. Twenty-five years younger than her husband, she is not, as Serkan first thought, a trophy wife. She is tall and tan and thin, a bottle-blonde with large blue eyes, but she is even smarter than her husband and more driven, a successful attorney who is always checking messages and has long jargon-filled conversations every night with her office in Los Angeles. Her iPhone, never far from her, lies on the table next to her glass of French pinot noir.

"Yes," Serkan says, "thank you." His lopsided smile and dark eyes often attract his foreign guests, especially the women. Glancing at his Heineken, he does not reach for the bottle—he has already spent their full fee and more. Pigeons are cooing somewhere nearby, and a flurry of small dark birds whirls in the light above the hotel's fairy chimney.

"We've booked a couple of nights in Crete and a couple in Rhodes before we head to the Holy Land," Jack says.

"But we'll still meet you in Istanbul to pick up our order on the twenty-third before we fly home," Clare adds.

The Californian sips his scotch and leans toward Serkan. "Perhaps," he says, "in the meantime, you can find something really nice for Clare. Another memento of our trip to Asia Minor."

Serkan's mind spins. "That's a nice idea," he answers to buy himself time. He has already sold them half a dozen of his sister's terracotta figurines. And the couple has also arranged to have his sister fashion a gold amulet for Clare—a unique design that she and Elif conceived together.

"Something old, of real, *lasting* value," Jack adds.

"Yes," Serkan says. "That's a *very* nice idea. And something I'm sure I can arrange." His part of the profit would help keep him financially afloat for another couple of months. As his mind clears, he turns to Clare. He prefers younger women, like the full-bodied Bavarian he is currently dating, but Clare is, he must admit, very attractive. "Yes," he repeats, "I have exactly the right contacts."

"Gold, also?" she asks.

"Yes. Of course."

"I'd like that, Serkan." Holding his gaze, she traces her forefinger around the rim of her wineglass. "That would be lovely."

Sipping his scotch, Jack smiles.

"Instead of my sister's amulet?" Serkan asks.

As Clare shrugs, her smile is coy. She gazes at her husband. *"In addition to..."*

Serkan tries not to look surprised. He needs a sip of his beer but holds himself back. "That can be arranged," he says.

"I would like something *ancient,* Serkan," she says, cocking her head and again holding his gaze.

He looks over at the fairy chimneys, focusing on one with steps carved from the same volcanic ash as the cone itself. The window above the door frames a large green vase holding sunflowers.

His smile widening, Jack says, "Clare tends to get what she wants."

Serkan tries not to show his excitement, but when he does finally drink his Heineken, beer almost fizzes out his nose. He stifles a cough. Sweat runs down his spine. After the Istanbul terrorist attacks and the failed coup, his private, high-end tour business, like everyone's, has gone into the toilet. Three years ago, he worked 297 days, last year 137, and this year only 29 in the first four months. To meet his ever-increasing costs of living, he has had to launch two new ventures—taking kinky clients to forbidden Istanbul locales and selling antiquities to wealthy foreigners. The former, which requires only au courant information and a bit of bribery, is far less complicated. In the latter, he is working on commission, a finder's fee actually, for a powerful and influential family with strict protocols. This would be his fifth sale, and by far the most lucrative.

"Whatever you like can be arranged." His voice doesn't crack, but he feels like he is outside himself looking in. "What do you have in mind?"

"Another amulet. Something from the Roman period. Or Hellenistic. Egyptian might do." Clare's smile is soft as she swirls the wine in her glass. "Or perhaps even older. Something my jeweler might turn into a pendant."

"We can find something you'll love, I'm sure." The word "we" is used loosely. He is an honors economics graduate who felt that an academic life, like that which his father has lived, would be dull. He is a man fluent in German as well as English and Turkish. A man bright enough to have learned in less than five years everything he needs to know to entertain worldly foreigners at sites historic and esoteric. And this moment, maybe his last chance to make his business work, is exhilarating. Suddenly, he's rising from the depths, ready to take wing among the fairy chimneys, to soar beyond the hot air balloons.

Jack puts down his scotch, leans forward with his forearms on the table, and, fixing his gaze on Serkan, asks, "Should we be talking to somebody else?"

His wife picks up her phone and begins tapping.

"No," Serkan says. "Absolutely not. My connections have a long history of trading in antiquities. Customers are *always* satisfied." This conversation has been so abrupt. There hasn't even been any mention of price. And, actually, the Hamits invite no outsiders, and certainly not him, into their inner workings. But their reputation is impeccable. If a sale ever went wrong, no one he knows has ever found out about it.

Still leaning forward, Jack says, "And customs? Will there be guarantees in place?"

"No problem," Serkan says. "No problem." He knows he needs to stop repeating himself. "All the paperwork is taken care of. Guaranteed." At least, that was what was done on earlier, smaller deals.

Clare sighs and places her phone on the table in front of him. "Something very much like this, Serkan," she says, "would please me."

He stares at the golden image of a goddess similar to some of those his sister has made.

"Or this," she says, flicking the phone's face.

Staring back at him is a svelte, ornately dressed golden goddess with the head of a lion.

 9

KAIKOS VALLEY, TURKEY

Five kilometers northwest of Bergama, six women in their twenties and thirties file up a steep, narrow trail toward a rock escarpment. The first and last carry backpacks; the middle four hold hand drums. The air is dry, the breeze tangy. The gibbous moon is past its zenith, and stars blink in the hazy night. The women do not talk, but their footfalls on the stone and dirt have a distinct rhythm. Traffic hums in the distance, and cicadas buzz close by. Somewhere in the Kaikos Valley below, a dog is barking.

When the women reach a niche cut into the rock formation, the leader, Elif Boroğlu, takes from her backpack a small figurine, an unpainted terra-cotta mother goddess with a headdress. As the women chant softly, she places the figurine reverently in the niche. After a minute, they start up the path again, but their low chanting continues. Their chant is, as always, spontaneous, and they pass the melody among themselves as they walk.

High up the escarpment, when the trail cuts back, the procession stops near the narrow mouth of a cave. A spring whispers from the rocks to their right. Though they are far enough from Bergama that the town is mute, the sightline to ancient Pergamon's acropolis is clear, the pale temple columns stark even at this distance. Still chanting, each woman takes off her clothes and piles them neatly on the rock next to the spring. In nakedness, they have learned, is honesty.

Elif, the only one of the women without tattoos, takes three more figurines, human rather than mother goddesses, from her backpack. One is painted dull black, the second the pale blue of the sky just before sunrise, and the third a glossy yellow. She places them as an offering on a horizontal stone shelf cut next to the cave's mouth. The women form a semicircle, and each begins to sway to her internal music.

The drumming starts slowly, the rhythm clear but not yet relentless. One woman double steps into the semicircle, twirls, raises her drum first to the night sky and then to the cave. "Oh, Mother Goddess," she calls out, "by every name you are known in every place, take the souls of those murdered in our ancient city! Take these innocents into your heart and purify them for their journey! Wash all of us of our impurities!" She lowers her head and beats her drum harder.

A second woman steps forward, takes up the beat, spins, stomps hard, and spits into the dirt. "We mourn the passing of innocence!" she sings. "We mourn the loss of families, of mothers and fathers and dear children and grandparents!" Her voice rises. "And we curse the violence of men! Their destructiveness! Their evil! Their stupidity! Their arrogance! Their narcissism!" She squats, spits again, and leaps wailing at the moon. "Oh, we curse their arrogance!"

A third, already weeping, calls, "Oh, Mother, help us understand what cannot be understood! We entreat you, help us comprehend incomprehensible evil!" She raises her arms and shakes her hands. "Give us the wisdom," she cries, "of the ages that we now need so deeply! Send us a cure for the pain that wracks our souls!"

The fourth woman shouts again for vengeance, and the fifth takes a list from a backpack and calls out the names of all of those killed on Bergama's funicular. She repeats the names of the eight-year-old twins again and again until their names become a single incantation. The women are all sweating now, each swinging, each calling, each beating time. The moon turns, and the stars rotate.

The women's rituals are never scripted, their actions never preset. Their incantations are always new, and, though they sometimes utter the names of the old mother goddesses—Cybele and Meter and

Isis and others—it is the current transgressions of humans that they bewail. And it is the sanctity of the earth, of the world *now,* that they honor, this moment in time. Often they step out of time, dance beyond time, but they remain present to this escarpment, this cave, this spring, this night, this air, and the dust they stir in this moment.

Finally, Elif takes up the black figurine and steps into the center of the tightening semicircle. The drumming around her is unrelenting, the passion still rising. "Hear our sadness, Mother!" she sings, her voice beautiful, high and haunting. "Hear our anger, oh, Mother! Feel our pain! Feel the ache in our hearts and in our town!" Her voice rises in pitch. "Lament with us the senseless horror that has been visited upon us!" She raises the figurine with both hands as she pirouettes. She then lowers her right hand that holds the figurine, turns, cocks her arm, and hurls it against the escarpment above the cave's mouth. It shatters, showering the dancers with shards.

"Give us hope, Mother!" Elif intones. "Give us strength! Give us the power to overcome! To carry on! To go forth! To make things right! To love!" Spinning, she can't catch her breath. "To love! To love!" Her voice rises above words, beyond language.

The others whirl with her but not in unison, each in her own universe. They are all sweating and panting, pale gleaming shadows hidden in the night from outsiders. Their voices rise with Elif's, but none speaks words. Their incantations fly well beyond the discourse of any dogma, beyond the languages of cults or tribes or nationalities, beyond any dialects of man. In the valley, dogs bark.

 10

BERGAMA

Tuğçe Iskan glances at the raspberry-colored steel door at street level before climbing the flight of concrete steps to the main entrance. The stone house—Greek, predating the 1923 Turkish–Greek population exchange—is the uppermost in the last line of private dwellings below the barbed-wire-topped, chain-link fence that encircles Pergamon's ancient acropolis. Iskan raps on the steel double door, also raspberry, and steps back. One steel-framed window is to her right, and two are to her left. Steel bars, also painted raspberry, protect all three windows. The stonework and masonry are exceptional and probably, if she felt that way about buildings, beautiful.

The door opens a crack and then slams shut. Iskan takes a deep breath and turns. The front porch provides a panoramic view of Bergama's red tile roofs and the Kaikos Valley beyond, where the morning haze is just beginning to burn off. Across the narrow cobblestone street, graffiti mars the windowless concrete back wall of the next property downhill of the acropolis. She knocks on the door again and waits.

Özlem Boroğlu opens the door, steps out onto the front porch, and says, "Good morning, Tuğçe." Her eyes are not as bloodshot as they were yesterday morning, but the bags under them are darker. "You might have called before you came."

"Good morning, Özlem Hanim," Iskan answers, her voice deep. "I did call, but there was no answer." Her blonde hair, though cut short, is not cropped. Her white shirt's crew neck and long sleeves cover her tattoos. "How are you?"

"I'm upset about the tragedy in my neighborhood. And worried that terrorism has burst the Bergama bubble."

"Yes, I understand. That's why I'm in town."

"Why is the Ministry of Culture involved in a terrorism investigation?"

"May we talk, Özlem?"

Boroğlu massages her temple with the fingers of her right hand. "Is this an official interview?"

"No, it is not."

Boroğlu takes a pack of cigarettes and a red lighter from her pocket and then says, "Join me in our rooftop garden."

The house's cobblestone courtyard is large and swept clean. An olive tree stands alone in the sunshine below the high, stone back wall cut into the steep hillside. To the right, a covered terrace has an outdoor oven and a long wooden table with six chairs. In an alcove to the left, small brightly painted terra-cotta goddesses line the shelves and stand wherever space is available. The old woman sewing on a bench in the shade near the stone stairwell does not look up as Iskan climbs the stairs behind Boroğlu.

They are greeted on the patio by dozens more of the polychromatic terra-cotta goddesses set on shelves. Some are tall, some fat, some thin, and some in the fullness of pregnancy. Some are praying, others dancing. Some are naked and others ornately dressed; each is unique, and none looks like she is derived wholly from any specific culture—Anatolian, Indian, African, or European. Iskan doesn't immediately discern the organizational scheme, but the pattern will, she knows, present itself to her later. Sixteen pots of herbs line the patio's low ledge, providing the area with a pungent fragrance in the light breeze. The view out over the valley is spectacular. Above and behind the house, the promontory on which the Altar of Zeus once stood is visible on the acropolis.

"My daughter is the artist," Boroğlu says as they sit at a round, glass-top table under a trellis covered by thick grapevine. "My mother is the herbalist." She makes a point of not asking Iskan if she would like tea.

"Your daughter's art is interesting," Iskan says. "Impressive." She is not merely making small talk; she has never been any good at it. The figurines really do speak to her.

Boroğlu lights a cigarette, takes a deep first drag, and blows the smoke over her shoulder at the grapevine. "Elif is talented," she agrees, "but as her mother I would, of course, rather she had a job and a husband."

"My mother, too." Iskan shakes her head. "But that life doesn't work for everyone." Again, she is not at all making small talk. She is divorced from the man in a neighboring village to whom she was betrothed. He was twice her age, saw her as his property, and used her hard for two years until she refused. Then, he beat her. Her father and brother eventually rescued her, and her incredibly high scores on the national university admissions exam earned her a belated scholarship. She considers herself lucky that she was not saddled with a child.

Her own mother, Boroğlu realizes, would agree as well, but she doesn't share that thought. She drags on her cigarette, holds in the smoke, and drums her fingers on the tabletop. As she exhales, she says, "So Tuğçe, why are you here? I thought the Ministry of Culture was finished with me. And you're not the sort of person to drop by for a social visit." Last year, a month after the coup attempt, Boroğlu came into possession of an eighteen-hundred-year-old letter written in Attic Greek on parchment. Although she is not perfectly fluent in Greek, she immediately understood the significance of the letter. She sent a copy to the Ministry of Culture, asking that she and her team be allowed to investigate both the letter's provenance and its content. Only three days later, Iskan appeared in Boroğlu's Bergama office bluntly informing her that their superiors at the Ministry in Ankara would like the original letter and would complete whatever investigation stemmed from its existence.

After nineteen years of leading the Allianoi and Bergama area excavations, Boroğlu knew better than to hand over anything of value to the Ankara bureaucrats without an extensive paper trail—and so she refused. Iskan appeared unofficially two weeks later saying that she, Iskan, had been removed from the case and that she, Boroğlu, was about to be summoned to Ankara to produce the original letter or her career was finished. Less than a month later, her position was eliminated, and one of the Ministry's minions from Istanbul has since been the acting administrator of Bergama's Department of Archeology and Antiquities. Only the fact that she had been the public face of Bergama's ceremonious elevation to a UNESCO World Heritage site likely prevented more dire consequences.

Now, as Boroğlu stubs her cigarette in the ashtray, Iskan reaches into the left pocket of her black jeans, takes out a carefully folded muslin cloth, and places it on the table. Boroğlu stares at the muslin until Iskan says, "Open it, please."

Boroğlu gasps when she first sees the gold coin and then stares at the profile of the Roman emperor Hadrian. The Hadrian Aureus is rare and quite valuable—in fact, too valuable to be carried in someone's pocket. This one isn't mint, but it certainly wasn't in circulation for long.

"I have been relegated," Iskan says, "to seemingly unimportant tasks in the Ministry as punishment for what the satraps say was abetting a rogue staffer—you."

"*Abetting* me?" Boroğlu coughs.

"I was sent here yesterday," Iskan continues, "to find out if there was anything about the attack that could embroil the Ministry in the investigation. No one expected anything." She shrugs. "This is the sort of work I am now assigned."

Boroğlu shakes another cigarette from her pack.

"I found this," Iskan says, holding up the coin, "in the boy's pocket."

Boroğlu drops her lighter. "The b…? Mehmet? The ten-year-old in the coma?"

"Yes."

"*You* found it?" Boroğlu points the tip of her unlit cigarette at Iskan. "How did *you* find it?"

"The boy's pants were bagged at the hospital. The investigators are still focused on the acropolis...the crime scene." Iskan leans forward and places her forearms on the table. "My Ministry special services ID got the attention of the hospital staff." Her smile is unfriendly. "And I took the time."

Staring at her cigarette, Boroğlu says, "Mehmet had an Aureus." She looks up at Iskan. "No one checked his clothes at the hospital. But *you* did."

Iskan stares across the table. "Of course." There is neither conceit nor irony in her voice. She carefully folds the cloth around the coin.

 11

RAQQA, SYRIA

As the air-raid sirens wail, the veiled woman standing just inside the closed apartment door grits her teeth. Clenching her gloved fists, she bites at her lower lip until she tastes blood. Sweat runs down her spine beneath her black double burqa. Her emerald eyes flash, and her head thunders even before the first bomb explodes. She loathes the kuffars, especially the French and Americans who attack Raqqa, but her anger has begun to run deeper. She is not afraid to go out, not at all. In a way, she welcomes the destruction.

As the wife of a Foreign Martyr, she has privileges—this apartment, intermittent electricity, running water once a week, a steady ration of food, and all of her husband's few remaining material possessions. But the caliphate forbids her to leave the apartment alone. Though she needs no protection, a state-assigned Guardian must watch over her every moment she is in public. She has no one else. The diabolical Assad regime murdered her father for speaking truth. One brother was banished, the other vanished. Her French-born husband made the ultimate sacrifice for the Islamic State, and the caliphate honored him by summoning her only son to the al Farouq training camp when he was eleven.

The floor shakes, and the boarded windows rattle. Pale plaster dust rains in the half-light. The coppery taste of blood in her mouth, she pulls off her thick black gloves and flings them against the locked door. The Guardian is always respectful, but he comes only twice each week to take her to markets that seldom have what she needs and never what she wants. And today, the Guardian will not come at all. He will cower in the bomb shelters like the other officials in the city. He would die for the caliph but never risk his life for her.

She crosses to her bed in which she is seldom able to sleep. Sitting, she stares at her quivering hands, which she has so often scrubbed. The ground shakes again, and the sirens blare. Fine dust swirls. Her fingernails are bitten to the quick, the skin around her cuticles inflamed, though not in this moment bleeding. She undoes the black niqab that covered all of her face except for her eyes. As she takes off her headscarves, she folds each of them on the bed beside her. Her hands still shivering, she begins to remove her hairpins. When she pricks her right thumb, she shakes her hand and sucks the blood.

She does not deliberately prick herself again, but the sting wakes her. Bees might be a good way to go. Her long hair, the color of chestnuts, falls around her shoulders as she takes out the rest of the pins. She lines the pins carefully on the scarves and then rubs her cheeks and temples. The pounding behind her eyes only gets worse.

Standing, she pulls the outer burqa over her head. The coarse material catches under her chin so she yanks hard, further entangling it around her neck. Gasping for air, she wrenches and twists until the burqa is free. She drops it on the floor at her feet and, panting, slumps back onto the bed. Her whole body quakes. She smells of sweat, an odor she once liked. Hanging is definitely not the way.

She yearns for her son whom she has not been allowed to see for more than a year. The caliphate forbids her to mourn her husband; she has been told repeatedly that he is better off in the hands of his Creator. There was never a body to wash, purify, and shroud. And no family to gather. No one except her son. Her Sunni faith runs deep, and white, she knows well, is the real color of mourning—but she is required by law to wear black only, even her inner burqa.

No graves can be marked, even for the Martyrs. As tears slip from her eyes, she swipes at them. Crying is also prohibited. No tears may be shed for the dead, but she will go on mourning the living, as she has every moment since the caliphate stole her son...every moment since the sheikh pulled the boy from her arms and rebuked her for her weakness.

She selects the longest of her hairpins, raises it in the floating dust, and gazes at this last vestige of her family, a wedding gift from her mother's mother who herself received it when she was betrothed so many decades ago. The silver pin with two small, smooth orbs at the top is the last of the items she possesses from her childhood, the final remnant of a family now disbanded, disbursed, destroyed.

The sirens fade, and her shaking subsides. The motes slow their winding descent. Without flinching, she clasps the orbs and jams the pin through the black inner burqa into her right thigh. Although pain fires, she makes no sound.

 12

BERGAMA

As Tuğçe Iskan strides up the walk toward the Bergama Ministry of Culture office, a mangy gray dog approaches her, its head cocked and its tail wagging. She stops and, leaning over, ruffles the dog behind its ears. The dog sniffles as though laughing, and its entire backside wags. "Ah, my dear," she says, patting her pockets, "I've got nothing for you except a coin worth a fortune." She stops herself, rubs the dog's chest, glances at the Ministry office, and heads instead toward the Bergama Museum's entrance. The dog follows but turns away at the door.

Once inside the museum, Iskan takes out her personal phone, the iPhone she uses only for private calls. No one from the Ministry office can see her in the museum's front hall, but she still goes to the inner courtyard, a square, sun-splashed area that can't be seen at all from outside the museum. A stone lion, seeming to leer, greets her. The head of its ruminant prey lies between the lion's forepaws. Behind the lion at the center of the courtyard, an ancient fountain with a cracked basin spews no water. She heads to her left toward the larger than life, headless, armless, legless statue of a Roman emperor from Pergamon's Temple of Trajan. A pithos, a large earthenware storage vessel, lies on either side of the truncated emperor. Standing by the museum's pale-gray concrete wall in the scant midday shade, she taps the Ankara number.

The phone is answered, but no voice says hello.

She leans her right shoulder into the wall and says, "Hello, Nihat Bey."

"Ah, it's time for me to have a Yenice." The voice is gruff, raspy from decades of smoking. The line goes dead.

Iskan smiles, gazes at the griffins facing each other on the emperor's chest, and spins the iPhone in her left hand. It's quiet in the courtyard, seemingly farther from Bergama's bustling town center than it really is. The only sounds above the hum of a generator are cooing close by and birdsong higher in trees she cannot see. In exactly ninety seconds her phone rings. "You are in the doghouse?" she asks.

"Again!" Nihat Monoğlu answers. "Smoking is such a dirty habit." He has been retired for a year now, and his wife does not let him smoke in their apartment. Last year, he blocked a scheme among some of his colleagues to transfer paintings from the Ankara Museum archives to private hands—and then he took early retirement before any reprisals could occur. He never made the scheme public because no *real* investigation would ensue in any case. And everyone, including those who would retaliate because they stood to have made millions of euros, knew that he lived by a code that they had broken, that he would hold onto the evidence against them but take it no further, and that if they came after him or his family he would fight them to the death.

"I need your advice," Iskan says.

"It is always good to hear your voice. Are you back in town?"

"I'm at the Bergama Museum."

"Bergama, Tuğçe? And?"

"I found a Roman coin, a Hadrian Aureus." She hears the click of his old Zippo lighter, but he doesn't comment, and so she continues. "In the boy's pocket. The one in the hospital." She knows what questions Nihat Bey will ask next. "The investigators recovered his phone, which was destroyed, but his shoes and pants were bagged in the hospital. And nobody took the time to check them." She switches the phone to her right hand and reaches into her pocket to make sure the carefully wrapped coin is still there. Her current boss never likes her providing so much information, but Nihat Bey is different. "The boy—his name is Mehmet—has severe head trauma. Broken neck. He's on a respirator. In a coma. Ribs and arm broken. Punctured lung. Prognosis is not good. But he lived because someone, his grandfather or someone else, apparently cushioned him in the moment of impact. Everyone else in the cable car died. Four people. His grandfather and three Chinese nationals. Two males in their sixties and one female, forty, the tour guide." She taps the larger pithos with the toe of her walking shoe and brushes her left forearm across her nose and mouth. "None of Mehmet's other relatives was on the funicular. The grandfather is—was—on his mother's side. But both families live outside the town. Farmers. Own land. The other investigators…" She stops herself because whatever the other investigators thought is conjecture—and irrelevant. She did not speak to any of them, only to the first responders at the scene and to the staff in the emergency room. "I've shown the Aureus only to Özlem Boroğlu. No one else."

"Why Özlem?" His question is no more gruff than anything else he has said.

"Because she would make the connection."

"And did she?"

"Yes."

"What did she say?"

"Nothing."

His deep-throated laughter is sudden. "No. She wouldn't. Especially not to anyone from the Ministry."

"She doesn't like me." Iskan's voice is flat, the statement not at all self-pitying. Liking or disliking an investigator was never important to Nihat Bey, which makes her like him. "What should I do?"

"The fact that you are calling me suggests that you know what you should *not* do."

"Yes." She will tell no one at the Ministry of her discovery. But what she has not told even Nihat Bey is that when the copy of the ancient letter that Özlem Boroğlu sent crossed her desk, she read it. She did not, of course, know Attic Greek, but she recognized the name "Galenus." And later, using an old dictionary from a forgotten shelf in the Ministry's outmoded library, she made a painstaking interlinear translation from memory. She trusts Nihat Bey more than anyone else in Ankara, but it is difficult for her to trust anybody absolutely. "Yes," she repeats. "That much I know."

"Put the coin somewhere safe," he says, "where not even you would look. Return to Ankara. Make the report expected of you. Do whatever else *you* need to do."

"And, if I need your advice…? Or help…?" Her voice trails off.

He does not answer immediately. "Then contact me." He pauses again. "And, Tuğçe…," for the first time, there is emotion in his voice, "do not do anything heroic."

 13

AEGEAN SEA

$A$s the young man passes the swimming pool on the yacht's aft deck, he tries not to stare at the three gorgeous naked women, two blondes and a brunette, treading water. The expansive salon he enters is all white oak and plush upholstery. The Russian sitting on the sofa with his back to the evening sun glances briefly at him and then goes back to keyboarding on his tablet. Four news feeds appear simultaneously on the muted LCD television's screen. Shostakovich's Seventh Symphony bursts from the six diminutive speakers.

The young man stands for more than a minute before the Russian looks up again and says, "I was expecting your father." His hooded eyes are dark; his voice is low, almost a growl. He speaks English because he has never bothered to learn Turkish.

The young man nods. His father told him that the Russian would try to intimidate him and that he should show no fear and stand up to the shithead. But his father failed to mention the three beautiful distractions stepping out of the pool. "My father sends his regrets," he says in English. He does not add a reason or excuse for his father's absence. In the family business, there are never excuses.

"Sit." The Russian waves his hand at the cushioned chair opposite him.

The young man takes a seat, crosses his legs away from the Russian, and looks around at the yacht's accoutrements and then at the uniformed steward standing at attention at the salon's portal and the guard, his back to the three women, standing at the stern cradling an AK-47 and scanning the Aegean. The thirty-eight-meter yacht, he has been told, is not the Russian's largest. He is to show appreciation for the trappings of the Russian's immense wealth but not be blinded by it. The young man's great-grandfather was doing a booming business in Hellenistic antiquities, lucrative private deals with English and German aristocrats, while the Russian's ancestors were farming potatoes.

The Russian is about his father's age, midsixties, less refined and less fit—though, according to the stories, even more ruthless. His slip-ons are handmade Italian, the pressed slacks tailored, the collared shirt monogrammed with gilded thread. His hands, although manicured, are scarred, his fingers knotted with arthritis; the gold, seventeenth-century-BCE Minoan ring with the bull's head figurine is certainly genuine. The young man himself wears no jewelry, but his shoes, shirt, and suit are all Italian. He's clean-shaven with short black hair and has the family's bright-green eyes. And he works out harder and longer, he's sure, than either the steward or the guard.

"I have been informed that your father has antiquities that may interest me."

In fact, the Russian made the first contact, but that is not something to quibble about here. "Yes," he says, "we have recently made exquisite acquisitions." He recrosses his legs. The word "acquisitions" isn't quite correct, but he will not mention that in this negotiation.

"I need something special."

"My family has never let you down."

The Russian gestures to the steward. "That's true." He makes a steeple with his fingers. "But I am looking for a *presidential* gift." His smile is unfriendly. "A gift to my countryman, the wealthiest, most powerful man in the world."

Aware that this information may well be true, the young man nods. "So nothing," he says, "that ISIL has looted." ISIL plunder has flooded the private antiquities market for high-end, secret acquisitions, but those artifacts carry a political significance that makes them in this case untenable.

The Russian's nod is dismissive. His face, tight around the eyes, has had a number of plastic surgeries. The steward places two champagne flutes on the salon's bar and turns a bottle chilling in a silver bowl.

"No mere Mycenean gold amulets," the young man adds. "And no hoards of gold coins. Something both singular and priceless."

"Yes. Preferably something never seen on the market."

"Perhaps, museum-quality sculpture?" The sun behind the Russian is setting, casting glimmering red and orange light onto the sparse clouds above the horizon.

"Museum quality is in museums," the Russian scoffs.

"Perhaps." The young man leans forward. He should not move beyond his father's directives, but he must also seize the moment.

"No Roman marble. Nothing terra-cotta," the Russian snarls.

The young man takes his cell phone from his suit jacket pocket. "And Hellenistic bronze?"

"It has all been melted down." Though the Russian scoffs again, he is leaning forward, too. A stubby finger pats the bull's horns on the ring.

"One would think."

"I *know*."

The young man taps his phone. "And I know that the finest Pergamene bronze ever sculpted still exists." He slides the phone across the table.

The Russian starts when he first gazes at the photo.

The young man's heart is racing, but he keeps his breath even and his face blank. "The perfect gift for a conquering hero."

The Russian sits back, runs a hand over his bald head, leans forward again, and says, "It's a fake." His dark eyes bore into the young man's face.

"I have myself verified its authenticity." Again, this is not exactly true.

"*You* have?" Disdain creeps back into the Russian's voice.

"As I'm sure you have been informed, I have a degree in Hellenistic Antiquities from the University of Chicago. And an MBA from Harvard University. My father does not like to brag so perhaps he didn't mention my three years in procurement in New York for the Metropolitan Museum of Art's Hellenistic department."

"So I am to take your word for its authenticity?" The derision deepens.

"Of course not." The young man takes the phone from the table. "We will provide you with a list of three independent evaluators whom you already know. You may select someone from the list. All in strict confidence, of course."

"It's a hoax." But the Russian's voice is no longer a growl.

"My family has never perpetrated a hoax." It's true. But the family has also never been willing to make the bold transactional moves that lead to spectacularly lucrative deals. Yes, his father netted six—and sometimes seven—figure earnings on particular items, but he never had an item that produced eight-digit profits. The sun flashes green as it disappears. The three women have vanished as well, but the guard remains at the yacht's stern.

# ✩ 14
BERGAMA

At 2:15 A.M., Elif Boroğlu inspects the terra-cotta goddess she has been sculpting. Turning it slowly, she uses a paintbrush to clean any residual dust. The figurine is fully robed; not so much as a shoulder or ankle is bare. She is squat, not pregnant, but thick around the middle. Her face is full, her expression dour. Three snakes emerge from her long, thickly flowing hair. One hand holds a short, single-edged sword, the other the severed head of a bearded man.

Elif must still glaze and paint and fire the figurine, but it is finished. It is not a copy of any particular statue of hers or anyone else's. Each of her figurines is always rendered anew, and each springs, like Athena from Zeus, fully grown from Elif's head. She never follows a mold—or even a plan. When she can, as tonight, be fully present, a statue appears in her mind, flows through her fingers, and forms in the clay. She is only a flume, a sluice, a channel.

What she experiences is not exactly a trance, but she becomes aware of only the sculpting, nothing else. The world outside the studio dissipates. She hears only the tanbur music in her earbuds and feels only the damp malleability of the clay. Her focus sharpens until something akin to light runs through her, binding her and the statue. And then finally the music fades, as does she herself. The sculpting is so clear and bright that she herself vanishes—only to find herself sometime later brushing dust from a figurine.

This small studio, clean and well lit, at least most of the time, is her sanctuary. On this side street at the edge of town near the ancient Aesklepion, it is quiet, except for the voices of the dear children in the day and the barking of the sacred dogs at night. Sometimes her cat, Sekhmet, joins her, but that is more Sekhmet's choice than hers. But she never invites friends or family when she is working through a problem. And she is having difficulty getting her heart and soul beyond the bombing of the funicular.

More facts about the attack have emerged, but none provides meaning. A number of people in the neighborhood noticed the killer in his pick-up truck. Five elderly women remember a man in a white shirt standing in the area minutes before the blast, but for the most part they averted their eyes. One of them did say that he was young and handsome, like a movie star. The killer was, however, identified —an Irishman, a drifter with a criminal record who went to Syria to wage jihad for Daesh and then came to Bergama to wreak senseless havoc. His life was undistinguished, and people are already forgetting his name but not his heinous crime.

How the killer got into the country is still not certain. The pick-up truck was stolen in İzmir a week before the blast, but where it was turned into a bomb and how it got to Bergama are also unknown. And the truck itself has provided scant physical evidence because it is now nothing more than mangled, burned-out shards. The cleanup of the debris is requiring most of Bergama's municipal workers, and there is already a debate growing about whether or not the funicular should be rebuilt at all.

The ritual that Elif and her friends performed at the cave was cathartic, but anger and sadness are creeping over her again. And although she erected a temporary memorial at the acropolis funicular's ticket office, she feels she should be doing much more. The Chinese and the families of the other murdered tourists have taken home the remains of their dead. Little Mehmet, the lone survivor, still lies in a coma.

The massacre's real toll, Elif realizes, will continue to rise. She accepts both the notion that war is in our blood and the fact that war is brutal. Massacres and scorched earth are often a result, perhaps even an inevitability. But what happened here was not warfare. Nor was it in any way heroic. The Irisher was a murderer not a martyr, and what he did here terrorizes only the innocent. It has enraged those in power, inspiring retaliation and retribution, but not fear. In Ankara and other national capitals, the "Bergama Bombing," as it is now known, is already being used by the powerful to pursue their personal political ends. The pain, the suffering, the trauma are being felt here in Bergama, which will never again be a peaceful market town where people go about their day-to-day business. Lives here have been shattered by the blast, but the powerful elsewhere have not and will not suffer, have not and will not *feel* pain, in any significant way.

As Elif blows on the figurine in case any speck of dust remains, the earth trembles a little—barely enough to register on seismographs, but enough to remind her that she is living on a faultline. Yes, even this studio, her sanctuary, is always at risk. Her sculpting gives her peace, though often it's only ephemeral. But she does not come here to run away from the dangers or the horrors of the world. Rather, she feels as though here she can enter the world more deeply, comprehending—at least for a few moments—the folly of men, the grave illness of the species. Sculpting gives her a modicum of hope even when, as now, it feels like society is foundering. But her work never blinds her to the evil in the world.

As she places the figurine on the rack, she is suddenly exhausted. Her neck and shoulders, wrists and fingers ache. Her eyes burn. After she cleans up, she could sleep here on her yoga mat, but she should go home. Her mother and grandmother are used to her nocturnal habits, but if she does not show up by dawn they will, given the current perturbation in town, begin to worry.

She stands up and stretches into tree pose on her right foot. As she switches to her left, her phone rings. She lifts her arms into a spire for three seconds before stepping back to her worktable. The number is her brother's, with whom she still has not yet spoken. When he calls this late, he has invariably been drinking. She should let the call ring over to voicemail, but she, as the older sibling, feels obligated to take care of him. After the fifth ring, she answers, "Good evening, my dear brother."

"Hello, dear sister," he says, "I knew you would be awake."

"Yes."

"How are you?" His voice is even, his tone deliberate. When he drunk-dials, he tends to speak too carefully in a futile attempt to keep her from noticing his inebriation.

"Not good, Serkan." She sits on her stool. "Upset. Sad and angry about what has happened here."

"I know," he says. "It's awful."

She says nothing. He doesn't know. He couldn't. If he did, he would have come home.

"I'm driving down tomorrow…today…after an important meeting in the morning…"

"Have you called Mom?"

"Uh, no…" He hesitates. "I wanted to surprise her."

Again, she says nothing. A quick cough in the background informs her that he is not alone.

"I should've called. I know." His voice is sincere. When he intermittently feels guilt about not keeping in closer touch with his mother, he is genuinely remorseful—but the pattern doesn't change. He tends to call her only when he needs money. "I've been in Cappadocia," he adds, as though that might explain the lack of contact. "And…," his voice rises, "I've got a great deal going!"

Taking a breath, Elif brushes her left hand down her face. The couple of times he has visited in the last two years, he has taken two dozen of her statues back to Istanbul to sell in boutiques, promising to split the profits.

"This is it," he says. "A game changer. A real breakout!"

She rubs her left eye, which is burning more fiercely than her right.

"The Americans you met," he says.

"Yes…" She hesitates. She did meet an older American couple, but they were only in Bergama for half a day—and Serkan didn't even stay long enough for them to meet his mother. The wife, Clare, has e-mailed Elif half a dozen times about designing a piece—a golden goddess amulet. Serkan knows about the project, but she isn't sure he understands that they're providing her with both the equipment she needs and the precious metal necessary.

"They want me to find them an ancient amulet," he says. "Something *really* old!"

"Uh, okay." But it's *not* okay! She opens both eyes wide.

"Something gold!"

"How? You can't… We can't—"

"I have connections!"

"What connections?" Their mother has discovered quite a number of priceless artifacts over the years, but none of them is hers. They all belong to the country, to the nation, to Turkey. As far as Elif knows, their mother *never* held out any artifacts from any site. "You don't—"

"I thought you'd be excited!" he says, interrupting her again.

"I…" She has no idea what to say, and this is clearly the time *not* to say anything.

"Don't tell Mom," he says.

She won't. She can't. Even Serkan's entertaining such an idea worries her. She takes a deep breath, exhales, and then rubs her hand down her face again.

# 15

KAIKOS VALLEY

When the burly man cradling the semiautomatic rifle steps onto the dirt track in front of Özlem Boroğlu's gray Dacia, she brakes quickly. The man wears combat boots, baggy camouflage pants, and a forest-green T-shirt. He is unshaven, and his cadet cap is grimy. The afternoon sun glints off his reflective sunglasses and his rifle's barrel. She taps her cigarette's ash out the window, turns the car off, switches on the dashboard camera, and stares silently at the man. They are one-and-a-half kilometers away from the main road between Bergama and Dikili. The track slopes slowly up and then winds behind a hill. The land behind her is flat, with rectangular fields in variable shades of green and brown.

"Stop!" the man shouts. "Go away!"

Even with just these three words, she can tell he is neither Turkish nor military. She has, of course, already stopped, so, saying nothing, she glares at him through the windshield. His thick neck and hairy arms are thoroughly tattooed.

"Go!" he shouts, gesturing with the rifle. "Get out! Leave!"

She takes a long, slow drag on her cigarette and exhales through her nose.

The man reaches up and begins to talk into the radio microphone clipped to his T-shirt's neckline. The language is a mixture of Georgian and poor Turkish. His thick hand adjusts the angle of the microphone, and, cocking his head, he speaks more intensely.

Sweating in her long-sleeved, blue cotton workshirt, Boroğlu reaches toward the passenger seat for her thermos. The man swings the rifle and points the barrel at her face. Very slowly, she raises her hand, palm open. He circles to his right and approaches the driver's-side window from just behind her view. Her heart pounds. She has stood up to and stared down many men in her life—but never a Georgian with an automatic rifle.

The man stays just behind her left shoulder. She places both hands on the steering wheel and tries to slow and deepen her breathing. Sweat runs down her chest and back. She can hear his quick, shallow, adrenaline-soaked breaths and smell his sour sweat. It's possible, she thinks, that this moment is even trickier for him than it is for her. Whatever he has been hired to do, he is certainly not being paid to blow the head off an unarmed older woman.

The white pick-up truck coming fast down the track leaves a trail of red-brown dust. She goes on counting her breaths—three seconds in and three out. The pick-up slows and stops twenty meters from her Dacia. A young man, perhaps Serkan's age, gets out slowly and deliberately, then quickly closes the door to the dust that is settling around him. He has on sunglasses but no hat. Unarmed, or at least carrying no unconcealed weapon, he walks calmly toward the Dacia. As he approaches, he waves his right hand at the guard and says, "Stand back. Cover me."

The young man is tall, but not Serkan's height. His shoulders are square and the line of his jaw strong. He is lean, but in the way of a country village, not a gym. Although they have never met, she feels as though she knows him.

He leans down, rests his wrist on the top of the window well, and says, very respectfully, "Good afternoon."

Boroğlu widens her eyes, looks into his face, and says, "Good afternoon, young man. What is going on here?" Her voice holds a mixture of equal parts confusion and irritation.

"This is private property," he answers, again respectfully. Smoke from her cigarette twirls toward him.

"Oh," she says as if she didn't know. He *must* recognize the Dacia as well as she does the white pick-up that has, periodically, followed her around the valley.

"It is…," he pauses, looking for a gentle word, "restricted."

"Oh," she repeats. "It is?" She looks out through the windshield at the hill, a washed-out green covered with wild grass and shrubs. Gray rock juts in irregular formations near the summit.

"You are…trespassing."

She purses her lips. "Who is the owner?" She already knows, of course. She has checked the property deeds, and one of the Hamits' holding companies is the owner of record.

"He…" The young man leans back. "It doesn't matter."

"It does to me!" She crushes her cigarette butt in the Dacia's almost-filled ashtray.

"And who are you?" Irritation is creeping into his voice.

"A resident of Bergama." Glancing back at the rifle still pointing at her, she adds, "I'm looking for an old friend who lived here."

"She… No one lives here."

Boroğlu holds up her pack of cigarettes. "Would you like one?"

"No," he says sharply, but then, momentarily disarmed, he drums his fingers on the window well and adds, "thank you." His fingernails are dirty deep into the quick. "You can't stay here."

"But what about my friend?"

"No one *lives* here!"

"She did. For a long time."

He drums his fingers more rapidly. "What is her…your friend's name?"

Smiling, she tosses the pack of cigarettes next to the thermos on the passenger seat and then gazes again at the hill. "Cybele Meter."

He doesn't react. He may be in charge here, but he's not an archeologist, not fully aware of what's really going on.

"No," he says. "No one by that name. No women are working on the site at all."

Taking a deep breath, she shakes her head as though she is becoming exasperated. "Perhaps I'm just confused." In fact, though, he has just given her the exact information for which she has come.

He looks over at the guard. "Maybe you are."

"I won't bother anyone. I promise."

He shakes his head as though she is already bothering him.

"Still, I'd like to look for her. It's important that I get in touch…"

"You…" He pulls off his sunglasses. "You need to leave. *Now!*"

His eyes are bright green, that sea-glass green of Mustafa Hamit's eyes. She drops her gaze, as if in submission. "But—"

"Now! *Immediately!*" He really could be Mustafa junior, except that, as she has learned, the Hamit scion lacks this man's roughness, his ruggedness.

She turns the Dacia's ignition key. "I will…," she begins but then hesitates. "May I speak to the owner?"

"He…they're not…" His eyes gleam as he leans in closer. "Leave. *Please!*" That last word is wholly a command.

"Okay, okay." She shifts the car into reverse.

The moment he notices the dashcam is on, she pops the clutch, and the old Dacia doesn't stall. He jerks his arm past her face to rip out the dashcam, but he's too late. The back of his hand slaps her as she pulls away. Though the Georgian guard does not shoot through the dust, she doesn't breathe until she is forty meters back down the track. And only when she has turned the car around and reached the Bergama–Dikili road does she smile. She has sent the Hamits a message they can't and won't ignore—and one that is absolutely false. With any luck, they will go on digging here for an eternity.

 **16**

PERGAMON; 159 CE

$G$alen pulls the silk thread taut, loops it, and ties off the final stitch. He wipes blood and sweat from his hands and forearms; his tunic is splattered, but there's nothing to be done about that. He reaches for the beaker of ointment, both analgesic and antiseptic, he has made to protect the wound. The gladiator, a stout, thickly muscled Syrian, breathes heavily and stares at the low stone ceiling of the colosseum's spoliarium. He gives no other sign of the pain caused by the deep sword wound in his thigh.

As Galen spreads the ointment, he says, "Rest now. You will be back in the arena for the next festival." The Syrian closes his eyes but doesn't otherwise move.

The ointment's aroma mixes with the stench of the spoliarium, which doubles as the colosseum's morgue. Galen wraps linen bandages around the wound, takes a deep breath, and stares at the candle he used to heat the ingredients with which he cauterized the wound. The stone walls thunder as the forty-eight thousand people above him cheer the beginning of the afternoon's final bout.

Galen is, at twenty-nine, the youngest man ever to be appointed Pergamon's physician to the High Priest of Asia's gladiators. He is certainly well-educated, having studied here under Satyrus and in Smyrna, Corinth, and, for eight years, Alexandria, the world's center of medical training. But none of his teachers' knowledge, their often contentious philosophies, their ineffectual treatments, their rudimentary understanding of anatomy, and their senseless appeals to the gods for mercy have prepared him for attending to the gladiators. Working on their gaping wounds has revealed to Galen an empirical world that his elders seldom considered—and never understood. He has discovered an anatomical universe of human veins and arteries, tendons and muscles, organs and intestines, hot and pulsing blood, and, when a treatment is erroneous, decay and putrescence. He has, unlike his predecessors, never lost a gladiator because of maltreatment.

Now, well into his second term, Galen is finally *experiencing* death. He has seen death often, of course, from afar and up close, in his work. When he attended the gladiatorial games as a boy, death was on display in the slaughtered animals and in the noxii, the Empire's condemned criminals and traitors who suffered spectacularly and then were dragged deceased from the arena. In his studies, he has dissected pigs and monkeys. The dying and the dead have been woven into the fabric of his life, but the only death that Galen has ever *felt* deeply was his father's.

When Galen was nineteen and beginning his study of medicine, Aelius Nicon wasted slowly from a disease that ran its devastating and irrevocable course with nothing of the arena's drama and fanfare. In Nicon's last months, Galen spent a great deal of time with him, but by degrees Nicon lost the ability to walk and stand, and then to write and speak, and ultimately to eat and drink. In the final week, all that was left to them was the fond, suffering gaze in Nicon's eyes and the sorrowful devotion in Galen's. During the interminable two days after his father became unresponsive, the man's soul departed so gradually that, despite Galen's constant vigilance, the process, enshrouded by grief, was imperceptible.

As the crowd above roars repeatedly, Galen peers at the second gladiator lying on a stretcher near the spoliarium's tunnel into the arena. Like the Syrian, he is clean-shaven, but he is taller and not as thick. His face is long like Galen's, and his nose Roman. Stripped of his helmet and armor, he wears only a loin cloth. His breathing is shallow, his skin gray. A bloodstained bandage covers the left side of his chest from his armpit to his nipple.

Wiping his hands again on a clean linen, Galen crosses to the stretcher, drops to one knee, and leans close to the dying man to check the wound. The sword's blade, entering at an angle in the narrow space between the shoulder and the armor, went deep. The thrust must have been perfectly timed and brilliantly placed. The wound is fatal, as any wound to the heart is, but the blade tore only the endocardium and not the ventricle. Galen has not closed the wound because if he did, the bleeding would become even more painful. The man is slowly bleeding out; his soul will depart his body soon, sometime in the next half hour.

As Galen takes the man's pulse, which has weakened, the gladiator opens his eyes and turns his head slightly so that their eyes meet, but he is stoic, giving no indication of the severe pain he suffers. After the crowd goes silent for a moment and then cheers even louder, the executor enters the spoliarium from the arena's tunnel. A large man dressed as Charon, the Etruscan god of death, carries the heavy mallet used to finish off dying gladiators. Earlier in the day, he was busy with the noxii and the damnati, but his business now is only the man on the stretcher.

"Go away!" Galen says. Neither he nor the gladiator looks away from the mallet's bloody, diamond-shaped head.

"The High Priest commands it." The executor's deep voice is devoid of emotion.

Galen stands so that he faces the Charon. "I said, leave this man be!" His voice is imperious. "He is dying. Beyond help."

As Galen's dark eyes bore into him, the executor takes a step back. He raises the mallet so that the iron diamond gleams darkly. "That is why it is ordered."

"Yes. But in his own time."

"I will report—"

"Do that," Galen shouts. "Tell the High Priest that I take full responsibility for this man's death."

The Charon backs into the mouth of the tunnel, turns abruptly, and stomps toward the thundering arena where the crowd is chanting the names of both gladiators. The final bout has obviously been a success.

Galen pulls his stool close to the stretcher and sits. The man's face is ashen, but he never flinched during the altercation. Galen knows him both from Pergamon's gladiator training encampment and from the parchment posters plastered about the city. He is not as infamous as those fighting in the day's final bouts, but he has a following. He is an auctori, a free man who originally chose the enslavement of the arena in order to pay off his debts. Noted for his fierce bravery in more than a dozen bouts, he was again granted freedom—but enslaved himself once more so that he could keep fighting in the arena.

"What is your name?" Galen asks, even though he knows it.

"Pectoris of Smyrna." The man's voice is hoarse.

Galen nods. The man is still rational. His lips are cracked and dry, so Galen offers him water from a clay cup. "I studied in Smyrna."

The man swallows water until the cup is empty.

"The light there is good," Galen adds.

The man looks more carefully at Galen. "Yes, it is." His eyes close for a moment, as though memory has taken him. When he looks again at Galen, he says, "I accept the mallet."

"I know. But I want you to die naturally. With dignity." He does not add, *So that I may experience it.* Galen takes a sponge and wipes the gladiator's forehead and neck. He remembers doing this for his father, but his father was withering and this man is not. His father's soul slipped away. This man's is not. As his heart weakens, his soul neither wavers nor shrinks. Most doctors believe that a man's soul resides in his heart, but it is clearly not so. This man retains an internal dignity that goes far beyond the gladiators' oath. Although Galen has forsaken the Olympian gods, he still believes deeply in the human soul. Every man carries within him a divine spark, and Pectoris of Smyrna's soul remains present, fully evident, even in his final moments.

The noise above and through the tunnel becomes cacophonous. A melee between factions must have erupted in the stands, as it sometimes does, but the plebeians trampled, beaten, or otherwise injured are not Galen's concern. Pectoris of Smyrna's heartbeat is fading, but his soul remains firm. Could the soul and the mind, the spirit, reside most deeply not in the heart or liver, as Aristotle had said long before, but in the brain?

# ✮ 17
## ISTANBUL

At six minutes to 10:00, Serkan Boroğlu takes a seat on the stone bench that runs along the outer wall in the garden of the Süleymaniye Mosque. A breeze rising from the Golden Horn stirs the heat. No one else is in the garden except for an old man with a cane tottering along the path toward Süleyman's tomb and a young couple, he in a white shirt and she in a red headscarf, sitting under a tree off to Serkan's right. He takes out his smartphone and waits for the next message, the third he will have had since 9:15. The first instructed him to move from the steps of the New Mosque to a café near the main entrance to the grand bazaar, and the second from there to this garden. This last move was uphill all the way, and, though he's not winded, he's sticky here in the sun—and not at all happy. He didn't really sleep last night, and the climb has made his headache worse. He has met with the Hamits' rep four times before, but there has never been this senseless faux-spy security where he has had to trudge from point to point.

The man who approaches him at exactly 10:00 is about his age, shorter but more lean. He is clean-shaven, and his dark hair is freshly trimmed. Both his pale-green sport shirt and his khaki pants are pressed. He is altogether handsome in a stylish, male model sort of way. "Hello, Serkan," he says when he comes close. "May I sit down?"

64

"Of course," Serkan says. He sees himself as a man of the world, but this guy is clearly more cosmopolitan, right down to his Italian slip-ons.

"Another perfect day in paradise," the guy says as he brushes off the bench. He doesn't give his name, but Serkan is sure he has seen him before in one of the after-hours clubs or, perhaps, on one of the online gossip sites.

Serkan doesn't quite know what to answer so he simply nods. Small pleasantries were never a part of the four earlier deals with the disheveled and disgruntled bald man who was his contact. When he glances to his left, he notices a stout, middle-aged man standing at attention fifty meters away on the path along the wall. He wears a dark, shiny suit jacket despite the heat.

"May I have your cell phone?" The guy's eyes are bright green, and his tone is so polite that it's menacing.

Serkan stares at his phone for a moment before handing it over. Without looking at the phone, the guy turns it off and sets it on the mottled stone between them. "You have some business for us?" he says, his voice oily. His fingernails are manicured. The breeze off the Golden Horn riffles his hair, and so he smooths it out.

Serkan takes a breath. He's not going to let this guy's superiority get to him. "I have *customers*," he says. "An American and his wife."

"His *wife?*" The skepticism drips.

"Yes. Definitely his wife." Off to Serkan's right, a younger, even more muscular man has appeared on the path. His arms are folded across his chest as he scans the mosque's grounds.

"And they have an interest in antiquities?"

"They do. Specifically, a golden amulet. Roman or older. The mother goddess."

"Demeter? Or Cybele? Or…?"

"I'm not… It doesn't matter." Deliberately not looking left or right, Serkan glances across the path at the light post next to three cypresses braced with wooden rails. "*Authenticity* matters."

"I…we will provide something that suits him and pleases the wife."

"They're pretty clear on what they want."

"And the price range?"

Serkan takes another breath and says, "They will pay for quality."

Crossing his legs, the guy gazes over at the nearest of the mosque's four minarets. "My family will provide something beyond their expectations." He picks absently at the crease in his khakis. "How shall we get in touch with him?"

"Them. *Her.* She, the wife, will make the choice."

"Ah, so they are a *modern* couple?" The guy's voice suggests irony and a touch of scorn.

"They are."

"And what is his name?"

"They are my customers." He knows he is repeating himself, but it's necessary. He can't let the moment slip away.

"They were. Now they are my family's."

"They will work *only* with me."

The guy starts to say something, but then stops and smiles. "Serkan, you misunderstand me. We will pay you a generous finder's fee. My family is always fair."

Across the lawn near one of the mosque's exits, four budding saplings are bent to the left as though some gale prevails. "Fair" doesn't seem like the right word. "I have previously worked on commission."

The guy takes a breath and shakes his head once, as though he needs to explain something obvious to a child. "Yes, Serkan," he says, "but now you are working for me. And I'm prepared to offer you ten thousand lira for simply introducing the Americans to me."

Serkan picks up his phone but does not turn it on. He made four thousand Turkish lira on the last sale, and that icon was worth less than a tenth of an ancient gold amulet. *Gold!* Ten thousand lira would pay off half of his credit card debt, but it's probably less than one percent of what they'll charge. Anybody can do the math—if they paid the same to some poor farmer who dug it up, they'd be making 98 percent, and Serkan and the farmer would split two percent. Jack and Clare know him, trust him. That's got value. He slips his phone into his pants pocket and then looks into the guy's eyes. "As I mentioned," he says, "the customers intend to work with me."

The guy does not look away. "All right," he says. "You've made your point, Serkan. I'll talk with my father. Perhaps, we'll raise your fee."

Serkan holds his gaze. "Thank you," he hears himself say, "but that's not the point." He has become every bit as polite as this condescending asshole.

"Yes, Serkan, it is the point." An edge cuts into the guy's voice; his eyes brighten. "You have nothing without me and my family." His smile is sharp. "And you'll have *nothing* in the future. But if this deal goes well, we may have a long and mutually beneficial relationship."

Serkan should just take the deal, of course, but his mind races to other options. He wants to buy time. "I understand," he says. And he does. This guy will use his family's wealth and political connections to bully him. Serkan was smart and a good basketballer so he was never bullied in school—but he never liked guys who picked on others. In his business the last five years, he never tried to muscle others out. It worked better to cooperate—at least, a little.

"It's a big financial deal for you," the guy goes on, "but for me, it's pretty small. Almost trivial." He waves his hand at the garden. "I can walk away…and never look back. How about you, Serkan?"

# ✪ 18
## BERGAMA

As the evening's final call to prayer echoes through Bergama, Özlem Boroğlu and her mother climb the cement steps toward the acropolis funicular's ticket office—and the impromptu memorial for the ISIL massacre victims. Although most of the glass panels were blown out, the massive facade of the funicular's main platform prevents a clear view of the devastation on the hillside. Demolition teams have been working from dawn to dusk to remove the shattered stanchion and the ruptured cables, but the work and the noise subside each night by this time. Still, an acrid vestigial odor of burnt earth, metal, and plexiglass cannot be scrubbed from the area.

At the top of the stairs, Boroğlu stubs out her cigarette. When four beige puppies sniff about the two women, Boroğlu's mother, in her floral scarf and a long, dark dress despite the heat, stops to scratch each behind its ears. They begin to leap about, but neither Boroğlu nor her mother has any food to give them.

Many mourners have begun to come to the memorial each day, but the only other person here in this moment is a stout, bald older man in a dark suit cupping his hands and whispering prayers in Arabic. A bed of red and white long-stemmed carnations lies at the base of the office wall. A dozen Turkish flags frame the photos of the victims taped to the office's boarded-over windows. Handmade placards—"We Will Remember" and "Death to Terrorists"—are fastened to wooden dowels. At the center of the memorial, the photos of the twin girls and their parents are larger than those of the Chinese victims surrounding them. Folded personal notes are affixed to the photos of the girls. Boroğlu recognizes Elif's terra-cotta rendering of the twins among the other gifts and tributes spread through the flower bed.

When the man finishes his prayers and lowers his arms, Boroğlu's mother steps forward, takes a small brown bag from her dress pocket, and sprinkles the memorial with a sacred combination of herbs. The man moves to one side and folds his thick arms across his chest. Özlem, standing near him, has no prayers and no tangible gift—and won't, at least for a long time—but tears fill her eyes.

As a blue sedan pulls off the road into the narrow dirt lot below the memorial, the stout man in the dark suit goes down the steps. A man in a gray T-shirt and sweatpants gets out of the driver's door, goes around the front of the car, and opens the passenger door. He is fit and in his late thirties; his black hair is cropped short and his dark beard trimmed. He helps from the sedan a woman with a white scarf and an ankle-length khaki dress. Together they head to the stairs. As they begin to climb, he puts his arm around her waist and steadies her. Both have their heads bowed when they reach the top. The puppies leap and bound.

As the couple approaches the memorial, the woman sags for a moment against her husband. Wisps of auburn hair, having escaped from beneath her scarf, curl across her cheek. Her hand trembling, she leans forward and touches the photograph of Mehmet's grandfather. "Father," she murmurs. "Father…? Why…?" Her voice cracks. "Why has Allah…?" Her shoulders shake, and her hand slips from the photograph. Before her husband can bolster her, she collapses onto the bed of carnations. Her husband reaches for her, but he is himself so unsteady that he can't lift her, and he slumps to his knees. She sobs uncontrollably. Both Boroğlu and her mother kneel by the couple. The woman pushes her husband away, clutches Boroğlu's mother, buries her head in the older woman's chest, and wails.

Boroğlu stands as a silver Mercedes pulls up next to the blue sedan. An overweight, middle-aged man in blue jeans and a loose, blue work shirt pulls himself from the car and rumbles toward the steps, leaving the door open and the motor running. He has a thirty-five-millimeter camera and flash attachment slung on a strap around his neck.

Boroğlu steps over to block the photographer's way. Her anger and frustration boiling, she hisses, "Get out of here! Leave them alone!"

"It's public property, hon," the photographer says in a low voice with a strong British accent.

"Leave us alone!" the husband shouts.

When the photographer raises his camera so that he can shoot over Boroğlu's shoulder, she steps forward and knees him in the groin with all of her might. He goes down hard, his camera crashing to the cement beneath his weight. Moaning, he rolls to his side, curls his legs, and grabs his crotch. The husband stomps the camera repeatedly.

"No," Boroğlu says, her voice low. "That will only make it worse." She goes down on one knee, grabs the camera, and, not quite choking the photographer with the strap, slides out the camera's memory card. She drops the camera next to the photographer's head and flings the memory card down the side of the hill into the brambles.

Mehmet's mother, oblivious to what has just happened, continues to bawl. The puppies yip, and the neighborhood dogs start to howl.

Boroğlu leans over the photographer, who still can't catch his breath, twists his ear, and whispers, "Leave them alone, you stupid kafir!" She yanks his ear. "If you're not gone in two minutes, I'll throw your car keys into hell."

 19

BERGAMA

When Özlem Boroğlu and her mother enter their house's courtyard, Serkan bounds down the stairs from the rooftop garden. He kisses his grandmother's hand and presses his forehead to hers. Then, he hugs his mother, who at first only holds him tentatively. Finally, she begins to let go of some of the fierce anger she felt when she took down the kafir cameraman at the memorial an hour earlier. She clutches her only son until his grip around her shoulders grows limp. They each step back and look at one another. Tears run down her face again. "My Serkan," she says.

He cocks his head and gazes at his mother but says nothing.

Özlem Boroğlu's mother wrings her hands and says, "I will make çay."

"I will help, Anneanne."

"No." She nods to the stairs as she says to him, "Talk with your mother. I will bring up the çay." Her voice, though little more than a whisper, is firm.

The night is still warm, but a light breeze on the roof rustles the grapevines. The garden smells of herbs, not scorched earth. Serkan brings a third wrought-iron chair to the glass table. Boroğlu lights a cigarette, takes a long drag on it, lifts a candle from the ledge, and lights it as well. She sets the candle on the table, exhales pale smoke, and asks, "To what do we owe the honor of your visit, Serkan?" She can't help that ire seeps into her voice.

"I just wanted to see you." He snatches a bunch of underripe grapes from the vine and takes the middle chair, but he doesn't look at his mother.

She takes another drag and, exhaling slowly, says, "Tell that to your grandmother. Tell me why you're really here. Do you need money again?"

"No. No, I don't need money." As he gazes at a dozen of Elif's terracotta statues perched on a shelf below the vines, a chubby black-and-white cat climbs along the trellis. The cat drops to the patio, sidles over to him, and rubs against his calf. "Hello, Sekhmet," he says, leaning down to stroke its head. The cat purrs, crosses the patio, and laps water from a bowl.

Özlem squeezes her lighter. "You didn't come home after the attack!"

"I was in Cappadocia. With clients. *Working.*"

"You didn't even call!"

"I didn't hear about it until…" He pulls two grapes from the bunch but doesn't eat them.

"The memorial service… You didn't call me then either."

"I had a deal going. My biggest…"

"You and your deals!"

"Look, I'm sorry."

She scoffs.

"I said I'm sorry." He looks into his mother's eyes for the first time. "How are you doing?"

"I…I just kicked a kafir photographer in his jewels." She coughs. "That's how I am."

Pulling another grape from the bunch, he hides a smile. "Did he deserve it?"

"That. And more." She shakes her head, almost herself smiling. Although she has always found it hard to stay mad at her son, she can't now let go of her fury. She has not felt this deeply angry since the government flooded the archeological site she ran at Allianoi. Or, perhaps, ever. "He was harassing a woman who lost her father. Her son's the boy who…the survivor. The one… But he's…" She stares at the smoke serpenting into the breeze.

Serkan nods. "How is Elif?"

"At least you called her! Finally." Her son's eyes remind her too much of her ex-husband, the father of her children, her professor who took her to bed, the man who ten years later took another student to the same bed. "She's not doing well. Everybody… We're all taking it hard."

"It is hard."

"Harder than you know, Serkan." She takes another drag on her cigarette.

When he hears his grandmother, he leaps to his feet. Meeting her at the top of the stairs, he reaches for the tray holding the teapot, three cups, and a plate with six biscuits.

"No, my dear," she says. "Sit. You're home." Still wearing her scarf, she sets the tray on the table and begins to pour the çay.

The three of them sit for a couple of minutes silently regarding the steam from their çay. Boroğlu stubs out her cigarette and then snaps a biscuit in half. Her mother gazes at Serkan as he stands and selects a small, thin, red-and-white goddess from the shelf. As he sits, he stares at the statue's finely wrought face of a lion.

"It's good to be home," he says.

"A home wrecked by terrorists."

"*Terrorists,*" he mutters. "They're killing my business… My clients left for Crete when—"

"They're killing *people,* Serkan! People in Bergama!"

He squints at his mother. "I know that! And I know it's tragic! I'm just saying it's bigger. They're killing tourism. The whole economy!"

Özlem's mother looks from her daughter to grandson. "They're killing something inside us," she says. "Something *in* all of us."

## 20

### ANKARA

Tuğçe Iskan is alone in her Ankara office at a time, 22:17, that she likes. No other people. No distractions. She stares at the computer monitor, not her own, but a colleague's, because the research she is doing in the Ministry's system can't be done on the clock—or on the record. She gleaned his password months ago to use in moments like this. Her half-liter bottle of Coke stands on a paper towel on the floor behind and to the left of her colleague's desk chair.

When she feels her personal iPhone vibrate, she slides it from her khakis' pocket—but no one is on the line. She doesn't get many calls, doesn't have many friends, and none in the office, but this phone has been exceptionally useful in her work. She never uses it when others are around, in fact, has necessarily kept its existence hidden from her office mates. The second time the phone vibrates, she answers, counts to twelve, and clicks her forefinger's black-polished nail three times against the receiver. When she hears three more clicks, she smiles, counts to twelve again, and says, "Hello, Nihat Bey."

"You are safe, I trust, my dear Tuğçe."

For a split second she thinks she may have heard affection in his gruff voice. He has always shown respect, even in the beginning when others in the Ministry did not, and perhaps... She shakes her head. She has read inflections wrong before, failed to notice social cues any number of times. "I missed you, Nihat Bey," she says. She does not mean that she longed for him. When she went to their arranged meeting at their kiosk in Genclick Park at 20:15, he was not there.

"Old friends dropped by unexpectedly."

She knows he means that he was being followed. He has never missed a rendezvous except when he detected tails sent by his "old friends" in the Ministry whose plans to defraud the Turkish people of hundreds of millions of lira he blocked. Embittered in their fetid swamp of greed and power, some apparently believe he still intends to use the evidence against them. "It seems your friends are stopping by more often," she says.

"It does, doesn't it?" She hears his lighter click and flare before he adds, "You are back in the office?"

"I am." Night is the best time to actually get work done here. She can roll up her sleeves and loosen her collar. She has reread all of the files about tumuli, particularly the robbing of the ancient graves in the State of İzmir dating from the present to a year before Özlem Boroğlu's Galen letter surfaced. The Ministry has a wealth of information to sift through on its system—memos and site reports and project summaries—but nothing mentions gold coins from the second century of the Common Era. And there's nothing, of course, about a letter from Ancient Rome's most famous physician to the son of an old friend in Pergamon. She needs to discover how Boroğlu got her hands on the letter without Boroğlu figuring out that she has done so—no easy task. Iskan didn't really expect to find anything in the Ministry's electronic file system, but she had to do the research to be certain.

She logs out and shuts down the computer. No one, she knows, can really multitask perfectly. Although she comes close, she'll give her mentor her full attention, not least because she wants him to tell her something he will definitely not say. When she stands up, she makes sure that she has left everything exactly as she found it. She adjusts the mouse and pushes in the chair. As she picks up the Coke bottle and the paper towel, her phone pings.

"And your friend, the emperor, is resting peacefully?" Nihat Bey asks.

"Safe and sound." She slips the paper towel onto her desk and sets the bottle on it.

"Working on an old case? Or a new one?"

She smiles, something she doesn't do much except when she is talking with him. "Both really," she says as she glances at the icon for the e-mail that just arrived.

"Ah," he says. "Sometimes those are the most interesting...and the most frustrating."

She nods, though she knows he can't see her. "Nihat Bey," she says, "I need to ask you something."

"Of course."

"You know the old case, the one I barely began before it was officially terminated? I've been receiving e-mails for almost four months from an anonymous source. I just received another a minute ago." She tries to unscrew the Coke's cap with her right hand but has to cup the phone and use her left to steady the bottle. "I wonder if you know who the source might be?"

"What do they say, these e-mails?"

"Nothing. They contain a lot of information. Records of transactions. Financials. Land deals, particularly." She takes a quick sip of Coke. "And photos. Recent and not-so-recent. Focused on one business. One family. An established one. Well-connected. The dealings and the people involved are all, as you would say, interesting."

"But the e-mails, they don't *say* anything? No messages?"

"No. Nothing at all."

"Perhaps someone wants you to make connections. Find the patterns."

"Perhaps." She smiles again. Thankful.

"Perhaps you should take a look at what you just received. Maybe it will include a message."

"Maybe." She taps her phone and then taps it again. As usual, the e-mail has no message, just an attachment. When she clicks on the icon, she finds a single photograph, another long shot of two men sitting on a stone bench in a park. But these two men are young and handsome. The one on the right is Mustafa Hamit's Americanized playboy son, also named Mustafa. It takes her a moment to recognize the clean-shaven almost equally handsome one on the left. She sucks in her breath. That these two are meeting is almost as startling as the Russian spy meeting with the boy's father. Her mind begins to race.

"Tuğçe, my dear," Nihat Bey asks, "Is there a message?"

*Not anything written,* she thinks, *but there is definitely a message.*

 21

BERGAMA

Elif Boroğlu looks up from her work when there is a knocking at the studio's door. She takes out her earbuds, rises from her stool, and cocks her head. As the door opens, she sees a man about her age, lean and handsome in a conventional way. He has carefully combed black hair, green eyes, and two days' growth of beard.

"May I come in?" he asks. His tone is polite, but she's not sure it's a question.

"You already are," she answers, her voice even, neither gracious nor sarcastic. The man's clothing is tailored, his wristwatch Swiss, and his shoes handmade. He wears no socks.

Shutting the door behind him, he glances about the studio. "I've heard you're talented," he says, "and I was just driving by."

Given that her studio, at the outskirts of Bergama near the military base and the Aesklepion, has no exterior sign and no listed address, his statement, though perhaps meant to be ingratiating, sounds absurd. Without answering, she takes a towel and covers the wax model she has been carving. Her black-and-white cat leaps down from the table to her right, stretches, sniffs the air, and sidles over to her.

"I'm Mustafa," he says. As he steps toward her, he extends his hand in a Westernized way.

She picks up her cat, tosses back her long braid that has fallen across her right shoulder, and then shakes the man's hand. He smells like he has just showered and put on cologne. He is good looking, but in a too carefully groomed, worked-out and worked-on way that doesn't attract her. Her boyfriend, an elite commando deployed somewhere near or beyond the Syrian border, has a jagged, seven-centimeter scar on the back of his left hand that she finds far more intriguing than this man's manicured fingernails. "I'm Elif Boroğlu," she says, her voice still noncommittal. "But you must already know that." She continues to hold the cat against her chest.

He strolls around the studio looking at the terra-cotta statues in various stages of completion. As he picks up a svelte, naked nymph that has been glazed and fired, he says, "You're from around here?"

It has the inflection of a question, but she thinks he's again inquiring about something he already knows. "Yes," she answers. "I've lived in Bergama since I was eleven."

He glances at the centrifuge she has borrowed from a friend but has not yet plugged in, nods, puts down the nymph, and smiles at her. "It looks like you've found your medium."

"For now." She leans over and slips her cat onto the floor. Purring, the cat rubs against her leg.

"So, what's for sale?" he asks as he selects another nymph, naked to the waist, and turns it slowly.

"The finished pieces. Most of them. Basically."

"Most?" He puts the figurine down.

"Most."

"But not all?" As the cat crosses the floor, the man reaches down to pet it, but the cat keeps moving away from him. It suddenly leaps to a high shelf near the kiln.

"What's his name?" the man asks.

"*Her* name is Sekhmet."

"Ah," he says, his smile genuine. "The Egyptian warrior goddess, the lioness. Fiercest hunter. Her breath created the desert."

Not returning his smile, Elif says, "Also the god of healing and arbiter of justice and order."

His smile twists. "And plagues. Don't forget plagues." Looking over at the cat again, he adds, "Your Sekhmet doesn't look all that ferocious."

She nods but does not continue the conversation.

He stares at her not-yet-fired rendering of the stout goddess holding the single-edged sword and the severed head. "This one's interesting," he says, pointing to it.

"Thank you."

"How much is it?

"It's not for sale."

He reaches toward it but doesn't touch it. "But when it's finished?"

"It's not for sale," she repeats.

His bright eyes fix on her. "Really?"

"Yes." She sells her terra-cotta figurines here in Bergama for fifty to eighty Turkish lira. Serkan peddles them to artsy boutiques in Istanbul for eighty to a hundred. The shops resell them for two hundred to two-fifty. Some of the more upscale places charge even more. Occasionally, as he did with the older American couple, Serkan arranges a special order for his tourism customers.

Still looking into her face, he waves his hand expansively around the studio. "What's the price of these?"

"It varies."

"But what? On average?"

She looks at his wristwatch and his clothes. "Perhaps, a hundred."

He points again at the stocky goddess with the snakes emerging from her hair. "What if I offered you a thousand for this one?"

Her eyes lock on his. "I'd tell you it's not for sale."

"Ten thousand?" His smile seems less friendly.

"Still my answer."

"One hundred thousand?"

She laughs but doesn't hesitate before saying, "I'd tell you that anyone stupid enough to pay me a hundred thousand for one of my figurines should never own one."

His eyes flash. He nods slowly. "I see," he says. He nods a second and a third time. "Well," he adds, rubbing the palms of his hands together, "it's very nice to meet you, Elif Boroğlu." His tone, though still polite, is no longer at all amicable.

"Likewise," she says. "I don't often get customers at my studio." Sekhmet leaps from the shelf to the floor.

"Do you have a card?"

"No." She laughs again, but not in an unfriendly way. "Of course not."

"Well," he says, "I know quality. And, I'll be back."

He does not look over his shoulder as he leaves the studio. She stands there for a moment, her head again cocked, wondering who sent Mustafa—and why. As she realizes he came of his own accord, she shivers. He wants something…something that isn't healthy for her or others in Bergama. And that look she saw in his eyes suggests he's used to getting what he wants.

 **22**

KAIKOS VALLEY

$T$he three men, the Hamit patriarch, his only son, and his nephew, stand in the shade of an olive grove seven kilometers outside of Bergama near the road that leads to Dikili and the sea. Although it is only an hour after sunrise, it's already hot. The cousins look enough alike to be brothers, but the son is more refined and, at this moment, far more tired. The patriarch, a trim, carefully groomed sixty-five-year-old with a receding hairline gone gray, takes a white cloth from his younger sister's oldest son. As he unwraps the cloth to reveal a small, exquisite gold amulet, Bora, his nephew, brushes his hand through his short black hair and beams like the father of a newborn.

Gazing at the amulet, the patriarch says, "Athena. Hellenistic." He glances up. "Site B-113?"

Bora nods.

"What else?" It's more a command than a question.

"That's the only gold. So far. I knew not to say anything on the phone." Bora nods at the amulet and scratches his chin. "But amethyst, carnelian beads, silver coins, a dagger…"

"Bones?" Mustafa, the patriarch's son, asks.

"Not yet. No skeleton." Bora turns to the patriarch. "We're close. You told me to be careful. Go slow. Not rush." Although Bora scratches at his throat, both father and son believe him. He is not holding anything out on them because he is blood but also because he knows that if he did his remains would be fed to the family cats.

"Careful. Yes, of course," Mustafa says. He is no older than his cousin, but he is much better educated and, he believes, exponentially more knowledgeable when it comes to Hellenistic gravesites. "The real treasure will be with the bones." His mouth is dry, and his head pounds. His father woke him at 5:30, only an hour after he got home. After arriving in Bergama, he checked out the old bitch's artsy daughter at her studio, then stopped by the apartment he has rented for Damla. She had a bottle of raki chilled and was more than willing to demonstrate how happy she was to see him again. He likes to have at least one woman in each city, and the family has a villa along the sea in Dikili so that they can keep tabs on their landholdings in the area. "May I see it, Father?" he asks, his tone ever respectful in front of his cousin.

His father gazes at the amulet, brushes an imagined spec of dirt from it, and hands the cloth to his son.

Mustafa smiles as he inspects it. His hand shakes only a little even though he has never before held a recently unearthed gold artifact. Athena is wearing a helmet and carries a spear and a shield fringed with snakes. Medusa's head hangs from her body armor. "Yes," he says. His headache doesn't vanish, but it slackens. "This is okay. It'll do." It's actually museum quality, perfect for his purposes, but he doesn't want his cousin to see his enthusiasm.

"Thank you, Bora," the patriarch says by way of complimenting his nephew. "And thank you for contacting us so quickly. Keep in touch."

"Of course," Bora says to him. "I'll use the code."

"And only that one phone," the patriarch adds.

As the cousin ambles away toward his white pick-up truck, the patriarch says to his son, "He's a good boy. Does exactly what I tell him to do."

Dropping their amiable expressions, father and son move a couple steps farther into the shade of the olive grove. The meeting was held out here at this hour because the patriarch's sources have informed him that yet another government investigation of the family's finances and business practices has begun; his calls are being monitored, and surveillance has started anew. He will be able to fix the problem, of course, but it is not yet clear who should be contacted and how they should be leveraged.

No one can eavesdrop here. The Hamits own all of the land surrounding the grove and a number of nearby plots. For years now, they have been, mostly through shell companies, buying up any arable land available around Bergama. Neither father nor son gives a fig about farming, but the land, leased back to farmers, turns a small profit and allows the family to launder a lot of money. And far more importantly, much of the wealth of ancient Pergamon remains in undiscovered tombs in the area. With advanced technology, including seismic and geophysics prospecting, they can systematically check sites like B-113 without any interference from the government or competitors. They can even work in broad daylight. Mustafa particularly likes the concept of an extra-legal, vertical monopoly on priceless Hellenistic artifacts.

"I'd like that back," the patriarch says, nodding to the amulet resting in the cloth.

"Of course," Mustafa says as he scrapes his loafers in the dust. "It's not like I was going to give it to Damla."

They rode here in silence, partly because Mustafa could not quite form words after so much raki and sex and so little sleep and partly because the patriarch was angry yet again at his son's lack of self-discipline. He has invested a lot personally and financially, and the boy is bright, very bright, a brilliant student. And as well educated as anyone in Istanbul and better than anyone down here in the hinterlands. But the boy definitely developed some bad habits in the U.S. "You've got to focus more on work," the patriarch says, "and less on your dick."

"I do." He folds the cloth over and, bowing slightly, presents it to his father. "I've already got a buyer for that in Istanbul."

"The American?"

"Yes."

The patriarch gazes again at the amulet. "What have you done about that bastard who's demanding a commission?"

"I've got it all working out." Mustafa smiles again. "He's Özlem Boroğlu's son. And I'm making him an offer he can't refuse."

His father looks alarmed for a moment, then surprised, and finally pleased with his son.

When his father doesn't pick up on the movie line, Mustafa adds, "I'll get whatever information she has *before* we finish with her."

"She's found the *Galatian*," his father says, a spark of anger in his voice.

"Not yet, she hasn't." Mustafa's voice rises. "She wouldn't be trying to get onto site C-174. She knows we're close."

"She seemed *too* interested." The patriarch refolds the cloth and slips it into his pants pocket. His son is incredibly well educated, but he still needs to learn a thing or two about people.

"Our tech's telling us we're onto something." There's almost no breeze here, and cocks are crowing somewhere nearby. Mustafa's head is pounding again, but he left his water bottle in the Range Rover.

"Boroğlu is clever. If she really thought we'd find the Galen cache at C-174, she wouldn't have been so obvious."

Sweat beads on Mustafa's forehead.

"And, anyway," his father adds, "your tech's not the only thing."

"Whatever information the old bitch has, I'll get."

"Is that another promise you can't keep?" the patriarch asks, the edge in his voice sharper. When his son doesn't answer, he adds, "We need something concrete. *Yesterday!*"

"Look, I told you I'm on it." Sweat runs down Mustafa's spine. "I've doubled the tech teams' shifts."

"You and your tech!" the patriarch says with disdain in his voice. "Do I have to—"

"I've got it all under control!" Mustafa's mouth is pasty.

"Just like you told Vlad the family has the Galatian statue!"

"I…" Mustafa balls his fists, starts to breath hard.

The patriarch stares into his son's eyes until his son, still hyperventilating, drops his hands to his sides.

"You smell like raki farts," the patriarch says as he turns away.

# 23

BERGAMA

Tuğçe Iskan knocks a third time on the raspberry-colored front door. While she waits, she slaps a manila envelope against her thigh. Graffiti covers the back wall of the house downhill; pale morning haze obscures the view of the Kaikos Valley beyond. Birdsong is punctuating the constant mumble of traffic down in the town.

Iskan raps a fourth time, quick and loud, clearly urgent. She has never fully understood the nuances of social interactions, but she has learned to follow them most of the time. This, however, is not the occasion for pleasantries or patience. For more than a day now, she has been trying to contact Özlem Boroğlu by phone, text, and e-mail. Coming here was absolutely necessary. She can't otherwise get the woman's attention, except, perhaps through legal channels which are too slow and will only further antagonize both of them. And anyway, she has shared exactly none of what she is doing with her Ministry colleagues or bosses. It's far too important to risk getting bogged down in the bureaucracy. And the endemic Ministry corruption and inevitable leaks would sabotage her investigation.

It's hot today, and the porch provides no shade, but she will stand here forever—or at least until neighbors come out to complain about the racket. She even called ahead this morning to inform Boroğlu that she had returned to Bergama and had in her possession photos Boroğlu needed to see, evidence that would matter to her family. And she is certain that Boroğlu is home. It's only eight thirty, and Özlem, like herself, tends to be a nocturnal creature.

The fifth time is harder, even longer, and clearly impatient—a clamor that neighbors must notice. She looks again at the graffiti wall. It is beige, the color of earth in this part of Turkey. There are darker gray spots where messages have been painted over... White slashes like scars where the concrete has been scraped away... A dark metal drain pipe... Chinks in the concrete down near the level of the street...

"Go away!"

The shout from inside the house is irate, but Iskan expected as much. "I have photos you need to see!" she calls back.

"Get the hell away from here!" The response is dark, even more emotional. "You lied to me again!"

"I'm not leaving till you see—"

"Rot in hell!"

Iskan doesn't answer. She doesn't know what Boroğlu means by her lying again, but she has Boroğlu's attention, and she's not going to hell or anywhere else.

"I said, *go to hell!*"

Boroğlu has no idea what hell would be like for Iskan, but Iskan knows that her knocking on Boroğlu's front door would be in one of hell's inner circles for Boroğlu. She looks again at the wall across the street at the names "Burak" and "Mehmet" and at the numbers that don't mathematically add up. She knocks a sixth time, and then she notices a young woman, seemingly lost in thought, coming up the street.

"I'll call the police!" Boroğlu shouts through the door, but Iskan knows she won't. None of this can ever involve the police.

The young woman is about Iskan's age and height, but she's thinner and prettier, Iskan thinks, with a small nose and long, silky black hair pulled back in a loose braid. The woman hesitates when she sees Iskan, but then she continues on toward the house's steps. Iskan shifts the manila envelope to her left hand and waits, making no response to Boroğlu's threat. "Elif?" she asks when the woman reaches the steps.

Elif stops, switches the small, black plastic bag she is carrying to her left hand, and asks, "Do I know you?" Her question isn't threatening, but her tone is wary.

Iskan comes down the steps. "I'm a very big fan of your work, your terra-cottas."

"Really?" It's a genuine question.

Iskan wipes her right hand on her jeans and then extends it. "Yes. The statues have…life in them."

Elif shakes her hand. "Thanks. I put my…" She stops herself. "Why are you here?" Her eyes, bleary, as though she has been up most of the night, fix on Iskan.

"I have to show your mother…" She taps the envelope against her right palm. "Maybe you can help me…"

Elif takes a deep breath.

"I'm not from the police or anything." Technically, Iskan is telling the truth. She has come here entirely on her own. "I just need your mother to identify—"

Elif shakes her head.

"You don't have to talk to me," Iskan insists. "I would, though, sometime like to talk with you about your figurines."

Elif seems to believe her, but still she says, "If this has to do with my mother's work, I really can't."

The front door is flung open, and Boroğlu barges out onto the porch. "Leave her out of this!"

Iskan waves the envelope. "I just need—"

"Get the hell away from us!"

Iskan reaches into the envelope and pulls out a photograph.

Boroğlu rushes down the steps. As she's about to tear the photograph from Iskan's hand, Elif says, "That guy was in my studio yesterday. He came to the studio!"

Both of the other women freeze.

"Who is he, Mom?" Elif's voice sounds stricken. "Who's that guy with Serkan?"

The photograph is the one of Serkan Boroğlu and Mustafa Hamit on the stone bench in the park. Iskan has identified the setting as the area behind the Süleymaniye Mosque in Istanbul. "Yes, Özlem," she says, "who is that with your son?" She hands the photograph to Boroğlu. "You know, don't you?"

Boroğlu's hand quakes as she glares first at the photograph and then at Iskan.

*If eyes were daggers,* Iskan thinks, *I'd be dead on the cobblestones.*

HOUSE IN BERGAMA

# ☆ 24

BERGAMA

Özlem Boroğlu's mother sits in a small lobby outside the intensive care unit at Bergama's hospital. A basket of food she has prepared rests on the floor next to her. Both of Mehmet Suner's parents are inside the unit, but she doesn't want to bother them. She could sit here waiting for hours, hands folded in her lap, but her daughter paces the corridor.

Boroğlu ignores the nurse at the station who stares at her. It's warm, too warm; the air is unmoving, dead. The murmur of electronic machinery and the antiseptic odor irritate her. She doesn't like feeling confined and detests doing nothing—and hospital waiting rooms entail both. They're not as bad as classrooms or airplanes, but this is too much like being stuck in an office pushing paper after doing field-work for years. She badly needs a cigarette.

As she paces, Boroğlu spins her lighter as though it's a short red baton. Finally, the ICU door opens, and Engin Suner, Mehmet's father, steps into the small lobby. When he sees the two of them, he is startled for a moment. "You...," he says, the word a mixture of a greeting, a question, and an accusation. In the hospital lights, the rings under his eyes are dark green. He is wearing a clean T-shirt but the same sweatpants and work boots that he had on at the memorial. He does not hug either woman.

"My mother has brought you food," Boroğlu says.

He looks blankly at the basket, as though his mind can no longer process ordinary information. "Yes," he says. "Thank you."

Boroğlu's mother stands and hands the basket to him, but he appears unable to figure out what to do with it.

"Thank you," he repeats as he bows his head to Boroğlu's mother. "Would you…"

"We don't want to impose," Boroğlu says.

He closes his eyes and squeezes the bridge of his nose. "It's…" Dropping his hand, he takes a deep breath. "No…Hafize… She has no one… Her mother is dead… My mother left for the day…," he pauses, seeming to have lost all sense of time, "an hour ago. Anyway, they don't always get along…." Turning again to Boroğlu's mother, he asks, "Would you like to visit?"

Boroğlu takes the basket from him.

"If it will help," Boroğlu's mother says.

"Yes," he says. "It could…" He presses the buzzer that opens the unit's door.

Boroğlu leaves the basket outside under the station nurse's watchful eye. She and her mother and Mehmet's father scrub their hands before entering Mehmet's room. Mehmet lies on his back, his eyes closed, a frail form under the pale sheet. His shaved head is immobilized by a brace with three pins driven into his skull. His face is waxen, even the purple bruises on his right cheek and temple. His arms, lying at his sides outside the sheet, look to Boroğlu like pencils. An intravenous feeding tube is attached to his forearm. Drainage runs from under the sheet to a bag clamped to the bed. Most ominous, at least for Boroğlu, is the tube affixed to a shunt at the crown of his head. A ventilator cycles, and an EEG monitor shows a low level of brain function with no spikes.

Mehmet's mother sits on the edge of his bed holding his right hand in both of hers. Her long auburn hair is pulled back in a tight braid. When she turns and sees Boroğlu's mother, she bursts into tears. Her skin is gray and the bags beneath her eyes dark. Still holding Mehmet with one hand, she reaches for Boroğlu's mother with the other. Boroğlu's mother leans in close so that Mehmet's mother can grasp her forearm and still hold her son. She strokes the younger woman's hair as they both weep.

Holding back tears herself, Boroğlu stands by Mehmet's father looking on for a few minutes until the women's weeping subsides. Then, she whispers to him, "A cigarette?" He puts his hand on his wife's shoulder and squeezes his son's free hand for a moment before leaving the room.

Boroğlu and Suner take the basket out the hospital's main entrance, turn to their right, and walk past the *kantin*. Around the building's corner, they finally find a quiet spot with three connected wooden chairs lined against the hospital's wall. A lone fir tree with a split trunk stands next to a ramp leading up to an unmarked emergency exit.

As Boroğlu and Suner sit down, small dark birds scatter from the fir's branches. She hands him a cigarette and slips one from the pack for herself. He takes her lighter and lights first hers and then his. His hands are rough, those of a working man, and more steady than she expected. As he returns the lighter, he takes a quick puff and then a slow, deep drag on his cigarette. She savors that first long inhalation.

"Thank you," he says, smoke escaping his nose and mouth. His brown eyes hold little light.

They sit silently for a moment until she takes from the basket two plastic bottles of water, a loaf of ekmek baked fresh, and a jar of her mother's pickles. "How are you doing?" she asks.

"Okay." He shrugs. "Okay...as long as my son lives."

A skinny white puppy with a dark muzzle ambles toward them. It wags its tail, sits, stands again, and sits once more. Boroğlu tosses a piece of ekmek that the dog scarfs without chewing. She opens the jar and puts it on the bench. "And Hafize?" she asks.

He looks out toward the road, but she is sure he is looking at something closer—or farther—which she cannot see. "She's strong," he says. "But..."

The dog sniffs the basket and licks Boroğlu's hand. She brushes it aside and then tears off a big enough hunk of the bread so that the dog slinks away with it. "It's a lot for her..."

"Too much... Her father *and* her son. Mehmet is her whole life."

He stares at the open jar and then at the thin line of smoke swirling from his cigarette. "We just need to hold on until he comes around. Gets better." He nods, more to assure himself than her. "He will."

Although she is fairly certain that won't happen, she smiles and says, "Yes." When he gazes off into the distance again, she asks, "Was it a special day, their visit to the acropolis?"

"Yeah. Yes, it was. His birthday…Mehmet's." His voice trails off, like he's having difficulty remembering something from the distant past. "Dede said it was a special surprise." He takes another long drag on his cigarette and then drops the butt and grinds it out with the heel of his boot. He carefully picks up the crushed butt and puts it into a white plastic container already more than half full of discarded cigarettes.

She leans forward. "What else did they do? I mean, did they go anywhere else?"

"No. I don't think so." Cocking his head like he himself is wondering, he takes a pickle and crunches it in half with his teeth. "I think Hafize walked him over to Dede's village." Chewing the pickle, he adds, "I don't know."

When the puppy comes begging again, Boroğlu pushes it away. It sits, cocks its head, and looks dolefully at her. "You're not far from his grandfather's?" she asks even though she already knows that the two villages are only three-and-a-half kilometers apart. The area between Bergama and Kozak, known for its rugged terrain, forests, granite quarries, small farms, pine-nut-processing plants, and now logging, has been populated for thousands of years.

Shaking his head, Suner raises the other half of the pickle but doesn't eat it. His hand begins to shiver for the first time. "He, Dede, came for dinner every Sunday. Other days, too. Since Hafize's mother passed… She was…is…an only child. Dede…they both needed… family." He rushes his words as though once he started talking he can't stop. "Dede still works his land. Gets around good. They…him and Mehmet walk the fields together. The hills. A lot. 'Exploring,' Mehmet calls it. 'Going exploring with Dede!' He's had real good offers for the land, but he says it's for Mehmet. I want Dede to sell…

94

Wanted him to sell. He could live with us…my family." His half-smile is painful. "Mehmet's going to be an engineer. He's good at maths. The best in his class."

Boroğlu nods but doesn't say anything.

As Suner sucks in his breath, his face darkens. "I'm going to get the people who did this to Mehmet! To Dede! To Hafize!" His voice trails off and then returns, even deeper and darker. "Mehmet's blood, Dede's blood will not be left on the ground!"

Boroğlu carefully says nothing. She understands the desire for vengeance, but she also knows that the father's energy and focus have to be on the boy as long as he is alive. And afterward, Hafize cannot have her husband succumb to a lethal obsession after she has lost her father and her only child.

Suner clenches his fists and glares out across the parking lot at the Ambulans Bufe.

**25**

RAQQA

The sheikh leans forward in the only armchair in the woman's apartment and says, "I alone can protect you."

The woman's emerald eyes flash for a moment. Her body goes rigid, and her hands, covered by her thick black gloves, clench in her lap. Her cheeks, hidden behind her niqab, flush. He is trying to sound paternal, but his nasal whine sounds nothing like her father's voice; it lacks the timbre, the authority, and, clearly, the rectitude. "Thank you," she says. "You have told me before."

She sits on the edge of the plain, straight-backed chair, her head bowed and her eyes averted, not out of respect for the sheikh, as he would expect, but rather so that he may not see what's there. He has visited her regularly since her husband drove the explosives-laden, Fiat delivery truck into one of Assad's military command posts. On each visit the sheikh brings her gifts, fresh fruits and vegetables unavailable in Raqqa's markets. But he is also the man who took her son from her and delivered the boy to the al Farouq training camp. She was expecting her Guardian when the hard knock on the door came, and, though she was fully dressed in her double burqa, she was still taken aback by the sheikh's arrival.

The sheikh's scalp itches under his black turban; beneath his black robes, sweat runs down his neck and chest and spine. The small apartment's living area is stifling, and his heart is racing. His two heavily armed attendants wait as instructed in the hallway. "The Guardian I have assigned you," he says, "informs me that you have stopped going to the market."

She looks into the sheikh's face. He has small, cold eyes. His eyebrows are thick and his nose wide. Scars pockmark his fleshy cheeks. Gray has crept into the stubble of his unkempt beard. "I have lost my appetite," she says.

"But you will eat these." He waves at the oranges in the net bag that lies on the small table next to her chair. The silver Rolex on his right wrist shines even in the room's dimness.

"Allahu Akbar." Her voice is flat. "I am grateful to Allah."

"The Guardian," the sheikh says, "he has not caused you any... difficulty...?"

"Never." She shakes her head. "He is not the problem."

The sheikh stands up and moves closer so that his robes are almost touching her bowed head. Speaking down to her, he says, "You need a husband."

The smell of peppermint on his breath disgusts her. She presses her right hand against her thigh and claws at the unhealed puncture wounds so that, even though she wears heavy gloves, the pain in her torn fingers weds that in her infected leg. "As you say."

He runs his right hand through his beard. "Soon!"

"I am still in mourning."

"The iddah ended...," he raises his voice, "more than a year ago!"

"And yet I mourn." She stares at his robes bulging around his midriff. He may be a sheikh, may even be, as he has informed her, the fourth-most-powerful man in the caliphate, but he has grown soft during these hard times in Raqqa. As the city is destroyed by the unrelenting air attacks and the people suffer immeasurably, the sheikh and his cronies grow fat. Brutes enforce the caliphate's stringent dictums, maiming or executing people over trifles, while the sheikhs themselves flout sacred Sunni customs and statutes.

"You are making a mistake!" His breath quickens as he takes a half step closer so that his robe touches her head covering.

"You know better than I." She shuts her eyes.

"Yes, I do!" He takes her chin and raises her head so that the cloth covering her nose and mouth rubs against his robe. His hand shakes and his voice cracks as he whispers, "It's either me...or *everyone.*"

Her eyes still closed, she gouges her thigh so that wedded pain fires through her. She takes a deep breath, grits her teeth, and yanks her head back so that he loses his grip.

His right hand grabs her neck. His thumb and forefinger press hard into the fold of her burqa. His voice high, he hisses, "You must not understand what's good for your son!"

Her eyes pop open. She glares up into his face, her loathing clear as dawn breaking.

"You stupid cunt!" He shoves her head back, makes a fist, and shatters her nose.

The world falls into deep night except for the gleaming meteor shower of the Rolex as he pummels her face.

# 26

ISTANBUL

Walking along the stone path in Gülhane Park, Serkan Boroğlu smiles wryly at a circular flowerbed planted to resemble a nazar boncuğu, the blue and yellow and white talisman that protects believers from the evil eye. Though the park runs for a long way below Topkapı Palace's outer fortification walls, he has never been here before. His clients always loved his tours of Topkapı Palace and nearby Hagia Sofia and the Blue Mosque, but none of them, *nobody ever,* asked to spend a serene hour or two strolling here among the tall trees and multihued gardens. And it never once occurred to him to suggest a sojourn here. His sister might like it—no, though it's peaceful, it is managed and manicured, not natural and not nearly wild enough for her. And his mother would want to dig it all up just to find shards of lost civilizations.

His trek here today again involved stupid security precautions— his crossing through the Blue Mosque's courtyard and circumnavigating Hagia Sofia's grounds before entering the park. This time it was less disconcerting and exhausting but even more annoying. Mustafa Hamit sits on a brown wooden bench at the top of a hill. His back is to Topkapı's high stone curtain wall. A vineless trellis runs above his head.

As Serkan scans the park, he sees only one of the bodyguards, the older one, sitting twenty meters to the left on a similar bench, a newspaper folded in his lap. The other one, Serkan figures, must have been trailing him and will appear soon enough. When Serkan approaches, Mustafa neither stands nor shakes his hand. The "arrogant prick," as Serkan has come to think of him, taps a message on his iPhone and, without looking up, pats the bench next to him twice. Children's laughter rises from a playground below them.

Serkan has gleaned from the Internet that Mustafa is the scion of the Hamit family, for four generations one of Istanbul's richest and most influential dealers of antique artifacts. Mustafa flaunts both his pedigree and education on his own dedicated website separate from the family's business site. His Twitter account has almost three thousand followers, and his tweets, a dozen or so each day, are self-congratulatory—though, obviously, nothing akin to this meeting is ever mentioned. It's all social, much of it photos of him with rich international friends and anorexic women.

Serkan shuts his phone off, sits, and stares at the wooden bench in front of them that's shaped like a snake. One of the curved slats is broken, revealing rotting wood and rusted struts. Mustafa reaches his hand, palm up, toward Serkan who hands over his phone. Mustafa places both phones on the bench between them and says, "Good morning, Serkan."

"Good morning," he answers but does not say anything more.

Mustafa takes off his Ray-Ban aviators and gazes down through the trees as though he is surveying *his* estate. "My father and I are prepared to make you an offer," he says, "that you will find more than agreeable."

Wary, Serkan sits back. Mustafa's face is a little pasty, a bit puffy around his eyes. Perhaps, Serkan thinks, after a long night he won't be at the top of his game. In any case, if the offer isn't agreeable, Serkan at least has Elif's amulet for the Americans.

As Mustafa turns, his eyes narrow. "Twenty-five thousand American dollars," he says. "In cash. And the promise of more deals. With one non-negotiable condition."

Serkan is blown away. "Twenty-five grand," as they say in movies. He'd be out of debt, maybe even able to get a lease on a new Audi. He takes a quick breath to hide his astonishment and then gathers himself. Suddenly, doing this deal straight seems like it may be the way to go. "And what is the condition?" he asks.

"Two, actually." Mustafa smiles. "Three."

"What are they?"

"First, the deal is only on the table today. Take it or leave it."

Serkan nods. That's to be expected.

Mustafa glances at his manicured fingers. "Second, we pay you one-fifth up-front. Today. I will handle any ongoing negotiations with the Americans, for whom I already have a perfect solution, an absolutely stunning amulet."

Whatever the amulet, Serkan thinks, the negotiations are going to be more complicated than Mustafa imagines. He may be well educated, but he's also smug. Jack and Clare have been doing business, making difficult and elaborate deals, for decades—and they will have an alternative to the amulet that the arrogant prick is unaware of.

"You can stay in the loop if you want," Mustafa continues, "but I'm the closer. My piece is awesome. Breathtaking. Authentic. Never seen on the market before. It'll sell itself the moment they see it."

Serkan nods again. "Yes," he says. "I'll continue as the contact, the go-between, but you'll do the deal—be the closer. That's fine by me." Though all of this is playing into his hands, he remains leery.

Mustafa fixes him with his eyes, which are abruptly less bleary. "And you need to do one more thing."

"What?" When Mustafa's gaze doesn't waver, Serkan looks away.

"Obtain for me and my family certain information, archeological documents, that your mother possesses."

"What...? My mother...?"

"Yes."

Serkan is almost speechless. "She's...retired."

"From her official position." Mustafa picks at an imaginary cuticle on his left middle finger.

"My mother?" Serkan repeats.

Mustafa looks into his eyes again. "She remains deeply involved in the search for antiquities. Especially for those that may be buried in or near Bergama."

"I don't think so."

Mustafa laughs aloud. "Yes, Serkan. Absolutely. You have no idea."

Serkan shakes his head, but he hasn't been home much since his mother was fired. He has no idea how she is spending her time or what she's doing. She was, though, a workaholic as he was growing up—couldn't stay at home doing nothing. She always had a project —or seven—going. But she's still his mother. He can't embroil her in any of this. He sits straighter, looks Mustafa in the eye, and says, "This doesn't—can't—involve my family."

Mustafa doesn't laugh in his face again, but his smirk is condescending. "Yes, Serkan, it can, and it does. No information, no deal. At all. Ever." Slowly and deliberately, he puts on his aviators.

Serkan stands, wipes his hand across his face, and says, "No!" Sweat is breaking on his neck and back. His chest feels hollow. "Leave my family out of this!"

"Serkan," Mustafa's voice somehow sounds even more patronizing. "She's already involved. Over her head. You'll actually be making her life safer. Much safer."

"No!" The light streaming among the trees in the park looks like fire.

As Serkan is turning to leave, Mustafa holds out the phone and says, "You forgot something." He cocks his head and smiles. "Oh, and Elif's studio is nice, very functional. But she's not much of a businessman, is she?"

Serkan, unable to breathe, is frozen in a raging sweat.

"Sit down," Mustafa says. "We need to talk. Man-to-man."

 ## 27

İZMIR, TURKEY

Nihat Monoğlu and Tuğçe Iskan sit on separate wooden benches in the dappled morning light near the jogging path in İzmir's Kültürpark. The clearing's three benches form a U that opens toward the narrow lane that runs along the park's periphery. Monoğlu has his back to the thick trunk of a palm tree. Iskan's bench, at a right angle on his left, is little more than a meter from his. A large tan dog with a green metal tag in its ear lies on the third bench across from Monoğlu. Above the three of them, the sky is Aegean blue.

From a distance, no one would likely even notice that Iskan and Monoğlu are talking. She is on her way to Bergama; he is traveling back to Ankara, his flight from Adnan Menderes Airport leaving in two-and-a-half hours. He holds a newspaper, she a cell phone. "She's up to something," Iskan says as she lowers her head and stares at her cell phone as if she is receiving a message.

Monoğlu does not at first answer. He folds the newspaper, places it on the bench's seat, and then takes a Yenice from his gold-plated cigarette case. "Of course," he says finally. "She's always up to something." Even his whisper is a growl. "But it's probably not illegal."

"Her son's involved with the Hamits." She randomly taps her cell phone with her thumbs. Three crows haggle in the upper branches of the conifer across from her.

He shrugs, lights the cigarette with his old Zippo, and drags on the Yenice. "Yes, he is," he says, smoke escaping his nostrils. "But you know better than to assume guilt by association."

"Tell me you've begun to believe in coincidences." The breeze is warm but not yet hot. She likes the smell of lit cigarettes, has ever since she was a young girl and sneaked out of her family's house to spy on the men who gathered near the plane tree in her village's center. Women like her mother mostly stayed at home, cooking and baking and cleaning and taking care of the children and the chickens, all the while gossiping with each other in one another's gardens. But the men gathered in the cafés, smoked, drank çay, and talked football and politics, always politics.

He waves his hand holding the Yenice. "I don't. Her son is in shit up to his neck. But I've known Özlem a long time. She's smart. Stubborn. Doesn't always follow Ministry rules. Butts heads with bureaucrats. And she can be both clever and conniving. Does that sound to you like anybody else you know?"

"I'm not conniving."

The tan dog raises his head during an outburst of distant barking, but almost immediately rests his muzzle on the seat again. His left forepaw dangles over the edge of the bench's seat. Birdshit stains the bench's slats just below the etched İzmir Büyükşehir Belediyesi.

Monoğlu smiles to himself. "No, you're not." He takes another drag on his Yenice. "But you've still got to remember that she hates Mustafa Hamit and his family for what they've done over the years. And what they'll keep doing if nobody stops them." Exhaling, he tugs at his right ear. "She'd never get into bed with him."

Iskan picks at the irritated cuticle of her right thumb. "Sending me that Galen letter... She ruined my career."

He taps ash onto the clearing's paving stones. "Did she?"

Somewhere over toward the children's Fun Park, a woodpecker looses a staccato riff.

Iskan says nothing because she has learned, mostly from him, not to take every negative comment as a personal attack that must be countered.

"She used you," Monoğlu adds, "but that doesn't make her a criminal. Or mean that your career is ruined."

"So honesty is what made her pass a copy of Galen's letter on to the Ministry but keep the original? Remember, she left me hanging. That was complete…" She doesn't want to swear in front of her old boss even though she has heard him spewing expletives any number of times.

"Of course, it's horseshit," he says. Smiling, he adds, matter-of-factly, "Perhaps, she wanted to get fired so that she could pursue it…the search for Galen's legacy. After Allianoi, her job became shuffling paper, petty stuff that almost anybody could do."

"And getting me in trouble was just an unintended consequence?"

Trying to keep his smile from his voice, he says, "Oh, I would bet it was intended. I haven't actually spoken to her in months, but my guess is that she thought you were the only one who would, *honestly*, follow up…" He takes a final drag on the cigarette. "Maybe, she thought …thinks…the best way to keep you digging into the case was to get you thrown off it." He lets amiable laughter slip into his snarl. "You're still on it, aren't you?"

She doesn't answer. The breeze, the sunlight filtering through the branches, the resting dog, though it's all pretty peaceful, she feels even more on edge than usual.

"You wouldn't be if you were actually assigned to it," he says. "Some of my old friends in the Ministry would have stolen whatever information you dug up and dismissed you outright."

She remains quiet for another minute before saying in a less antagonistic tone, "So that's what you're doing, too? Taking retirement so you can hunt out corruption in the Ministry."

"I'm retired," he says, "so that I can enjoy my grandchildren." He stubs the cigarette on the sole of his shoe and places the butt on the bench's black steel arm. "And irritate my wife with my bad habits."

Hearing the same quick gait she noticed when they were first talking, Iskan glances back over her left shoulder as a gaunt man with matching pale blue shorts and a T-shirt runs along the path. His sweating, shaved head bobs. She takes a deep breath and says, "You're the source of the materials and photos being sent to me, right?"

"What materials?"

"The ones you figured I'd show to Özlem Boroğlu to stir things up."

"I don't have any idea what you're talking about."

"And the photos on the net of *The Dying Gaul*, was that you, too?"

He shrugs, seemingly unaware of what she is talking about. The photos, which first appeared just before the bombing in Bergama, show a bronze statue of a naked warrior with a chest wound.

She taps her cell phone's screen until it wakes up again. "Well, if you do meet the guy, thank him for me. It definitely worked." She pauses again. Across the narrow lane, the two-story, blue-and-gray sports center has silhouettes of athletes painted on the windowless exterior—a blue tennis player, a green weight lifter. "I've taken a two-week leave."

"I see," he says. "You have time in the bank...?"

"Of course. You know I—" She smiles, realizing he is teasing her. Last year, she never took a day off, not once. "My boss was only too happy to sign off on my request."

"He doesn't appreciate your...tenacity?"

She smiles again. "And tell your friend the evidence—I've found a lot more—shows that for a long time the Hamits have been buying up land around Bergama. And out toward Dikili. And up toward Kozak. Through dummy corporations. Purchase and lease-back deals with local farmers. Since even before they dammed Allianoi. But lately, after Galen's letter, the number of deals in the valley and up in the hills has really spiked."

He takes another Yenice from its case. "I'm not surprised."

She looks over his right shoulder at the ten-meter-high, white fence of a tennis complex. "I still haven't been able to track the Aureus."

"Maybe there's nothing to track."

"Huh?"

"I'd bet that Özlem thinks the coin came directly from the boy or his grandfather. One of them found it." He taps the cigarette against the case. "If it's from anybody or anywhere else, other coins would've surfaced. Or at least there'd be rumors of them."

Iskan looks up from her phone and rolls her neck, then stares down at the cigarette butts ground onto the pavers. Tufts of grass are growing between the stones, and pine needles litter the unswept areas around the bench's steel legs. She will not, just as Monoğlu won't, bring up the fact that the boy, little Mehmet, is dying. The doctors are going to pull the plugs on the life-support equipment sometime in the next day or two.

"Sounds like you've hit a wall on that," he says, his voice far more somber.

"Not entirely." Her thumbs tap furiously.

"What if the two of you worked together?" There's no irony in his voice.

She stops tapping. "Me and Boroğlu? Did I mention she hates me?"

"And you're not overly fond of her. I get that. Just the same…"

She looks into his eyes. "One of us would probably wind up dead."

"But what's that I've been hearing about women…it takes a village?"

She shakes her head and looks up at the morning sunlight in the branches of the trees. "I've never been very good at being a villager."

He lights his cigarette and exhales slowly. "I know. And neither has she…"

"And neither," she says, "have you."

"Well, at least you've still got the Aureus coin safe."

"What coin?" she says.

# 28
### KAIKOS VALLEY

At 3:23 A.M., Elif Boroğlu hides her bicycle behind a clump of bushes just off the two-lane country road seven kilometers outside of Bergama. The night is warm and mostly cloudy, the moon hidden. Rain is forecast by morning, but she should make it back to town by then. It will be the first rain in two weeks and will likely cover any tracks she leaves. Wearing black hiking shoes, black pants, and a black, long-sleeved T-shirt, she shifts her dark backpack to balance its weight and then heads across a field recently plowed under. The night smells of fertility.

When Elif was young, she often went to the Allianoi excavation with her mother. She liked the archeological work at the site, particularly the painstaking preservation of artifacts, but she enjoyed even more wandering the nearby hills scavenging. Sometimes her younger brother, Serkan, went with her, but he quickly became bored with the tramping and returned to the site, where he was particularly taken by the statue of the water nymph. She gradually came to feel, to learn, to know the contours of the earth as though it was a mother's living body—which, she has now come to understand, it was and is.

While in high school, she began to go farther afield, often alone and at night. She had friends, both at school and in town, but her explorations were solitary—though not ever lonely. Her brother seemed not even to notice, and her mother, perhaps due to her own upbringing, turned a blind eye on the excursions. Over the years, Elif discovered two ancient cult sites around Bergama, one of which she has shared with her friends. She is, however, the only person to have visited the second site in two millennia. The earth has also disclosed to her dozens of gravesites including four that were entirely undisturbed, which out of respect for the deceased and the land itself she has not revealed to anyone, even her mother. Özlem was, until recently, always busy with other archeological projects, and Elif believed that so many graves were being desecrated by robbers that she would not add to the list.

When she is alone like this in the hinterland late at night, the earth sings to her. Not just the hum of insects and the distant barking of dogs, but the land itself. The songs are sometimes chants, sometimes dirges, and, more recently, anthems, but to her all of them are holy and all ground hallowed.

After crossing the field, she climbs two low hills, passes through a narrow valley, and reaches a rocky, crescent-shaped ridge. Near a boulder the size of a Fiat Ægea, she opens her backpack. In the gathering breeze, she catches the first scent of the approaching storm. She hears a rustling off to her right, and two large dogs, one tan and one chocolate, rush at her through the brush. Both leap at her. She throws her right arm around the darker dog's shoulder as they tumble together to the base of the rock. "Quiet, Gula!" she whispers as the dog pins her and licks her face. The tan dog is on her, too, slobbering. She holds back laughter as she fends them off. She is clearly trespassing in their territory, but they have been friends, she and the dark bitch and her son, for years.

Elif rolls to her side and, with both dogs still bounding about, gets to her feet. "Stay!" she says as she removes a plastic bag from her backpack and pulls out a frozen beef bone with scraps of meat still on it. The bitch seizes it and turns away. Her son takes his bone but settles at Elif's feet and manipulates it with his paws as he gnaws at it. Both dogs lie in darkness, but their bushy tails catch shadows as they wag. As the dogs, who belong more to these low rolling hills than to the local farmers who sometimes provide them with food, attack the bones, Elif pulls her long, tousled hair back into a ponytail and hefts her backpack. She used to come this way in daylight, walking about and sharing treats with dogs, but her recent visits have been, out of necessity, nocturnal.

Through terrain that is increasingly rocky, Elif and the dogs, proudly carrying the bones in their mouths, trek along another ridge that rises gradually toward a steep rock massif. Gula stays close, but her son periodically runs off after a scent or sound that Elif can't detect. After twenty minutes of climbing, she stops by a narrow cleft in the rock. Gula sniffs about while her son marks territory. Elif stands still for three full minutes, letting her senses sharpen. She then looks closely at the area around the cleft but finds no tracks, no signs that others have been here. She is not a geologist but knows that the cleft was never the tomb's entrance. She glances up at the escarpment, the wall of rock. The earth quakes frequently around here, not in human time, but in its own. The crust heaved at some point, perhaps during the great quake of 262 CE that demolished much of Pergamon, sheering the escarpment and sending down a cascade of boulders, rock, and scree. Elif is reasonably sure that this area was once a necropolis, and the landside that covered this and other tombs also created this cleft.

As Elif puts down her backpack, Gula, who first discovered this place while chasing hares two years ago, settles near her. Elif takes out her miner's light, adjusts it on her head, and breathes deeply. Getting into the tomb is for her frightening, though the tomb itself is not. She scratches Gula behind the ears; whispers, "Guard the door, my dear"; crouches; and wedges herself into the crevice. She then squirms at an angle to her right, scraping her chest and shoulders against the rock. She extends her left arm high above her head, finds a handhold, and pulls herself upward.

When for a moment she becomes stuck, unable to move up or down in the darkness, she fights panic. The fingers of her left hand claw the rock; the toes of her shoes kick and grip. She snakes toward a ledge she knows is there but cannot see. Her hand finally finds purchase, and she pulls herself into a narrow tunnel. Breathing hard, she switches on her lamp and crawls deeper into the earth.

Her headlamp sweeps the tomb, half the size of her studio with a stone ceiling so low that she has to stoop. It dates from the second century of the Common Era so there are no lavish displays of wealth—no bronze and gold armor or weaponry, no finely wrought gold chains, no precious stones, no gold death mask. But the skeleton lying on its back was once a wealthy aristocrat, a leading citizen of Pergamon. A bronze box lies on a low marble pedestal near the skeleton's feet.

Kneeling in front of the box, she begs for forgiveness. She then lifts the box's lid, her headlamp shining on the rolls of parchment. When her hand shifts the parchment, the five gold amulets, each worth a fortune, gleam. She picks up the exquisite rendering of Athena. Each line, including the facial features and hands, is precise, close to perfect. Her own work, she fears, isn't comparable. She squeezes her eyes shut and re-opens them. Still holding the goddess between her thumb and forefinger, she looks about the tomb at the human remains, the rock ceiling, the sealed entrance, the dusty floor.

She has only once in all of her rambles in this territory removed an item from any tomb—this one. The document, she believed, had little monetary value but might be of historical importance. Her mother had sunk into a lethargic slough after decades of productive work both at Allianoi and in Bergama. When her mother then received the document anonymously, she was, in fact, reenergized—or, rather, her obsessions were reignited. But Elif failed to account for the depth of the darkness of the human spirit. She should have known better. At least, she has now learned enough to realize that this amulet, which would seemingly solve her brother's immediate problem, would create still more grave risks for him and the rest of her family.

 29
BERGAMA

As Recep Ateş leaves the Ministry of Culture office building on the Bergama Museum grounds, he hears his name called. When he turns, he sees Tuğçe Iskan standing to his left on the garden path among large remnants of ancient pillars and friezes, architraves and sarcophagi. He stops on the bottom concrete step below the thick grapevine on the arbor overhanging the building's porch. He has forgotten how striking she is—the short blonde hair, pale skin, high cheekbones, and bright eyes—but not how irritating she can also be. "Hello, Tuğçe," he says. He does not ask how she is doing.

"Can we talk for a minute?" she asks.

He leaves the office promptly at five each afternoon, and, no doubt knowing this, she has trapped him. He has another meeting out near the Aesklepion in half an hour so he answers, "This isn't something we could've talked about earlier in the office?" It's pointedly not really a question.

"It's about an investigation."

"Yours or the Ministry's?"

"Both."

"What investigation?"

"You know I can't tell you." She realizes that she should have brought coffee or some other peace offering.

"And it can't wait until tomorrow?"

"Not really." She waves at the bars and cafés directly across the street from the museum. "Can I buy you a beer?"

Though an Efes would go down really well right about now, he says, "No." Then, aware of how curt he's being with a colleague from Ankara, he gestures toward the table and chairs in the garden to her right. "Will five minutes do?"

"Yes," she says. If he's not too evasive, it will be more than enough time.

They settle in two of the white wrought-iron chairs surrounding a round marble-top table in the shade of the garden. He has his back to the Ministry office; hers is to the street. This side of the building has large windows but no security cameras, which fits her purpose. She wants to be seen here but doesn't want what she's asking to be on video. Her mind is registering everything. The glare in his eyes. The frown. The spot on his right cheek he missed while shaving this morning. The thinning hair. His forehead and neck sweating, though it's not all that hot this afternoon. His rumpled shirt. His bulk in the chair that makes him look like a circus bear on a stool. "I need to ask you a favor."

"I figured as much."

"I'd like to look at any files you have on grave robberies and rescues in the area over the last year."

"It all goes to Ankara. Everything."

"Yes, I know. But I also know that sometimes things fall through the cracks."

"Not likely. Esen, my administrative assistant—I think you've met her—is both capable and responsible."

"Just the same." She forces a smile.

He does not return it. "And this wasn't something you could've requested in the office?"

She gazes at a large cement oval, like a spoked wheel, set on a ledge against the building's wall. The center is the sun's face, and twelve rays shoot to the periphery. She can't tell if the face is smiling, but the shape of the fiery rays holds her attention. "I thought," she says, "it might be better for everybody if—"

"So this *visit...,*" he practically spits the word, "is *unauthorized.*" He leans forward, shifting his weight so that he looms in front of her. "You're poking your nose where you shouldn't again."

"I'm not after you."

"No, you're just causing my office more work and possibly embarrassing my staff."

"I'm not trying to cause anyone any embarrassment."

"No, but you will. And you'll pester me for an eternity if I don't do what you want." He shakes his head. "Come back tomorrow if you must. We'll see what we can do." He places his large hands on the table and presses himself up so that he is standing over her.

Unfazed, she asks, "Do you still have your weekly meetings with Özlem Boroğlu?"

"Officially, no."

"Have you noticed anything strange about her?"

"Özlem *is* strange!"

"Any difference *lately?*"

He leans closer, blocking out her view of the archeological pieces lined against the building's wall. Off to her right, red roofing tiles are piled against the adjacent building's wall.

"Yes!" he shouts, sputtering. "She's very upset about the bombing! We all are!" He glares at her. "But we'll spend half a day tomorrow on your bureaucratic shit!"

"Before that," she says. "Before the bombing, any change?"

He leans back and takes a breath. "Why do you ask?"

"An investigation may lead—"

He cuts her off, shouting, "She's honest!" Sputtering again, he adds, "Too honest for her own good!"

"I wasn't suggesting—"

"Leave her alone! Hasn't the Ministry screwed her enough?"

Iskan pauses. "Yes." A motorcycle screams along the street. She gazes up at a tall pine bending into the sky. All of its branches have been cut except for those at the very top. "But that doesn't mean she isn't involved in something...."

"She's not!" His spittle strikes her arm. He wheels without another word and lumbers off toward the gate.

She wipes away the saliva.

 30

BERGAMA

Elif Boroğlu tries to ignore the knocking on the studio door. She has been deep in her work, finally getting the wax model to exactly the point that she wants it. When the hammering continues, she looks to see if the deadbolt is set, which it isn't, covers the mold with a white cloth, and takes out her earbuds. As she goes to the door, she shouts, "Who is it?"

"Tuğçe Iskan!" she hears. The voice, though a woman's, is deep.

*Who?* Elif thinks, unsure if she knows someone by that name. She opens the door to the young woman from the Ministry that her mother detests. Her mother, though, loathes a lot of people, and this woman was, in an awkward way, trying to help the family when she showed them the photograph.

The two women stand silently, facing each other across the studio's threshold. They are both tall and fit, but they are not at all mirror images of each other. Iskan wears black jeans and a short-sleeved, blue T-shirt that reveals the tattoos on her forearms. Because her studio is climate-controlled, Elif has on yoga pants and a lightweight, gray sweatshirt. She is thinner than Iskan. Her skin is darker, her features softer. Her brown eyes are warm, and her braided black hair falls down her back almost to her waist.

After half a minute, Iskan says, "Hello, Elif. How are you?"

Elif doesn't answer, partly because it is complex and partly because she can feel her focus, having been interrupted, slipping away.

"May I ask you a couple of questions?" Iskan says in a voice that is not at all a command.

Elif takes a breath, nods, turns, and moves back to her stool. Iskan hesitates before following her. There is nowhere to sit so Iskan steps over to the table holding the figurines, finished and unfinished, and gazes at them. Elif remembers that when they first met, Iskan complimented her on her work. Sekhmet leaps down from atop the kiln and, purring, moves toward Iskan. The neighborhood dogs are barking, and the gypsy children up the side road are shouting and laughing as they play in the street. Their voices are high and lyrical.

"Please shut the door," Elif says. "I need to keep the place cool."

Iskan closes the door, returns to the table, and picks up the stout goddess with the single-edged sword and severed head.

"Mustafa Hamit liked that one, too," Elif says.

The image of all the figurines at Özlem Boroğlu's house wells in Iskan's mind, and she is suddenly aware of the pattern or, rather, the lack of pattern, in the arrangements both in the house's courtyard and on the rooftop garden. Here, all of the figurines are new, and all are Elif's. There, mixed into the array were a few ancient goddesses that Elif or someone else must have had discovered. Not many, only four or maybe five, ancient Anatolian mother goddesses were hidden in plain sight among the modern figurines.

"He offered me a lot of money—way too much money—for it," Elif adds.

Iskan nods. She has been building her case against the Hamits carefully. She has more than enough evidence of the family greatly adding to their fortune in recent years by delivering ISIL plunder to the wealthy of the world. She has pretty much concluded that Serkan Boroğlu is just another of the Hamits' disposable pawns, a dupe serving some finite end. And though it's not yet entirely clear, his mother's involvement is probably adversarial.

Using the only cup in the studio, Elif fetches water from the cooler.

Sekhmet rubs up against Iskan's calf and then saunters over to Elif, who stoops and lets her drink from the cup.

"It was a bad idea for your brother to get mixed up with the Hamits," Iskan says. She has never been any good at winding around toward the topic about which she wants to ask someone.

"That's not a question," Elif says, but her tone is not negative.

Iskan puts the figurine down, looks around the studio, and picks up another heavyset, robed goddess with snakes entwined around her staff. "Now that he has, it's likely that he's headed for some sort of fall."

"You think my brother's in danger?"

"The Hamits have been using people, chewing them up and spitting them out since the Ottoman Empire."

Elif sips water from the cup. "Is there something I can, *should be,* doing?"

Iskan doesn't at first answer. "Not now," she says finally. "Not yet." She draws her finger along the statue's staff. "I'm more concerned about your mother."

"I told you before that I won't talk about her work." Elif licks her lips. "Anyway, I don't really know anything."

"The Hamits. They think there's a huge treasure near Bergama— the Galen cache. And they think your mother has found it. Or, she's about to."

"She hasn't."

Iskan eyes her. "We know that."

The cat comes back over to Iskan and rubs up against her leg again.

"Wait. How do *you* know that?" *And who is we?* Elif wonders.

*"How do you know that?"*

Both suddenly guarded, the women stare at each other. Neither looks away. Finally, Iskan says, "Because we don't think it exists anymore."

"But the letter my mother got? That's authentic?"

"The letter, it probably is. But nobody else has seen the original." She leans down and strokes the cat's neck. "But the destruction here over the centuries. Devastating earthquakes. Invading armies. Arabs sacking the town. Fires. Greeks. Far more than a thousand years, the city went without records. There may have been a cache, but…only stone remains." She shrugs, then quickly refocuses on Elif. "How do *you* know your mother hasn't found it?"

"Because I've lived with her my whole life. And archeology is…has been her whole life."

"Archeology and her children?"

"Archeology, and then her children." There is no resentment in Elif's voice. "If she'd found something big—even if she were trying to hide it from the world—she'd have been bubbling over at home. And, since she lost her job…really, since the government flooded Allianoi…she's been unhappy. Angry. Except for the first few weeks after she got that letter… She's been much worse since the attack on the funicular." She starts to sip more water but stops herself.

Iskan wants to ask how Boroğlu got the letter but holds herself back, and the two women become silent again. Surveying the studio once more, she asks, "What are you working on?"

"Something for a client."

Iskan nods toward the new centrifuge and the vacuum table with the bell jar. "Precious metal?"

"Why do you ask?" Elif's voice is clipped.

"Just wondering…" It's as close to a lie as Iskan can muster.

Elif stares at her and says nothing.

"I'm interested in the lost wax method." This is not a lie. "I have been for a long time."

"I did some metal casting after university, but it was too expensive."

"But you're back at it now?" Aware that she is pushing too far, Iskan adds, "I'm sorry. I didn't come here to pry."

With no point in pretending that the new equipment could be used for terra-cotta figurines, Elif stands and says, "I've got to get back to work. Thanks for stopping by."

# ✫ 31
## PERGAMON'S AESKLEPION; 168 CE

$A$s Galen takes his patient's pulse, the aging, over-weight man hyperventilates. He is as tall as Galen but bald and shaped like an egg. The two sit in a private underground chamber in the Aesklepion's main treatment facility. Located outside Pergamon's walls beyond the base of the citadel, the Aesklepion, named for Aesklepios, the god of medicine, is the world's most famous healing center. More than four hundred years old, it has in this century returned to prominence because of Emperor Hadrian's vast rebuilding program. It boasts this circular curing center with pools and fountains, a columned portal, two sacred springs, a library, three roofed colonnades, a theater that seats 3,500, and a temple modeled after Rome's new Pantheon and dedicated to Zeus Aesklepios. Galen's father, the project's lead architect, designed the renovations but did not live to see all of them finished.

The patient's rapid pulse and breathing reinforce what Galen has already concluded—a serious illness of the psyche. In his second year home after seven successful years in Rome, Galen has spent most of his time writing his epic study of Attic Greek, editing his medical treatises, and tending to business related to his father's—and now his—estate. He is, however, being consulted in this case because the patient is wealthy and powerful, one of Pergamon's leading citizens and an architect that was once his father's protégé. The man's three daughters are married, but he never had a son. His recurring nightmares have driven him to seek treatment in the Aesklepion and then to ask for Galen's intervention. But there is no one moment, no single trauma, that has brought on his dread, this psychosis—and it has only worsened during his stay at the Aesklepion.

"I tell you," the man says, "Atlas can't keep it up any longer!" He gnaws at his already torn left thumbnail. "It's only a matter of days!" His tone is urgent, as though some power is forcing him to share a dark premonition of imminent destruction. "Hours!"

Galen nods as the man's pulse quickens even more. The diagnosis is easy; the cure will be difficult, if not impossible. These maladies of the soul are always the most difficult to treat. "Let's go outside, take a walk in the courtyard," he says. The chamber is peaceful, cool and fairly dark, lit by a single torch, but Galen has to find out immediately how deeply disturbed the man's soul is.

"No!" the man screams. "It's not safe! The crash! It's coming at any moment!"

"Who told you this?"

"*Atlas!*" The man repeatedly picks at the sleeve of his tunic. "Atlas himself!"

"In your dreams?"

"Yes. No! Not just in dreams! He talks to me! Speaks in my ear! 'It's too much!' he says. 'Too difficult!'"

Galen runs his fingers through his beard. "What is?"

The man gasps. His eyes go wide. "His job! Holding up the heavens! It's too much."

One of the Aesklepion's sacred dogs wanders into the chamber. Tail wagging, it sniffs the patient who is too distraught to notice.

"But your dream?" Galen asks. "Last night's dream that has brought me here?" The dog comes to him and licks his right hand.

The man starts to shiver. "He's giving up! I saw him! His face was contorted. Veins in his head and neck bulged. Moaning, he shut his eyes. His shoulders slumped, and his hands dropped! He's letting go! And…"

"And?" Galen scratches the dog behind it ears.

The patient grasps Galen's wrist. "That's when I woke up."

"Screaming?"

Shaking his head, the man lets go of Galen, shrinks into himself. "I don't remember…" His voice becomes a weak whisper. "That's what they tell me…" His spirit withers before Galen's eyes.

"You were screaming," Galen says, his tone reportorial not judgmental. "For a long time. Hysterically. Woke other patients."

The man swallows hard. "My throat is sore," he admits. He grips Galen's arm even more tightly. "Help me," he croaks. "You can! You're the only one! Please, help me!" This man, whom Galen once saw as robust, whimpers, "Please!"

"I will," Galen answers. His work is renowned throughout the Roman Empire. If anyone can help, he can. "I'll prescribe a course of treatment for you." He has already sent one of his slaves to get the ingredients for his secret calming potion. The dog curls at his feet. "And I promise that Atlas will continue his work," he adds, as though it were a fact that Atlas existed and diligently performed his duty.

The man sobs. Tears run down through the stubble on his flaccid cheeks.

Galen listens to the water streaming from the nearby fountains. "Do you hear anything?" he asks. "Tell me what you hear."

Pinching his forearms, the man murmurs, "I hear…Atlas is moaning… He's trying to tell me…"

"I am the only other one here with you."

"There's someone else. There's groaning. Atlas is groaning under the weight."

"The only other one who could be here is Aesklepios."

"Aesklepios?"

"This is his sacred ground. His healing power resides here."

"I know. I know." The man is weeping. "But it's not him."

"Has *he* ever spoken to you?"

"No. Never."

"Well, he does to me." And, indeed, he does—in Galen's dreams.

Galen's reputation is, justifiably, built on his ability to note symptoms and to notice patterns and to make inferences and to predict the course of disease and to discern which treatments and curatives will work and which will not. And, of course, to debunk all that is specious—omens and auguries and astrology and divination through the entrails of birds. But he also believes that our highest rational soul resides in us and speaks to us, especially through our dreams. Some dreams are clear messages from the soul, from the gods. And some of his own dreams have come from his ancestral god, Aesklepios. The practice of medicine and the work of Aesklepios are not in his mind antithetical. Healing always involves both the body and the spirit. They are two sides of the same Aureus. "He spoke to my father and told him that I should become a doctor. And he saved my life when I was twenty-seven. Came to me in two dreams and gave me a cure, showed me how to cure myself."

The man's head is shaking as he shivers and pinches himself, raising welts on his forearms. "It's too late! It's all over!"

"And while you're here, Aesklepios will speak to you. You just have to listen. You must accept the treatments and—"

A muscular, dark-haired young man wearing a toga fringed with scarlet stands at the entrance to the chamber. A parchment is rolled in his right hand. The dog stands, ears pinned back, but does not growl.

"No!" the patient screams. "Dis Pater! It's not time! I'm not ready! No!"

Galen, who left instructions that no one should interrupt this session, shouts, "Be gone!"

The young man remains standing, silent, in the archway.

"I said..." And in this instant, Galen realizes that the messenger has come for him, not the patient. This is the summons from Emperor Marcus Aurelius that he has dreaded. This is the summons back to Rome, back into the service of the Empire. He should be gratified to become the emperor's personal physician. It is the highest honor that a doctor can receive in Rome's society—and brings with it great wealth and exalted status. But Galen loves this, his father's treasured city, and he fears that his duty to the emperor will take him into harm's way—not just the unending treachery of the Roman aristo-crats but worse, far worse. Wars with the northern Germanic tribes in some godforsaken frozen forest. Or the plague that soldiers return-ing from Aquileia are spreading through the empire and bringing back to the Eternal City. The churning within him, the perturbation of his soul that suddenly grips him, is not at all like the psychosis of his patient. It is the product of the rational recognition that he will not be able to stay in Pergamon to finish his classical studies or, even more importantly, to complete his tribute to his father and to the cul-ture of this city that he loves so deeply.

 32

KAPIKAYA, TURKEY

Özlem Boroğlu follows her daughter Elif down the trail toward the old stone bridge that crosses the stream. Both mother and daughter wear hiking boots, long pants, and long-sleeved shirts. Özlem has on her floppy black hat. Two water bottles are clipped to Elif's backpack. At first light, they started out from Bergama along the road that leads up to little Mehmet's village in the pine forest, but they parked the Dacia less than five kilometers out of town on a steep incline in a wooded, sparsely inhabited area. They hiked down through the woods along a winding path that has taken them into this valley a long way from the road. The sun is beginning to rise above the crest of the rocky escarpment to the east, but the morning is still cool. The scent of pine is strong.

The stone bridge is neither large nor elaborate. Moss covers much of the stonework almost to the capstone. Somewhere out of sight upstream, an axe is striking wood. Closer, a cock crows by a ramshackle white cottage with orange roofing tiles. A large tan dog starts to amble over, but a rodent skittering by an old cement trough steals its attention. Barking, it gives chase but isn't nearly quick enough. The stream is murky beneath the bridge, but not far downstream it runs fast and white over the rocks.

Elif stops at the foot of the bridge to let her mother catch up. They talked little on the way here. Elif learned early in life to let her

mother have her second morning cup of coffee and her third cigarette before attempting any meaningful conversation. She and her
mother have not hiked together in more than a decade, but Boroğlu
asked Elif to guide her to Kapıkaya, the ancient sanctuary dedicated
to Cybele, the Earth Mother. Elif agreed because the area is isolated
and the terrain unusually rough—and someone no longer used to
making difficult ascents clearly shouldn't go alone.

Once a year on the vernal equinox, Elif and a couple of her friends
make the climb to Kapıkaya because she believes the cave there and
the spring are holy. Any relics—terra-cotta figures, ceramic vessels,
lamps, and coins—are long gone, taken by diggers, legal and illegal,
but the sightline back to Pergamon's acropolis is still clear. The site's
inaccessibility has in a sense saved it from further exploitation and
destruction. In fact, Elif believes that three years ago she was the
only visitor to the site. Boroğlu, who has only climbed to the site
once, seventeen years ago, did not explain to her daughter why she
wants to go now. But Elif knew that, given the situation, she had to
accompany her, whatever the reason.

The stone bridge, which has no walls or rails, is wide enough
for a cow but not for a car. Although the two women could cross
together, Elif lets her mother go first, before again taking the lead.
The path forks almost immediately, and they follow the higher trail
that heads up through the pine forest and around the jagged peak
that stands between this valley and Kapıkaya. After only twenty minutes, Boroğlu calls for Elif to stop. She takes off her hat and fans her
face that is already sweaty. Elif unclips both water bottles and hands
the pink one to her mother. She herself drinks from the green bottle.

Boroğlu takes a series of deep breaths, looks up the steeply rising
trail, and says, "Enough."

Elif cocks her head. It is getting warmer, but it's not yet hot.

"Let's head back!" Boroğlu says.

Elif wipes her mouth but doesn't answer. Her mother has never
given up this easily on anything.

The two women stare at each other until Boroğlu says, "I mean it."

"I thought you wanted to visit Kapıkaya."

Boroğlu pulls her red lighter and her pack of cigarettes from her shirt pocket.

"Mom, don't!" Elif says. "Please don't."

"I'll be careful. I'm always careful."

"I know that, Mom, but...the forest..."

They stare at each other again. Birds are calling, and, though the sound of the axe is no longer audible, somewhere in the distance downstream a chain saw is revving. Finally, Boroğlu says, "All right," and puts the cigarettes and lighter back in her pocket.

"Why are we here, Mom?" Elif's tone is not petulant, but there's an edge in her voice. A day away from her studio is, at this point, a day lost.

Boroğlu glances around. "I need to see the area."

"And you've seen enough of it already?"

"No, but we don't need to go farther."

"Why are we really here?"

"To look around."

"For what?"

Boroğlu looks into her daughter's eyes for the first time. "The remains of a villa."

Elif shakes her head. "Out here?"

"Near the stream. Maybe." Boroğlu waves at the trail ahead. "I don't know. But not farther up. Not more remote." Her hand goes to her pocket, but she doesn't take out her cigarettes. "Back along the stream, I think."

Elif clips her water bottle. "You should've told me the truth."

As Boroğlu hands the pink bottle back, she says, "You wouldn't have come." Her tone is matter-of-fact.

Elif doesn't answer. Her mother is probably right. If she had not mentioned Kapıkaya, Elif would not likely have agreed to come. Her mother's obsession with unearthing human artifacts is hers alone; Elif's work is focused on the earth itself and on creating images that might hold meaning. Their only juncture is ancient sites, like Kapıkaya, that are, at least for her, sacred. Without saying anything more, she turns back down the trail.

 33
KAPIKAYA

Still not speaking, mother and daughter backtrack to the fork above the bridge, where they pause again by the trunk of an uprooted tree. Someone has carefully arranged stones of various sizes and colors among the exposed roots, creating both a trail marker and a cairn. Slipped in among the torn and gnarled roots are a large gray stone, two pale white rocks the size of loaves of bread, and numerous smaller stones—gray and beige, golden and speckled. Elif walks down toward the stream, examines the ground, and selects a flat, russet rock about the size of her mother's lighter. She returns, studies the roots, and places the rock in a niche where a root corkscrews into air. Finally, she runs her fingers over a bright white shard wedged into a smaller space and then turns back to her mother and asks, "A villa?"

"Yes. Built in the second century. Well outside Pergamon."

"But up here? Not down in the valley?"

"It's cooler up here. The water's clean."

"And?" That's not enough evidence for one of her mother's archeological hunches. And her mother, in her work and in her family life, always knew more than she told others.

Boroğlu doesn't answer. Nor does she look into Elif's eyes.

"That damned letter you got!" Elif says, scolding herself in her mind. "What did the letter say?" She really doesn't have any idea.

Boroğlu takes off her hat, wipes the back of her hand across her forehead, and gazes downstream.

"Mom, what did the letter say?"

Boroğlu runs her index finger along her hat's rim. "That Galen's villa, the villa his father built, was outside the city."

"And?"

"Elsewhere, Galen wrote that his father had been drained by his constant civic responsibilities, Pergamon's day-to-day administrative and bureaucratic duties. He built the villa to get away."

"But why are you looking up here?"

"Others are looking in the valley."

Elif smiles to herself. She and Serkan used to joke about their mother's many unstated rules. Number seventeen was "Never Do as Others Do."

"But that doesn't—"

"Stop cross-examining me!" Boroğlu snaps.

"You invited me! If we're going to go on, you need to…" Elif's eyes lock in on her mother's face. She knows neither to push her mother too hard nor to surrender. "I need to know."

Boroğlu waves her hat like a fan. "Little Mehmet had with him on the funicular something he found from Galen's time. Or his grand-father had found."

"What?"

Boroğlu hesitates. She has told no one. "A coin. Roman. Gold. Very rare."

"Who told you that?"

"I *saw* it!"

Elif pauses again, thinking about who might have shown her mother an ancient Roman gold coin. Boroğlu puts her hat on, a signal that the conversation is finished, at least for her.

"But why bring me?" Elif tries to hold her gaze. "Why trick me into coming?"

"Because, my dear," Boroğlu says, her tone becoming less com-bative, but still resentful, "you've become better at reading the earth than I ever was."

Elif scrunches her face. She and her mother look at the world far differently—the earth itself, people, life. *Everything,* it sometimes seems. An artist is not an archeologist. Her mother looks for what is dead and buried; Elif feels for what is living. Her mother searches. In her sculpting, except for the current project, which has required almost a dozen models so far, Elif waits and becomes, at least sometimes, connected—a conduit. "I don't know about that," she says finally.

"I do," Boroğlu retorts. Then she sags, as though she is tired, and says, "Walk with me. For a couple of hours at least."

Elif takes a long, deep breath. Her mother's abrupt mood shifts worry her. Although she and her mother can't possibly recover the openness of their walks when Elif was a child and her mother was flying high about her team's Allianoi discoveries, it was those walks, that sense of wonder, that started her on her own journey. She looks back down at the bridge. Beyond it on the other side of the stream near the cottage with the orange tile roof, an old woman is loading firewood into a blue, plastic laundry basket.

"Wait here, Mom," Elif says as she begins to hike down toward the stream. When Boroğlu follows her across the bridge, Elif pauses and looks back into her mother's eyes that glare at her.

The old woman lifts the laundry basket, swings it over her right shoulder, and then, holding it with both hands, leans forward and starts for the cottage. Her large, tan dog trots along ahead of her. When she sees the two women approaching, she stops by three solar panels set at an angle in the scrub grass. An orange electrical cord leads from the panels toward the building. The dog ambles over to Elif who scratches it behind its ears with both hands.

"Hello, Child," the stout old woman says to Elif. Her paisley headscarf is tied tightly. A black sweater covers her mammoth drooping breasts, and her baggy şalvar has a purple floral pattern.

"Hello, Mother," Elif says. "May I help you?"

"No... Yes, thank you, my child," the woman says as her round face breaks into a gap-toothed smile.

Elif reaches out and takes the basket with both hands. Her shoulders slump with the weight.

The old woman's eyes well.

"This is Özlem, my mother," Elif says.

Boroğlu takes off her hat and nods. The dog sniffs at Boroğlu and then returns to Elif.

The three women and the dog head around to the far side of the building where a corrugated metal roof shades a small cast-iron cooking stove, two brown plastic chairs, and a clutter of cooking equipment. The woman squats on a cinder block next to the stove. As Elif sets the basket near her, she looks up, her eyes welling again. A cooking grate and utensils hang from hooks driven into the cottage's white-washed, cinder block wall. Half a dozen ears of corn hang from the roof as do three white plastic bags. A large, metal cooking pot placed below the edge of the roof serves as a cistern. Boroğlu stands by a row of metal buckets filled with earth and growing herbs. Five chickens mill and cluck off to her right.

"I am alone," the woman says to Boroğlu as tears begin to serpentine among her wrinkles. She takes a split log from the basket, uses it to stir the embers glowing in the stove, and then carefully sets the log among them. "Your daughter visits me sometimes. Brings me gifts. Statues I keep inside. And chocolate."

Boroğlu looks at Elif and says, "Yes, she is a good child."

For once, Elif can't hear any irony in her mother's voice.

Waving her pudgy, age-spotted hand at the two plastic chairs, the woman asks, "Can you stay? Sit with me?"

"We would love to visit with you, Mother," Elif says. "But after our walk, if that is all right."

Looking up again at Boroğlu, the woman says, "My son died." She chokes back more tears, takes another piece of firewood, and sets it at an angle over the first. "My husband is long dead."

"What happened to your son?" Boroğlu asks.

The woman swipes at her tears. "He never really came back after his Service. Lived in the town." She begins to shake her head. "A motorcycle accident between İzmir and here." Her thick chest heaves. "He was driving too fast at night. He had a daughter, but I barely know her."

"How long have you lived here?" Elif asks, though she already knows approximately.

"Many years." The woman's smile is sad. "Since I was eighteen." Her eyes glazed, she glances up at Boroğlu. "I came here from my village when Bulent married me. He's gone, even before my son. Lost to cancer. Our goats, gone, too. Everyone."

Boroğlu's eyes narrow. "You've lived here about seventy years?"

Shrugging, the woman pulls at the corner of her scarf.

"And your husband was a goatherd?"

"Yes. He loved our goats."

Boroğlu stares at Elif for a moment before turning back to the woman. "This is your land?"

The woman shrugs again. "My husband's family. Some of it. After he died, I herded the goats for a long time. But I got too old. My son, he didn't come back." She sobs twice. "He died."

Boroğlu looks again at Elif, who says to the woman, "My mother is looking for large stones. Smooth ones. Cut. When your husband and you were herding your goats, do you remember seeing any? Arranged in rows?"

"Yes." The woman leans over and nudges the upper log until it starts to flame.

Boroğlu takes the chair closer to the woman. "Cut stones? Three or more together."

"Oh, yes."

"Upstream or downstream?"

"Yes. In the meadows."

Boroğlu leans forward. "Both? Upstream and downstream?"

The woman's eyes focus through her tears. "Three. In the meadows where the goats fed."

"Mom," Elif says. "I think she's trying to tell you that there are three places. Three sites."

The woman looks up at Elif, smiling and nodding thankfully— but her tears keep running.

 34

ISTANBUL

At dusk, the two powerful and influential business-men in their mid-sixties sit at a table at the Ciragan Palace Hotel's posh terrace bar overlooking the Bosphorus. They are about the same height, but the Turkish patriarch is far more fit and trim than the Russian oligarch. The Russian drinks Krug Vintage Brut 2000, the Turkish patriarch Perrier. The three closest tables are empty, and the ring of tables beyond are occupied by bodyguards. The oligarch insisted that the meeting be on his yacht, and the patriarch countered with a demand to use his plush Istanbul apartment. Both men are deeply concerned that the subject of the negotiation be private, but neither is willing to enter the other's domain, and so this neutral site was a compromise, arrived at only an hour earlier. The Russian's name and his reputation for tipping extravagantly convinced the maître d' to locate other patrons away from the immediate area. Neither of the two men is a politician, and so they can be seen together in public, but the subject of their conversation is not fodder for social media.

"The boy has done nothing," the Russian says. "Nothing at all." His voice holds superiority as well as belligerence. "Fucking nothing!" He leans forward, his elbows on the table. His neck is fleshy, but the skin of his face is taut, as though it has been stretched. His hooded eyes are dark. "I have heard *nothing*. Not one fucking word!"

"Have we ever disappointed you, Vladimir?" the patriarch asks. Unlike the Russian, he will not stoop to vulgarity. Both men speak English because neither has deigned to learn the other's language—and English is the language of international business. They have done deals before that benefited both exceedingly, but they have never done a deal of this magnitude—and they have never been amiable. The patriarch gives up invaluable artifacts but retains a deep sense that Anatolia is the cradle of civilization and that Russia is a dreary wasteland. The oligarch covets the artifacts but does not receive from the Turk the obsequiousness that his incredible wealth and power demand.

The Russian sips his Krug before answering the question. "No, Mustafa, *you* have not. And *your* willingness to take this meeting is, finally, a step in the right direction."

The patriarch looks over at the hotel's infinity pool where wealthy foreigners are frolicking with their screeching children. The emphasis on the words "you" and "your" is another deliberate slight toward his son, which he should, in the name of profit, ignore, but he cannot. "*We* are making significant progress."

"Your son made promises. I assumed he was speaking for you."

The patriarch's green eyes flare. His receding hair may have gone gray, but the fire in his belly when his family, his *name,* has been insulted is still stoked. Barely able to keep his tone civil, he says, "My son speaks for my family."

The Russian pulls at his gold cufflinks, leans back, and smiles maliciously. "The boy makes promises he doesn't keep."

The gilded monogram on the Russian's shirt pocket has always provoked irritation, but now it proves even more maddening because his statement has some truth to it. "The situation is complex," the patriarch says.

"So, there is no statue? No *Dying Gaul?*"

"There is," the patriarch says flatly. "Absolutely." He is not blowing smoke. Like his son, he believes the statue still exists. There's the photo circulating. And, the statue was specifically mentioned in the document. Not as *The Dying Gaul,* of course. That name was given to the statue by Europeans only a couple of centuries ago. But *The Galatian* and *The Galatian and his Wife* were both referred to in the letter, a copy of which was forwarded to him from the Ministry of Culture shortly after his highly placed sources there learned of it. "There is another player." Though it isn't quite true, he adds, "And a second bidder. But *your* deal, will, as always, be honored, Vladimir. *Yours* first. Yours *always.*"

A tourist boat playing traditional music is passing on the Bosphorus. The Russian inspects his manicured fingers and then gazes at his ancient Minoan bull's head ring, the only one of its kind known to exist outside a major museum. "You understand," he growls, "that the deal must not fall through. The statue is to be a gift for the President. I clearly made that point to the boy." He lifts his champagne flute and glowers across the table. "This deal has to be your priority. If it isn't, your business, your family will…" He waves his hand dismissively.

The patriarch nods but does not answer. He is not one to forget—or forgive—a threat. He folds his hands on the table, careful not to clench them. This Russian, no matter how prominent he is, will have to be dealt with—but only after the deal is done.

"I certainly hope the boy is aware that *nothing* can fucking go wrong," the Russian says.

Yet another insult directed at his son. But the patriarch merely nods again because he knows that the way to manipulate a narcissist like this shithead is to flatter him rather than combat him—and with each of the Russian's insults the price of the statue, already eight figures, is rising. "We will deliver, Vladimir. And the piece will exceed your expectations." His tone is factual and pragmatic, not defensive. He gestures toward the ring the Russian is fondling. "You, of all people, know that."

The Russian stares across the table, but his eyes are losing their ferocity. The surgically tucked skin around his eyes and the unnatural red-orange hue of his facial skin suggest some deep insecurity beneath the imperious meanness. The patriarch wonders if procuring the statue is so crucial because Vlad's influence with the Russian president is waning—if the man's position, his entire financial empire, is in jeopardy. You can, the patriarch knows, amass immense wealth and surround yourself with opulent trappings and heavy security but still live in fear—especially if you're Russian. In a country where there is, essentially, no real rule of law, you can lose *everything* —the yachts, the dachas, the London real estate—in an instant if you displease the leader. You can become the envy of all the babushkas, be seen on All-Russia State TV as powerfully influential as well as supremely rich, but you cannot save yourself should you fall from grace.

"I hope, for your son's sake," the Russian says, "that you're correct." He then smiles sourly and adds, "If you need help in eliminating competition…"

Although the statement is an even more direct threat against his son, the patriarch says only, "Thank you, Vlad. If this was an international issue, I would gladly call on your expertise and advice. But it's a local dispute, and we will deal with it." The simple-minded bullying of these Russian oligarchs makes them in some ways even easier to manipulate than the European aristocrats his father and grandfather once dealt with, but their deep insecurities also make them far more dangerous—and it's best to keep them at a distance. "We will do whatever is necessary, Vlad. You know that, too."

 35

BERGAMA

Serkan Boroğlu spins the floor safe's combination lock again and then tries his own birth date, but that doesn't work either. Frustrated, he rises from his knees and smacks the heel of his hand against the closet door. He is in his mother's bedroom, which has doubled as her home office for as long as he can remember. He has already checked her desk's drawers, sifted through the file folders piled on her desk, and inspected the two hundred or so books and journals on the shelves that line two of the room's four walls. Everything is related to archeology, especially that of the Aegean area, but only two journals, both in German, are dated this year—and nothing suggests what specifically she is working on these days.

Nine of the twenty cardboard file boxes piled five high against the bedroom's windowless back wall dug into the hillside are labeled "Allianoi." Most of the others have "Akropol," "Red Hall," and "Aesklepion" written boldly in his mother's clear script. Two of the boxes in the top row have "Tumuli Rescues" scrawled across them in heavy black marking pen, but one has the date "2014" and the other "2015." He has hidden the fifty American hundred-dollar bills in his Istanbul apartment, and he has got to give Mustafa, that arrogant prick, something tangible—but he doesn't want to provide anything that might actually damage his mother's work, whatever it is.

When he hears the front door closing, he places the two German journals back in the stack on the desk, scans the room to make sure he has not altered any of the usual clutter, and steps out into the courtyard. As he passes the long table where his family often ate as he was growing up, his mother and grandmother stand glowering by the front door. He is used to the expression from his mother but not from his grandmother. "Anne!" he exclaims. "Anneanne! Surprise!"

His mother huffs, and his grandmother blinks back tears.

"Where have you been?" he asks. "I've been looking for you."

Both women are wearing long dresses and floral-print scarves. They have been in the village up near Kapıkaya where little Mehmet's funeral was held. Being women and outsiders, they did not, of course, participate, but they stood on the periphery with some of the other women from neighboring villages as the Imam said the prayers. Then, they remained at the mosque as the village men escorted the boy's body to the cemetery.

"Why are you here?" Serkan's mother asks, anger in her voice.

He smiles. "I just came home. Do I have to have a reason?"

His mother's eyes continue to harden. His grandmother bows her head. As she crosses toward her bench in the courtyard's corner, she takes one of Elif's statues from the alcove's shelves.

"What?" Serkan says to his mother.

"What's going on, Serkan?"

"What? What do you mean?"

"You know what I mean." She is using the tone she used during cross-examinations when he was a boy.

"I have no idea what you're talking about." She can't possibly know.

"What were you doing?" Her voice is ice.

"When? What do you mean?"

"Now. Right now!"

"Nothing."

"*Nothing!*" She mimics him in that voice he used to hate.

"I was just..." He stops, memories of confrontations with his mother flooding his mind. Sweat breaks on his forehead and neck. He glances at his grandmother, who continues to stare at the terra-cotta goddess she is holding. He moved to Istanbul after university partly to get away from this look of condemnation on his mother's face. He always made good grades and was a starter on his lise basketball team, but she still berated him if he stayed out too late or came home with the smell of beer on his breath. When he went to university in Ankara and lived with his father, he didn't have to answer his mother's sorts of questions. His father, who had a new wife, his third, provided Serkan with a place to live but little else. Serkan's years there were essentially free of constraints, much less regulations. His decision after university to try to make it on his own in Istanbul was easy, even obvious. But whenever he returns to Bergama his mother just keeps nagging him about her strict house rules.

Shaking her head, Boroğlu lifts her cell phone from her purse and taps a number. "Your brother's here." She pauses. "Not sure... Yes..." Glancing at her mother, she adds, "I don't know... Up to no good, I'm sure... Okay." She clicks off the phone and turns again to him. "Elif needs to talk to you."

"Fine," he says. "Is she in her studio?"

"No. Yes, but she's on her way here."

"Good." Elif often stood up for him when they were younger, and she has, it seems, offered to help him now.

"You are so much like him!" His mother's voice is venomous. "So self-involved!"

He has heard this all before, of course. Too often. It makes him seethe, but he certainly knows better than to answer. He will not give her an opening to start ranting again about his father.

"Wait on the porch," Boroğlu says. "We need to show you something."

It sounds too much like an order, but there's something else in his mother's voice he can't quite identify. Something more than ire. Agitation? Unhappiness? It might even be sorrow.

Alone on the rooftop patio, Serkan looks out at the haze hanging in the sunlight over Bergama. The town, the whole area, needs rain. He crosses the patio to where his grandmother's herbs are lined in pots. The soil is dark and moist—she must have watered them this morning. Still sweating, he needs a Bud or Coke or water or something—

but he's not about to call down to ask for anything. He feels like he did when he was in trouble as a boy, but he hasn't done anything. Nothing at all, really.

He can't keep his hands still. They drum the railing along the periphery of the porch, a hollow sound. He looks down across the street at the concrete wall where, when they were children, Elif sometimes left him secret messages. "The graffiti wall," they called it. Now there are names, "Burak" and "Mehmet" and others, scratched and marked there. The town keeps patching the concrete and whitewashing it, but new messages keep appearing. It all seems so anachronistic —and so innocent.

Sekhmet drops from the arbor to the glass-topped table and from there to the tiled floor, but she doesn't come over to him. Doesn't rub against his leg as she usually does. The haze feels heavy, the air close. Down the street, Elif is pedaling her bicycle toward the house. Her head is down, as though she can only see the cobblestones. She should look up and wave, but she doesn't.

# 36

BERGAMA

Özlem Boroğlu taps the manila envelope against her left palm before passing it across the patio table to her son. Elif, sitting between her mother and her brother, folds her hands on the table's glass top and stares at her thumbnails painted black with silver skulls. Still drumming his fingers, Serkan doesn't touch the envelope. He leans back in his chair, looking at nothing rather than at either his mother or his sister.

"Get your head out of your ass, Serkan," his mother says.

"What is this?" he asks, his anger rising again.

"Photographs," his mother hisses. "Look at them!"

"Not those!" he shouts, hammering the envelope. "This!" He waves his hand in the air. "I feel like I'm on trial for something I don't even know about."

Elif leans forward and presses her hands on the table. "Please look at the photographs, Serkan," she says. Her tone is more hurt than hostile.

He glances at his mother for a moment before picking up the envelope and bending the metal clasp. As he slides the photographs out, he sucks in his breath.

His mother reaches over and spreads the photos on the table.

Serkan's neck and back stiffen as he stares at the pictures. "Where... where'd you get these?"

"What's going on, Serkan?" Her voice sounds more calm, a mother wanting to help her son, except that Serkan thinks he knows better.

He grabs the edge of the table, glances at Elif, and then looks back at the photos. "Where'd you get these?"

"Who is he?"

Serkan is sweating again. "Where'd you...?"

"Serkan!"

He brushes his hand across his face. "He's...he's a business associate."

His mother clears her throat.

"He's a guy I'm doing a deal with..."

She coughs loudly. Elif looks up at the grape arbor. His grandmother comes out onto the patio carrying a tray with four teacups. As she sets the cups on the table, no one says anything or makes eye contact. When she sits in the fourth chair, her dress swishes. She gapes for a second at the photographs, which she has not seen before. She begins to say something but then stops herself. Traffic mutters down in Bergama.

"He's just a guy...I don't really know him." Serkan shakes his head. "Where'd you get them?"

"The Ministry... The police, Serkan." His mother's voice is sounding to him like ice. When he was young, this was even worse than the fire of her outbursts.

"I told you, I don't really know the guy."

Boroğlu takes a cigarette from her pack. "You know who he is."

"Kind of..."

"Kind of?" She mimics him again. "Whatever you're doing, the government's got you under surveillance."

"No... Not me, they don't!"

"Don't be stupid!" She taps the photographs with her cigarette. "An investigator gave these to us. If something illegal is going on, which there must be, who'll take the fall? Who, Serkan? That rich, connected boy? Or you?"

He doesn't answer.

Boroğlu lights her cigarette and inhales deeply. "What were you doing in my room, Serkan?" she asks. Smoke escapes her mouth and nostrils.

"I wasn't... What do you mean?" He runs his forefinger along the rim of his cup, but the tea is too hot to drink.

Elif bites her lower lip. Her grandmother stares at the photographs.

"I can smell that you were in there," Boroğlu says.

"Wha...? Nothing." His voice sounds to him like it's going to crack like it did when he was twelve. "I wasn't doing anything."

Boroğlu fixes him with her gaze. "The safe's lock was at a different setting."

Elif's eyes fill as she says, "The guy came to my studio, Serkan." She blinks back tears, but her tone is firm.

"What?" Though he already knows that, he shakes his head to fake confusion. "No..." His concern, though, is real as he looks into his sister's eyes.

"You heard her," Boroğlu says.

"Did...did he threaten you?"

"Not exactly." Elif's eyes harden. "Implicitly."

Boroğlu's mother does not say anything, but she looks intently at her daughter and her grandchildren as each speaks.

Serkan continues to shake his head. "What'd he do?"

"Tried to buy my soul."

He winces. "Huh?"

"He tried to get me to sell what's not for sale." She keeps staring at him. "Kept offering me more money."

Serkan's stomach sinks. He feels like she somehow knows the depths to which he is plunging. He has always thought that he was the smarter sibling, even though she did better in school. And he was smarter out there on the street, in the world. But now they're in territory he's less sure about. Elif needs to stop staring at him, though her look is not a righteous glare like their mother's. Not at all. But she is looking into him, and it's even more unnerving.

"You've really done it this time," Boroğlu says. She takes a long draw on her cigarette, exhales slowly, and only then looks at him again.

"We might be able to fix this, but you've got to be honest with us. The whole truth. For a change."

He nods, but he can't tell them *everything*. Not about his after-hours tours to kinky clubs. And certainly not the part about taking the five thousand dollars from the arrogant prick for the introduction to Jack and Clare—and to spy on his mother. But he can't think of any credible way to explain why he was trying to crack her safe. All three women are staring at him, burning holes. His palms are clammy, and the back of his neck prickles.

"The truth, Serkan!" Boroğlu says, her voice severe.

"It's the only way we can help you," Elif adds.

"That day…," his grandmother whispers as she taps one of the photographs. "I saw him when…" She shivers, and her breathing becomes shallow. "Maybe not him… Him but not *him*." Her family turns toward her. "The morning of the bomb…the attack on the funicular …I saw him in town!"

# 37

ROME; 192 CE

$A$s the Great Fire smolders, Galen of Pergamon trudges up the Sacred Way next to the Horrea Piperataria, the immense warehouse that was, until a week before, the commercial heart of the Roman Empire. Soot covers his toga, and damp ash blackens his sandals and feet. A storm has finally doused the flames, but the pungent smell of burnt incense and spices hangs in the air. The odor is so strong that even he, one of the most rational men in this city of three million, can't help but think he is attending a funeral—and he certainly is, at least that of his own material wealth.

While he was moving his residence to a new estate in Campania, he stored his gold coins, fine silverware, and medical records, including the lists of debts owed to him, in this colossal warehouse. He did so because it had a military guard and, of greater import, *it could not burn*. The entire structure, one of the largest in the world, was built of stone. Only the doors were wood. What neither he nor any other of Rome's wealthiest patricians and merchants considered was that when the Great Fire reached the area, the stone buildings would serve as ovens for the almost five thousand tons of incense and spices stored there.

A collapsing roof somewhere to Galen's right thunders, and the ground shudders. A cloud of black smoke and ash darkens the sky. A bent old man near him wails as he hobbles away. But there is no longer danger except for those foolhardy enough to be inside the warehouse digging through the thick, sodden, still-simmering ash for remnants of their lost fortunes. He will no doubt have to treat some wretched merchants whose hands are scorched by their desire to retrieve that which cannot be.

Galen wipes sweat and grime from his bald head. The bitter taste of ash clings to his throat and mouth. His own greatest loss is not gold or silver or a list of debtors. He has dedicated his life to learning— medicine, of course, but also philosophy and the arts. He has recently, even at age sixty-two, been training himself in a variety of medical and philosophical fields, and the conflagration has consumed many of his books and much of his research. The complete manuscripts of his first two books of *On Composition of Drugs According to Kind* are smoke sent skyward to gods he does not believe exist. Gone too are the rare medical substances and ingredients he acquired while acting as personal physician to the emperor Marcus Aurelius. And the medical remedies gathered from around the world—all smoke. And all irreplaceable. The unique collection of medical instruments that he had designed for the various surgeries he and no one else was able to perform has, no doubt, melted to sludge, perhaps even vaporized by the immeasurable heat. Even his study of the vocabulary he collected from ancient Athenian comedies is lost to the world. Much of what he has left—all of the classical Athenian manuscripts his forefathers saved, his own early medical treatises and those he collected during his travels, and the Attalid Dynasty art and statuary —is in Pergamon awaiting his return, which in this moment he feels might never occur.

He recognizes that what matters most—his life, his very soul— has not been scorched by the fire. Still, the weight of his personal loss presses in on him as he looks up the Sacred Way at the devastation. Beyond the Horrea Piperataria—the Temple of Peace, housing untold treasure from conquests abroad, among them the menorah from the razed Hebrew Temple in Jerusalem—is demolished. The round Temple of Vesta, the very soul of Rome, is now desecrated debris, and the Imperial Palace, charred rubble. He understands in a way few others will that his own calamity, as deep and pervasive as it is, pales in comparison to the city's catastrophe. This greatest of cities will, he believes, never recover its full glory.

He is the personal physician to the current emperor, Commodus, a man who is anything but the stoic his father was. Marcus Aurelius charged Galen with the task of keeping his heir healthy. And he has attended well to all of the heir's physical ailments for more than two decades now. But the current emperor's mental state is more precarious—and far more difficult to treat. As Commodus's vast personal wealth and power have increased, he has become ever more narcissistic and delusional. He has even taken to dressing like Hercules and fighting as a gladiator in the Colosseum. He is convinced he is invincible and that, in any case, Galen can instantly heal any wounds he might suffer. All Romans of every rank know, of course, that the Great Hercules's foes must always, inevitably be vanquished.

And now, even before the ashes have cooled, Commodus has begun ranting about rebuilding the city in his own image. In his megalomania, he has declared himself the new Romulus and plans to rename the city after himself. Although Rome's wealth has been decimated by the Great Fire, the emperor rages on.

 38

BERGAMA

At half past nine in the morning, Özlem Boroğlu descends the stone steps to her house's cellar. She passes through her kitchen to the dark pantry that, dug into the acropolis hillside, stays cool even on these hot mornings. Pulling hard, she shifts the old wooden cabinet used to store her mother's pickles and tomatoes. She lowers herself to one knee, jimmies free a stone the size of two loaves of ekmek stacked one on the other, reaches into the darkness, and grasps the aluminum tube. Holding the tube carefully, almost reverently, she rises to her feet, crosses back through the kitchen, and climbs the stairs first to the courtyard and then to her rooftop garden.

Boroğlu places the tube on the linen cloth she has spread on the glass-top table. Earlier, she moved her cigarettes, lighter, notebook, and cup of tea to the patio's ledge near her mother's herbs. She also swept the patio after the night's contentious family meeting, as much to clear her mind as to clean the space. Serkan left early in the morning for Istanbul, and Elif returned to her work at the studio. Serkan was not completely forthright with her, and she, for her part, withheld a lot of information as well. She did, however, give him the copy of Galen of Pergamon's last letter that she was keeping in her office safe. She also provided him with photocopies of twenty pages from her current notebook, but her notes—written in her personal, idiosyncratic and, therefore, almost indecipherable language—will not help the execrable Hamits.

She is close to the Galen cache, weeks or, if she has been lucky, only days away. She has only returned to the area near Kapıkaya twice since Elif introduced her to the old woman. She brought the woman oranges the first time and chocolate the second. On the first visit, she searched downstream and found a site that has real possibilities. Only a few andesite blocks protruded from the rocky terrain, but the view back toward Pergamon's Acropolis was clear and direct. There was also nearby a huge stone that might once have been part of a mausoleum. On her second visit, a site upstream was not as promising, but still needs to be investigated further. She did not spend much time at either site, except to log their exact coordinates. Far more time-consuming was her search in Bergama for land deeds and in the German Archaeological Institute's office for early records to determine if either site had ever been worked. In the institute's old-fashioned library near her house, the meticulous German records revealed that the lower site had been surveyed in 1911 but never excavated. The upper site was never mentioned at all.

Galen's reference to the scent of pine led Boroğlu out of the Kaikos Valley into the hills rising to Kapıkaya, and poor little Mehmet's possession of the Hadrian Aureus confirmed that she is on the right track. And now, she has these two specific sites. She even gave Serkan the detailed geological map of the valley around Pergamon that she had painstakingly made. Let the Hamits dither around on their extensive land holdings in the valley. They, especially Mustafa, the overeducated, pompous son, have no real understanding of archeology and no chance of finding Galen's treasure on their own. The Hamits have always stolen artifacts or gypped poor farmers or bullied and even killed competitors—never themselves doing the painstaking labor archeology requires.

Boroğlu sits at the table, wipes her hands on the edge of the linen cloth, puts on clean white gloves, and breathes deeply three times. She then uncaps the tube and slides out the rolled parchment. This is only the third time she has ever touched the letter. As soon as she received it as an anonymous gift, she understood its cultural significance. She photographed the document, took the necessary steps to preserve it, and hid it in the cellar's pantry. Holding the parchment written by Galen steals her breath. She feels, as she has needed to after her son's betrayal, the bolt of energy that possession of ancient documents has provided over the years. When she unrolls the parchment, her hands quiver and her eyes water. Warmth spreads through her body. As she reads, she barely breathes at all.

*Aeneas, son of my Beloved friend, I am returning to Pergamon, the home of my birth and the city I love. Rome is the greatest city in the world, but it has never been my home. I have had an extraordinary life, but now I am old and do not have long to live. I miss your father, a great friend and patron, whom I knew well as a boy. I have travelled the world in search of treatments and medications. My thirst for knowledge, which began at a very early age, has never been and will never be quenched. I have been the personal physician to emperors, and I have outlived those emperors and also my contemporaries. Very few of the Empire's doctors were competent, and their outdated ideas and outmoded procedures have died with them. I have been the Finest of the Roman physicians, and my discoveries, my treatments, and my medications must live on for a thousand years.*

*Now, I want only to live out my final days at my Paternal villa in the presence of my father's collections of art and literature. I desire to gaze again at the beauty of our native sky and to smell once more the rich scent of pine. I am bringing with me my writings, those books that survived Rome's great fire, and my personal library of medical texts. I will combine my works with those of my father's Athenian philosophers and dramatists and all those manuscripts that his father and grandfather saved when that lust-besotted fool, Marc Antony, presented the Pergamon library to the megalomaniacal Cleopatra in Alexandria. When I arrive, we will also take from safe storage the Attalid Dynasty's bronze statues of the conquered Galatians that my father saved when the Temple of Athena was constructed. I am bringing with me my designs for a permanent home for all of these collections. The building will be splendid, a museum befitting the treasures it will house. The Library of Pergamon will again be renowned. The learned will again come to Pergamon to further their education just as I once did at Alexandria.*

*My mind and soul remain strong, but my body has become worn. My villa in Campania is beautiful, but I still miss Pergamon, the Temple of Trajan, which as you may remember, my father built, the majesty of the Great Altar dedicated to Zeus, and the theater where your father and I enjoyed the classical Athenian comedies with their wonderful play on words. Even more deeply, I miss the Aesklepion's healing spring waters, the sacred dogs and the snakes that resided in the tunnels, the evening light flowing above the healing rooms, and the fragrance of roses in bloom.*

*I would like to die where my father died. I want to release my soul where he released his. He was my first and greatest teacher. He sent me on my life's journey, for which I remain infinitely grateful. I trust that my father's villa is still kept up well. I have been faithful in sending funds to keep it thriving. I look forward to seeing you and your family.*

*The voyage at this time of year may, indeed, be difficult, but I cannot wait. If I do not survive the journey, leave my father's treasures in their chambers. It is better that they be lost to the ages than that they be looted or sold off or otherwise degraded by men.*

 39

BERGAMA

Özlem Boroğlu breathes deeply, stares at the letter for another moment, and then slips the parchment back into the tube and caps it again. Although she realized that the words would be identical to those she read a hundred times on the photocopy, she expected, yearned for, even craved a greater message, something that would lead her to the cache. Galen believed he received messages from Aesklepios and from his own soul—messages that helped him heal himself and others, messages that informed his practice, messages that merged into his writing—*messages that guided him.*

But here in this moment, *nothing.* She shakes her head. Light drips through the trellis and vines. Artifacts have spoken to her at times during her career, but this letter is as mute as its photocopies. She has gleaned enough from the letter to know where the villa is not, but she is still missing something that would lead her to the cache. The day is heating up, and her tea has cooled. She needs a cigarette.

As she takes off the gloves, stands, and turns toward the ledge, her mother comes out onto the patio. Boroğlu takes her lighter and the pack of cigarettes from the ledge, taps one out, and lights it. Her mother, wearing a loose purple şalvar, a blue blouse, and a red floral headscarf, holds an empty cloth shopping bag.

"You're working?" her mother asks.

Boroğlu exhales slowly through her nose. Her mother's words sound to her more like an accusation than a question. Of course she's working. She's always working, and her mother knows it. "What?" she says. It's not a question either.

Her mother lays the empty shopping bag on the table. "You didn't say goodbye to Serkan."

Carrying her notebook and the ashtray, Boroğlu returns to the table and sits down. "I was asleep. I'd been up much of the night with him."

"Yes." Her mother nods and then glances at the notebook on the table. "Are you sure you should have let him go?"

It isn't a real question either. "How was I supposed to stop him?"

"You *sent* him back." The skin of her mother's face is wrinkled and her crow's feet deep, but her blue eyes are intensely bright. "It's dangerous."

Boroğlu glares at her mother, who usually doesn't question her about her relationships with her children. Although the two had their share of disagreements when Boroğlu was growing up, her mother has been far more reluctant to criticize her in the decade they have lived together after Boroğlu's father's death. "He put us all in danger!"

"That's true." She waves at the notebook. "But what you're doing is the root of it!"

"The *root* of it is that Serkan got into bed with the Hamits."

Her mother turns the bracelets on her right wrist. "But you're making it more dangerous. Giving the grave robbers information…"

"Nothing useful." She takes another drag on her cigarette.

"That won't make it less dangerous for Serkan!"

Boroğlu shrugs.

"It looks like you're competing with them!"

"I am!"

"And Serkan's a pawn?"

Boroğlu squeezes the cigarette's filter. It's another non-question. "I haven't made him a pawn!" Her voice rises. "*They're* paying him to spy on me!"

"And Elif?" Her mother's eyes narrow. "It's not some game! He's your son! They're your dear children!"

Boroğlu taps ash into the ashtray on the table. A motorbike is whining up the hill. Dogs are barking. "They've got to be stopped!"

"By you?"

"Who else?"

"The gov—"

Boroğlu snorts. "The Ministry works *for* the Hamits!"

"Not everyone!" Her mother's tone is sharp.

Thinking that her mother must be referring to Tuğçe Iskan, that young woman who notices everything but understands nothing, Boroğlu doesn't answer. She takes another drag on her cigarette and looks across the patio at the pale sky above Bergama. The noise of the motorbike has stopped, but the dogs are still barking.

"So, it's you against the world?" her mother asks, yet another criticism masked as a question.

When Boroğlu still doesn't answer, her mother steps to her herb garden, stoops, picks a sprig of mint, and touches it to her tongue. "What makes you so much better than the Ministry?" she asks.

As Boroğlu grinds out her cigarette, she says, "I don't steal artifacts for myself or my friends!" She flicks the butt into the ashtray. "You saw what those bastards did to me! Destroyed Allianoi...my site... my career!" She picks up her notebook and then flings it back on the table. "And when I got Galen's letter, they screwed me again! Took my job! *Eliminated me!*" When her mother still pretends to fuss over her plants, she shouts, "I'm trying to *save* the artifacts!"

Her mother turns and looks her in the eye. "And take the credit, get all the attention for the discovery."

Boroğlu meets her mother's gaze. "Yes," she says, her tone not at all conciliatory. "And what's so wrong about that?"

Her mother cocks her head. "Nothing! I'm proud of what you've done, but..."

"But what?"

"What about the risks? What's more important? The artifacts or your children?"

"That's not fair!" Boroğlu clenches her fists.

Her mother steps toward the table and grabs her shopping bag.

"It's not either-or!" Boroğlu yells. "It's not!"

Her mother stops with her hand on the shopping bag. "Are you sure about that?"

Boroğlu's fingers drum the tabletop. This time, it's a real question —and one she doesn't have a ready answer for. Her mother scoops the bag from the table, turns, and heads down the stairs, her shoes clumping a refrain.

40

ANKARA

Tuğçe Iskan stands in front of the associate minister's spacious mahogany desk. Nothing at all is on the desk except a telephone console and an iPad—no files, no pens, no notepads, no family photos, *nothing* for her to take notice of and store in her memory. Nothing on the walls either, except for enlarged framed photos of Ataturk and the current president. The minister sits behind the desk in a burgundy leather armchair. His hair, combed forward, hides much of his baldness. The hair on his temples has gone gray. His eyes—narrow, brown, and intense—scan her, taking in her height and hair, her bright eyes, pale skin, and large nose. His eyes pause for just a moment on her neck, which shows just a couple millimeters of her tattoo above the collar of her plain, white long-sleeved shirt. The eyes pause again, longer, on her chest.

The minister, Iskan notes, is cleanly shaved except for a tiny crescent of silver whiskers on his jaw beneath his left earlobe. A dark mole rises on his right cheek, and a small oval scar is at the base of his chin. His tie is maroon, his shirt a crisp white. His hands, folded on the desk, are hairy. His wristwatch features multiple dials.

"Sit, please," he says, gesturing to one of the two leather-cushioned chairs set at angles in front of his desk.

She does as she has been told. She has never met one-on-one with anyone this high up in the Ministry, and she is unclear about what an associate minister does much less why she was summoned or how she should act. She was instructed to bring with her any files she retained on the Galen letter and on her earlier truncated investigation into the Hamit family finances. She has no paper or digital files on either, and the voluminous materials she has gathered on the Hamits in the last month are neatly filed—but only in her brain.

"How are you, Tuğçe Hanim?" he asks, his voice deep and his tone, she believes, unfriendly.

"I'm good. And you?"

He tilts his head and nods but does not smile. "You have taken leave?"

She smiles nervously. "Two weeks, long overdue… My department head has been…encouraging…me to." Her left foot is dancing so she strokes her sweaty palms on the thighs of her black pants and roots the offending foot into the plush carpet.

"But you have not gone on holiday?"

Iskan is not sure it is a question so she merely shakes her head, glances over his shoulder at the portrait of Ataturk gazing into the future, and, trying to slow her mind down, forces a smile.

He looks her in the eyes for the first time. "And yet you have been to Bergama twice."

When she told Nihat Monoğlu that she had been summoned to the Ministry, he suggested to her that she should not lie—but also not actually tell the associate minister anything he didn't already know. "Yes," she says, "under a directive from my department head."

"Your new department head."

"Yes. The department I was transferred to last November."

"The first time." He clears his throat. "The second visit, there was no directive from your department."

"No." She feels herself flushing.

"You contacted Recep Ateş. What was that about?"

She focuses on the minister's mole. "I found some inconsistencies in the numbering of reports the Bergama office submitted to the Ministry."

The minister takes an iPhone from his pocket, glances at the screen, looks at her again, and says flatly, "But you were not instructed to do so."

"I wasn't." she smiles, this time not forced. "I don't like inconsistencies." It's entirely true, of course. "I'm always very careful to straighten things out."

"I am, too," he says. "What did you discover?"

"That three were misdirected. But it was relatively easy to put everything in order."

"Good." He taps his fingertips together. "Did you see Özlem Boroğlu while you were there?"

"I did."

"Well?"

She looks at him as though she does not understand.

He places his hands flat on the desk. "*Why?*"

"She thinks…thought…I caused her firing. I wanted to set the record straight on that, too."

He leans forward and stares at her. "And did you?"

"No." She looks down at her hands, which she realizes she is wringing. "That was *not* easy. She is bitter. Hates me."

He leans even farther forward, as though he is going to leap on her. "But you saw her on your second visit, too."

"Just on the street." Technically, it is true. "She was just as bitter." She remembers Boroğlu stomping away when she asked her about the photo of her son and the Hamit boy. "Wouldn't speak to me at all." She is becoming less nervous. This is, it seems, all about the Galen letter, which she knows little about, and the Hamits, whom she will not talk about.

He nods. "So you did not speak to her about the earlier matter, the Ministry's letter she has stolen. Either time in Bergama."

She shakes her head. "I did not."

"But you did handle the letter?"

"The copy the Ministry received, yes. I was the first to see it."

"And?"

She knows that she is supposed to tell him something more, but she is not about to mention that she translated the document so that she could determine its contents. "Once I realized what it was," she says, "I passed it on to my superior."

He presses his palms on the desk and stares at her. "Did you alter the letter?"

"What? No." Genuinely taken aback, she takes a quick breath. "Of course not."

He keeps staring. "It was altered, the translation. After it arrived here."

She makes eye contact. "I don't know anything about that."

He holds her eyes for a moment before saying, "Okay. What about the photo?"

"What photo?"

"The one of the statue."

He's fishing, but for what she isn't sure. Becoming irritated, she struggles to keep her tone respectful as she says, "I don't know anything about that either."

"You haven't seen it?"

"No." She is aware that a photo of a long-lost bronze Pergamene statue is circulating on the web, but it wasn't her concern. "I've been focused on my work."

"It's real, the photo," he says matter-of-factly. "Boroğlu never mentioned it to you?"

"No. As I told you, she hates me. Won't speak to me."

He sits back in his chair. "The woman hates a lot of people in the Ministry."

Iskan says nothing. This man is political and therefore dangerous, but he is not as well informed as he thinks.

"There's another matter," he says as he slips the phone back into his pants pocket. "One of your cases."

She makes what she hopes is a quizzical expression.

"The Hamits. Antique dealers selling ısıl contraband. Antiquities."

"Yes?" She wonders if her expression has held. "I barely got started..."

"Did you retain any files?" He is leaning forward again eyeing her.

"No," she says, nodding as though she is trying to be helpful. "I gave everything to my supervisor. Before the New Year."

"You have no more information?"

"Files? None." Checking out the mole on his cheek, she adds, as though it should explain everything, "The case is closed."

"Nothing?" His eyes are intense once more. "Nothing digital or paper?"

Although she has much in her memory, including how and where to relocate all the relevant information, she can be wholly truthful. "I turned in everything I had." She pauses, for the first time, genuinely curious. "Should I have saved something?"

He smiles, which, she thinks, might actually be genuine. "No. I just needed to find out." He presses his hands again on the desk, but his expression has become abruptly friendly—and it seems to her that she may have just passed some sort of test. "Your work, your skills are being buried in your department, aren't they?"

Because the question also seems friendly, she is unsure how to respond. "I do my best," she says. "Always."

"I'm sure you do." He sits back, hooks an elbow over the back of his chair, and looks at her from a different angle, seeming to appraise her. "I...we should find a position that will better suit your skills."

She nods, confused not only by the change in his expression and voice but also by the implications of what he is saying. Unable to form a response, she feels her face flushing again.

"With some additional training," he says, "you could do excellent work. Provide real service to our country."

She can't be sure but thinks he might be leering again.

"Well," he concludes, "that's a conversation for another day." He rises from his chair and comes around the desk. By the time she stands, he is next to her. He is about her height and more muscular, much more fit, than she thought. "It has been good talking with you, Tuğçe," he adds as he puts his hand on her shoulder.

She flinches. Since her experience with her husband, she has not liked men touching her. When she was a child, her father seldom hugged her. He was fair to her, never harmed her, but he was really only interested in his son, her older brother, who was an excellent footballer. When she was young, she played with the boys sometimes and was often able to keep up on the pitch, but any contact was just part of the game. By the time she was a teenager, boys no longer let girls play. And she never had a boyfriend. She was too smart in school, too isolated, and, when it came to all the social intricacies of teen-aged courtship, too clueless. Her husband…well, his touch was *never* pleasant, and she learned to flee to a private garden in her mind.

The minister's hand lingers too long on her shoulder, but she does not brush him off. As they turn toward the office door, he says, "Yes, Tuğçe, I am glad to meet you." He places his hand in the small of her back as though he is escorting her. She can feel him gazing at her profile. "I'm sure we can find a position that better suits your abilities."

 41
ISTANBUL

Clare, the American lawyer, takes from the coffee table the gold amulet that rests on the black cashmere cloth in the center of the three flutes bubbling with champagne. As she inspects the gleaming image of Athena holding the head of Medusa, she says, "It's beautiful." Her hand is steady even though she is impressed with the piece—in fact, covets it. She looks across the posh apartment's coffee table at the impeccable young man with the bright green eyes and adds, "And it's just the sort of thing I was hoping for."

Mustafa Hamit, who has been entrusted by his father to close this deal, smiles and nods. He has not even negotiated the price with the Americans, but he believes he has already got them. He lifts the flute closest to him, sips the Krug, and smiles at her.

She returns his smile and then turns slowly to her husband who sits with her on the plush beige couch. "Do you think we should take it, too?" she asks.

*Too?* Mustafa's back stiffens and his smile freezes.

"Maybe," Jack says without glancing at Mustafa. "If we can make certain arrangements."

*Certain arrangements!* As he slips the flute back onto the table, Mustafa looks from the wife to the husband and back. This meeting was called on short notice and set up for the brief period of the Americans' stopover in Istanbul before the couple's return flight to Los Angeles.

It was all seeming too easy, the couple so amiable and so willing to meet here at the apartment the family uses only for its especially private deals. And at the time he suggested. Adrenaline starts pulsing. "You have acquired something else in your travels?" he asks politely.

"We have," she says, still smiling at him. "A Sekhmet amulet. I identify even more with her than with Athena."

Mustafa nods. This woman may look like an aging Barbie doll, but she identifies with the Egyptian warrior goddess, the fiercest of hunters, the Powerful One whose breath created the desert, the one who once in her bloodlust almost annihilated the human race, who only stopped the carnage when she became drunk on seven thousand jugs of beer colored by pomegranate to look like human blood. This deal could prove more difficult—*and more interesting*—than he expected. He knows from Serkan Boroğlu that when the couple cut short their Turkish tour, they visited Rhodes and other Aegean islands, but an ancient Sekhmet amulet shouldn't have been available—or, if there was one on the market, he and his family should have known about it. His tone becoming even more polite, he says, "I didn't know you visited Egypt."

"We didn't," Clare answers. She cocks her head and looks into his eyes. "The piece is from the Bergama area. Finely wrought gold."

Mustafa masks his rising anger. There is no way in hell a piece from Pergamon could have, should have, escaped his family's notice and control. "A Sekhmet amulet?"

Clare holds his gaze. "Why, yes, an exquisite miniature similar to the statue being reconstructed at the Red Basilica in Bergama. Do you know it?"

"Yes," Mustafa answers. He doesn't add, *Of course, you stupid bitch!* Instead he says, "That's very interesting. You bought it from a local dealer?"

"Yes," Clare says, but she doesn't add that she had the Sekhmet piece made for her. She inspects the Athena amulet closely, almost fondling it.

Mustafa looks at his manicured fingers as his mind races. His tone remains friendly, almost conspiratorial. "Did you have it authenticated?"

Clare's smile turns up at the corners. "Oh, quite!" she says. "The provenance is clear."

Mustafa keeps his voice even, although the ire inside is simmering. "The provenance can be, as you say in America, doctored."

Clare glances at her husband who is leaning forward staring at Mustafa. "Oh, we know that, Mustafa!" she says. Her smile is fixed, but something in her voice is changing. Not unfriendly, but more businesslike.

"Would you like me to take a look at the piece?" Mustafa asks. "My background is in Hellenistic antiquities. And a Sekhmet piece from Pergamon is rare, indeed."

"We know that, too," she answers. "And we appreciate your expertise. In fact, we're counting on it." She touches Medusa's severed head with her forefinger. "But we trust our source."

"And, may I inquire—"

"No," Jack interrupts him. He doesn't add any American claptrap about protecting sources or the importance of confidentiality. The issue is, quite simply, not going to be discussed.

Mustafa reaches for his flute but then stops himself. The Americans have not touched their champagne, and this deal certainly isn't closing as he expected. He nods again, but his mind is boiling. *There have been no recent government-authorized digs near Bergama. None. And any artifacts from the area discovered more than a few months ago would have come to his attention. Bora, who oversees the family's current clandestine digs, is the most likely suspect. But he, more than anyone else, would understand the consequences. No amount of money would have been worth it. Some stupid farmer gone rogue? No. None would have any access to clients like these Americans. Serkan, that social climbing shit? He would not have access to anything as valuable as a Sekhmet amulet. Unless… Unless Serkan's mother has discovered a cache. Yes, someone must have. And that old bitch has got to be the one. She can't have done it alone! One of the family's government sources in Bergama or Ankara should have, must have, known about it, even abetted her. Heads are going to roll…*

"Mustafa!" The American husband is speaking to him, has already said something to him.

"Yes," he answers, his voice courteous even though he has no idea what the man said.

"Keep your fucking head in the game, boy!" the man growls. He is leaning forward, red-faced.

In his meetings and negotiations for the museum in America, no one ever spoke to Mustafa that way. There, he dealt mostly with Ivy-educated money, who understood the etiquette. In fact, no one other than his father has ever called him "boy" in that demeaning way, but he remains outwardly calm. He uncrosses his leg and leans forward, both attentively and aggressively. He knows his place in the world; he just needs a moment to think through his position here. One of the family's Georgian bodyguards is stationed outside the apartment door, but this is not the moment for the family's old heavy-handed ways. He's smarter than that. Appeasement galls him, but he needs information from this old fart—and he needs this deal to work *now*. "You were saying?" he asks, his tone anything but servile.

The American glances at his wife, shakes his head—*condescendingly,* Mustafa thinks—clears his throat, and grumbles, "I was saying that Clare and I made time to meet with you today in order to purchase the amulet. She wants it. We intend to pay a fair price, but there is one stipulation."

*A stipulation... Money,* Mustafa thinks, *it's always about money with Americans.*

"You must deliver Athena...," the old fart points to the amulet that his wife is putting back on the black cloth, "to us in Los Angeles."

Mustafa starts, but only for a second. He was ready to negotiate price. But this... He is no one's delivery boy. And he is not going to be theirs.

"We," the old fart asserts, "aren't taking any antiquities out of Turkey, even if the provenance is perfect and you have received assurances that all will go smooth."

His wife is smiling at Mustafa again. "Not in the current political climate," she says, almost sweetly. "I'm sure you understand, Mustafa."

He does, and a week or two in LA, especially if it included a Las

Vegas excursion, would relieve the tedium of overseeing the search teams and, far worse, the diggers here. But the Russian business isn't yet resolved—and it must be. There's also the American's insult—he is *no one's* errand boy! "My schedule," he says, not quite able to keep his voice cordial, "will not permit me to travel to the U.S. in the near future."

The old fart rubs his palms together and then twists his signet ring. Shrugging, he says, "That's unfortunate." He turns his head to his wife. "At least you have Sekhmet, dear."

Her smile fixed, Clare continues to stare at Mustafa, seeming to size him up as a possible trophy.

# 42
## ISTANBUL

Mustafa Hamit slouches in the Istanbul apartment's armchair. His father paces by the coffee table where the Athena amulet still rests on the cloth in the center of the three champagne flutes. The Krug no longer bubbles.

"You told me you'd close the deal in under an hour," the father says, glancing at his gold wristwatch. "That didn't happen."

"They'll be back," Mustafa says, his tone defensive. "She wants it."

The patriarch stops pacing and stands over his son. "But it will take another day. At least. We've got more important work to do."

"I know."

"But have you thought it through? What will you do when they tell you they'll only take the deal if it's COD when the amulet is delivered in Los Angeles?"

"That won't work!"

"Of course, it won't!" His father starts pacing again. "But what the hell are you going to do when they make it a stipulation?" He practically spits the last word.

Mustafa's head jerks up, and his jaw tightens.

"Say that your schedule won't permit it?" There's clear disdain in his father's voice.

Mustafa jumps to his feet. "You were listening?" He looks wildly around the room. "You bugged this place? *My meeting!*"

"Yes, I did. It's business." The patriarch presses his hand into his son's chest, quick and hard, so that Mustafa slumps back into the chair. It doesn't hurt, physically, but Mustafa glares up at his father.

The patriarch waves at the crystal flutes. "They weren't drinking, and you had champagne!" He shakes his head.

"I'll fix it." Mustafa takes out a pack of Marlboros. "It's a done deal!"

"Not in the apartment!" his father says.

Mustafa tosses the pack onto the coffee table. "I'm going to get the bastard who sold them Sekhmet!"

His father shakes his head, not unlike the way the old American did. "Yes. Of course. But it's not the priority."

Mustafa clenches his fists. "That Sekhmet amulet's got to be fake!"

"I hope so," his father answers. "For your sake." He grabs the pack of cigarettes, crushes it with his hand, and drops the mangled pack back onto the table. "But what if it's not a fake? Have you thought about that?"

"What does that mean?"

"Have you thought about the possibility that despite all of your fancy equipment, somebody's beaten you to the Galen cache?"

"It's that old bitch!" Mustafa grabs the arms of the chair. "And Serkan. I'm going to—"

"I thought you were already *taking care* of her." His father's voice is sarcastic.

"I've handled it!" Mustafa gapes at his father. "It's all set up. Perfectly!"

"*Perfectly!*" His father mimics Mustafa in a high voice.

"I said I've—" Mustafa wipes his mouth that has suddenly gone dry.

"And then you plan to fly off to America again?"

"Only when I've taken care of what needs to be done here."

"You'll do the American's bidding?"

"Yes." He looks up at his father. "No! I'll only go when the time is right for the family. I'll make the deal work. And make the family a lot of money."

His father scoffs at him. "We can send somebody else."

"Who? I've already got the visa. The language. Good reasons to travel back and forth."

*"The connections,"* his father says with an edge. *"The sophistication."*

"I can evaluate that Sekhmet amulet. Track the bastard that sold it. Even develop new markets for our surplus Syrian artifacts."

His father's eyes narrow. "You're right," he says as he leans over the coffee table. "You're the right man for *that* job." He carefully folds the cloth and puts the amulet in his pants pocket. His voice devoid of emotion, he adds, "You can certainly do all that."

Mustafa knows the abrupt change in his father's tone is ominous. His father is rethinking—or has *already* rethought—his role, his usefulness here. "I'll only go *after* we're done with the old bitch. And the deal with the Russian is wrapped up."

His father glares at him. "Go sooner if you want. I'll deal with Vlad. I've already met with him."

"What? You did? But—"

"As you say, you'll have the opportunity to evaluate the Sekhmet amulet. And set up other conduits for our Syrian antiquities. Bora can oversee the field work here."

Mustafa feels as though he has been slapped. "Bora? He doesn't know anything about antiquities...except what I've taught him."

"You've been an excellent teacher."

Mustafa looks up at his father, trying to discern any more sarcasm. It could actually be a compliment.

"And Bora likes to get his hands dirty."

This, Mustafa believes, must be mockery. He stands up again, facing his father.

"And he's absolutely loyal."

"And I'm not?" Mustafa's voice rises.

His father neither steps back nor pushes his son into the chair. "Of course, you are," he says, his voice still even. "I know that. But much of what needs to be done here is beneath you. You're far too valuable to risk..."

"Are you saying I'm not tough enough?" Mustafa takes a quick breath, balls his fists. He is almost a head taller than his father, stronger, and more fit.

His father takes half a step back, not giving ground, but getting a better angle to look into Mustafa's eyes. "I did not say that." His tone suggests to Mustafa that his father meant exactly that.

Mustafa is about to argue the point, but he sees in his father's eyes a coldness, a hardness that he has seen only a few times before. Although his father has provided him with so much in his life, he has never given in on anything when this look comes over him. Mustafa takes a full step back, in his mind not capitulating but rather de-escalating the situation.

"You will go to America in a couple of weeks," his father says. "In the meantime, you'll still direct the search. Bora will do the daily hands-on work. I'll deal with the Russian."

"But—"

"The decision has been made." His father continues to stare at him.

Mustafa feels like he needs to defend himself. "I can—"

"It's final!" his father interrupts him. "Final, final."

# 43

## KOZAK, TURKEY

On the third morning after young Mehmet Suner's funeral, fourteen women, packed into the sitting room of his family's house in their village, are murmuring prayers. The TV, switched off, serves as a stand for two black-framed photographs, one of Mehmet posing gleefully between his parents and the other of him hugging his grandfather. The parlor's walls are decorated with more photos of the boy—kicking a football, driving an old tractor, and cavorting with two large dogs.

All the women wear headscarves and long traditional print dresses. Hafize, Mehmet's mother, sits on the divan between her cousin and her mother-in-law. She is slumped to her right so that her head rests on her cousin's shoulder. Her long auburn hair is bunched and pinned beneath her white headscarf. She is too exhausted to sit up alone and too grief-stricken to sleep. Her closed eyes are puffy, and her face is pale, waxen, gray-green. Whenever she falls asleep, she starts, goes rigid, and begins to weep again. At the funeral, she barely made it through the Imam's prayers and, as is the custom, did not accompany her son's body to the cemetery for burial. She returned to the house where women from the village stayed with her through that night and the next two.

Hafize's cousin has her arm around her shoulder as though she is bracing an injured friend. Her mother-in-law, hands raised in prayer, whispers in somber piety. Özlem Boroğlu and her mother sit across the room near the folding table stacked with pide and dishes brought by neighbors and relatives. Boroğlu's mother's basket rests on the floor next to her. They arrived in the Dacia just after dawn, thinking others would want to sleep, but no one has left yet. Boroğlu's mother recites prayers, but Boroğlu does not—and will not. She is deeply sad for the family, but she asks for neither divine intervention nor divine assistance. The boy was murdered by an ISIL suicide bomber. That's it. God may indeed be great, but the corruption in this world is the work of men. And so, too, is any measure of justice.

Engin Suner, Mehmet's father, wearing dark pants and a white shirt with a collar, stops for a moment at the doorway to the left of his wife and mother. As soon as Boroğlu notices him, he nods and vanishes. She waits five minutes and then leaves the parlor for the family compound's courtyard. Although the village is only nine kilometers from Bergama, it is high in the mountains on the road beyond Kapıkaya. The ground is hardscrabble; electrical wires crisscross above her. Smoke swirls from the outdoor wood-burning oven's chimney. The morning is bright and hot, and so Suner stands smoking alone in the shade of a cinder block storage building with a flat metal roof. The only other person around is a thin old man sitting on a wooden bench in the shade of an even older building with a roof topped with four solar panels.

Suner's eyes are bloodshot, and his beard has grown out. His hand trembling, he takes a pack of cigarettes from his shirt pocket, jiggles out two, lights both from his lit butt, hands one to Boroğlu, and takes a deep drag on the other. He grounds the old butt against the sole of his black shoe and cups it in his left hand. Only then does he exhale.

"Thank you," she says. "Hafize is not any better?"

His eyes brimming, he shakes his head. "She will not recover. Never." He leans back against the shed's wall, which has recently been whitewashed. "While Mehmet was with us, she held hope for the impossible... Pleaded with Allah... But..."

They smoke in silence for a minute. A cock crows somewhere in the village. A large beige dog meanders over to them, sniffs Boroğlu's shoes, and then settles in the shade.

"And your mother?" Boroğlu asks, looking over at a bright-blue plastic tarp covering a motorcycle.

"Angry at everybody. At Allah, for *everything*. At me for letting Mehmet go with Dede on his birthday." He shakes his head again. "At Hafize for getting all the attention. My mother needs to be consoled, but she also needs to be strong, which makes her mad."

There is no breeze at all, and smoke spirals from their cigarettes. Boroğlu taps her ash onto the ground. "And you? How are you?"

"Angry, too. But not at Hafize or my mother."

"At Allah?" she asks.

"No."

"At Daesh?"

"Yes." He shakes his head more vehemently. "No. More at the men who brought the kafir here. At whoever helped the terrorist."

"And the police?"

"They have done nothing." His voice rises, the bitterness starting to pour out. "Nothing! They say they have found nothing!"

She nods. "Or nothing they will say."

"I am the father! But they tell me *nothing*." He glares at his cigarette.

No one has told her anything either. But then, they wouldn't. She has a pretty good idea, of course, but it's too soon to tell Mehmet's father.

"*They ask me questions!*" The ire in his voice runs deep. "Here," he says and steps around the corner of the shed.

She follows him around the side of the shed to a small herb garden where a high, crumbling brick wall provides additional shade. The smell reminds her of her own rooftop patio. An old tin can with the label removed stands next to a hand trowel and garden fork. His hand still quivering, he drops the extinguished butt into the can. His shoulders slump, and his eyes become bleary again. "I…," he begins, but then stops himself. "I need to…" He tugs at his shirt collar.

Boroğlu takes a final drag on her cigarette, stoops, puts it out on the side of the can, and drops it in with the others. Whatever he needs to tell her is going to take time.

He runs his hand through his beard. "Hafize... She... It makes her too sad to go to Dede's village, to his house. The house she grew up in... So I have been cleaning it... After the...attack...but before Mehmet was taken from us..." He lowers his voice. "I needed sometimes to get away from the hospital and this house. Work is good for me." As with the last time they spoke, his words begin to stream. "I must stay busy. I am not able to do nothing. Sit in a café, no. Drink çay, no. It hurts too much. The sadness..." He pauses, seeming to look for the right word. "It steals my breathing." He clutches his beard under his chin. "Strangles me. So I walk to Dede's—it's less than three kilometers—and clean." His smile is sad. "It doesn't need it. He is... was...very organized. But I still do it. In a box in his room, I find land deeds. He bought land when Mehmet was born. Even before. Before the dam. Before land cost too much. Not just farmland. Land far up in the hills."

Boroğlu nods. She has seen Hafize's family name on three of the land deeds she researched.

"He never spent money. Always saved. Fixed his own tractor and truck." His smile is again weak. "Sewed the holes in his socks. He didn't tell Hafize about the land. Didn't tell me. Bought more land when Mehmet was five." He waves in the direction of the steeply rising hills. "You are the archeologist..."

She cannot tell from his voice if his words are a question or a statement. "Yes," she says. "I was in charge of archeology in this area for years."

He nods. His cigarette has burned down to his fingers and so he drops it in the can. "He...Dede... I told you before at the hospital that he kept saying the land was for Mehmet..." His eyes fill again. "For Mehmet to go to university."

Boroğlu reaches out and puts her hand on his arm. Even through his shirt, she can feel the nervous energy, the exhaustion.

"I thought…we…me and Hafize thought that he was just talking about the farm…pastures…trees with pine nuts."

She pats his arm, something she did with Serkan when he was upset.

"I found a bigger box…hidden… It has old things…things I need you to explain… I have no one else." He pulls his arm away from her and takes from his pants pocket a crumpled red cigarette pack. "You will not tell…"

Again, it could be a question or a demand. She looks into his eyes, at once sad and angry, exhausted and excited. "I will tell no one," she says. He is trusting her, and there is no one other than perhaps her mother and daughter to whom she would speak. And both of them are, at this moment, furious at her. And at this point, she would not tell Serkan anything. Or anyone in her old office. Not Recep Ateş. Certainly not Tuğçe Iskan. No one.

He looks over his shoulder back toward the house, but nobody is watching them. "These," he says, "these were in the box." He opens the cigarette pack and shakes two coins into his left palm. Even in the shade of the herb garden's wall, the gold is brilliant. He reaches out his hand as though he is offering the coins to her.

Her breath catches, but she does not touch the two Hadrian Aureus coins similar to the one Iskan showed her. She looks around also and then folds his fingers over the coins. Both of their hands are shivering.

"They are old?"

"Yes," she answers. "And very, very valuable." She takes a deep breath. "And there will be more, others, wherever these came from." Her voice takes on a sense of urgency. "Put them away now. Hide them. Not with the other things." Her mouth has gone dry, and she is suddenly very thirsty. "I will come to see the other things tomorrow. Later. In the afternoon. After a meeting. But hide these *separately!*" As he slides the coins back into the cigarette pack and stuffs it into his pants pocket, she asks, "You have the land deeds?"

"At Dede's."

"Bring them here and put them somewhere safe." She takes his arm again and turns her head toward his. In a whisper, she asks, "Has anyone approached you about selling Dede's land?"

"Yes," he says, "two men last week."

"Who?"

"I did not know them. Younger men."

"From here?"

"Not from this village. And not from around here. Or Kozak. One had a fancy watch. And fancy shoes."

She nods. "What did you tell them?"

He brushes his hand through his beard again. "That Mehmet was very sick, and I could not think about it."

"When they come back, and they will, tell them you will sell, but it's too soon. You are still—"

He pulls himself away from her. "I will *not* sell!" His voice is irate. "*I will never sell!*"

She holds his gaze. "No," she says. "No, you won't." As his eyes cloud, she adds, "But do not tell them that. Do not make them angry."

"I am angry!"

"I know. You should be." She takes another long breath. "But don't let them know that."

 44

BERGAMA

Özlem Boroğlu walks up the Sacred Way toward the ruins of the Aesklepion, Pergamon's once-renowned hospital and health center. A stray dog follows her along the path that was eighteen hundred years ago a colonnade, roofed and lined with busy shops and stalls that sold votive offerings. She is wearing boots and jeans and a loose, blue work shirt and her dark floppy hat—her work clothes from her years on site at Allianoi and at the local tomb rescues. She has walked all the way from her house on the hill below the acropolis because she needed to think. Though she is regularly followed when she drives the Dacia out of town, no one trailed her on foot as she took the higher, more direct route through the Alevi enclave, the Kurdish and Gypsy neighborhoods, and along the trail by the Roman amphitheater, one site she has never had any interest in excavating. Finally, she passed Elif's studio on the way to the Aesklepion's front gate, but she knows better than to disturb her daughter when she is working. Tricking her into going out to the area around Kapıkaya, which significantly altered the search for Galen's family villa, was one thing; actually interrupting her work in progress is quite another.

Boroğlu's meeting at the Aesklepion's theater isn't for another hour, so she has time to meander through the sacred grounds, but she stops first in the shade of an old conifer because she is sweating and out of breath. She used to be able to trek the area's hills and the site at Allianoi all day, but in recent years and especially since she was fired, she has had too much coffee and too many cigarettes and too little exercise. Only in the last few days at Kapıkaya and in the DAI library has she felt her old excitement and energy returning, but her body hasn't really caught up with her mind.

She takes off her hat, wipes her forehead with her sleeve, and slows her breath. Although a row of restored columns runs nearby and the entrance to the Aesklepion's main tunnel is marked, the ruins here are far less impressive than those on the acropolis. Aware that the neglect of the site has in some sense saved it, she smiles. She has dedicated her life to archeology, and she feels that this place, only partly restored, is trying to speak to her. The light and the breeze are whispering but in a language she can no longer quite comprehend. She needs a staff with an entwined serpent. Or a single-edged sword.

Galen once walked in this sacred precinct, restoring people's health. Indeed, death was officially forbidden at the Aesklepion. The terminally ill and women in the later stages of pregnancy were prohibited. Needing Galen to speak to her now, she lights a cigarette and inhales deeply. But all she hears is hammering from the military base that abuts the property, the rumble of a tractor on the hill beyond the theater, the faint breeze in the branches, and, intermittently, the call of a songbird.

Smoking her cigarette, Boroğlu passes a pool, once used for mud baths, where two turtles bask on rocks. The healing center's sacred spring still burbles, and so she settles next to it and listens to the water coursing. The place is tranquil, unmarked by the terror in town, but she herself, scarred by what has happened in Bergama, finds little peace. The Aesklepion's ancient treatments focused on consistent gentle exercise, massage, music, theater, and quietude. Water was integral for drinking and bathing but also for its soothing sound. Central to all else was the interpretation of dreams. In her recurring nightmares, Boroğlu is the last priestess on earth standing with a staff entwined with a snake before an immense wall of water that is about to engulf her sanctuary and drown her. Interpretation of that particular dream is obvious. She was the director of the Allianoi Archeological Excavation and Restoration when the government ordered the valley in which it lay to be flooded to make a reservoir so that wealthy landowners could become filthy rich. She was forced to look on as the ancient site—another lesser-known healing center farther outside of Pergamon—was inundated. Since the terror attack on the Bergama funicular, the dream has altered in only one detail—the liquid wall heading toward her is fiery, a lethal brew of toxic chemicals and radioactive waste killing all life along the way.

She douses her cigarette's butt under the spring's constantly running spigot, places the butt on a stone, and lights another cigarette. She is aware of the peace that dwells here, but she is not a part of it. In fact, the Aesklepion's treatments other than the interpretation of dreams might well do her good, except that she doesn't really want them or the tranquility they might bring. Agitation, she believes, is necessary in her present situation. She is again hard on the trail of an archeological discovery, likely the most culturally significant one in Anatolia in a century or more. And her need to make this discovery separates her from this holy precinct. In her mind, she must make amends for her failure to save Allianoi, and, frankly, she savors the thought of showing up the crooks and kleptocrats that destroyed her site and then later fired her for wanting to follow up on the nation's best archeological lead. And she can't help but be obsessed with the idea that the bombing in Bergama was anything but random.

Suddenly, two large hands cover her face from behind, blinding her. Screaming, she swiftly raises her cigarette to burn the hands. She catches only the wrist of the left hand, grazing it, not pressing the cigarette's tip.

"Özlem!" The deep shout is one of pain and surprise. She wheels to find her old friend Recep Ateş crouched on one knee and clutching his wrist with his right hand.

"Shit!" he mutters.

She springs to her feet and yells, "Recep! What are…?"

"Shit! Shit! Shit!" Grimacing, he lets go of his wrist. A small white crescent-shaped blister is already rising.

"I'm so sorry!" Upright she isn't much taller than he is kneeling. She drops the crumpled cigarette and grinds it into the stone. "Here," she adds, reaching for his hand.

He smiles through the pain. "I should've known better than to try to sneak up on you!" His hand, roughly twice the size of hers, trembles.

"Here," she repeats.

Still holding his hand, she turns and guides it toward the water flowing from the spring's spigot. He leans forward, his right hand on the ground, and stretches so she can guide his left hand into the water. He flinches when the swelling blister reaches the cool water. Then, almost immediately his shoulders relax and his face softens. He shifts so that he can sit cross-legged near the fountain and keep the water running over his wrist. She sits back, her rear on her heels, folds her hands in her lap, and watches his face, the frown slowly melting.

"Stupid man!" she says with some affection.

Shaking his head, he gazes at her. "I do know better," he says. "Even lost in thought, you're a lioness."

"Keep your hand in the water!"

This is the first time they have seen each other since the morning after the bombing. Their meeting at the Aesklepion's theater is a walk-through for the upcoming National Psychotherapy Convention meeting during which she is a featured speaker. Her topic, "The Past, Our Future," is supposed to present the significance of the Aesklepion's treatments in light of recent findings about the nature of wellness.

Boroğlu and Ateş sit quietly for a couple of minutes before, to take his mind off the pain, she asks, "How are the twins?"

"Studying for their university entrance exams. Which is to say, not in very good moods. How about Elif?"

"She's burying herself in her work."

"I wonder where she gets that from?" When Boroğlu doesn't answer, he sighs. "I heard about the boy…"

Boroğlu looks away at the Aesklepion's ruins. "Yes," she says. "The last of the bombing victims to die." She doesn't add that the families and friends of those killed, here in Bergama and elsewhere, are victims as well. The ill effects will ripple through the town for a long time. Certainly young Mehmet's parents and a lot of other people have lost both the measure and purpose of their lives. She has thought a lot about it, and she doesn't want to pursue the point at the moment. "Let's look at that," she says, waving at his wrist.

He keeps his hand under the flowing water. "It's okay," he says. "At least you didn't go for my eyes."

"I didn't mean…," she says but doesn't finish her sentence. She has since she was a girl reacted fast and only later tried to piece together what she did.

He smiles ironically. "I came early because I was hoping to find you."

She cocks her head.

"Tuğçe Iskan paid me a visit at the office. She wanted to review the records of our tumuli rescues. Communications with Ankara. Other stuff. Everything."

"She is by nature and practice a pain in the ass."

He nods. "She was also asking about you."

"Me?"

He inspects his wrist and then shoves his hand back into the water. "For some Ankara investigation."

Boroğlu thinks of the photos of Serkan with Mustafa Hamit. Her mind leaps ahead. *Does Iskan believe that she is involved with the Hamits, too? Iskan must know better! Or is that stubborn ass building a case against the Hamits for raiding the Bergama area's tumuli? Does she think that Serkan has been feeding those crooks information about grave rescues for a long time? It's absurd, but Iskan is too obsessive to notice the inherent absurdity of what she's doing.* "That bitch!" Boroğlu says.

"She is," Ateş says. "She's also tenacious."

"She told me—" Boroğlu stops, aware that continuing the conversation might lead Ateş to suspect Serkan's involvement with the Hamits. "That bitch!"

# ✰ 45
ANTALYA PROVINCE, TURKEY

All day, the van drives fast along the highway in the stifling heat. The boy hidden under the carpets in the back of the van cramps from dehydration, but he remains silent, uncomplaining. Although he is slight for thirteen, with only wisps on his chin and the shadow of a mustache, he is the one who has been selected for veneration—and paradise! The sheikhs' repeated kicks in the stomach and the regular thrashing with sticks have toughened him. He was not the most clever boy at the Al Farouq training camp and certainly not the biggest, but he was the most zealous, the fiercest of the lion cubs. He made up for his small size by being the first to obey every order, the first to complete every task with honor. When they beat the barren Zahidi woman until her face was pulp and her ribs and pelvis were crushed, he did not stop until she was long beyond screaming.

He was honored to be one of the chosen as executioners of the five Kurds, those abominable slaves of the Western kuffars. Given clean camouflage fatigues and a new black-and-white headband, he held the 9mm pistol proudly. The Kurdish dog knelt before him in his orange boilersuit, his head bowed in absolute submission. The boy had seen the videos of the public executions, cheered with the other cubs in the camp. The heavy gun became light in his hand as he raised the weapon above his head so that the cameras could record his supremacy.

When he pulled the Kurd's head back for the cameras, the eyes were already dead. And when the command was given, he felt divine power surge within him. Bracing the gun with his left hand as he had been trained, he aimed carefully. He pulled the trigger, on guard not to yank it, and the 9mm recoiled. The Kurdish dog jerked forward. As the head hit the ground, blood pulsed from the skull and erupted from the cheek below the left eye. The sheikhs and the other cubs shouted praise, and the cameraman crouched close to shoot the spurting blood. As he lowered the gun, the acrid smell filled him with irreproachable pride.

Now, as he is relentlessly jolted at every bump in the road, something begins to jostle his sense of honor and duty and fealty. He sees again his mother's eyes brimming when the sheikh came to take him to the special training camp. She said nothing as she wrung her hands and tears ran down her cheeks. He must remember that, as the sheikh said, she is only a woman and therefore unable to understand that he has become Allah's sword of righteousness and retribution. He will make her proud. She *must* be proud to have both her husband and her only son martyred, both esteemed beyond measure in heaven and on earth.

At night, the van stops along a deserted side road. The driver pulls him from beneath the carpets. Too cramped to stand, he collapses at the feet of two men whose faces are covered with gray scarves. The two men laugh, but they do not kick him. When he left Al Farouq days before, his orders were clear and simple: obey whoever is transporting him to his sacred destiny. He knows nothing of the mission itself—except that he dies for the greater glory of God.

As the driver bickers with the men in a language the boy does not understand, feeling returns to his legs. He struggles first to his hands and knees and then, wobbling, to his feet. He is dizzy, thirsty, disoriented. The two men wear work boots, dirty jeans, and dark T-shirts. He glimpses one man's face, which has only stubble, not a full beard. The language, Turkish, the boy guesses, sounds harsh and unfriendly. As they argue, all three men ignore him. They seem nothing to him like mujahideen.

Without a word to the boy, the driver stomps to the van, turns it around, and drives away. One of the men takes the boy by the shoulder and shoves him toward an old, open-bed produce truck. The other throws baggy shorts and a T-shirt at him. They yank off his black headband and then force him to strip off his combat boots and fatigues. The shorts and the T-shirt, which are way too big, stink of cigarette smoke.

Together the men push him up and into the truck's bed. The man who grabbed him gives him a plastic liter bottle of water and gestures for him to lie down. Flies have found the few split watermelons still on the truck. He tries to keep his focus on his glorious mission, but the buzzing and the stench of rotten fruit distract him. He downs half the water as the men return to the truck's cab. When the truck pulls away, exhaust from a broken muffler mixes with the other smells.

The road is rough, the night air heavy; clouds cover the moon and stars. He guzzles the rest of the water before realizing he has none for his ablutions. Although he is exhausted, he remains vigilant, barely sleeping, and then waking suddenly from disjointed dreams of his childhood. He scratches his itching skin and scalp. Unable to stand, he is at least able to take off his underpants before he pisses himself. Nothing about any of this feels noble or triumphant.

At first light, the truck stops in a remote valley. One man blindfolds him as the other binds his wrists and tethers a rope so that he can lead the boy like a prisoner or a donkey. Neither of the men says a word. They walk a winding path for what must be most of an hour. His saliva becomes gummy. Rocks cut his bare feet, but the pain helps him keep focused. Though he smells freshly turned dirt, he can't tell what's growing in the fields. Birds sing, and periodically an engine rumbles farther off. He trips often but only falls once, scraping his forehead and elbow. Cocks crow, and his ears buzz.

Finally, he is led down creaking stairs into a dirt cellar. His blindfold is removed, his wrists are untied, and he is left alone in the dark. The dimness gradually takes shape. The foundation walls are crumbling brick, the beams above rough-hewn. The odor of decay sticks in his nose and throat, but he sees nothing that's rotting. There are no footfalls above him.

After a while, a third man, taller than the others, descends the stairs carrying a cloth bag in one hand and a rolled mat in the other. The door is left open so that light filters down. Dust motes float in the musty air. The man's face is covered like the others, but his blue jeans and button-down shirt are clean. Even in the cellar's low light, his eyes shine like the boy's father's. His hands are not those of a workman. He sets the bag in front of the boy and says, "Drink. You need strength to complete your mission." His Arabic is rudimentary but clear, and his voice is not unfriendly. "Go slow."

The bag contains a loaf of bread and a bunch of grapes as well as three liter bottles of water. The boy's hands shake as he twists the first bottle open and lifts it to his mouth. As he sips the water, slowly as he was ordered, it feels like the water is washing down his throat and spreading through his chest and stomach and arms and legs, cleansing him.

"Listen carefully," the man says as he lays the mat next to the boy. "Your mission is so important and so secret that you must stay here for three days, unseen by anyone. Two men will be here at all times to protect you."

The boy picks one grape, rolls it between his fingers, pops it into his mouth, and chews. The grape is, he thinks, the sweetest taste he has ever experienced.

"You must never go outside," the man says in a more commanding voice. "Never make noise. Do whatever the men say. Do you understand?"

The boy nods as he reaches for another grape.

"Look at me! Say it!" The man's voice is imperious, like those he has heard the past three years.

The boy drops the second grape into the bag. "I must always obey orders," he recites. "Never go outside. Never make noise."

"Good." The man's voice softens again. "No one must know of your presence until the holy hour of your sacrifice comes round."

 46

ISTANBUL

As Serkan Boroğlu rides the trolley down Istanbul's İstiklal Caddesi, a heavily muscled man takes the seat next to him. When the man leans his bulk into him, Serkan shifts closer to the window. The man leans harder, jostles Serkan, and mutters, "Get off at the next stop."

"Wha...?" Serkan says. He turns so that he can look at the man, who has a shaved head and small dark eyes. Black stubble covers the man's cheeks, chin, and thick neck, which slopes to his shoulders like a bodybuilder's. His tattooed arms bulge from his black T-shirt, and his hands, folded in his lap, are the size of toilet seats. "What?" Serkan repeats. "Move! Get away from me!"

The man opens his left hand to reveal in his palm an old-fashioned, single-edged barber's razor. He turns toward Serkan, his maniacal smile revealing crooked, nicotine-stained teeth. "Get off at this stop," he growls. "Now!" His breath is fetid. "Do what I tell you, and you won't get hurt."

The man's accent is strong, but Serkan can't place it. He glances around, but neither the trolley's other passengers nor the pedestrians on the avenue nor, for that matter, the rest of the world seems to notice what's happening. As the trolley slows for the Tünel Square stop, the man stands in the aisle and steps back so that Serkan can get up. "Mustafa Hamit needs to talk to you," he says into Serkan's ear.

Shaken, but still as angry as he is frightened, Serkan climbs down from the trolley. The man, who is half a head shorter than Serkan, grips his arm above the elbow and steers him across the avenue toward Galip Dede.

"Let go of me!" Serkan snarls.

The man obliges but first jostles him again and then presses his massive hand into the small of Serkan's back. They pass the gift shops and the ice cream parlor near the entrance to Galip Dede and head up the narrow street. Serkan is seething but says nothing. He has often been in the trendy bars and upscale restaurants in this part of Beyoğlu, and it's normally not dangerous. Last night he stayed over again at his Bavarian girlfriend's apartment near Taksim Square, but Mustafa could only have known about his taking the trolley if they had been following him long enough to have learned his routines. This is more than just Mustafa's faux-spy bullshit—much more. And Mustafa himself, that arrogant prick, is apparently unaware that the government is surveilling *him*.

This whole deal has become a mess. Serkan should have taken the original offer and been done with it. Now he somehow has to extricate himself and keep the women in his family safe. When his mother questioned his grandmother about seeing Mustafa on the morning of the funicular bombing, his grandmother was sure that the man she saw looked like Mustafa but was not him. The man's eyes were different, not green. Still, Serkan remains genuinely sorry that he has dragged the women in his family into this.

Serkan has kept his part of the bargain, providing Mustafa with documents, including some his mother gave him from her safe, and two days ago arranging Mustafa's meeting with Jack and Clare. Serkan would have been willing to take this meeting with Mustafa, but not after this heavy-handed crap. It's not only unnecessary but stupid. The irony is that Mustafa, in his attempted intimidation, is no doubt providing more information to those who are watching him.

The man takes Serkan's arm again, the grip tight, and stops in front of the arched steel, stone, and stucco gateway into the Galata Mevlevihanesi, the museum dedicated to Rumi, the thirteenth-century

Sufi mystic. "In the back," the man mutters. "In the garden." He gestures toward the entrance but does not himself enter.

As Serkan walks through the shaded passageway that opens into a courtyard, a calico cat saunters along next to him. On Sunday afternoons, Serkan often brought clients to the Mevlevi museum's whirling dervish performances. Occasionally, some clients also toured the museum's exhibits, but they never took the time to sit in the garden. The gravestones in the cemetery to his right have cylindrical tops shaped like the hats that whirling dervishes wear. Beyond the ablutions fountain, Mustafa Hamit sits on a wooden bench, his back to the courtyard wall. To his right, a tree provides shade. Off to his left, another man, built like the thug on the trolley, stands with his hands folded in front of his crotch. This guy, though, is older and better dressed in dark pants and a short-sleeved blue shirt with a collar. He is bald, but his head is not shaved. His arms, covered with tattoos, are as thick as logs. As Serkan approaches, Mustafa continues to text on his iPhone. He is, as always, impeccably dressed; his aviators are perched on his head.

When Serkan stands over him, Mustafa still ignores him. "What's going on?" Serkan says, glaring down at him.

Mustafa barely glances up. "Sit, Serkan," he says as though he is training a dog.

"You're having me followed!" Serkan wipes his mouth to keep himself from spitting. "The guy had a razor!"

Mustafa continues texting.

"What the hell is going on?"

Mustafa stops texting. Glowering up at Serkan, he says, *"You're* asking *me* that?" All of the false amiability of their earlier meetings is gone. "Shut up and sit down!"

Serkan does not sit. Mustafa puts his phone away. Only then does Serkan realize he no longer has his phone. "Shit!" he mutters as he pats the pockets of his jeans.

Mustafa smiles for the first time, a superior, unfriendly smirk. "Our Georgians are rough around the edges, but they are talented—and dependable. And we need to check your call log."

"I want my phone back!"

"Shut up!" Mustafa shakes his head slowly. "Crossing my family is stupid, Serkan. Very stupid!"

"What? I haven't crossed anybody." And, technically, he hasn't. He sits on the bench, looks at Mustafa, and then studies his own hands.

"*What?*" Mustafa says sarcastically.

"I sent you everything I could get of my mother's." Again, the truth—technically. "Some of the materials I got from her safe."

"Those things were useless! We've had the translation of the letter for months. The map is incomplete. And the notes are a mess."

"I kept my end of the bar—"

Mustafa slams his hand on the bench. The powerfully built man to the left unclasps his hands and takes two steps forward before Mustafa waves him off. "You've fucked with the wrong people!"

"What the…?" Serkan starts to say but then stops himself. He sits back. "I don't have any idea what you're talking about! You owe *me* money!"

Mustafa stares at him as though he can't believe what he is hearing. "And if I *want*, you'll be dead in five seconds."

"We had a deal!"

"You stupid fucking idiot." Mustafa cocks his head and looks at Serkan. "We had a deal, all right. And my family honors our deals." His voice is lower, not amicable, but factual, informational. "And we deal *harshly* with anyone stupid enough to sabotage the deals." His phone pings.

Serkan is not stupid, and Mustafa calling him that is getting to him. Mustafa is the fool here, acting tough when he's the one being surveilled. A young couple is working their way slowly through the cemetery, seemingly inspecting the gravestones, and he wonders if they are the watchers.

Serkan takes a deep breath so he doesn't lose control, which, he finally realizes, could get him killed no matter how much surveillance there is. He's frightened, not so much of Mustafa, but that he himself will say or do something to this arrogant hemorrhoid that will bring the Georgians down on him. He looks around at the plain, white, two-story back wall of the Mevlevi lodge and at the lush trees and flowers and at the ablutions fountain, where a skinny elderly man is washing. For the first time since he got here, Serkan can hear birds. He should have come here before, come here with his wealthy clients, especially the younger, more attractive women. He measures his voice as he says, "Mustafa, I don't have any idea about this…" He does not add the word "shit." "No idea."

"What about Sekhmet!"

*Sekhmet?* Serkan looks blankly at Mustafa but does not say, *What in hell does Sekhmet have to do with any of this?*

Mustafa stares at him, then shakes his head, looks up at the clear sky, takes out his phone, reads the text, and fires off a reply. When he finally looks at Serkan again, he says, "The Sekhmet amulet."

"What Sekhmet amulet?"

"You're even more stupid than I thought!" Mustafa's smile is disdainful. "You're being played by your own mother."

Serkan feels his face flush, but he controls his words. "The Sekhmet amulet?"

"The one your mother is selling to the Americans!"

"Clare and Jack?" Except for the insults, Serkan feels like Mustafa is speaking some foreign tongue. "My mother? No! She's never even met them!"

"*Yes, your mother,* you clueless piece of shit!" Mustafa laughs. "At least *I* offered you a finder's fee!"

"Leave my mother out of this. She's not involved!"

Mustafa's continued laughter is derisive. Serkan stands up, feels his eyes welling and his head thundering, stomps over toward the ablutions fountain, brushes both hands through his hair, and, his whole body sweating, turns back. *His mother? Selling antiquities? Impossible!* He's not sure he even mentioned the Americans to her. Elif, yes. When they were in Bergama—it feels like centuries ago—Clare bought a half a dozen of the figurines as gifts for friends. She also talked with his sister about Elif making something new for her, but he doesn't know if anything came of that conversation. And, his mother? He may have mentioned… But it's not who she is. She would never…

The old man has vanished from the courtyard. The man to the left of the bench has again dropped his hands and stands poised, as though waiting for a signal. The couple in the cemetery have turned away and seem to be deliberately studying one of the headstones. Serkan stands over Mustafa. "Leave my mother out of this! Stay away from her."

Looking up at Serkan, Mustafa, now the calm one, says, "Oh, I will. I no longer have anything to do with it. I'm here in Istanbul doing business as usual. A lunch meeting…," he glances at his phone, "in less than an hour." A gleam in his eyes, he adds, his voice almost soft, "Thanks to your stupidity, your mother is already being dealt with." Actually, the plan has been in place far longer, and he himself has been in charge of the whole operation, planned it all himself, right down to this moment when he gets to savor sticking it up Serkan's ass.

"What does that mean?"

"I don't know," he lies. The edge of his mouth turns up in a sneer as he looks into Serkan's tearing eyes. "But it can't be good."

"I need my phone!" Serkan shouts. "I want my phone!"

"Get out of my sight, shithead," Mustafa says, his tone now one of boredom. He lowers his head and begins to text again.

# 47

BERGAMA

As the boy pulls his knees closer to his chest, the thick vest prevents him from wrapping his forearms around his shins. Though scant light marks the far end of the narrow stone tunnel, the darkness gathered around him unnerves him. He brushes his middle finger across the triggering device. He avoids putting any pressure, but his finger trembles. His breathing is shallow, a huffing he struggles to control. Soon he will enter paradise, but time is moving too slowly now. He is alone in the gloom with no weapon but himself.

The plastic water bottle he was given when his headband was returned to him is empty. He feels around in the darkness until his fingers touch it, and then he pushes it farther away so he does not later crush it by mistake. He must make no noise until the moment is upon him. Reaching up, he adjusts his headband. His forehead is clammy, but he can't help that. Voices outside speak Turkish and English, that most detestable of the infidels' languages. Amplified voices start, stop, start, stop—startling him. He has been told that this would happen and that under no circumstances should he go until he has heard a woman's voice speaking for the count of two hundred. His bones ache against the rough stone so he shifts his weight but makes no sudden movement.

Time played tricks as he spent the days in that dark cellar, and he lost track. One of the two guards brought him stale bread and spoiling fruit and bottles of warm water, enough to drink but not to wash, and a plastic pot in which to piss. Though he was too far in the country to hear the call, he prayed regularly. He exercised diligently, for what seemed to be hour upon hour, pushing himself as hard as the sheikhs had, but still he slept poorly and woke to dreams of his mother and father leaving him stranded and starving in a strange forest. He was relieved when the guards again blindfolded him and pushed him back into the open bed of the truck.

When the truck stopped, his blindfold was not removed. The night air was warm, the smell of horses close by, and the hum of a city somewhere off in the distance. As he was strapped into the heavy vest, the first cocks crowed. Strong tape was wound about him repeatedly so that he could never remove the vest. Though he prayed fervently for continued courage, the sharp shriek of the tape being torn from the roll caused his legs to wobble as they had when he was removed from the van at what now seems like such a long time ago. He was taken over two more hills and pulled through a cut in a barbed-wire fence that pricked him in the shoulder and thigh. When he yipped, one of the Turks cuffed the side of his head—and he made no further sound.

The two guards said nothing as they pushed him through a small rectangular opening into the stone tunnel. He crouched, disoriented, for a moment before a stern voice, similar to that of the tall Turk who spoke Arabic, ordered him to take fifteen paces. When he stood to his full height, he bumped his head. As he felt his way along the curving tunnel, the stone was coarse and cool. The bright light that preceded him outlined the blindfold's edges. After exactly fifteen steps, he was told to sit.

When the man removed the blindfold, the sudden brightness caused the boy to squeeze his eyes shut and turn his head. He kept his eyes averted as the man wired the trigger to the vest and taped it to his wrist. As the man's rough hands worked, he repeated all of the earlier orders in a clipped whisper. The man's voice was sharp in his ear, and the smell of beer and cigarettes was vile. When the man finished, he turned the boy's chin to face him. The headlamp flooded his vision and sent flashes of pain behind his eyes and through his head. Molten red and yellow spots pulsed and popped—and the shaking began.

The man commanded him to stop, but he couldn't make himself do it. The man said something harsh in Turkish, and then his tone suddenly changed. Whispering again, he reminded the boy that soon he would join all of the other venerated martyrs in heaven. He tousled the boy's hair as his father had, and then he returned the black-and-white ISIL headband, placing it firmly on the boy's head as though it were a crown. When the man handed him the water bottle, the light was too brilliant for the boy to see anything. The man took a long deep breath and then patted the boy on the side of his head.

His grip tight on the back of the boy's neck, the man reiterated that the boy must wait until the woman spoke two hundred words. And then the man let go, and the light began to back away. The man whispered, *"Allahu Akbar,"* but it sounded distant, an afterthought. The light receded around the bend and then vanished, leaving only the weaving spots.

Now, the boy's left calf is cramping, but he can do nothing but grit his teeth, clench his left fist, and press the ball of his foot against the dusty stone. A woman's amplified voice sounds nothing like his mother's —the tone and the language both all wrong. His mother's voice was soothing, especially when she spoke or sang him songs in his father's French. His own French is gone after his many months at Al Farouq. Yet somehow at this moment, his mother is calling him for dinner, waving to him along a long dusty street. Her headscarf is green and red, and her long dress is blue, the color of her eyes. Though he waves curtly, he goes on kicking the Coke can against the crumbling stone wall. She apparently cannot see that he is training himself for a war she doesn't comprehend. She continues to call him in French and Arabic and then in languages he doesn't know.

With his heel, he stomps the can flat, turns toward her, takes three steps, and stops, stricken. Her headscarf writhes with scorpions, and her face is contorted in unspeakable pain. Her eyes flash purple and then crimson. Red ants swarm her dress and cover her twitching feet. Flames lick her raised hands, her neck, and her hair. She is screaming hysterically. Her face dissolves into that of the disfigured, dying Zahidi woman. And then the kneeling Kurd snaps his head back against the 9mm's barrel. Blood splashes the boy's face, streams down his neck, and drenches his hands.

Darkness strangles the boy. His head falls back, striking the stone wall. Screams reverberate. Stars burst. *That voice…!* His mother isn't screaming. It's the woman's voice speaking, amplified—the target of his mission. And he has not been counting, has no idea if she has spoken two hundred words or two million. Was he the one who screamed? His fingers twitch on the trigger. He stinks of fear. The gloom, thick as shit, is drowning him. He pushes up from the wall and stumbles through the tunnel.

 # 48

BERGAMA

Özlem Boroğlu takes a breath before delivering the conclusion of her speech. Standing behind the podium, she looks out from the stage at her audience in the Aesklepion's ancient theater. The psychiatrists and psychologists gathered from all over Turkey and the Aegean islands have filled the stone seats rising toward the crest of the hill. Her friend Recep Ateş is seated in the front box with Bergama's mayor, a tall, heavy man who still looks small next to Ateş. The early evening light paints the trees gold; the wind has fallen, and a thick heat is settling in the theater's bowl.

"We are meeting here today on what people through the ages have believed is holy ground," she says, her voice rising. She turns slightly to her right and waves her hand. "This spring has been providing healing water for more than twenty-five hundred years. Galen, the father of both pharmacology and psychiatry, practiced here. In fact, he grew up here. His father was the architect of the renovation and renewal of this Aesklepion in the second century of the Common Era. Galen no doubt accompanied his father often. He almost certainly played in this theater as a child, listened to lectures here as a medical student, and spoke here as a renowned physician." She pauses, a moment of understanding welling as it sometimes did during her years at Allianoi. "Perhaps he even sat in the very seat where you now sit."

As her epiphany deepens, a strange nervousness, part excitement and part anxiety, washes through her. "Galen believed in the soul, the human spirit, which he called 'psyche.' He understood, as you do, that there is really no absolute distinction between physical and mental illness. The Aesklepion was a healing center designed to last through the ages, and those practicing medicine here twenty-five centuries ago knew that health required both physical and mental balance."

She scans the audience again. Her mother is there in the last row, her focus locked on her daughter. Tuğçe Iskan is there as well, standing behind the last row, her arms folded across her chest and her expression, as usual, void of affect. But she is, Boroğlu knows, committing every word to memory. Elif is not present, which is tremendously disappointing. They have spoken cordially, as mothers and daughters do, but since that morning at Kapıkaya, Elif has spent little time at home—as though she is now living in her studio. She said she would come to the Aesklepion for the speech, but she is not here.

"The soul, Galen believed, was part of the body," Boroğlu continues. "One couldn't be healed without also treating the other. In this sacred place, the analysis of dreams was as important as surgery. Exercise and massage and diet and even music and theater were critical to the healing process." She waves her hand slowly over her audience. "What played out here where you are now seated mattered to the health of the patients.

"We have, of course, come a long way in twenty-five centuries." She pauses again. "Or, have we?" Letting her question sink in, she looks out over her audience. "We have created any number of technological miracles. Great empires have risen and fallen. Political upheavals, wars, massacres—and through it all the Aesklepion's spring still flows. The human spirit, the psyche, is still central to any deep understanding of our health, individually and as a society!"

She pauses a third time, shifting her notes on the podium, though she doesn't need them at all for what she is about to say. "As an archeologist, I am, like you, concerned with—my mother and my daughter would say *obsessed* with—understanding the psyche, the human spirit. We archeologists, like you, search for meaning, for the spirit of an age. In my years of work at Allianoi that I have told you about, we discovered invaluable artifacts, but what was most important, what I was really after, was an understanding of that place and time.

"Yes, our site at Allianoi was drowned, flooded over by those in power in order to create a reservoir that served narrow economic ends. My work was seemingly nullified. But I studied and sweated and fought for all those years so that I might come to know something that would help me, help all of us, comprehend not just that age but also this age in which we live.

"Archeology, like psychiatry, helps us to discover who we are. And our age is frightening—an age of horrifying strife, of wanton violence, of the destruction of whole cultures, of the fragmentation and dissolution of nations that are our neighbors. Our town, as you know...," she waves her hands more expansively in order to bring all of Bergama into the Aesklepion's theater, "has recently suffered a deadly terrorist attack that has traumatized us as individuals and as a community. But we are by no means alone in our pain." She fully understands that, in what she is about to say, she is moving beyond the purview of her speech. But she must. It's necessary. Her arms gather the audience to her.

"Our amazing technology alone cannot protect us, cannot save us. We need more than ever the commitment of those like you who treat the human psyche, who heal our collective spirit. Together, we can use the wonders of our age not as ends in themselves but as tools that serve our skills as healers.

"Those of you who have, like Galen, dedicated your lives to providing the remedies for our individual and collective illnesses must recommit yourselves to the task. We must act now to discover meaning so that we can keep the darkness at our borders—and within each of us—from flooding our culture and drowning us. I call each of you to action, to an endeavor in which we use the wisdom of this Aesklepion to stand together against violence and terror." She nods to her audience. "Thank you!"

The applause, at first uncertain, builds quickly. Boroğlu acknowledges the plaudits, nodding again and smiling, but her mind is already elsewhere. Not actually elsewhere, but here, in another time, two millennia ago. This theater and this healing center with its tunnels and baths is the still point, the nexus. Of course. Here all along. Of course! Why didn't she recognize it earlier, months ago? Years ago?

Recep Ateş and the mayor and a well-dressed, wrinkled, elderly woman carrying a red bouquet are coming up on stage. Iskan is not among those clapping, and neither is Boroğlu's mother. But her mother is pleased, Boroğlu thinks. She is smiling. Her arms are not folded across her chest, nor are her hands clamped to her hips.

When the shriveled woman turns to present the bouquet to Boroğlu, there is a clattering off to Boroğlu's left. Glancing over, she glimpses a skinny, young, dark-haired boy in a lumpy vest climbing the stone steps to the stage. He is rushing, his face contorted.

Abruptly, Ateş shoves the mayor into Boroğlu, knocking both of them and the podium off the front of the stage. As they sprawl into the theater's front aisle away from the boy, Ateş is already wheeling his bulk toward him.

"Allah…!" she hears the boy shout.

Ateş lunges at him, knocking the boy backward off the stage. Their momentum carries the man and the boy into a stone recess next to the theater's wall.

A galaxy of silver stars swirls around Boroğlu. Pain engulfs her. Pinned beneath the mayor's weight, she cannot breathe. Her eyes squeeze shut as a brilliant light flashes an unfathomable white. Her world snaps into darkness.

THE AESKLEPION'S THEATER

 **49**

BERGAMA

The hard knocking on the studio door does not stop. Elif, who has been completely immersed in molding a rotund, poly-breasted, terra-cotta mother goddess for her grandmother, stares at the locked door as her awareness of the world outside rushes back. She yanks the buds from her ears, stands, and takes a deep breath. Her neck is stiff so she rolls her shoulders as she goes to the door. She hears sirens as she lifts her hand to the knob. "Who is it?" she shouts.

"Tuğçe! Tuğçe Iskan, Elif!"

The voice holds far greater emotion than Elif has heard in it before. Elif rolls her shoulders once more and opens the door. Iskan's blue eyes are huge. Sweat beads on her forehead and runs down her temples. She is sucking air as though she has just run five kilometers at speed. An ambulance is screaming by on the road from the army base and Aesklepion.

"Your mother!" Iskan gasps. "The Aesklepion! Another attack!"

"My...?" For a moment, Iskan's words are runes. Then, Elif feels herself collapsing. She grabs the knob and slumps against the door.

Iskan takes Elif by her right shoulder and buttresses her. "She's alive," she says. "The paramedics, they're working on her!"

Elif gulps air, holds herself upright. "What...? What?"

"Come!" Iskan says.

Nodding, Elif glances back into her studio. She then pats the pockets of her yoga pants, though she has no idea what she is looking for. When she takes a step, the world starts to spin.

Iskan throws her left arm around Elif's shoulders and with her right hand pulls the studio door shut.

The evening light blinds Elif. Even soft, it's far too sharp. She sees only a burst of colors. Noise—sirens, honking, shouting, barking, even the neighing of spooked horses and a buzzing like locusts—floods her mind. Both overheated and deathly cold, she slips her right arm around Iskan's waist and tries to calm herself, which she cannot.

The two women hurry along the road crowded with people rushing to and from the Aesklepion two kilometers away. Waves of images of the acropolis bombing crash in Elif's mind—the toppled stanchions, the mashed cable cars and tangled cables, and the scorched earth. There is no stench of burned plastic, but an acrid odor scratches her throat and nostrils. Her tears are streaming, and her breathing is erratic, quick and shallow and then long gasps and more huffing.

"Mom's okay?" Elif asks.

"She's alive."

Half a kilometer from the Aesklepion, the road is blocked by a green military jeep and a covered troop transport. Only emergency vehicles are being allowed through the checkpoint. Heavily armed soldiers are turning everybody else away. Iskan steers Elif toward a barrel-chested, clean-shaven officer wearing fatigues but no helmet or cap. Elif teeters as Iskan pulls her Ministry ID from her jeans pocket. While showing it to the officer, she says, *"The speaker's daughter."*

The officer looks at the ID, glances first at Elif and then at Iskan, and waves them quickly through the cordon. Confusion reigns within the Aesklepion grounds. The flashing emergency vehicles' lights snatch Elif's thoughts before they fully form. None of the shouting makes any sense. She looks around feverishly but can't keep anything in focus. No flames or smoke, but billowing dust. The scratching in her throat sharpens. "She's alive, my mother?" she yells in Iskan's ear.

"She was when I came for you." Iskan is looking ahead at the menagerie of emergency vehicles.

Triage is set up near the ancient spring under the wide canopy of an old fir tree with horizontally spreading branches. As the two women begin to angle toward the theater, Iskan stops. With her free hand, she points to their left. Six people, four men and two women, sit in the tree's shade. A single paramedic is walking among them giving out cups of water. Elif's grandmother stands alone next to the group.

"Anneanne!" Elif shouts as she lets go of Iskan. She has been so overwhelmed by what's happened to her mother that she completely forgot that her grandmother was planning to attend the speech.

With both her hands shaking, her grandmother is holding a paper cup to her lips. She does not actually drink, and she does not look Elif's way.

"Anneanne!" Elif shouts again. The cacophony recedes. The flashing lights dim. Elif moves to hug her grandmother but stops abruptly. The old woman is standing so stiffly and so awkwardly that Elif doesn't dare embrace her. Instead, she places her hand on her shoulder. Her grandmother does not respond at all. "Oh, Anneanne!" Elif says in a lower voice. Her tears flowing again, she brushes her fingertips along the older woman's cheek.

The paramedic, a fit, strong-jawed man about her age, comes over to them.

"My anneanne," Elif says through her tears.

He nods. "We'll get her to the hospital when…," he looks around at the bedlam, "when we can."

"Thank you. I will…I can…" Elif realizes that there isn't much she can do other than stay with her grandmother. "Anneanne!" she says more loudly. "It's me, Elif!"

Her grandmother finally looks up but says nothing. Her face is vacant.

Elif takes the cup so that her grandmother can hold Elif's other hand with both of hers. She seizes Elif's hand and grips it hard but doesn't otherwise move. Her eyes gaze at the ground. Elif gives the cup to the paramedic and looks around at the chaos. All of the clamor and the glare crash around her again—as though the sky itself is falling. Her breath coming in gasps, she roots herself with her grandmother under the tree's canopy. She stands there for a minute or a century, not stepping beyond time but simply confused by its erratic passing. Finally, she notices Iskan hurrying back toward them from the area closer to the theater.

Iskan, again sweating and breathless, shouts, "She's gone!" Then, apparently aware of how her words must sound, adds, "She's been taken to the hospital! Emergency surgery!"

# 50
BERGAMA

As Serkan Boroğlu paces the small, private family waiting room at Bergama Hospital, he shakes his head and mutters, "I came as fast as I could...I didn't have my phone!" He still wears the sandals, blue jeans, and Anadolu Efes basketball T-shirt he had on when he left his girlfriend's Taksim Square apartment in the morning. He stops in front of his sister, who is sitting in an overstuffed blue chair with thick wooden arms, and says for the fourth time, "The bastard stole my phone!"

"You told us," Elif answers.

Sitting stiffly in the adjacent chair, her grandmother holds Elif's right hand in both of hers. She looks up at Serkan but does not say anything. Turning her head, she stares across the room at a roiling red and green blob on the wall. Since the carnage at the Aesklepion, she can't form clear thoughts, much less articulate them. She is dizzy, and her ears ring. Light, even the softer light of this waiting room, hurts her eyes. She realizes at some level that, although her life is not in danger, she needs medical attention—but she will do nothing until they get word about Özlem.

"I came as fast...," Serkan repeats. "I..."

"Serkan!" Elif is angry at herself, not at him. Although she knows she could have done nothing to stop the bombing, she feels guilty that she was not there. She *chose* to continue doing her work at her studio. And in some deep way, what happened to their mother is *her* fault. *The Galen letter...* The horror in Bergama began with Elif's discovery of the letter... No, that's not true either. It all began long ago, even before history... But her gift to her mother is the current catalyst for this senseless mayhem. And now, she is able to do exactly *nothing*. Except wait. Time is sticky here in this windowless room in this interminable night. She has altered time in her studio, flowed through it on her bicycle rides and hikes in the hinterlands, and, occasionally, stepped beyond it during solitary moments and, even more rarely, in meetings with her friends. But this...

"I drove as fast as I could! Made record time!" Serkan scratches the stubble on his cheek. "I did!" He makes a fist and slaps it into his left palm. "I tried to warn Mom that the Hamits..." His shoulders slump. "I didn't know what... The Georgian bastard stole my phone. I tried..."

"Yes," Elif says. "Yes, Serkan." Serkan has just arrived, perhaps twenty minutes...or half an hour...ago, but she and her grandmother have been shut in this room for...for what? The *duration* of Özlem's surgery... At the Aesklepion, Tuğçe Iskan somehow conscripted a car that took the three women to the hospital on the outskirts of the town. Once they were informed that Özlem was already in surgery, Iskan ushered Elif and her grandmother to this private waiting room—and then vanished.

"I had no idea about the bombing...about what was going to happen," Serkan says, his voice rising. "But I knew that something... It's my... I should've..." Wide-eyed with anger and frustration, he begins again to pace. "I bought a phone!" He pulls an inexpensive single-use phone from his jeans pocket. "I tried to call. I did." He claws at his throat. "I didn't have Mom's *new* number. It's in my contact list, but that Georgian bastard..." He stops, stuffs the phone back in his jeans pocket, and turns to face his sister and his grandmother. "I called you, too, Elif! It went...it went straight to voicemail. Four times. No, five."

"Yes, Serkan," Elif says. "My phone was off." Her phone, as always when she is working, was switched off and stowed in her backpack. It still is.

"I tried. I really did."

"Serkan," Elif says, "I wasn't there either. And I have no excuse."

"I came as fast as I could," Serkan repeats, turning away from the two women. "The traffic... I couldn't get here any faster. I couldn't!"

Elif looks up at the television mounted on the wall near the ceiling. The teaser said that an updated report on Bergama's second bombing was next, but there are still only adverts for paper products on the screen.

"Near Baliksehir, I began to hear the radio reports." Serkan swallows hard. " 'The terrorist attack at the Bergama Aesklepion.' The 'ancient curing center,' they called it." He glances back at Elif and then stares down at the room's beige carpeting. "Multiple fatalities! The Hamits had them killed just to cover... I should have...!"

"Serkan!" Elif's voice is sharp. "Daesh claimed responsibility!"

"It's not Daesh!" he retorts. He shakes his head vehemently. "It's the Hamits! Mustafa...I'm—"

"Serkan!" Elif snaps. She waves him over to the chairs, but he stands rigidly, glaring at the carpet.

Finally, on the monitor's screen, the video, taken from the center of the Aesklepion's theater just above the box where the local dignitaries were sitting, begins with a shot of Özlem Boroğlu smiling as the audience applauds. It then zooms out to include the backs of the three people, two large men in dark suits and a petite woman in a dress, climbing the stairs on the left of the stage. Just as they reach the podium, the small woman raises a bouquet of red roses to give to Boroğlu.

As shouting erupts off to the side, the camera pans to the right where a young, dark-haired boy is climbing onto the stage. Silver-gray duct tape, wound heavily around a vest, covers his chest. He wears a black-and-white headband. When he reaches the stage, he hesitates, seemingly disoriented, as though he is listening to some distant voice. In that moment, the camera quickly zooms out again. Near the podium, the larger of the two men pushes the other man so hard that he and the speaker and the podium all tumble off the front of the stage. The large man, with the dexterity of an athlete, then pivots and hurls himself across the stage. The camera pans to follow him. As the boy, his face now contorted, begins to rush forward, the man plows into him, taking them both off the stage and out of sight. The camera focuses for a second on the top of a stone recess next to the theater's exterior wall. Then, a flash of light causes the camera's lens to career wildly and go dark.

Although she has seen the video twice before, Elif's breath catches. Her grandmother's hands are trembling, her breathing quick and shallow. Serkan stands transfixed. "He saved Mom!" he says to the television. "Recep saved her!" He squeezes his hands into fists. "And the Hamits killed him! Killed them!"

Elif rises from her chair and approaches him, but the veins in his neck are pulsing and she does not at first attempt to touch him. "Yes," she whispers, "Recep saved a lot of people...Mom, too... Maybe...I hope..." She reaches for her brother's hand. "But the Hamits didn't kill him..."

Fists still clenched, he pulls away from her.

"It was Daesh!" she says, reaching for him again. "The boy had on a Daesh headband!"

He yanks himself free of her. "The Hamits did it," he shouts. "I should never have... My deal started...!" He hyperventilates and then, not able to catch his breath, screams at the TV, "Not Daesh, you fucking idiot! The Hamits!"

Someone knocks on the room's door. As Serkan gasps for air, Elif reaches out a third time.

He jerks away. "My deal... I couldn't...didn't stop them!"

"Shut up!" Elif whispers fiercely to her brother as she glances at the opening door. "Shut up!"

He wheels and smashes his right fist into the yellow cinder block wall.

As the short, sturdy fortyish doctor in pale-green scrubs enters the waiting room, Serkan grabs his hand and averts his eyes. She stares at him for a second, turns toward Elif, and says, "Hello, I'm Doctor

Mutlu." Elif nods, but she can't find words. Her grandmother sucks in her breath and bows her head. "Özlem Hanim came through the surgery," the doctor continues. She takes off her surgical cap, revealing thick strawberry-blonde hair, and then gestures for Elif and Serkan to sit with their grandmother.

Elif takes the remote control from the wooden end table and turns off the TV. She then sits next to her grandmother and pats the chair on her other side for Serkan. He remains standing, his left hand still covering his right. The doctor sits next to Elif and then leans in toward Elif and her grandmother. Serkan takes a step closer but still does not sit down.

"Özlem Hanim," the doctor says, "has suffered a severe traumatic brain injury." She looks up and nods at Serkan, who looks away. "She has not regained consciousness, but she is stable."

Özlem's mother again takes Elif's hand in both of hers and squeezes hard. Tears slip down her cheeks. Elif, who has been holding her breath through the doctor's information, exhales.

Shifting her position, the doctor pats Elif's and her grandmother's wrists. "She's not at all out of danger," the doctor says. "The next twenty-four hours will be critical. Her brain is still swelling. There are significant contusions and at least one hematoma." Seeing the confusion on Elif's grandmother's face, the doctor pauses. "I'm sorry," she says. "Her brain crashed back and forth inside her skull causing bleeding and at least one blood clot." She shakes her head. "She'll have to remain sedated for days, except when she's brought out periodically for neurological tests to evaluate her condition. We have to be careful to avoid overstimulation." She pauses, seemingly measuring what to say next. "Seeing her may be a little shocking. Her face is badly bruised and swollen. We've had to drill into her skull to insert a brain oxygen monitor and, separately, an intracranial pressure catheter. The pressure of her skull on her brain as the tissue swells may still have to be relieved through another surgical procedure."

Elif's grandmother leans into her, energy ebbing fast now that there has been news of Özlem's condition.

As Serkan looks away again, he chokes, "My deal...I..." Shaking his head, he begins to cry. Elif isn't sure if he is weeping for their mother or himself.

Elif asks, "If she lives... Is there...will there be...permanent brain damage?"

The doctor frowns at Serkan before saying, "It's too soon to tell." She takes a breath and looks into Elif's eyes. "In some cases, there can be a full recovery. But at best, it's always a long, difficult road."

 51

KAIKOS VALLEY

"It was stupid!" the Hamit patriarch says, his voice sharp. "You are not stupid, but you fail to think things through!" As the sun rises over the Kaikos Valley he drives the black Range Rover fast along the two-lane road between Dikili and Bergama. Mustafa, his son, holds his iPhone up by the windshield and frowns. The reception out here in the middle of nowhere is barely one bar. Although he has not worked out or showered, he feels much better, *physically*, than the last time they made this drive. He knew enough not to visit Damla when he arrived at midnight, and he didn't have a beer, much less any raki. His father, however, is on his case worse than ever.

"I did think it through," Mustafa answers. "And it worked!"

"She's alive!"

"She's virtually dead! We're rid of her!"

His father slams the palm of his right hand against the steering wheel. "What does that mean?"

"She won't survive."

"That's not what my man at the hospital told me."

Mustafa waves his phone at his father. "You talked to your source *last night.*" He struggles to keep his tone respectful. "My source texted me *ten minutes ago!* She's in a coma. Paralyzed. Unable to speak. A fucking vegetable!"

Mustafa's father shakes his finger at the telephone. "You and your tweets."

"They're not…" Mustafa stops himself. His father doesn't even understand the difference between tweets and texts. He doesn't get how the world has changed. How the nature of their business has changed with it. And how the opportunities to make money are exponentially greater.

"You've made a mess of it!" his father growls.

"It's supposed to be a mess!" And that's exactly the point. The old man doesn't understand that the more the news reports are contradictory, the better. Özlem Boroğlu's death was never going to go unnoticed. And now there's so much conflicting information, so much disinformation, that no one will figure out what really happened. The family will, as always, be fine. Untouchable! It might even be good if the old bitch lives a few weeks, keeps the media frenzy focused on her rather than on the family's business. "There's no evidence," he says, "nothing that connects us. It looks like a fucking Daesh attack!"

His father turns his head, but the old man's trademark glare does not reach Mustafa through his aviators. "The reporters will swarm here like flies!" the patriarch shouts.

"Exactly!" Mustafa retorts. He reaches to the dashboard and turns on the air conditioning even though his father's window is open. "Isıl has already claimed responsibility. The bomber's identity was leaked to the media twenty minutes ago."

*"He was a child!"*

"He was a Syrian. The son of a foreigner, a Frenchman. A Daesh operative trained at the Al Farouq base in Raqqa." There's no way he's going to admit to his father that those ISIL assholes didn't tell him they were sending a boy to do the job.

"He screwed up!" His father is spitting mad. "He didn't cleanly take out the target!"

"It's better this way. Better if the old bitch lingers in a coma like that boy in town did!" He, too, is angry about the Syrian boy hesitating, giving that hulking moron a chance to be a hero, but he won't on this point give a millimeter to his father. He's got to change the narrative, spin it so that this operation, *his* operation, is a winner. Just like all his other deals. "You told me after we saw that letter that we'd have to rid ourselves of the old bitch if she got too close to the Galen cache. That's what we had to do, and that's what we did!"

"*We?*" His father squeezes the leather-covered steering wheel and rolls his wrists like he's shifting a motorcycle. "I told you that getting in bed with ISIL would be bad for the family."

"You told me I was in charge of day-to-day operations." He glances at his phone, but reception is still too weak.

"And look what's happened!"

"Yes, look what happened! We've more than tripled our revenue in the last year!"

"By making deals with ISIL! The family has always stayed out of politics."

"You mean, paid off whoever was in power!"

"Not extremists! Never! They're too unstable. Can't be trusted... I've told you that!"

His father has—too many times. "We've made a fortune selling artifacts we've gotten from them. Huge profits!"

His father turns the Range Rover onto the narrow road that cuts through one of their larger properties. "You've gone too fast. Haven't thought—"

Mustafa can't listen to this any more! "Or maybe, you've gone too slow!" he shouts. "We're making more money than—"

"It's all too risky!"

"It's all working!"

"You don't even know who you're making deals with!"

"So I need to get to know people like that Russian bastard Vlad!"

"Yes!" The patriarch shakes his head. "No! But you need to be able to read them. Men like Vlad—"

"Read them?" He holds up the phone. "In three minutes I can get as much information, personal and professional, as I need."

"It's not the same!" the patriarch says. "You don't *know* who you're dealing with."

213

Two hundred meters ahead, Bora and another younger cousin stand next to a white pick-up truck parked on the side of the road by a stand of poplars.

"You should've known not to promise Vlad something you couldn't deliver."

That again. "I'm going to deliver!"

"You're *going* to Los Angeles!"

"Not for another two weeks!"

"Twelve days!"

"Yeah. I've got almost two weeks!"

"You're going to lie low. Not draw any attention to yourself—or the family."

Mustafa's phone pings. He looks down at the message.

"Got that?" his father shouts as he slows the Range Rover.

Mustafa nods more to the phone than to his father.

"*Got that?*" Saliva sprays from his father's mouth.

**52**

RAQQA

The sheikh is sweating heavily by the time he reaches the top of the stairs. He shifts the potted orchid to his left hand. With his attendants stationed on either side, he pauses before the woman's door, wipes his forehead, and adjusts his turban. Since that day when she inflamed his rage, he has sent her a dozen gifts including antique gold Lydian jewelry. She has thanked Allah but has barely acknowledged him. Her mistake is, however, about to be corrected.

He will certainly not tell her that he traded her son's life for the jewelry. And he will absolutely not inform her that her boy is already dead, a martyr like her husband. He will instead insist that her son's future safety depends solely on her submission to him and his wishes. He pulls in his stomach, thrusts back his shoulders, and raps on the door.

Even though she has prepared herself for this moment, she is startled by the knocking. The doctor the sheikh sent the day after he ruined her face and who still attends her regularly has let her know a little of the sheikh's plans for her. The doctor, who was kind to her, also told her that her nose will never again be straight and that her fractured left cheek is permanently marred, but she does not care at all about any of that. The swelling has receded enough that she can see clearly out of her right eye; the vision in her left remains blurry.

Both eyes averted, she opens the door and steps back. She is wearing her double burqa and niqab, even though it is not a day for her Guardian to take her outdoors. She does not, however, have on her heavy black gloves. Her chafed hands fold, and her torn fingertips dig into her palms.

He shuts the door behind him and, remembering that he was not going to berate her for the problems she caused last time, offers her the orchid.

Her head bowed, she takes the plant, murmurs, "Allah Akbar," and sets it on the floor next to the door. Then, she stands again silently before him.

He locks the door's deadbolt. Her submissiveness arouses him. "I bring you news," he says, his voice firm and authoritative.

She nods but does not answer.

"Your son is safe." *As are all of those in paradise.*

"You will return him to me?"

"No…" His arousal blocks him from the answer he rehearsed. "Not yet…" But then the words come to him. "But I assure you that he is no longer in danger."

Her neck stiffens. Her hands, folded in front of her, tighten. There is, as always, deceit and arrogance in his voice, but now there is something more. *Smugness. Supremacy!*

He looks across at the table where his other gifts are stacked. Only the jewelry box has been opened. He can't help but smirk—women are so weak. They can be bought with baubles. His voice cracks as he adds, "I alone can keep him *safe.*"

She nods again. His words are all fraudulent, always. As her mind fixes on the way he said "safe" and on the phrase "no longer in danger," the fingers of her right hand go to the cuff of her left sleeve. The air-raid sirens begin to wail, but like her wounds, the noise, the external threats, mean nothing to her.

"I *alone* will make you safe again." *She will succumb,* he thinks. *When you are powerful, you can do anything you want to women.* He reaches up and unfastens her niqab. His fingers tremble as he touches the cloth. And that face that was once so beautiful, so alluring to everyone, has become even more so because it is now his creation. The still-bandaged nose, the left eye a plum, the gray-black bag beneath the right eye, the lumpy discolored yellow and purple of the left cheek. The split and swollen lips. He has planned every moment, but he is becoming so excited that he might have to take her right here on the floor. And he realizes that he should have remembered to have her water turned on so that he could properly clean himself afterward.

As he holds her niqab open, she stares at the shining silver band of his wristwatch. Her mind flashes to the meteor shower of pain, but she neither gasps nor shudders. Her fingertips brush the two spheres at the top of the ornate golden hairpin in her sleeve. Cold, dark energy fills her chest as her fingers clasp the pin. The iciness rises in her throat and suffuses through the hot devastation of her face. Her mind stone-cold, she keeps her head bowed and her eyes cast down. "How soon may I see him?" she asks.

"Soon." The blaring sirens are a distraction, but he will not let them ruin this. Her stitched lower lip quivers, which makes her that much more enticing. His breathing becomes heavy, his mouth dry. She has to be feeling much of what he is. When his cell phone rings, he lets go of her niqab and mutes it. Nothing is going to interrupt this moment of conquest.

One of his attendants is shouting something through the locked door, but the rushing in his ears drowns the words. He lowers his hand to her right breast which, even through the coarse garments, is ripe to his touch. The holy book states that foreplay is proper so he squeezes the breast hard. Heat rises within him. Sweat runs from his temples into his beard.

She grips the hairpin, her fingers locking around the two spheres. She takes a long, deep breath.

His lower back arches as he twists the breast; his breath quickens. He can feel that her breathing is changing, too. He grabs onto something firm…her nipple?…and pulls. Both his attendants are shouting outside, but this moment's siren song is all he can hear. He throws his head back and gapes at the cracks in the ceiling's plaster, sure that there is a divine message there. Glass rattles when the first bomb strikes nearby.

The thick beard that scratches her wounded face smells of cigarette smoke. He is yanking at her burqa's seam, rocking on his heels, mewing. She bites her lip. Tastes blood.

A second bomb, even closer, shakes the room's bare furniture. He lets go of the burqa, runs his right hand down her side and hip, and then clutches the back of her thigh.

Their eyes meet for the first time. She sees lust and imperiousness and misogyny. He sees her submissiveness turn suddenly to contempt, a look so fierce and so filled with loathing that he is momentarily frozen by it.

As he lets go of her thigh so that he can cuff her to her knees, she slides the hairpin from her sleeve. Far more swiftly than he can react, she plunges the bright golden tip through her left eye deep into her brain. Blood spurts in his face. She is already convulsing as she lurches backward away from him.

# 53
## BERGAMA

With his left hand, Serkan Boroğlu slides the empty bottle of Efes Pilsen onto the rooftop patio's glass table. "No," he mutters, "I don't want to talk. Not to you…or anybody else." In the two days since the attack on their mother, he has become increasingly guilt-ridden and sullen. He has finally changed his T-shirt, but he hasn't showered or shaved. The soft cast on his right hand protects his two broken knuckles and fractured middle finger.

Elif, who sits across from him with the saucer of sliced apples she brought out for them to share, looks at the figurines on the shelf. She has just showered, and her damp hair gleams in the day's last light. Her cat, Sekhmet, lies in her lap purring. In less than an hour she and Serkan will return to the hospital for their third visit of the day, though she believes that her mother does not even know they are there.

The doctors say the swelling has slowed, but there's no evidence that her mother's condition is improving—or that it ever will. And there isn't much Elif can do for her mother except hold her hand and hope. Eventually, perhaps even tonight, she will get her grandmother to come home and rest from her constant vigil. But, here, now, there is something else she needs to do. She fixes Serkan with her eyes. "Look at me," she says to him.

He doesn't.

For two days, she has been trying to bolster him, telling him the attack was not his fault. Which it isn't. It's far more her fault, something she is acutely aware of and must herself do something about. But first she has to get him out of this swamp of self-pity into which he plunged after he smashed his hand into the hospital waiting room's wall. She takes a slice of apple, bites it in half, and chews it. "I've been thinking," she says, "that you're right. It *is* all your fault."

He glances at her, then looks away again. His Bergama basketball T-shirt, which has been in his drawer since high school, is much too tight.

She eats the other half of the apple slice. "If you hadn't gotten involved with the Hamits, hadn't gotten greedy, Mom would be fine!"

He glares at her as he wipes his mouth with the back of his left hand. But he still doesn't answer.

She picks up another apple slice and points it at him. "You endangered me, too. If it weren't for you, Mustafa Hamit would never have come to my studio." She bites off a small piece of the apple without the skin and feeds it to Sekhmet. "So what are you going to do about it?"

He stares at the table.

"You keep crying into your beer—literally." Her voice is even, feigning disdain.

He sniffles.

"If you really believe the Hamits sent the boy to kill our mother, you should be up in Istanbul hunting down Mustafa!"

He dabs at his eyes with his left hand, but he still says nothing.

"You know that, but you keep telling yourself that Mom needs you here. Why? She's not responding to any of us. Not yet, anyway."

He looks out at the dying light.

"You're the man of the family. You should be wreaking vengeance!"

He doesn't respond.

"That's how it's supposed to work. You take charge. You sharpen your sword! Gird your loins for battle!"

He looks down at his cast.

"But you're not. You're cowering here." She strokes Sekhmet's neck. "Are you afraid of Mustafa?"

He shakes his head.

"Why, then?"

Again, he doesn't answer.

She leans forward and places her palms on the table. "Serkan, why?"

"They'll kill me," he murmurs.

"Who? Mustafa?"

"His Georgians! Steroidal maniacs."

"And you can't handle them?"

He wipes his eyes again. "Not those guys! Nobody can! They'll gut me and then have soguk for lunch before I've even bled out."

She nods. She thinks Mustafa will want to kill him—and maybe her—in any case, just to shut them up. But at least now, she's finally breaking through to Serkan.

He starts to sob. "It won't do you or Mom any good if I go off and get myself killed. Though it might be better."

"Getting yourself killed helps no one!"

"I've fucked up everything!"

"Maybe," she says, "but you need to be a man! *We* need you to."

"I'm sorry."

*"You're sorry!* What good does that do?"

He shakes his head. "I'm so sorry!"

"Stop it!"

He shakes his head more slowly. "I've messed everything up."

She holds his eye contact. "You've said that. And maybe you have… *but what are you going to do?"*

"I don't know. I…"

"You what?" Elif asks after a moment.

He takes an apple slice from the saucer but doesn't bite it. For the first time, he meets her gaze. "I want to do something, but I don't know…"

Sekhmet mews, leaps from Elif's lap, and darts for the stairs. The empty beer bottle begins to rattle on the tabletop. Elif's figurines tremble, and the grape arbor above them creaks. Serkan stands, glances about wildly, and grabs the beer bottle as it begins to pitch off the table. An entire row of the figurines on the top shelf topples like bowling pins. The statue closest to the edge of the shelf—a svelte, naked, polychromatic terra-cotta goddess—plummets and shatters on the floor tiles. Elif leaps to her feet, snatches a black goddess before it, too, pitches off the shelf, then turns and spreads her arms to shield the other clattering figurines.

The second tremor causes the arbor to groan. Grapes rain on the table, bouncing and rolling. Serkan moves out from under the arbor, plants his feet, and raises his arms as though he's getting ready to rebound a basketball. Elif leans over the shelf as her goddesses bump and grind. Their grandmother's pots shimmy on the floor, their herbs swaying. One of the neighbors is screaming.

When the third tremor is weaker, Elif straightens up and Serkan lowers his arms. They can barely feel the fourth, but their conversation has fragmented, their words splintered. Serkan's eyes are wide, and his breath is ragged. Whatever thoughts were coalescing in his mind have disintegrated.

As Elif begins to stand her goddesses upright and arrange them again on the shelf, Serkan says, "Can I help?"

"Get a broom," she says, her tone more curt than she intends.

# 54

## BERGAMA

$E$lif Boroğlu pedals past the Aesklepion's gate toward her studio. The hazy night feels heavy, but the gloom, she knows, is mostly in her heart. It is not late, not even midnight, but after the third of the day's visits with her comatose mother she needed to ride her bicycle hard, well out into the hinterland. The ride did not, though, as it usually does, lift her spirits. She did not feel that potent sense of flying that she sometimes has when she's on a long nocturnal ride in the hills beyond the valley. But at least she has gotten a full body sweat going.

When she slows at the corner, she sees a figure sitting in shadows near the entrance to her studio—a woman about her size. While she gets off her bike, Tuğçe Iskan stands and brushes off the seat of her jeans. She has nothing with her, no manila envelope, no Ministry materials, nothing. She must have been here quite a while because the neighborhood dogs aren't barking. Somewhere down the street, someone is playing a guitar. And farther on, an overwrought sportscaster is ranting about some football match.

Elif wipes sweat from her face and nods but doesn't say anything. She unclips her water bottle and drinks until it is empty. In the last five days, a couple dozen people from outside Bergama, police officials and reporters and politicians, have talked at her, offering condolences but really trying to get a sound bite or photo op. It's not, Elif thinks, that they are cynical but rather that they are self-obsessed, honestly glad that her mother is surviving but also trying to use her family's and Bergama's tragedy to further their own ends, whatever they are. Iskan, on the other hand, vanished from public view after having provided so much aid.

"Was the ride...? Did it help?" Iskan asks.

"Not enough," Elif says as she wheels her bicycle past her. She unlocks her studio door, opens it, and flips the light switch.

Iskan turns but does not follow her.

"Come in..." Elif steers her bike through the doorway. "Please."

Once they are both inside, Elif leans the bike against the wall and then turns the new deadbolt. "Thank you," she says, "for everything. I... We..."

Iskan nods.

Sekhmet stretches and leaps from her perch on the supply shelf. While Elif wipes her face, neck, and shoulders with a blue hand towel, Sekhmet rubs up against her bare, damp legs. Iskan surveys the figurines again before picking up the stout goddess holding the single-edged sword and the severed head.

"I'm still not sure what I'm going to do with that one," Elif says as she refills her bottle at the cooler. She guzzles all of her water, refills the bottle, and gestures toward the stool by the workbench.

Iskan shakes her head once. "I'd rather stand. I've been sitting most of the day."

Elif picks up the studio's one cup and offers it to Iskan.

"I'm good, thanks," Iskan says. "Your mother, she is improving?"

"The doctors are satisfied with her progress. But..." Elif drinks again from the bottle. "But, as I'm sure you know, she's still sedated, still in traction, still paralyzed, still unable..." Her smile is pained. The water has brought on a secondary sweat even though the studio is cool. "Or unwilling to speak. Her eyes open occasionally." Elif shakes her head as she realizes how much she actually wants to talk with this woman. "Twice, I've seen her follow somebody's movement with her eyes." She raps her knuckles on the workbench. "The swelling is down some. No seizures."

"That's good," Iskan says. Her tone suggests she's not just trying to be polite.

"My grandmother, who has two broken ribs herself, refuses to leave the hospital even though visiting hours are limited." Elif shakes her head again. "They've actually set up a cot for her down the hall."

"And your brother?" Iskan asks. "I saw him at the memorial for Recep Ateş. He looked...upset...sad and angry at the same time..." She looks for a word that might not be offensive but can't think of one. "He wouldn't talk to anybody."

"He goes to the hospital, but mostly he stays at home. Drinks beer until he falls asleep. Blames himself for what happened."

"It's not his fault," Iskan says. "Both attacks were carefully planned, which takes a lot of time. Certainly more time than your brother has been working with Mustafa Hamit."

"I've...we've told him that. But..." Elif puts down her water bottle, pulls the elastic bands from her ponytail, and begins to comb her fingers through her hair. "He wants revenge, wants to make up for what's happened, but he's too scared even to return to Istanbul." She massages her scalp. "Are the Hamits done with him, with Serkan?"

Iskan doesn't at first answer. Given her new position in a clandestine unit within the Ministry, she knows the answer but has to be careful about how much information she shares. Finally, she shrugs and says, "It's unlikely."

Elif leans down and strokes the cat's neck. "So you think he's still in danger?"

"I think you all are."

"And that's why you're here? To warn me?"

Iskan nods. "Partly."

"And there's nothing the government can do? I mean, about the Hamits."

"Nothing the government *will* do. The boy was Syrian, but he was never seen in Turkey. And the Irisher. Same thing. Somebody very good at smuggling both people and equipment had to be involved. But there's no evidence in either case. Nothing. Whoever ran the logistics was very good at it. Has been doing this sort of thing for a long time." Her own deep anger creeps into her voice. "Even if there was evidence, it would somehow get lost."

Iskan clears her throat and then continues, "The first attack was ISIL terrorism. As they lose territory, they're getting more desperate. Exporting terrorism. Trying to destroy other cultures, especially UNESCO sites." She shifts the figurine, clenches it in her left hand. "But this attack on your mother and her friends, it's different. It's business. ISIL may have provided the boy, the bomber and the bomb, but this was planned by someone who was targeting your mother. ISIL doesn't work that way. The amount of stolen treasure ISIL has traded for cash and weapons is monstrous. Crime organizations like the Hamits, they've been all too willing to partner up. Not just in Turkey."

Elif pours water into her right hand and wipes her face. "So there's no way to stop them, the Hamits?"

"I didn't say that. Governmental agencies aren't going to stop them. They're too deeply infiltrated, too deeply *indebted*." She pauses again, takes a breath, returns the figurine to the table, and gazes at Elif. "Even your mother's friend, Recep Ateş, the hero of Bergama, had a hidden bank account, one he made significant deposits into, monthly, for four years. Through the end of last year."

"Recep worked for the Hamits?"

"I didn't say that. But someone was paying him off...for a long time." She steps away from the drying racks and table, moves closer to Elif. "Look, no one will ever know about the bank account. Recep Ateş is a hero. We need heroes right now. But the point is that the Hamits are conspiring with ISIL, committing treason, and killing Turkish people. They've used the system for too long, and the system goes on protecting them. Somebody's got to stop them."

Elif turns on her stool and leans back. "What does that mean?"

The women's eyes lock. Iskan takes another step closer. "The Hamits are protected by a system they do not respect in any way. They never have, not in the entire history of our country. For that family, everything is transactional. Everything has a price. Everything is simply bought and sold. Even the law...it's just another negotiable factor. People, the same thing. But as my friend says—" She stops herself, surprised she used that word. "Their strength, that everything can be bought and sold, is also their weakness, their Achilles' heel." She reaches over and again picks up the figurine holding the sword and severed head. As she lifts the statue and holds it before Elif, she adds, "In your world, in the world you sometimes enter, they're weak. They don't understand that the world is so much more than a series of financial transactions." She hands the figurine to Elif. "There's power in your work. I saw it, felt it, when I first visited your mother's house." She points at the goddess. "How did you design this?"

"I didn't," Elif answers. "It just comes to me. I sit here, and I find it." Elif's smile is for the first time in nearly a week neither painful nor ironic. "Or, it finds me."

Iskan waves her hand at the table and the shelves filled with figurines. "These," she says, "they come from inside you. The Hamits can't possibly understand that. For them, everything is about winning. Always. They, the father and the son and the cousins and the nephews, believe your mother discovered the Galen cache. Gold artifacts. Bronze statues. All of it. And that she already sold an invaluable Sekhmet amulet to a rich American couple."

Elif winces. "The Americans knew what it was. That it was modern. They provided the gold. Paid for the equipment."

"The Hamits don't know any of that."

Frowning, Elif doesn't say anything.

"The Sekhmet amulet," Iskan says, "had nothing to do with the attack on your mother. The planning would have been well along by then."

"Since she received the Galen letter?"

"Yes. They assumed she had additional, specific information about the gravesite."

"She didn't."

"You would know."

Still holding the figurine, Elif leans over and slides the water bottle onto the floor next to the leg of the workbench.

"Look," Iskan says, "the Hamits believe that she, that your family, will ruin their business. Outsell them. Turn them into losers. They think it's already happening. And they're obsessed with controlling the market. They're already making mistakes. Especially the son. Their obsession is their weakness. And you, Elif, have the power to destroy them."

Elif stares at the figurine in her hand. She turns it slowly and then gazes at Iskan. "And this," she says, "is why you're here."

Iskan nods again. "Did you hear your mother's speech at the Aesklepion? The speech she was giving?"

"No." She shakes her head. Tears are welling for the first time since the night of the attack. "Why were you there?"

"A friend asked me to go." Iskan picks up the brown ceramic cup, draws water, and drinks. "You should listen to it, the speech. It came from inside her."

"I will."

"You'll know what to do."

 55
BERGAMA

Özlem Boroğlu strokes toward light. Just as she reaches the surface, she is sucked under again, towed into darkness. She swims toward sky, and the backwash yanks her down. She is worn out, utterly enervated, but she will not let herself drown in the pitched void. Each time, she moves a little farther into the brightness, and each time darkness reclaims her.

Finally she treads in light. The gleaming world around her begins to take shape. Sharp corners. Hot spots. Yellows and greens. Blues. Whites. But she hears no sound. Only a ringing in her ears. And an odor. A scent too clean, too strong. And no feeling, nothing tactile at all. The taste is metallic—copper? Bronze?

And no pain, no feeling at all. And no memory. Only of her starting a speech at the Aesklepion's theater. Standing before an audience of psychologists and psychiatrists. Talking about her work at Allianoi, the tedium, the red tape, the discoveries, the honors, the exhilaration. And, ultimately, the loss, the destruction of her work, of her site, of the ancient spa that healed so many. Everything swallowed by the flood.

Yes, the flood. Images are returning, swirling. An inundation she herself has submerged for years. But the flood this time was light not water, and instantaneous not gradual. A breaking wave of light.

Özlem feels something—a hand pressed on hers, clasping her. But silence still, except for incessant noise in her ears that annihilates all other sound. Softer light, and another dark shape that has no sharp corners. A flowing of energy above her, energy streaming through her, energy that is holding her, pulling her free of the undertow. Her eyes blink, but it's too bright to see, like staring at the sun on Dikili's beach.

And now a form, two forms, in the light flowing darkly but not dark. Gradually, one form becomes her mother standing over her and the other, Elif, her mouth moving but no words emerging, no meaning, no sense. Özlem has no memory of anything except the tsunami of light.

The stark brilliance exacerbates the headache, the throbbing pain that doesn't hurt but steals her focus, her concentration. She is safe, out away from the flood, but the world is blinding and nothing works, neither her body nor her mind. And maybe that's good, though it doesn't feel good—doesn't feel at all. She has no idea where she is or what she is doing or why she is lying here. She wears a flimsy gown decorated with inscrutable glyphs. For fleeting moments, she can move her eyes but nothing else. She doesn't seem to need to move her arms and legs. Doesn't really care to. Her mother and daughter are with her but are merely mimes, unable or unwilling to speak. The swimming into light has exhausted her, the light itself blinded her.

When she wakes again, she is in a hospital bed, hooked to silent machines. Or, maybe machines she cannot hear over the ringing. Her mother is here, weeping silently, and Elif is holding her hand in both of her own, a transfusion of energy. Everything is still too bright—the shining machines and gleaming walls and glowing sheets that cover her. An antiseptic odor scrapes her nostrils. And the bitter taste of metallic shavings.

She still cannot move anything other than her head, or won't try. A tube runs into her arm. A plastic bonnet squeezes her head. A straw shoots a cutting wind up her nose. When she closes her eyes to dim the glare, images flash. Elif's figurines battle in the rooftop garden among her mother's herbs...blades slice limbs, and truncheons crush skulls...dogs yelp and geese squawk... Iskan's photographs of Serkan and the handsome young man come alive and leap about in the melee stomping animals and statues alike...water nymphs scream in a deepening gyre...young boys hurl themselves into the battle only to be slaughtered...she pleads for calm, for sense, but the chaos escalates... Recep, mammoth and terrifying in his bearskin cloak, lumbers among the others until he turns with a maniacal gaze toward her as though he might tear out her eyes and rip out her throat. He instead flings her aside and crushes a young boy holding a bouquet of venomous snakes. Recep...*Recep?*

Serkan has left the battlefield, though the handsome young man continues his rampage. Serkan stands here now in the room with Elif and her mother. Time's stream is disrupted, dysfunctional, but Özlem is aware that her son is present. He weeps, the tears real, but they fall away from rather than to her. He mouths words, silent words, empty words. Although both her children linger above her, each has very different energy. Elif's sluices into her, nourishing her, but Serkan's spirals about, only touching her tangentially, barely brushing here and there. And something ominous lurks beyond, perhaps not in him, but around him. She is upset with him, deeply angry, but she doesn't know why and can't seem to care.

If Özlem could think at all, she might welcome darkness. Instead, she drifts in and out of moments. Other forms, male and female swathed in pale shimmering tunics, hover about her. They speak, seemingly soothingly, but their words don't reach her. They are at once too close and too far. There is not even an echo, only monotonous droning. A whiteboard is thrust in front of her, but the board glints with dark lettering in a language she once knew. Or didn't. The world out there is far too brilliant for her, the darkness inside too excruciating, though she still can't actually *feel* the pain.

Something, both fair and foul, orbits beyond her mother and children, at the far edge of her world. It comes into view, passes overhead, slips away. Returns. Within her world, the battle rages, the fire and the fury, the mayhem and the butchery. It should matter. She should care.

 **56**

BERGAMA

The hammering on the studio door is hard enough that Elif hears it even with her earbuds in and the music thundering. She has been sitting here at her work table for well over an hour, thinking, not really working. She has not begun anything new since her mother was attacked, cannot yet concentrate on anything other than her mother and her brother and what must be done.

Elif's hair is pinned back and piled loosely on her head. She is wearing the same black jeans and bright-blue tank top that she has worn after her hospital visits both nights since her conversation with Serkan was interrupted by the earthquake out in the Aegean Sea. She glances at her phone to see that it is 1:01 in the morning, takes a long breath, removes her earbuds, and slowly, deliberately goes to the door.

The pounding continues.

"Who is it?" she shouts through the wooden door.

"Open up!" The voice is male, deep, angry.

"Who is it?" she repeats even though she knows.

"Mustafa Hamit! Open the damn door or I'll kick it in!"

She takes another deep breath, leans against the door for a moment, takes a step back, braces herself, and turns the deadbolt.

Mustafa opens the door slowly and scans the studio to see that there is no one there except Elif. "Shit!" he mutters and then turns to her and, his voice cold, asks, "Where is that bastard?" He is wearing clean, creased blue jeans and a tight, green short-sleeved shirt that accentuates his biceps and complements his eyes. He is, though, unshaven, and his hair is tousled.

"Serkan?" she asks.

He glares at her. "Yeah! Who do you think? Burak Özçivit?"

She steps back as though she's frightened. "He's not here."

"Obviously."

She wrings her hands but doesn't say anything.

"What was that fucking call about?"

"What call?" she asks, though she is the one who told Serkan to make it.

He glowers at her more harshly. "That complaint he made to the Istanbul police about two Georgians mugging him in Tünel Square."

She shrugs. "I don't..."

He looks at her, seeming for the first time to actually notice her in her tank top. "Does he want to die?" As with the statements he made the first time he was in her studio, it's not a question.

Wide-eyed, she shakes her head. "He...hasn't talked to...me...people since Mom... I don't know what he wants...what he's thinking."

"He wants to fucking die." There's disgust in Mustafa's voice.

"Maybe I can..." She takes her phone from her work table. "I'll try...," she adds as she taps numbers.

As she lets the phone ring, he looks around the studio. The work table is clean, the centrifuge covered, and the kiln off. At least a dozen of the figurines are gone. The cat is nowhere around.

"Nothing," she says. "He won't answer my...anybody's calls. He wasn't at the hospital when I was there."

"I know," Mustafa says. "I've got a man waiting for him there."

"Maybe... He's been drinking. A lot." She pauses. "All the time."

When he spots the squat goddess with the single-edged sword and severed head, he picks it up. "You're here late," he says as he runs his finger along the sword's blade.

She looks away from his eyes. "I can't sleep," she says, careful not to sound flirtatious. "My work…" She pauses, seeming to be thinking, and points at the figurine. "Do you…do you still want that?"

His smile is grim.

"I've…" She rakes the back of her left hand with the fingernails of her right hand. "You… You can have it."

The corner of his mouth curls up. "I thought it can't be bought."

"It can't. Not with money." She pauses again, apparently still thinking. "But my brother… His life…"

"Is he in danger?" The question is anything but a question.

"He's broken. No danger to anybody. But *he* thinks he is."

Still holding the figurine, Mustafa takes a step closer to her. "And what about you? Are you in danger?"

"Of course." She looks down at the squat goddess in his manicured hand. "You're here." Before he can say anything, she adds, "But I do have something to trade for my safety. And my brother's." She fully understands the risk she's taking.

"This?" he laughs, holding up the figurine. His watch glints in the overhead light. "You'll need a lot more than this."

She looks down at the floor. "I've been walking, hiking in the hills around here since I was a little girl."

"So?"

"I've discovered two sites. Not worked, not disturbed like Marmurt Kale or Molla Mustafa Tepesi. Ancient sanctuaries still unknown to others."

"Sanctuaries never hold anything of value." His tone is gruff.

"True." She glances at his face and then turns away quickly. "Nothing of monetary value. But the sites were…are sacred."

Shrugging, he moves a step closer to her so that the figurine is almost touching her. "Trash," he says. "Broken bits of terra-cotta."

She finally looks into his bright eyes. "But I've also found a number of undisturbed gravesites. Ones of wealthy Pergamene citizens."

"Bullshit!" He stares back at her. "You would have told your mother."

"I did…if they were already desecrated. But not the ones that are undisturbed. They're sacred. She doesn't understand that. I've left them be."

"You expect me to believe—"

"No!" she cuts him off. "I expect you to believe me when you put on the rings and hold the gold coins and jewelry. That's what I'll trade for my life. For my brother's life. For me, it's an easy choice."

"So what exactly are you offering?"

"I'm offering to show you four undesecrated gravesites, each containing a fortune in artifacts."

He shakes his head and smirks. "And all you want is…?"

"A guarantee of my brother's safety—and mine." She doesn't trust him at all, but she keeps herself calm.

"No," he says flatly. "We…I don't make deals like that. I don't need to."

"But you're here, aren't you. You've come to me."

He grabs her arm tightly enough that it will leave a bruise. "Why don't I have friends of mine convince you to *give* the information?"

In this moment, she understands Serkan's fear but, more importantly, that Mustafa likes to have others do his dirty work. She wonders if he also likes to watch. "Sometimes, Mustafa," she says, her tone becoming as cold as his, "I like it rough." She looks hard into his eyes. "But that won't work here. Even if I told you or your friends where they are, you couldn't find the sites. They have gone undiscovered for two thousand years. Until I found them." She smiles angrily and yanks her arm free.

"The Galen cache," he snarls. "You know where it is?"

"No. As far as I know, it doesn't exist."

"Bullshit! Your mother's letter—"

"The letter. It's *from* Galen. And, it's real. But—"

"I've seen the evidence!"

"No, you haven't." She's not sneering, but she lets her voice become even colder. "Evidence, as you know better than anybody, can be faked. There is no Galen cache!"

"You don't think so just because you've never seen it!" He starts to grab her again but stops. "Who do you think you are, the god of these fucking hills?"

She holds his gaze. "No. I'm the person who's spent her life in, as you say, 'these fucking hills.'" Raising her arms, she adds, "I'm the one who's found a number of tumuli. Including four undisturbed sites with immense treasure. And I'll give them to you for a price, the right price, *my* price. Take it or leave it."

He rubs his free hand through his hair. "Suppose I want to do the deal? When do we start?"

She shakes her head as though she's trying to figure it out. "Next week. Maybe. And then a new one every six months."

"No. Too late." His voice is calming, becoming that of the tough-minded, big-time dealmaker again.

"My mother's in a coma! Isıl—"

"It's still too late." His voice may be under control, but his eyes are gleaming.

"Tomorrow...night?" She hesitates. "After visiting hours."

"Tonight. The first one. The proof that you're not lying to me."

"Right now? I can't—"

"Yeah. *Now.* Or no deal."

She looks down at his Sketchers. "Getting to the tomb is difficult! Getting into it is *really* tough! You're not... It's *too* tough!"

"I'm..." His smile is frozen as he glares at her. "Tonight or never. Take it or leave it."

"You're not... You can't..." She seems to stumble over her words. "You're not even dressed for—"

His smile twists. "Do you want to save your brother's precious fucking life?"

# 57

KAIKOS VALLEY

The black Range Rover stops on a deserted road far out in the Kaikos Valley. As Elif Boroğlu gets out of the vehicle, she is careful not to leave any fingerprints. She circles behind the Range Rover, pulls on her black hooded sweatshirt, and points toward the escarpment beyond the hills. The sky is star-swept, the Milky Way clear, and the sliver of moon low in the west. The day's heat has dissipated fast, and the breeze feels fresh and dry. A couple of farmhouses are nearby, she knows, but none has lights burning.

"It'll be easier and faster if we follow the streambed," she says as she leads him back along the road. After almost three hundred meters, she swings from a culvert and drops onto rocks in the dried streambed. He pauses for a moment before following her. They do not speak as she guides him farther into the hinterland. Their eyes gradually adjust to the dark, and she keeps up a brisk pace, strenuous but not exhausting, for half an hour until the Range Rover is nowhere in sight. She does not rush, and she does not rest. Twice they climb steep rock faces that would make their trail difficult to follow even for a trained tracker. She has one miner's lamp with her, but they won't use it until they reach the tomb.

Elif begins to breathe deeply and regularly as she loves to do when she is out here on her own at night. Mustafa keeps pace, but in this terrain his Sketchers work far less well than her lightweight hiking boots—and the climbs are taxing. They hear lizards skittering, though they can't see them. Elif misses her two dogs, but she has deliberately taken Mustafa on a different, more circuitous and difficult route toward the escarpment she is seeking. The earth does not sing to her as it often does, but the land whispers, urging her on. They trek along the ridge that rises toward the high, dark wall of rock. From where they are, they have a clear sightline back to the acropolis above Bergama, but she only furtively glances in that direction and he does not look at all. "Careful," she says. "Watch out. The rocks slide a lot."

When they finally reach the right place, she touches his sweating arm and whispers, "The cleft." She points toward a tapering, more deeply dark tear in the rock face. "Once we're in there, we can use the light."

"It's about fucking time!" he snarls. He's not out of breath, but he is breathing hard.

"It will be worth it."

"It better be." He peers into the cleft, which looks like a dead end. "This is the only way?"

"Yes." She wipes sweat from her forehead. "We can come back in a couple of days."

"Hell, no. Get going."

"Later, at first light, you'll see better."

"Get fucking going!"

She exhales slowly. "Do you want the lamp?"

"No. You lead." He grabs her shoulder and pushes her toward the cleft.

She turns from him, puts on the headlamp, and adjusts it—but does not switch it on. "Stay close," she says as she ducks down and squeezes into the cleft. She lifts her left arm, finds the slot, pulls herself up, and turns on the light. "There's a handhold," she says, slowing her breathing. "You'll feel it." She wiggles her way forward into the narrow tunnel.

He follows her but gets stuck almost right away. His breathing becomes ragged.

"Slow down," she says to the darkness behind her. Though she can't see him struggling, she adds, "Stay calm. Relax!"

As he fights his way toward the tunnel, he mutters, "Shit... Fuck!"

She listens to him sucking air. "Just stay calm!"

"I am calm!" he hisses.

When he finally makes it into the tunnel, she is careful not to shine the light in his eyes. "It's easier from here," she says over her shoulder.

His arms extended in front of him, he serpentines along the tunnel, scraping his elbows and shoulders and knees on the rock walls. After he bumps his head a third time, he panics, grabbing at her boot.

"Let go!" she says. "We're there." She kicks herself free. "You've almost made it!" She can smell his rank, fear-ridden sweat.

When she reaches the gap where the tomb's wall was breached during some ancient earthquake, she rises to her knees and waits.

"That was hell!" he mutters when he catches up to her.

"I told you."

Seeing the tomb in the arc of her light, he pulls his smartphone from his jeans pocket and turns on the flashlight app. Holding it in front of him, he starts to pan the tomb.

"The box," she says.

He gets to his feet, hunches down, and scuttles across the tomb. He only pauses when his right hand brushes the top of the finely wrought bronze box. As he opens the lid, he whispers, "Yes, yes... Yes!" Still holding the phone in his left hand, he scoops with his right.

She can hear the coins jangling as she crouches near the breach.

His breathing becomes more erratic. He bows his head lower over the box, and he lifts one of the amulets, glistening, between his thumb and forefinger. Leering, he holds it to the light, then grabs a second and third. And a fourth and fifth. He raises all five in his palm, and, both hands shaking, he holds them close to the phone's light. Only after he has kept the amulets aloft for more than a minute does he place them back in the box.

Without closing the box, he turns toward the skeleton. The phone app's light is unsteady as it moves from the gold rings to the necklace to the crown of precious stones. "A woman," he murmurs. He lowers himself to one knee and fondles the gold filigree of the necklace. His fingers shiver as he touches the edge of the crown. His breathing quick and shallow, he runs his fingers across the crown's jewels.

Elif leaps, swinging the oblong stone with all of her might, and strikes him just above his right ear. He sprawls sideways, away from the human remains. His phone falls onto the tomb's floor, the light facing down so that it forms a glowing ring around the phone but does not illuminate anything else. Dust motes swirl.

Breathing hard, she crouches above Mustafa, who lies on his side. Blood seeps from the gash in his skull. She drops the stone next to him and kneels. She can't control her breathing, but her eyes are clear and her hands barely shake. She feels neither elated nor dispirited. Touching her fingertips to his neck, she finds a pulse. She presses her palm to his chest, which heaves. She lifts the rock but does not hit him again. It would be fitting to strike him once more for each of those who died in the attack on her mother. And then again and again for the dear children who died in the ISIL attack on the funicular, even if Mustafa had only a little to do with it. But she won't. She is no avenging angel, and this moment is utterly personal.

She bows her head and asks forgiveness—not for striking Mustafa but for bringing evil here and leaving him alive in this sacred place. She wants Mustafa to go on living for a while in pain and darkness so that he will sink into despair. He will almost certainly make deals with himself and whichever false gods he worships. When she realizes he might also in his anger further desecrate this place, she retrieves the stone. Raising it above her head, she smashes first his left hand and then his right. His body twitches, but he does not come to. She strikes his wristwatch until it is shattered. Finally, she slams the smartphone with the stone. Even after the light goes out, she continues to beat it relentlessly, making sure it is obliterated. She takes no pleasure in any of it.

Still hunched over, she replaces the rock where she found it near the breach. She then rearranges the box's contents and closes the lid but does not touch the skeleton even though the necklace has been shifted slightly and the crown is askew. As she takes Mustafa's pulse one final time, tears run down her cheeks.

In the tunnel, she fears the earth will not let her go, but she does not get stuck at all. She emerges from the cleft into the night's vast stillness, the air and the darkness itself grazing her skin. Openly weeping, she clambers up the slope above the cleft until she reaches rocks the size of the box in the tomb. With the heel of her boot, she sends one and then another tumbling down. Scree and smaller stones slide, too, and as she climbs, she repeats the process until the cleft is completely covered. She sits for a moment on a rock the size of a wheelbarrow and slows her breathing. She wipes her eyes, sniffles, and swallows. She will not tell Serkan or her grandmother or her mother, if she regains consciousness, or anyone else what she has done.

As she takes the long hike by a far different route back to her studio in Bergama, the wind falls. Adrenaline melts away. The Milky Way fades. She is thirsty, and her gummy saliva tastes bitter. Though the air is not hot, she cannot cool down. Her hands twitch periodically. The earth begins to sing to her, at first an anthem but then, far more loudly, a dirge.

# 58

## KAIKOS VALLEY

Mustafa Hamit lies in agonizing darkness. He has no idea where he is. A hot spike is being driven into his skull. Fiery nails pierce both of his hands. He remembers only the fear of crawling through a dark tunnel. But this is worse. In the tunnel, a light guided him, and help was close; here he is alone in an excruciating void. His hands are mangled. His mouth is dry. He tries to swallow his panic but cannot.

When he raises his head five millimeters, pain radiates from an epicenter above his right ear. The left side of his face falls against stinging grit. Slowly, because any movement is torment, he lifts his right hand toward his head. Flames that shed no light arc among his fingers. When he touches his skull, finding sticky blood and matted hair, the juncture detonates. He jerks his head away, creating more misery. His head strikes the stone and grit again. Waves of nausea follow the blast.

He vomits.

The smell is unspeakable. The taste sickens him more, but he can't even wipe his mouth. He has to remain rational, think his way out of this hell. The guiding light from the tunnel grips his mind. His watch…his watch is giving off no light at all. But there was a light. A woman? There was a woman. The woman led him into— The bitch!

The bitch must have hit him. And left him…where? His phone! He's got to find his phone! His phone will tell him.

He doesn't have his phone. But he did. He was using the phone's flashlight app in a cave. No, not a cave! A grave! He's in a fucking tomb! Injured. Badly. His head and hands smashed. Alone. Without even his phone. This can't be happening. The bitch could not have done this to him. A woman… No. It's not possible. A woman! The bitch! She wouldn't. Couldn't. Evil fucking woman! She's left him, horribly hurt, entombed in…in fucking nowhere. Left him mutilated. Left him to die.

Knowing where he lies is even worse than not knowing. Far worse. He doesn't deserve this. *Persecution,* that's what it is. He has to get control. The phone…his phone is the key. When he finds it, he can get out, call for help. Then, he can go after the bitch with a vengeance, with fire and fury like the world has never seen. But everything hurts so much. So very fucking much.

He tries to stand but can't balance himself with his crippled hands. He finally makes it to a squat, wobbles, arms askew, and rises fast. His head strikes the tomb's ceiling, and he collapses in an eruption of pain. He screams, chokes, vomits again. His mouth fetid, he moans and moans. He whimpers for a time, though time itself has stolen away, leaving him in this hell.

He's cheek down in puke and grime, gasping, unable to catch his breath. Something warm… His blood! Blood is trickling along his forehead, around his right ear, into his right eye. Pricking his eye. He tries to blink it away, finally raises his arm enough to wipe it with his short sleeve. Not that he can see anyway. The world is black, the horror infinite. Darkness ubiquitous. Pain crushes him.

But he won't give up, won't give in to the bitch. He'll live so that he can have her tortured to death. And her brother. And her grandmother. All of them. His phone must be here, somewhere in the dust. Movement is agony, but he wills himself to move his right elbow, scraping an arc in the dust. Nothing. He sucks in his breath, shifts his body half a meter, scrapes his elbow, still feels nothing.

On his seventh shift, his elbow nudges something hard. But it's jagged, not smooth. He rubs his elbow back and forth. Yes, something, but it can't be his phone. He begins to shift his weight again, but stops. Despite the acute suffering, he taps the object repeatedly. It's the right size but not the right shape. Wracked with pain and utterly enervated, he begins choking, sobbing again. The bitch has destroyed his phone, completely demolished it. He is alone, absolutely—more than he has ever been.

He howls. The echo assaults him.

He is going to survive, though, going to make it home. He must. His father... His father will save him! He'll come looking for him. He'll organize a search party. They'll find the Range Rover. Follow the tracks. Discover the cleft. His father will be irate, but the treasure will appease him. The treasure! Priceless amulets—five of them. And invaluable jewelry on the bones. Bones...skeletal remains, desiccated, covered with dust. It's all here, all around him...treasure and bones and dust. A shiver runs through the blazing pain.

He wanted to show his father that he could, alone, find immeasurable treasure. He wanted to see his father's face when he laid the artifacts in front of him. But now he just wants to see his father's face, even incensed, one more time. He told no one where he was going, who he was meeting, who he was going to *convince* that he had an offer for the Galen cache that she could not refuse. And she didn't. The bitch! He'll have to get out on his own. And bring the treasure with him. Maybe not all of it at first. But something. Something that proves he did it. His plan—not really a plan but an *idea*—worked.

He needs to shake his head to clear it, but it hurts too much. It's all too much, too much effort and too much pain. It's not finite like it is when he's working his abs in sets of ten reps on the machine. This pain doesn't stop. He has to be logical, mathematical, but stringing even two thoughts together is almost impossible. He'll make a grid, cover each quadrant until he finds the tunnel. Yes, that's it. A grid, like those at archeological sites. But where should he start? A wall...or a corner would be even better. He slides his elbows out in front of him and slithers in the dust. In only a few seconds his left elbow reaches rock. Gulping air fouled by puke, he creates the grid in his mind.

But wait, he doesn't even need a grid. He can just follow the wall. It's all so simple. He has wasted so much time making it more complicated than it is. He can do this. It's easy. The only question is, how can he take the artifacts? His jeans have pockets, but his hands don't work. He begins to ponder but stops himself almost immediately. Cogitation is worthless. He'll come back for the artifacts. His father won't believe him, but so fucking what. He's found incalculable treasure, and there's more. The bitch said there were four undiscovered tombs, and this was the least of them. The last must be the Galen cache.

He finds the tunnel quickly, even more easily than he imagined, and the discovery energizes him. But once he's in it, fear returns, stealing his breath and the newfound energy. He has to move slowly, like a centipede, but without legs. A worm. The stench is awful, and it takes him a couple of meters to realize it isn't coming from the tunnel. But he's alive—the smell and taste and pain all attest to it.

The walls close in. Dust he stirs chafes his nostrils, scratches his throat, singes his eyes. Time fucks with him again. Is it morning? Have they found the Range Rover? Is anybody looking for him yet? Has anybody even noticed he's gone? The thoughts exhaust him. He just wants to stop and sleep, but he doesn't trust himself to wake up.

His breathing is quick and shallow as he wriggles his way along. Shouldn't he be seeing light—a *literal* light at the end of the tunnel? There was a ledge they had to reach up for, and some light should make it that far. Maybe it's still dark out. Or dark again. He has no way of knowing. He's lucid, he's sure. He's not hallucinating—no apocalyptic nightmares, no dragons, no aliens, no fires or floods, no devils except for the bitch who abandoned him here. There is only this hellacious, contracting, suffocating world of pain and fear and darkness.

Finally, he comes to the end, or what should be the end. The tunnel veers sharply downward at an angle of at least seventy degrees. But there is still no light. None. Only dust and infinite darkness. His scraped elbows lie on the edge of the shaft. There's no fresh air either.

Just more choking dust in his nostrils, his throat, and his eyes. He lays the left side of his head on his shoulder and bicep. This isn't right. It's all wrong. Tears run from his burning eyes. He's worked so hard, fought off enormous fear, stayed rational, yet here he is on a precipice above some void.

He's nowhere, with no end in sight. He can't stop his chest from heaving. His whole body begins to shake, intensifying his suffering. He can go on. Pitch himself forward and hope. But he holds no real hope. Ahead is only darkness. No air. No light. Going backward is physically impossible. And certain death. He can remain here, but here is the same. Here is hell.

 **59**

BERGAMA

 Serkan Boroğlu is sweating as he climbs the hill toward his mother's house carrying a twelve-pack of Efes. His head is down partly because of the exertion and partly because the morning light playing across the Kaikos Valley beyond Bergama only makes him more sad. He didn't make it to the hospital last night—his mother is still comatose, still paralyzed, still deaf, still entombed within her battered body. Neither Elif nor his grandmother came home last night. He hasn't been able to decide which is worse, waiting alone in the house while Elif's figurines taunt him—chanting at him that he is a stupid, worthless ingrate—or seeing his sister, whose energy shames him. She convinced him to report the incident with the Georgian and the razor to the Istanbul police, but what good will that do? The few times his grandmother has come home since the attack, she made dishes for the doctors and nurses. He himself is useless, building castles of remorse out of empty beer cans.

As he is approaching the front steps, he stops dead near the signal wall that he and Elif used as children. He gasps as though he has been gut-punched. His sweat goes cold. There, scratched in the wall is *Aytul + Zeynep*, A–Z, their newest signal, their *only* new signal: *Danger! Alert!*

The plastic bag holding the beer slips from his left hand and clunks to the pavers. Looking around, he rubs his hand through his uncombed, unwashed hair. He has no idea if the message was there earlier when he went out. He hasn't even noticed the wall since yesterday afternoon.

A skinny, gray-brown dog lopes along, but no people are on the street. Cocks are crowing, and light is splashing on the hill above the house. Somewhere, not all that close, a dog is barking. He pulls the phone from his pocket, cradles it in the soft cast that covers his right hand, glances about, and says, "Shit!" He scoops up the beer and, muttering "shit!" repeatedly, hustles toward the house's street-level kitchen door. After fumbling with the keys, he makes it into the kitchen, kicks the door shut, and slumps against it. On his third try, he successfully taps out Elif's number.

"Don't say anything," she hisses, her voice intense. "Listen!"

"Yeah." Fear ripples. "Okay." The sink's faucet is dripping. He must not have completely turned it off...yesterday...or the day before. With his free left hand, he turns the handles until they are tight and then goes on squeezing them even after the dripping has stopped.

"Don't go to the hospital!"

He wasn't really planning to, but he doesn't tell her that.

"Mustafa's men," she says, "they're waiting for you there!"

"Mustafa?" He tries to take a deep breath but can't.

"No!" She seems to be trying to gulp air as well. "His men."

"The Georgians?"

"I don't know. Just don't go there!"

She sounds like she's out of breath, which makes him all the more nervous. The rhythm of her voice is uneven, sometimes louder and sometimes softer, as though she is walking fast, even faster than her usual brisk pace. She must be somewhere out in the hinterland. "Is Mom...?"

"No change." Her tone is brusque.

"And Anneanne?" His hand holding the phone is quivering.

"She's okay. Listen, Serkan, you need to go away! Hide!"

Not knowing what to say, he looks out the kitchen's one barred window. From this angle, all he can see is the wall with the message.

"Get out of town," she says. "Immediately!"

"I could go to Dad's and—"

"No!" She cuts him off. "Not to any relatives! Or friends. Not to Istanbul! Or Ankara!"

"I...Aunt—"

"No!" she shouts. "No relatives!" She pauses, sucks in her breath, and lowers her voice. "Nowhere connected to anybody you associate with now. No one the Hamits might connect you to."

"What? Why?"

"Do you want the Georgians to find you?"

Feeling trapped, he stares out the window at the graffiti. A fleeting shadow causes him to duck. As he listens, he hears birdsong over his own breathing. The birds wouldn't be singing if someone were there. "But what about Mom?"

"I've...we've...Anneanne and I have got her."

"But—"

"They're after you, damn it!" She is shouting again. "Disappear!"

He glances around the kitchen but has no idea what he's looking for. "I could go—"

"No! Don't tell me," she interrupts. "Just do it. I don't want to know!"

He starts to speak but stops himself.

"Where are you now?" she asks, her voice lower.

"At our...," he chokes on his sadness. "At Mom's house. I saw the signal!"

"Get out!" she yells. "Get out, now!"

"Okay."

"Now!"

He looks out the window. A shadow causes him to duck again, but it's just a passing cloud. "Can I at least—"

"Now, Serkan!"

"Okay. Okay." He feels for a moment that she's talking down to him, acting like their mother. It's a tone he has never reacted well to, but he doesn't say anything.

"Look, Serkan, you need to vanish for awhile." Although she lowers her voice again, the urgency remains. "Mustafa's men are looking for you. They're *after* you!"

"I..." He takes a breath. "Are you okay?"

"I'm fine." Again, the answer is curt. He can hear her breathing, as though she has been running or walking a long way. Even farther than usual.

"What's wrong?" he asks.

"Nothing!" she says. "I'll call you when I get a new phone."

"What? Why?"

"They...I...they may be after...all of us."

"Then I should—"

"Serkan, you *should* disappear!"

"But—"

"I'll call you at six," she says. "Tonight. Please, please, just get out of the house. Go away. That's all you can do right now."

"But—" he repeats.

The phone goes dead. He stares at it, then looks at the bag of beer on the floor, starts to push redial, and stops himself. He realizes that tears are mixing with the sweat on his face.

# 60
## KOZAK

The knocking on the family compound's steel outer gate is loud. It is late in the afternoon, but most of the men in the village are still out in the fields or at the quarry or the pine-nut processing plant. Having himself just arrived home, Engin Suner is standing in the parlor's doorway. His wife, Hafize, is curled on the divan. The television is on and her eyes are open, but he thinks she is not really watching it. He isn't sure she even sees it. She hasn't acknowledged him at all.

Suner keeps the gate unlatched because Hafize's friends and relatives still visit her daily, but they also fail to rouse her much. His mother stops by once a day, but she orders Hafize to cook and do chores and then scolds her when she doesn't. Özlem Boroğlu's mother has, understandably, not come to visit since her own child was attacked.

As two men push through the gate, Suner steps out of the parlor door. He hasn't even had time to wash since he finished work. His shirt and pants are dirty. He hasn't shaved all week. Wiping his hands, he meets the men near the outdoor oven. The younger, more muscular man came to the house before, but the older, pudgy man in the white shirt and dark tie is new. Outside the gate, a third man, large and dour, leans against the side of a clean black sedan. He wears dark sunglasses, and his thick arms are folded across his chest.

"Good afternoon," Suner says, blocking the men from coming farther into the compound's courtyard.

"Hello," the older man says as the younger nods. "Thank you for seeing us," he adds as though he has been invited.

Although Suner is thirsty, he does not offer these intruders anything to drink. He remembers what Özlem Boroğlu told him after the funeral and on the morning she examined the artifacts, which turned out to be priceless: *Do not sell to anyone, but pretend that you are willing to do so in the near future.* She also told him to be nice, but he is exhausted from his work and, more so, from the unrelenting anger and sadness he feels whenever he is in his house.

The pudgy man takes a billfold from his pants' back pocket and extracts a business card embossed with gold lettering. Suner has never heard of the company, Anatolia Enterprises, that the man represents. When the man smiles, his double chin becomes more prominent. He wears a gold ring on his stubby right pinky finger. He smells of cologne. His shirt, though tailored, protrudes over his belt. "May we talk for a moment?" he asks, his voice oily.

"It's not a good time."

"Yes, our condolences. How is your wife?" His double chin bulges.

Suner shakes his head once hard. He is not going to talk about Hafize with any stranger, much less this man he already dislikes.

"Yes," the man repeats. "We understand. We would just like to talk with you for a moment only."

Suner does not say, *And I'd like you to get the fuck off my land right now!* He does, though, bend the card in half as he folds his arms.

"Your father-in-law's property," the fat man says. "We are prepared to—"

"Not now!"

"Hear me out…," the man wipes his fingers along his sweaty jowls, "for just a minute." He takes a pack of Marlboros from his pants' front pocket, flips the top, and offers a cigarette.

Suner looks at the cigarette but says, "No… No, thank-you."

"We are very interested in two parcels your father-in-law owns…

owned in these hills. The parcels are not arable. They're of no use to a farm—"

"No!" Suner interrupts. "I will talk to you later about selling my place." He's losing his patience. "But Dede's farm belongs to my wife! And she is not in any condition to talk yet!"

The man's eyes narrow. "May we come in for just a moment?" Sweat is forming on his upper lip.

"No!" Suner tries to soften his voice, but his head is starting to pound. "Not today!" He shakes his head vehemently. "It's time for you to leave."

"Mr. Karan," the young man says, "has come all the way from Istanbul. Just to meet you. His offer is well above the market."

Suner glances at the young man, who has grown a well-trimmed beard since he was last here. "Yes," he says, his anger billowing, "I'm sure that it's a good offer. And I'm interested." He rubs his hand across his mouth. "But the land belongs to my wife. The time is not good. She is not ready… Not healthy enough to—"

"Perhaps," the fat man interrupts, "you would be interested in a very generous offer for both properties. Yours and your family's."

"Get…!" He stops himself, hears himself say, "Very interesting." He glances at the large man who is now looming just inside the gate, clenching his fists. "But not today! I—"

The fat man smiles. "The proceeds would allow you and your wife to live elsewhere." He takes a step forward. "To forget all about—"

"Get off my land!" Suner's vision darkens around the periphery.

"Your wife—"

Suner hits the fat man in the mouth, splitting his lip. As the man reels, the young man coldcocks Suner, who staggers backward. The large man in the sunglasses is already coming at him fast. When Suner swings at the young man, the large man punches him in the ear. Suner, feeling like he has been hit by a fence post, slumps to his knees and then falls to all fours. The young man kicks him in the balls. The third man gets him in the ribs. Gasping, he curls on his side, his cheek in the dirt. Waves of pain and nausea break against each other in the pit of his stomach.

The fat man, bringing a bloody handkerchief to his mouth, sputters, "On our nechst vishit…," he dabs his battered mouth, "you'll remember to ashept our generoshity!" He kicks Suner in the stomach, knocking out what little breath he still had. The ringing world fades in and out as he watches the three pairs of shoes turn and walk away—the glossy, black dress shoes, the pale cross-trainers, and the dark steel-toe boots.

# ⭐ 61
İZMIR

The scrawny, gray-brown dog lies on a remnant of gray carpeting just inside the Otogar, İzmir's main bus terminal. As Serkan Boroğlu passes the dog, he thinks, *At least it has a home, a place to lie down and feel safe.* He is carrying only the backpack he tramped around Turkey and Europe with in his university days. He has not since he left Bergama noticed any followers, but almost everyone everywhere has looked in some way suspicious. After talking with Elif, he stuffed a change of clothes in the backpack and left town— a bus to Dikili, another to Aliaga, and a third to İzmir. None of the same passengers were on all three, but that doesn't mean he's not being tailed. He has seen all of the spy movies and, for that matter, the old gangster films. Mustafa may even be sending a woman to make the hit.

Still jittery from the Red Bull he bought in Aliaga, he turns right and heads toward the men's room. When the chubby man with lottery tickets heads straight for him, he stops in front of one of the shops selling sweets and trinkets. He pretends to be studying the racks of blue heart-shaped name tags, but the name "Mustafa" keeps jumping out at him. A man in a dark uniform pushes a Terminal Café tea cart past the mostly older people sitting in the gray-green steel chairs along the windows. The café's name alone causes Serkan to keep surveying the concourse.

Before entering the men's room, he stands under the red, white, and blue TUVALET sign for more than two minutes, scanning for…he's not sure what. No one, man or woman, is loitering nearby. Everyone except him seems to have some clear destination. He pays the one-and-a-half-lira fee and rushes to the toilets that are in a room separate from the urinals. Three T-shirts hanging on a line block most of the window's light. After choosing the stall at the end closest to the window, he closes the door, flips the latch, and hangs his backpack on the hook on the back of the door. Doing everything left-handed aggravates his headache. He got rid of the soft cast in Dikili for fear it made him more conspicuous, but his right hand is still swollen, still discolored, still pretty much useless.

The stall is neither clean nor well-lighted, but, breathing through his mouth, he tries to settle on the seat. The water on the floor makes him wish that he had shoes other than the sandals he was wearing when he left the Istanbul apartment…in that other life before the Georgian pulled the razor on him. When he hears someone enter the room, he clinches. There's shuffling and then the latch on the door of the next stall clicks. The smell of his cold sweat mixes with the stench of shit.

Choking down panic, he leaves the stall without relieving himself. Splashing water on his face in the room with the sinks calms him but only for a moment. It's all gray here, too, except for the bright pink of the liquid soap in clear containers on the wall. He looks into the mirror at the water dripping through four days growth of beard, at the dark rings under his eyes, and at the disheveled hair. But what really daunts him is the haunted look in his eyes, that of an indigent, a fugitive, an animal about to be cornered. His sweat goes cold again.

When an older man, shorter and skinnier than he is, enters and says hello, Serkan bolts for the door. He then remembers his backpack and doubles back to the toilets. He holds his breath until, the backpack slung over his shoulder, he passes the man taking money at the door. His breathing is quick and shallow as he enters the terminal's cavernous main concourse. Scores of ticket counters line the entire length of the wall to his left. He can, from this terminal, quite literally, flee to anywhere in Turkey, but the choices are overwhelming, as is the noise of the milling crowd. Light blasts through the wall of windows to his right. The killers could be almost anyone. Two Otogar policemen in dark uniforms, pistols in holsters at their sides, are walking toward him.

He turns and heads toward the exit again. He doesn't *need* a ticket —he's going to take a dolmus to Bostanli where his university friend, Zafer, has an apartment he can use. Zafer is in Çeşme with his family for the next week. Serkan, too, would like to be with his family, anywhere, but he knows he's toxic, pure poison for both his family and current friends. His mother will probably live, but she'll be a quadriplegic, at least for some time, and, knowing her, will not let him forget it's all his fault. In any case, he can't forget and can't forgive himself for involving her in his scheme. And Elif, she did nothing but help him, and she's in danger now, too.

Serkan can't contact his father. That would put him and his two young children in jeopardy. He's also afraid that Mustafa's Georgians are still watching his Bavarian girlfriend's apartment. He doesn't even want to think about what they would do to her. At least he has a safe house, an apartment he can hide in for a week. But what's he going to do then? Given the Hamits' connections, he can't get a job where tax records will be kept. He can't go home, and he can't go to either Istanbul or Ankara without endangering those he cares about. And it's only in the last few days that he has even realized how much he cares. He's alone, isolated—and he has no one to blame but himself.

He stops again outside the terminal. He needs a beer to calm himself—he can almost taste that first cool draught. A beer would do him a world of good. Just one. That's all. He'll be able to think, and he needs a plan. He circles the outdoor area which, of course, has no bars, no place that sells beer at all—and so he settles on Okibar. There's too much glass here, too, but he goes to the one corner table that's best protected, at least on two sides. He orders a Coke from the thin, dark-haired waitress who, in his other life, might have attracted him. He would normally scoff at the restaurant's orange plastic chairbacks and the cheap tiles on the floor and walls, but here he feels anonymous, not having to constantly look over his shoulder. He'll stay vigilant, of course, but maybe he can avoid the anxiousness that followed Elif's morning call. The music video on the restaurant's large television monitor still disconcerts him. Young men singing soulfully wander around a mansion's grounds as a young woman in a bikini swims laps in the pool.

When the waitress returns with a Coke, a straw, and a glass, he finally begins to relax. The Coke fizzing in the glass is no Heineken, but for hundreds of years, caffeine has helped men make clear decisions—and he needs clarity. He's where he is because he got greedy. He should've taken Mustafa's first offer for the hookup with the Americans and been done with it. Or would he have been? They were *his* clients. Mustafa knew, or must have known, that he was his mother's son. It could've been—*it was*—a setup from the start. The arrogant prick was using him from the beginning. It's even more deeply his fault that his mother lies in a coma. Were the Americans, Jack and Clare, in on it? That's impossible…but were they?

He pops the straw into the Coke. He never uses a straw, but he places the tip of his left forefinger on top of the straw. As he pumps it like a piston, his eyes catch two muscular, dark-haired, square-faced men pausing as they pass Okibar. One, wearing a black, sleeveless T-shirt, has hairy shoulders and a tattoo of a dagger on his forearm. The other is smoking a brown cigarette. They seem to be talking, but he can't tell if the language is Turkish. And they are standing so that they almost block the door. A Nutella advert is on the tv.

Greed got Serkan into this, and now he has no money at all. He has the five thousand American dollars from the Hamits hidden in his Istanbul apartment, but trying to retrieve the cash would be suicidal. His debit card is almost maxed, but that doesn't really matter because he can't use it anyway. Purchases would leave a trail for the Hamits to follow. Just to get to İzmir, he had to borrow money from the bronze box his grandmother keeps in her underwear drawer. He took only half of the money, a little over half, and he left her a note saying he loved her and would pay her back. And he wants to. But how is he ever going to do that?

The two men start to walk away, the one waving his cigarette as if to emphasize a point. As Serkan's eyes dart, searching for whoever else is out there, he sucks Coke through the straw. He's sweating again even though Okibar is air-conditioned. The math concerning the cash he has left is like some sixth-grade story problem from hell. He had to spend almost a fifth of the money on the three bus tickets and the Red Bull and the doner in Aliaga. He'll last on what's left for two weeks, maybe three if he doesn't eat out or drink. And then what? Washing dishes in a kebab joint? Sleeping on Zafer's couch until he kicks him out? Nutella and ekmek forever?

The two men are coming back. Heading straight for the restaurant's door. No longer talking. No cigarette. Hard faces. Narrow eyes. No obvious weapons. A tattoo on the larger man's knuckles as he reaches for the door handle. The two men take seats at a table where they can see the TV *and him*. As the waitress approaches them, Serkan drops a ten-lira note on the table and grabs his backpack. He's out the door, moving fast, not looking back, hunched and waiting for the blade or the bullet.

 **62**

BERGAMA

Holding her mother's limp hand, Elif Boroğlu leans farther forward. "Mom," she whispers, "I know that you can hear me…that somewhere in there you're listening." Her mother does not stir. She has been taken off the respirator, but the other equipment in the private room the hospital has provided for her continues to hum. Elif's face is stony. She has not slept much in recent days. She cannot cry over her mother, over anything at all anymore, but she means what she says. "I love you. We all love you. We *need* you." Elif squeezes her mother's hand—nothing. She rises, leans over still farther, and kisses her mother's forehead below the bandages that hold the tubes for the brain oxygen monitor and the intracranial pressure catheter in place. *Nothing.*

Elif's mother's color is not much better than the room's pale-green walls, but what disturbs Elif far more deeply is how diminished her mother is. She looks to be withering under the sheets. Her cheeks are shrunken, her face gaunt. That energy, that fierce energy that drove her, is gone. Her energy was not always positive, Elif knows, but it was always *evident*. This person lying on this hospital bed is drained, enfeebled.

Elif takes her phone from her jeans pocket and watches yet again the video of her mother's speech at the Aesklepion. She has viewed it more than twenty-five times since Tuğçe Iskan suggested she do so.

She has viewed it both before and after she led Mustafa Hamit to the ancient tomb. Iskan wanted her to hear her mother's conclusion, her call to action, but that is not why Elif has become obsessed with it.

She scrolls back through the video until she finds the spot where her mother told her audience that they were all meeting on holy ground. As Özlem talks about Galen growing up at the Aesklepion, studying there as a medical student, and practicing as a physician, she watches intensely—not the video itself, but her mother's facial expressions. First, there is the burst of brightness in her mother's face when she mentions Galen sitting in that very theater. The moment of epiphany, similar to those at Allianoi and other sites, occurs whenever her mother realizes something that she must have known on some deep level all along.

Then on the video, her mother's face tenses, her eyes narrow, and her lips thin. This would seem strange to people, given her epiphany a moment earlier, but Elif knows that for her mother any exhilaration is followed, immediately or soon after, by a stunning anxiety. She is wrung out by distress that someone else might understand as well and by foreboding that some sinister force would obstruct her or, even worse, steal the credit for her discovery. The irony in this video is, of course, that once the bomb exploded, no one, except Elif herself who was not actually there and had to depend on the video to figure out exactly what happened to her mother, would remember anything but the explosion.

Finally, there is the distant look in her mother's eyes during the applause at the end of her speech. Again, anyone noticing at all would guess that Özlem's mind is elsewhere. But Elif knows that nothing could be further from the truth. Her mother is still very much there, already digging, going deep, *obsessively*. And that explains why her mother reacted to the boy's attack less swiftly than Recep. Again, ironically, her uncharacteristic hesitation probably saved her life. Elif believes that, if not for her mother's abrupt journey from joy to dread, her mother, not Recep, would now be celebrated as Bergama's martyred hero.

"Mom," she says aloud, "You're right! It's all right here! It has been here all along. Look!" She holds up the phone so that her mother, were she not comatose, could watch. She listens to her digital mother speak to her present mother who cannot, and maybe will not, listen: "Perhaps he even sat in the very seat where you now sit..." Elif's hand is steady as she moves the phone a little closer to her mother's face. "...The human spirit, the human psyche is still central to any deep understanding of our health, individually and as a society."

Elif continues to let the speech play. "You did it, Mom," she says. "You figured it out. Everyone seeking the Galen cache, in whatever age, has been searching for his father's villa." Elif shakes her head at yet another irony. "After all, his father built the villa to house the Attalids' treasures that, if it were not for him, would have been melted down during construction of the Temple of Trajan!"

Elif stares at her mother's drawn and cadaverous face. The machines keep up their humming, but her mother remains immobile and insensate. A beeping in the hallway does not break Elif's focus. When the applause begins on her phone, she asks, "And here, Mom, you're already excavating, aren't you?" She pauses the video the moment the boy reaches the stage. Although she has viewed the speech so often, she only watched the ending those two times that first night in the hospital. It's seared into her mind, and she has no desire to ever view it again.

As Elif puts the phone back in her pocket, she notices her mother's doctor standing in the doorway. She is wearing sky-blue scrubs. Her strawberry-blonde hair is pulled back under her surgical cap, and her surgical mask is tied loosely around her neck. She holds the tablet she has had with her whenever she visits her mother.

"What are you doing?" the doctor asks, nothing critical in her voice.

Elif shrugs, her smile sad. "I thought that if anyone could reach my mom, *she* could."

Nodding, the doctor asks, "Her speech at the Aesklepion?"

"Yes." Elif shakes her head slowly. "A call to action... Her final words before..."

The doctor comes into the room and pats Elif's hand that is still holding her mother's. "She'll come around. Her vitals are strong. You've just got to give it, give her, time."

They both gaze at Özlem for a moment.

"I know," Elif says, though she is not at all sure. "I know." She is not being curt. She likes the doctor, credits her with saving her mother's life…such as it is. She looks away at the light streaming in the room's only window. In less than an hour, she'll need to make her daily one-minute call to Serkan, who is still hiding in Bostanli. As she glances again at the patient in the bed, she says, "That's just not my mom."

# 63
## KOZAK

Tuğçe Iskan and Nihat Monoğlu leave the rented Fiat Fiorino at a respectable distance from the compound's two-meter-high steel gate. The late morning is bright, hot, cloudless—with not enough wind to stir the dust. The only other people on the cobblestone street are three elderly women in baggy floral salvars, loose blouses, and bright headscarves who are shuffling toward the plane tree at the center of the village. The dogs that barked when Iskan and Monoğlu pulled up have quieted down.

As Iskan and Monoğlu approach the gate that slides sideways like a panel at a factory loading dock, she asks, "Are you sure this is a good idea?" Though she was only recently transferred to the shadowy unit that most people in the Ministry do not even know exists, she has been placed in charge of this operation. Given her obvious lack of experience, she was also provided with Monoğlu as a "temporary consultant."

"It's your idea," Monoğlu says, his voice guttural.

"That's why I'm asking."

He clears his throat. "With Mustafa Hamit and Serkan Boroğlu both gone, it's your only way to get to Hamit fast." When he knocks on the compound's gate, the three women stop and look back.

"But we're inciting this man," Iskan says, "putting him in harm's way after all he's been through."

He nods. "He's already in danger. And you can pull the plug on the op whenever you want…"

"But you've got his back, no matter what?"

"I've told you, I've called in favors." He knocks again—louder. "From old friends."

Engin Suner, little Mehmet's father, slides the gate open just far enough so that he can see the two people standing outside. "Go away!" he shouts. "Get out!" He stands stiffly, his left hand gripping the gate. His shaking right hand holds an axe handle.

Iskan and Monoğlu step back. Monoğlu holds up his hand, palm toward the house, and says, "Good morning." His tone is gruff. Although he is now in his mid-sixties, his shaved head, thick neck, grim expression, and broad shoulders make him look powerful and, at times, he knows, threatening.

Iskan focuses on Suner's face. The man's right cheekbone near his eye is swollen and discolored. The eye is half-closed.

"You do the talking," Monoğlu says to her without looking away from the axe handle.

Iskan holds up her hand and smiles. She is not used to taking the lead, and this op, she has been told, has, because of its urgency, not yet been officially sanctioned. "We're from the government," she says. She is, technically, telling the truth, at least in her case. "We need your help."

"I'm not selling!" he shouts, his face going red. Blocking the entrance, he holds the axe handle at crossarms.

"And we're not here to buy anything." Her voice lacks the empathy she hoped to communicate. "We just need to ask you a couple of questions."

"Leave us alone!" Standing even more stiffly, he strikes the palm of his left hand with the axe handle and then winces.

"We aren't…" She pauses, takes out her ID, and holds it up in front of him. It's hot here in the sun, and getting hotter by the minute.

Suner stares at Monoğlu, glances at Iskan, and looks again at Monoğlu. "Do I know you?"

"We haven't met," Monoğlu admits.

"What do you want from us?" Suner's voice is low, not quite as hostile.

"We're here to help you if we can."

Suner cocks his head, seeming to measure those words against all the other lies he has been told.

"How is Hafize?" Iskan asks, the question genuine. She wonders how people feel after this sort of devastating loss she has never experienced.

Suner raises his eyebrows.

"Is she sad?"

His shoulders slump. "Very." He looks down as he adds, "Too much."

Monoğlu gestures toward Iskan. "Is there anything we can do?"

Suner pauses before shaking his head. "Nothing. Nothing anybody..." He looks up. "Find the bastards that did this to us."

"That's why we're here," Monoğlu says.

Suner lowers the axe handle and steps out of the gate, but then stands even more awkwardly.

Iskan wonders if his ribs are fractured. As she taps the side of her face, she asks, "Who did that to you?"

He doesn't answer.

"Are the photographers still bothering you?" Monoğlu asks.

"No." The anger in his voice rises. "Men wanting to buy Dede's land." He wipes his mouth. "And mine. My land!"

"Did they threaten you?" Monoğlu asks.

"No. Not at first." His look is sheepish. "Not until I hit the fat man in the mouth."

Monoğlu hides a smile.

As Suner tries to lean over to put the axe handle down, he recoils in pain.

"Here, let me hold that for you," Monoğlu says, extending his hand.

Suner stares at Monoğlu for a moment before handing it over.

Monoğlu sets one end on the ground and braces his hip with the other as though it were a flying buttress. He nods for Iskan to talk.

"We're investigating the attack on the funicular," she says.

"You tell me nothing!" His voice becomes angry again. "When I ask, nothing! It's the Irisher and ISIL! But nobody else."

"We're part of a special team. A top-secret group that's still investigating…" Again, technically, she's telling the truth. They're just not exactly a governmental entity.

"We will find the others," Monoğlu says. He does not hesitate at all before adding, "The traitors who murdered Mehmet and his grandfather."

"Good." Suner drops his eyes again. "I can't… It's not a good time for you to come in. Hafize can't…"

"That's fine," Monoğlu says. "We can talk here. Or, perhaps, in the shade would be better." He still has not told him either of their names —and won't, as much to protect Suner as themselves. This conversation will have never happened.

"Here," Suner says. He steps back and ushers them into the compound. After shutting and latching the gate, he leads them across the hard-packed dirt to the shade of a storage shed's slanted roof.

"We think," Iskan says, "that a crime family, the Hamits, were involved."

At the mention of the name, Suner glances quickly away.

"Did you," Iskan continues, "or your father-in-law have any…contact…with them?"

"No! Never."

His answer comes too quickly, Iskan thinks, way too quickly.

Monoğlu takes out his smartphone and begins to scroll through photos. His thick, right thumb is crooked, having twice been broken, once while he was a wrestler and once in his work. Frowning, he glances up at the brilliant sky.

"I have the card," Suner says. "The card the fat man left. I will get it." Monoğlu gives back the axe handle. As Suner turns and hobbles toward the parlor, Iskan says, "He has had dealings with the Hamits."

"Probably something petty and unrelated," Monoğlu answers. "And not with the patriarch. He does not waste his time on working people." Monoğlu takes a pack of Yenice Régie Turques from his pocket. "I shouldn't," he says as he shakes a cigarette from the pack.

"Wait," Iskan says, "he'll join you."

Monoğlu smiles at her.

Suner walks unsteadily back without the axe handle. The card has been crumpled and then flattened again. When he gives it to Iskan, Monoğlu offers him a cigarette. Monoğlu's lighter, an old Zippo, flares immediately.

Holding the card by its edges, Iskan scans the information. She has seen the company name before, one of the shell operations the Hamits use. "Last night," she says, "was that when you had the…ah …visitors?"

Suner nods but then grimaces as he inhales.

"Who was here?"

"Two men…three…" He exhales slowly. "I hit the older, fat one when he said that Hafize…that we should move away. She will not. Never."

"The other men?" Iskan asks.

"A young man. Dark hair."

"And they've been here before?"

"No…yes… The young man was here before. Not the fat man, no."

Monoğlu gazes at a black motorcycle parked under the eaves of another shed. "And, he's the one who beat you?" Smoke escapes his nostrils when he speaks.

Suner nods but says, "No. The young man *and* the third man. They came in a big car. The third man—"

"A bodyguard?" Iskan asks.

"I don't know. He was big. A bodyguard or a driver, maybe." As he shrugs, his expression goes dark. "All three of them kicked me once I was on the ground."

"Could you identify the bodyguard?"

Suner taps ash into the dirt. "No. Maybe. He was very strong." He touches the side of his head. "He stayed by the car until I…until they beat me."

"Was he Turkish?" she asks.

He looks at her for a moment. "I don't know. He didn't speak."

"But the young man, you've seen him before?"

"Yes. He came before…"

"About buying your land?"

"Dede's land. This time, both places. Dede's and mine." He takes another drag on the cigarette and exhales before saying, "They said they were coming back. That I would take their offer then. That I would sell."

"The other man?" Iskan asks. "The one before. What was he like?"

"Rich."

She cocks her head.

"The two men looked alike. Both young. Brothers, maybe. But he had on fancy shoes. His hands were soft, like he did no work. And he had a fancy…very fancy…watch."

Monoğlu turns his phone toward Suner. "This man?"

"No. I know him. He grew up in town. The archeologist's son. But I have not seen him in years."

"You know the archeologist?" Iskan asks.

"Ah, yes…" Suner looks away. "Her mother was good to Hafize. To us."

Turning toward Iskan, Monoğlu asks, "The Russian?"

"No!" she snaps, as though he should not have brought up the Russian. She and Monoğlu agreed earlier to mention an anonymous Russian so that if any information about this meeting ever got back to Hamit, he would be misled.

Monoğlu scrolls his phone's screen again. "This man?"

"Yes." Mehmet's father's eyes grow wide as he looks more closely at Monoğlu. "That's him. How did you…?"

"But he did not come last night?" Iskan asks.

"No."

"Have you seen him, that man?" she asks.

"No. Not since…whenever that was."

"He has not come by at all in the last few days?"

"Not at all." He gives her a quizzical look. "No."

"His vehicle," Monoğlu says, "was found in the valley a few kilometers from here yesterday morning. But he wasn't in it."

"You haven't seen him?" Iskan repeats.

"No."

"We thought," Iskan says, "he might have been on his way to see you."

"He never came here." Suner's voice holds tension again.

"Okay," she says. "Can you describe the fat man? The one you hit."

"He has a bloody lip."

Monoğlu smiles. "And?"

"He had a Turkish stomach."

Monoğlu pats his own belly. "And?"

"Nothing special. Older, bald." Suner smiles for the first time as he adds, "But nothing like you. He was soft. A ring on his little finger. Gold." He shrugs. "Shiny shoes."

"The ring, any markings?" she asks.

"I didn't..."

"Where did it happen, the fight?" she asks. "Can you show us?"

"They came in... They just came onto my property without asking... Over there," he says, turning toward the parlor.

As the three of them walk back toward the parlor, Iskan hears a television tuned into some talk show. She says, "Get close. But don't walk on the spot."

"There," he says, pointing with his hand holding the cigarette. "Right there."

Three dark splotches of dried blood form a triangle in the dusty soil.

# 64

DIKILI, TURKEY

Wearing a blue tracksuit with white stripes, the Hamit family patriarch paces in the garden of his villa along the Aegean Sea near Dikili. It is early morning, the sun just risen, forty-eight hours after his son's Range Rover was discovered parked along a side road seven kilometers out in the Kaikos Valley—near, but not all that near, three of the family properties. The patriarch has not shaved, which he normally does early each morning. This time of day is usually when he thinks most clearly, but he is struggling to link thoughts together. His son has disappeared before, once from Istanbul and twice from Chicago. All three were gambling binges, Monaco first and Las Vegas the next two times. But in all three cases, social media posts and credit card receipts left a trail. But now, nothing. The patriarch's nephew, Bora, is checking the social media sites every half hour, and his banker has promised to call the moment there is any activity on the card. There's absolutely nothing there either.

Although birds are singing, the patriarch doesn't notice. His mind keeps jumping from scenario to scenario, all of them bad. The breeze is light enough that the leaves of the trees barely rustle. With villas to the north and south, the property is not isolated, but only bluff and beach stand between the villa and the Aegean. The smell of the sea only forty meters away does not reach him. He does not even hear the fountain gurgling next to him. The property's two-and-a-half-meter walls topped with black iron rails and concertina wire are impregnable, but that's no help whatsoever in this situation in which he needs news from the outside to reach him.

The local gendarma wanted to tow the Range Rover, but the patriarch sent Mustafa's two Georgians to retrieve it. The crew he had dust the vehicle found only his prints, his son's, his nephew's, and those of the Dikili slut that his son bangs whenever he's in town. The investigators he sent out into the fucking valley discovered Mustafa's shoe prints leading from the driver's door back onto the road where the car had been parked, but that's it. And Mustafa's phone, which he's never without, has had no GPS signal since the Range Rover was found. Mustafa did not tell the two Georgians assigned to protect him anything about where he was going when they last saw him while they were staking out the Bergama hospital. They assumed he went to see his slut, which he did most nights. She was still asleep when the Georgians barged in on her an hour after the car was found. She admitted, under duress, that Mustafa said he was coming over, but he never arrived.

The patriarch's cook, a bent old woman who served his father, brings out a steaming cup of tea and sets it on the glass-top table near the fountain. Still standing, the patriarch drops a single sugar cube into the cup. His shoulders are tight so he rolls his neck. While he stirs the tea with a demitasse spoon, he thinks again that someone Mustafa knew and trusted must have picked him up. But that's absurd. The boy knew few people in the area—and trusted no one except family members, his bodyguards, and, maybe, the slut, who doesn't even own a car. If there was any sign of trouble, he would have called his father. He always did whenever he was in a tough spot.

As the patriarch is sipping his tea, Bora comes out of the villa's French doors, shaking his head. "Still no contact," he says. "Not on any of the sites."

The patriarch nods but doesn't say anything. Although Bora has been dutiful the last two days, as he always is, he hasn't turned up anything either. He reminds people of Mustafa, but the patriarch knows the two boys are not all that alike. He admires Bora's willingness to take on any task assigned to him, no matter how difficult or unpleasant. The boy is bright, too, in his own way, but he's not brilliant like Mustafa. And he lacks sophistication. He could never be the face of the family that the patriarch has groomed his son to be—the fifth generation of the Hamit Enterprises leadership.

When they hear shouting by the villa's back gate, the patriarch knows by the anger in the voices that it's not a celebration of Mustafa's return.

"I'll check it," Bora says as he heads along the garden's path.

The patriarch sets down his tea which tastes bitter despite the sugar. He stares at a bee hovering around the rosebushes. The petals' red, the color of the Turkish flag, is brilliant in the morning light, but it fails to stir him. He has spent his adult life taking care of business, solving problems, making things happen, and he feels useless—worse, helpless.

Bora, who really does at a distance look like Mustafa, returns along the path leading two of the Georgians manhandling a scruffy man in rough jeans and a blue work shirt. The larger Georgian has the man's left arm bent sharply behind his back. The shorter has the barrel of a Glock 19 jammed into the nape of the man's neck.

"They found this," Bora says, "trying to enter the gate after the gardeners." He doesn't add that he knows the man because he does not want his uncle to know about what happened two days ago when that fat turd from Istanbul fucked up the buyout.

The Georgian wrenches the man's arm as he pushes him to his knees in front of the patriarch. Blood leaks from the man's nose and lower lip.

For a moment, the patriarch thinks the man might have news of Mustafa.

"He was carrying this," Bora says, holding up a knife with black tape wrapped around the haft. The fourteen-centimeter blade glints in the morning light.

"Why are you here?" the patriarch asks, his voice as even as he can make it.

As the man looks up at the patriarch, his eyes gleam with hatred. His face is swollen and discolored, which can't be the work of the Georgians just now.

When the smaller Georgian kicks him in the stomach, the man falls over, curls up, and gasps for breath. The patriarch waits until the man, still panting like a dog, uncurls. "I asked you a question," he says. As the Georgian plants his foot to kick the man again, the patriarch shakes his head once. "Are you here about my son?" The patriarch nods, and the Georgians raise the man again to his knees. "Are you?" the patriarch repeats.

The man's eyes, squinting with pain, fire. "*Your* son?" He spits blood onto the flagstones and tries to catch his breath. "My son!"

"What?" The patriarch fails to keep his voice cold.

The man coughs up more blood. "You murdered my son!"

The patriarch has had the sons of his enemies dealt with over the years, but he has no idea who this man is. Turning to Bora, he asks, "Any ID?"

"He's the father of the boy killed in the ISIL bombing at Bergama's acropolis," Bora says.

The patriarch clenches his fist and screams, "Where is my son?"

Still bent over, the man raises his head. His eyes meet the patriarch's. "*My son is dead! You* murdered him!" There is no fear in the man's eyes. None.

Bora cuffs the man's head with the back of his hand.

"No!" the patriarch says, glowering at Bora. "Let him speak!"

The man cocks his head, glares at Bora. "The funicular! You had my son murdered. My father-in-law. All of those people. You destroyed my family…"

"I had nothing to do with…," the patriarch begins, but then stops himself. He never explains himself or his actions to anyone, and certainly not to some farmer from out in the valley.

Bora punches the man in the ear.

The man does not fall over again.

"Stop!" the patriarch shouts at Bora. "You…," he says to the man, his voice gone cold, "who told you that?"

The man glowers up at him, sniffs at the blood, but does not raise his hand to wipe it away.

"Who told you that?" the patriarch snarls.

The man does not blink. "The investigator from the Ministry."

"What investigator?" The veins in the patriarch's neck bulge. "What ministry?"

"The woman from Ankara."

"A woman?" The patriarch's tone is both angry and skeptical.

The man looks from the patriarch to Bora and back. "Yes." He starts to smile through his bloody teeth, as though his words are the blade of a knife cutting toward truth. "They did not give me their names." His eyes do not blink as the blade twists. "She showed me her ID, but so fast that I didn't see the name."

The patriarch runs his upper teeth over his lower lip. "They?"

"An older man was with her. Worked for her."

"You're sure?"

Still unblinking, the man says nothing.

The vein in the patriarch's neck pulses. "The man worked *for* the woman?" The possibilities—the probabilities—are vile. He has been warned that the current investigation comes from high up, but it was supposed to be stopped already. Politicians—they are inherently untrustworthy, always serving their own interests first... Not as bad as extremists... But this! He has paid a lot of money for a long time to *protect* the family's interests. Retribution must be swift and fierce.

The patriarch's breath catches in his throat. Could Ministry agents have picked up Mustafa out there in the valley? Was there a meeting? Is that what happened? The log of Mustafa's cell phone showed no calls after he left the Georgians outside the hospital—and really nothing but routine calls before that. Are Ministry agents trying to turn Mustafa? He wouldn't cave... But Mustafa, for all of his excellent qualities, does have weaknesses. Could he stand up to intense interrogations? Death threats? Will they find out that Mustafa and Bora were providing logistical support to the ISIL terrorist? "You lost your son in the bombing?" he says to the bloody, kneeling man. It's not really a question. "Your only son?"

The man doesn't say anything, but the answer is in his eyes.

"You won't believe me," the patriarch says, his voice low, soothing, "but I'm sorry for your loss." He finds himself almost believing his own words. He looks down at the man. He has that rural toughness that the patriarch's own grandfather had. He'll never tell them more than he already has, never bargain, never plead, never grovel. His grief has made him dangerous. The patriarch takes a breath before glowering at the larger Georgian. "Take him to the farmhouse," he commands. "Do not hurt him unless he struggles. We will need to speak to him again later."

As the Georgians lift the man to his feet and turn him, the patriarch leans close to Bora and whispers, "Break him. Then, kill him." His voice is weary. "He knows too much." He can finally hear the fountain. Even the bees. He is no closer to understanding what has happened to Mustafa than he was before the man appeared, but he is at least finally doing something—fixing a problem for the family.

 65

KAIKOS VALLEY

Bora, the Hamit patriarch's nephew, paces behind the ramshackle farmhouse. He stops near the rusted wheel of a broken-down farm wagon and looks at the cell phone he only uses for family calls. Unable to get any more than two bars anywhere in the vicinity, he calls his uncle, even though he knows the poor reception will anger the man. When he hears a scream, he glances at the open cellar door. The farmhouse is isolated, far out along a dirt road, and so the screams don't matter. There are no curious neighbors, and vehicles only pass this way once in a while. In the time the Georgians have worked the farmer over, they have gotten almost no information out of him, but Bora has to make his report anyway.

When the patriarch answers, Bora asks, "Is there any news?"

"No."

Although Bora waits a few seconds, his uncle says nothing more. "We've got something here," he says.

"What?" Again, there is nothing more.

Bora sets his left cross-trainer on the wheel's rim. Tall, yellow wild-flowers wave on the fallow land beyond the decrepit barn. "The farmer admitted there was a Russian."

"A Russian?" Ire surges through the phone.

"Yes." Before his uncle can interrupt, he adds, "He's not coherent…"

The screams from the cellar have stopped—for the moment. "But a Russian's definitely involved...somehow."

"Vlad? What fucking Russian?"

"No name... Just, 'the Russian.' The investigators apparently mentioned the Russian a couple of times." Bora isn't sure how many times, but he will not let his uncle know that. He looks over at the van they used to transport the farmer and, earlier, the Irishman. They have parked it between the barn and the olive trees where it cannot be seen from the road.

"Find..." Bora's uncle says more, but it's indecipherable over the phone's static.

Afraid to ask his uncle to repeat himself, Bora says, "Okay. Okay!"

The line goes dead. Bora waits for his uncle to call back, but he does not. *Find out...what?* he wonders. He stuffs the phone into his jeans pocket. *Something...something more!* But getting more information out of the farmer will be like squeezing juice from a turnip. The man won't survive much more of the Georgians' work, and he probably doesn't even know anything more. His description of the woman—blonde, athletic, intense, authoritative—doesn't fit anyone in any of the higher levels of any of the ministries his uncle deals with. And, the description of the man—stocky, bald, tough—fits practically everyone.

As Bora heads down the dilapidated wooden steps to the cellar, four figures rise out of the wildflowers. Each is dressed in camouflage, each has his face covered by a ski mask, and each carries in a gloved hand a 9mm automatic pistol with a sound suppressor. The figure on the left also has an M416 carbine, the one on the right an MP7 submachine gun.

The cellar's twilight outlines the farmer, stripped to the waist and trussed between two pillars, as though he has been crucified in midair. His ankles are bound, and, no longer able to stand, he sags forward and to his left. Each wrist is tied, the ropes extended to the pillars, but all of the farmer's weight hangs from his dislocated right shoulder. Four of his fingers are also dislocated, bent backward at angles, the result of a series of questions the farmer failed to answer. His head is bowed, and blood runs down his chest over the burn marks made by the smaller Georgian's cigar. The farmer's breath rattles erratically.

Bora nods to each of the Georgians, who have themselves removed their shirts and pants so that their clothes don't get splattered with blood. Without the use of high-tech gadgets or, for that matter, any equipment, even pliers, they have already reduced the farmer to something far less than a man. Their torture is fast, simple, efficient—and brutal. They did not put out the farmer's eyes or cut off his ears because Bora wanted him to experience the mutilation with all of his senses. The farmer has pissed himself and shit his pants, but that's to be expected.

Shadows dim the light from the door. Six quick pops, and both Georgians collapse into the cellar's dirt. Bora barely turns before bullets strike him in the left eye and chest. The convulsing stops within seconds. The leader gestures for each of the two men on his flanks to go up the stairs and maintain the perimeter with their fourth teammate. They all keep their masks on. "All clear," he says into his body mic. "Send in the investigator." He surveys the cellar with his body cam, but touches nothing, not even the wretch who is strung up.

As Tuğçe Iskan descends the steps into the cellar's dimness, she is met by gunsmoke, the odor of rot, the smell of men—living and dead—and the stench of piss and shit, new and old. She scans the place carefully, noting the detritus: the dusty, discarded, plastic liter water bottles; the blue plastic pail; the crumpled brown-paper bags; and the three bodies akimbo in the dirt.

"Nothing," she asks the team leader, "has been disturbed?" She has never seen any of the team members' faces. She came in a separate black suv that halted two kilometers from the site. Although there was radio contact, she saw nothing. All she knew, all she knows, is that the men, including the paramedics who will arrive any moment, are retired special forces veterans.

"Nothing," the team leader says. "We will clean the place as soon as you are finished here."

His voice sounds familiar. She looks at his eyes—brown, narrow, intense—and is sure she has seen them before.

Looking away from her, the team leader steps back into the shadows.

She follows him with her eyes. She thought this was her op. She was told it was. Or was it just an audition? At least, it was her idea. Or was it Nihat's? She can remember exactly where they had the conversation but not exactly who said what. And in any case, the execution of the op was entirely out of her hands. She rode in the command vehicle, but she gave no commands. She wasn't even a spectator to any of it. And now—now Mehmet's father hangs half-dead before her. She is responsible for him—responsible, too, for the corpses on the floor.

As Iskan approaches Engin Suner, each wound, each burn and cut and bruise and break and dislocation, sears itself into her brain. At least, he is still breathing. Broken, mangled…but breathing. Carefully, delicately, she lifts Suner's chin. His face is a quagmire of tissue and blood. His eyes are open but unfocused. She cups the side of his head with her right hand. "I'm sorry," she says. "We came as fast…" She is unable to finish the sentence. A void, an emptiness, billows in the pit of her stomach. She doesn't actually even know if they came as quickly as possible—and the team leader is already gone.

When Suner hears her voice, his eyes clear, but only a bit. Choking up blood, he murmurs through his shattered teeth, "K…kill me."

She continues to cradle his head. "An ambulance is coming," she says in the softest voice she can muster. "Will be here…soon." This is her op, her mission, and this is what she has wrought. "Help is coming. Hold on…"

Suner's eyes focus on her face. His look is one she has never seen before. "Kill me," he repeats.

 ## 66

BERGAMA

As Elif Boroğlu closes the door to her mother's private room in Bergama Hospital, Tuğçe Iskan is walking along the hospital's corridor toward her. "Hello," Iskan says. Her voice is low, almost a whisper. Her face is gaunt. Her khaki pants are loose on her hips. In the five weeks since the bombing at the Aesklepion, she has lost seven kilos.

Elif nods to her, saying, "It's not a good time…" Her voice is also quiet. Her hair is cut short, even shorter than Iskan's. Her eyes are badly bloodshot, as though she no longer sleeps at all.

"No time would be good for her to see me," Iskan says. "I was just stopping by to check on her progress…"

Elif shakes her head. "What progress?" she asks both Iskan and herself. "She won't respond to *anyone.*"

"She might respond to me." Iskan's voice is heavy with self-deprecating irony, something new in her life.

As the two women head together past the nursing station, Elif says, "Her vitals are better, much better, but she isn't. She can't…or she *refuses* to communicate. Even with my grandmother and me." Her tone is both sad and angry. "It's killing Anneanne. I think Mom's aware that she's paralyzed from her neck down, but she won't acknowledge it." When they reach the elevator, Elif, her hand shaking, presses the button. "Why," she asks, "are you really here?"

"I need to talk with you."

"That's why you came to Bergama?"

"No," Iskan says. "My new boss sent me to check on the renovation work at both the bombing sites. And some other stuff."

They ride to the ground floor and walk out the hospital's main entrance without saying anything more. When they get outside into the morning's heat, Iskan looks across the circular drive at the back of the statue of a seated man with his left arm resting on a stack of oversized books. To the statue's right, the Turkish flag droops on a pole. "Can we talk," she asks, "for a little while?"

To their left an ambulance, lights flashing, is pulling up to the hospital's emergency entrance. Elif points to the orange and white kantin sign to their right.

An awning shades the kantin's patio, but it is not air-conditioned. The air is still. Each of the dozen tables, the color of mud, is surrounded by four plastic chairs. A cheap tin ashtray lies on every table. One elderly couple sits smoking at a table near the kantin's entrance, but no one else is on the patio. A tan, mangy dog sleeps on the patio's brick floor. While Iskan goes inside to get Elif and herself a carton of ayran, Elif finds a table away from the stench of cigarette smoke. Just to her left, an orange, coin-operated phone charger stands on a pedestal. Fifteen different plugs hang on wires like tentacles.

When Iskan returns with the ayran, Elif says, "You have a *new* boss?" In recent weeks she has become as bad as Iskan at small talk.

Iskan opens her carton. "Yes. I was transferred to a special unit just before the Aesklepion bombing." She does not provide any more information. She will not lie to Elif, but she can't tell her everything.

"And what does your new boss really want you to do here in Bergama?" Elif leaves her carton untouched.

"Tie up loose ends." Iskan takes a long pull on the straw. "Find out things."

"So this is an interview? An official visit?"

"No. I have questions, but I—"

"Ministry questions?"

Iskan stares at Elif's face. Much of the light has gone out of Elif's bloodshot eyes. The rings beneath them are dark and puffy. Her clear skin has become pale and chafed, especially her cheeks, as though she has become more troglodyte than human. Her once-beautiful hair looks like Elif herself chopped it down. "No," Iskan says. "Not a word either of us say will be in my report. Nothing." She bends and crimps the top of the carton. "I need to talk *with* you. I don't know who I trust anymore."

Elif's laugh is sharp, almost mean. *"You don't!"* A siren from a vehicle they cannot see is approaching the hospital fast.

"I feel like my mentor, my friend, may have set me up to do things that I...that caused me to..." Iskan squeezes the top of the carton. "I've done what I've done. What happened was my doing, my operation, but I didn't think it through...all the consequences." She tries to muster a smile but can't. "It was necessary, the op. And I ran it. But he..." She doesn't think she can tell Elif much of what happened.

"Is your mentor your new boss?"

"No." She has wondered, though, if Nihat Monoğlu is really running the entire operation to put the Hamits and their governmental cronies out of business. "My boss...he's ex-special forces...I think... I don't really know. The unit is cracking down on the illegal trafficking in artifacts. Not just the usual public-relations bullshit like what I was involved in before, but hitting them hard."

"You would be good at that." Elif reaches for her carton of ayran but stops her hand before she touches it.

Iskan can't tell if Elif's statement is a compliment. "I am. But I don't know... I've already done things..."

"Evil men have suffered?" Elif makes no reference to her own actions.

"Not just evil men." She pushes her carton aside, folds her hands on the table, and leans forward. Her blue eyes light as her voice becomes a whisper. "But evil men, yes. Definitely. A Russian oligarch, a really bad guy, burned to death when his yacht was blown up in the Aegean. Though the media reported the murder as typical Russian infighting among Putin's perversely corrupt friends, it was Mustafa Hamit's vengeance. Since his son, his *only* child, disappeared, Hamit has been out of his mind." She looks into Elif's bleary eyes, which don't blink. "His favorite nephew disappeared, too, along with a number of his thugs."

Iskan gazes out at the *Ambulance Bufe* beyond the hospital's circular drive. Scores of cases of water bottles are stacked next to the shed-like building. "Hamit thinks he's been betrayed," she continues, "and he's hell-bent on getting even. A governmental minister, pretty high up, one of Hamit's ex-cronies, died in a car crash on his way to Bodrum. That was in the news. Two other ministers, even higher up, have vanished. That wasn't in the news."

Leaning forward as well, Elif says, "Yes, there've been disappearances around here, too." Her face is stone, but a vein in her neck pulses.

Iskan turns her carton 180 degrees and then turns it again. "How's your brother?"

"Fine," Elif snarls, then checks herself. She drums the table with the fingers of her right hand. "I don't have any idea where he is, if that's what you're supposed to find out."

"I'm not supposed to find out anything." Irritation seeps into Iskan's voice for the first time. She looks at Elif's hand, which is rougher than it was when they met before. The fingernails are all cut—or bitten—down. The right forefinger's nail is cracked. "I was just wondering."

At first, Elif doesn't say anything. She drops her hand into her lap and then looks into Iskan's eyes. "Serkan's a mess," she says finally. "I really don't know where he is or what he's doing, but he sounds awful." She glances at the phone charger. "We talk for less than two minutes once a week." She lifts and waves her hand as if to dismiss the subject. "So you're winning the war against the Hamits?" she asks.

"Maybe." Iskan nods but looks away. "It doesn't feel like it."

"There's no winning," Elif says. She drums the table with both hands. "Are we safe, my family? Safe from the Hamits' wrath?"

Iskan holds her gaze. "Not Serkan. Not at all. If you are, which I believe you are, it's only because he thinks you're inconsequential. A woman artist."

The two women fall silent again. The two old people rise from their table and, still smoking, totter toward the hospital's main entrance. They follow the plastic yellow path set in the sidewalk's stone. The mangy dog looks up briefly but then settles back.

Elif presses the palms of her hands onto the table and asks, "Did Hamit kill Mehmet's father?"

"No." Again, Iskan offers no more information.

"My grandmother has seen Mehmet's mother wandering around town muttering about her husband being murdered like her father and son."

"Engin Suner is alive."

"Nobody here has seen him."

Iskan stifles the urge to lie, then admits, "Mustafa Hamit tried to have him killed." She wipes her left hand across her mouth. "Suner's in Istanbul. Recovering in a...private...rehab facility." "Recovering," Iskan knows, isn't the right word. Engin Suner will not be the man he was. The physical and emotional damage is too severe.

"Has she been told that?" Elif asks, pressing Iskan.

"Yes. But she doesn't believe it. She's not...in her right mind."

Elif leans farther forward so her face is close to Iskan's. "Are any of us?" she asks.

 67

BERGAMA

Elif Boroğlu struggles to remove the rubble block-
ing her way through the tunnel. Dust motes swirl in the arc of her
miner's lamp. She is covered in grime—boots, jeans, work gloves,
shower cap, and hoodie. Although it is not hot this far underground,
her face sweats beneath her goggles and dust mask. She is not sure
whether she is under the Aesklepion or the hillside pasture beyond the
theater. She has been working her way through this tunnel for close
to a month, having chosen it because it had once been wide enough
to transport large objects. It is connected to one of the theater's pas-
sageways—but not the one from which the Syrian boy emerged. The
whole theater is still cordoned off, though no investigation continues.

Elif has worked here every night from one o'clock to five o'clock.
No one, she believes, has seen her come and go from her studio or
noticed the secret entry, obscured by a fir tree's branches, she has
cut in the Aesklepion's outer fence. The Aesklepion's dogs, which
she has known since she opened her studio six years ago, greet her
quietly and sometimes escort her as she slinks through the curing
center's grounds.

Elif's days are still spent going to the hospital with her grandmother
to visit her mother. She has told her anneanne that she is working
in her studio at night, which, in a sense, she is—though she has not
sculpted a single figurine since her mother was attacked. She washes

herself and her clothes before dawn each morning at the studio and then sleeps there on her yoga mat for three or four hours—only to wake from nightmares of her decapitating rows of kneeling men in headscarves. She uses a single-edged sword that stays sharp despite all of the carnage she causes. The severed heads' unblinking, sightless eyes stare up at her. She cannot scrub their blood from her hands.

Elif loosens the largest stone and pulls it free. When she inserts her arm into the hole, she feels *nothing*. For a moment, she forgets to breathe. She can't fit her face and her lamp into the void at the same time, but she catches a glimpse of what might be a vaulted ceiling. Forcing herself to slow down, she yanks at the next stone below the hole. She has made breakthroughs in tunnels before, but she has never been searching for something in particular. Her tunneling has always been an adventure—exploration. Here it is obsession. She starts to claw at the smaller stones, widening the hole. Her breath quickens, and sweat runs down her temples. If it weren't for the gloves, her fingers would be bleeding.

She stops herself, once again realizing how much she has been affected, is being *infected*, by her mother's obsession. Slowly and deliberately, she leans back, takes off her right glove, and lowers her mask. She unclips her canteen from her belt and drinks deeply. Choking, she coughs up a mouthful of water. After taking another, smaller sip, she recaps the canteen and returns to work. As she enlarges the hole she can see that the chamber's ceiling is, indeed, vaulted, though parts of it have collapsed. Clearing a path through the tunnel is similar to what she did growing up, but what she's doing now *feels* fundamentally different. She is agitated, not excited.

When she widens the hole still farther, she thinks she might be able to squirm through, but she stops herself yet again. Even at an angle, her hips won't make it, so she returns to the task. Dust whirls and falls in the arc of her light. Finally, extending her arms ahead of herself, she wriggles into the gap, scraping her shoulders, breasts, and hips. And then she is sliding and skidding head first. She finds herself panting, facedown, on a slope of debris. She swings her legs around in front of her and plants her feet so that up is no longer down.

Although she straightens her lamp, goggles, and mask, she can, at first, see nothing through the dust storm she has created.

She tries not to move until the dust settles. Turning her head, she pans the light. There is something…shadows and contours…definitely something…ahead. When she finally can see recessed shelves cut into the rock, she rises slowly from the rubble, adjusts her goggles, and approaches as though she were on a precipice in a blizzard. There on the recessed stone shelves blanketed in dust are rolls of parchment —a lot of them. To her right, there are more shelves, some collapsed and some near the bottom buried. She reaches out but doesn't touch anything.

This is quite a find, whatever it is. The Aesklepion had its own library, but she is under the wrong part of the curing center's grounds, if she is under the Aesklepion at all. Marc Antony supposedly gave Pergamon's library to Cleopatra, but no one has ever been able to show that all—*or, really, any*—of the parchments were shipped to Alexandria. Pergamon's leading citizens like Nicon, Galen's father, had private libraries. Galen also sent books, his own and classic Greek works, back to Pergamon. Clasping her hands behind her back, she leans her face close to the shelves. Too many of the parchments are dust shrouded, but what little writing she can see looks to her like Attic Greek—but that may be wishful thinking.

Coughing into her mask, she remembers the problems her gift of Galen's letter caused her mother. It was really the source, the taproot, of much of the pain. She scans the shelves—there must be hundreds, *thousands,* of texts here, most intact. Already torn about what to do—or not do—she stares at the shelves. Her breathing is coming in gasps that draw the mask against her lips, but she is only now realizing it. She is shaking, unable to touch the parchments or turn away. And she is already past her deadline for leaving the tunnel undetected.

 **68**

BERGAMA

When Elif Boroğlu finally pulls her attention from the rolls of parchment and turns to her left, her miner's light catches something bright in the dust near the floor. The far end of the chamber is completely covered with rubble, but the pile tapers toward the area where she is standing. She takes three steps closer and stares down at a bronze left foot shrouded in fine dust. As she kneels and gently wipes away the grime, she begins to shake again. The perfectly wrought toes look alive, as though they belong to someone extant beneath the debris. The ankle bone shines in her light. The leg rises at an angle of about forty degrees. The calf muscle is that of an athlete, practically the size of a man living today. She recognizes the pose as that of one of antiquity's most famous Hellenistic statues, long thought lost. Still kneeling, she uncovers the leg to the thigh. Although the bronze kneecap is dinged, it is intact.

Elif sits back on her haunches and looks up. The ceiling a couple of meters behind the statue has collapsed, but the arch directly above has not. It may be that the rubble covering the statue is mostly dust that during an earthquake poured over it or accrued like sand spreading across the floor. She doesn't know so she keeps clearing the grit away. Sweeping beneath the left knee, she finds the right foot and lower leg lying horizontally on their bronze base—a warrior's shield.

As far as she can tell, the right foot is perfect—the tendons, the veins, the arch, the toes, the space between the toes, each toenail. And the left thigh above the foot but not touching it is muscular, but not idealized, not exaggerated. She is choking up, not at the beauty of the statue, though it is the most beautiful she has ever seen, nor at its grandeur or even its authenticity, but at its sheer *humanity*.

Unaware of time's passing, she keeps exposing more of the statue. She has in Italy seen a marble copy of the statue, but this is wholly different. The marble copies have mass, gravitas—this has vitality, vibrance. *The Dying Gladiator*, the Europeans called the statue until they deduced from the torque, the warrior's twisted metal neck ring, that he must represent a Galatian whom the Pergamene kings conquered in the third century BCE. *The Dying Gaul* that she is unearthing seems to be living on here in Bergama long after the empires, the conquerors as well as the conquered, have vanished.

Her work becomes feverish. Like a dog, she uses both hands to scoop the earth back between her legs. Dust eddies. When she lays bare the scrotum and penis, she remembers that the Galatians fought against Hellenistic armor naked, which was courageous but essentially stupid. Sandy grit sifts down over the shoulder and arm. As she moves larger chunks of stone, she finds that the left shoulder is damaged, as is the back of the head. The statue's hair is spiky; the torque around the neck has bulbous ends. The undamaged face is tilted down.

She sits back on her haunches again, her legs quivering, and gazes at the face. The Galatian's brow is heavy, his cheekbones high, his nose prominent, his mustache trimmed. Pain shows, but his expression is impassive, impenetrable. She leans forward, turns her head, and stares into his eyes, but they do not look back at her. In his moment, he is, as her grandmother was after Özlem was attacked, focusing on something beyond. He seems to see across the centuries what Elif cannot.

*The Dying Gaul* is mute, utterly silent. He does not, as some of her figurines have, speak to her. But they were her creations, and this man is not. His moment is beyond speech, and she is deeply moved, touched to her core by his silence. His life is ending, but here he is twenty-three hundred years later. His dignity in the face of death keeps him alive for her. Defeated, yes. Damaged and buried. Yet undestroyed. But for how much longer? In the brief time since Bergama's funicular bombing, there have been two deadly earthquakes nearby, one on Lesbos and the other on Kos. And others will come, not just in geological time but in her own.

She glances over her shoulder. Hundreds of rolls of parchment lie in the dust she has stirred. There must be more. And what else is interred here in this cultural tumulus? What else does the rubble conceal in this room ruptured by earthquakes? Knowing this chamber exists could well save her mother, reinvigorate her. Or, more likely, kill her. Or get both Elif and her killed. Elif's taking Galen's letter from the tomb in the hinterland caused havoc. What chaos would a thousand rolls of parchment wreak? And this statue, in and of itself, with whatever else lies in this chamber—what strife would ensue? The Galatian belongs solely to his caretaker, Mother Earth.

Elif rises to her feet. She will take nothing from this cache and tell no one about it. But she also understands that she is incapable of just walking away. She is wholly taken by this statue, this Dying Gaul, Pergamon's vanquished enemy that the sculptor filled with life, with humanity and dignity even in the face of death. She has made no attempt to render her enemy, and she feels no shame in the murder she committed. It was a necessity. She had to save her brother's life and perhaps her grandmother's and her own. Mustafa Hamit had little humanity and less dignity. His soul was lost long before she took his life. But she herself was also diminished by her action. In that tomb, she lost whatever purity her soul possessed.

Elif drops again to her knees. Dust still sifts over the shoulders and down across the torso. Her presence here will, sooner or later, draw others. Inevitably. She must go now. Must have been gone already. But she cannot turn away from the statue's bowed head. She stares again at that face that remains inward, private, solitary. She is no longer shaking. She could stay here until her lamp's battery dies. She could wall herself in and live out her life here, wasting away. She is, she thinks, every bit as alone, as isolated, as the Galatian. Utterly entranced by a twenty-three-hundred-year-old bronze statue, she is stuck here in her own time without whatever saving grace the ancient sculptor gave the Gaul.

# ☆ 69
BERGAMA'S HINTERLAND

Just after midnight, seven women file up the cliff-like ridge's steep trail. When they reach a sharp cutback near the crest of the ridge, their leader veers away toward a sheer stone wall. Though none of the others has ever been to this place, they follow, clambering over boulders until they reach a narrow plateau just wide enough for the women to congregate. Water trickles from a cleft to the right of the waist-high mouth of a cave. The night, lit by a crescent moon and an expanse of stars, is clear, but the air is humid, a heaviness devoid of wind. The journey up here has been arduous, taking the women far away from the road, any road. They climbed quietly along sloping forest trails and across outcroppings for over an hour. As they undress, they begin to chant softly.

Tuğçe Iskan, the new member of the group, turns and gazes for a moment at the ancient stone columns of the Temple of Athena on Pergamon's acropolis eight kilometers across the Kaikos Valley. She is breathing hard, her stamina reduced by her current anxiousness and by a recent, sudden weight loss, the byproduct of the constant stress in her new job. She chants along with the others but not in a language she knows. The sounds and the rhythms seem to her both ancient and modern, in and out of time. The moon has cycled three times since the bombing at Bergama's funicular that for her seems a lifetime ago. Her left hand clasps little Mehmet Suner's gold Hadrian

Aureus coin that she retrieved from under the pithos in the Bergama Museum's inner courtyard.

As the women form a semicircle facing the cave's entrance, their voices lower to a murmur. Elif Boroğlu, their leader, her dark hair chopped short, steps into the middle of the group. Turning slowly, she raises aloft a figurine—a dark heavyset, robed goddess holding a single-edged sword in one hand and a bearded, severed head in the other. Three snakes emerge from the figurine's thick hair. Elif raises her other arm, grasps the statue with both hands, and says, "Forgive us, Mother, our offenses against you and each other." She stretches into the night sky. "We cannot reclaim our lost innocence, but we can try to restore the balance. We can hope that those broken by violence, by the meanness, the greed and arrogance, of men, may begin to heal. We cannot make any of us whole again, but we can accept the broken among us. And we can dedicate ourselves, each in her own way, to creating the balance that we so deeply need."

But Elif knows, or rather, she is learning, that restoring balance and becoming whole again are not easy. Incantations may help, as does having like-minded friends, but she herself is not healing. Her soul is not what it was, and she has begun to question her own leadership. Her nightmares have not abated; she still cannot sculpt any figurines. The clay in her studio has dried up and cracked. Clare, the American, has commissioned her to make another gold amulet, but Elif has not yet finished even a single wax model.

Elif's boyfriend has been home on leave, but even with him she has vacillated between listlessness and aggressive anger. His job is to defend their country, killing whenever it is necessary to do so, which is, she believes, exactly what she did, but she hasn't been able to bring herself to tell him what happened in that grave in the Kaikos Valley or to ask him how he finds balance given what he has to do each day. And holding back from him, from her mother, from everyone, the news about what she has discovered beneath the Aesklepion is both eating away at her and, paradoxically, energizing her. She is the only person in the world who knows *The Dying Gaul,* speaks to the ancient bronze statue, waits for the statue to speak to her. Maybe, she thinks, she doesn't really want to heal. Killing Mustafa Hamit was traumatic, not at all a thrill, but knowing then that she had to do it and now that she can get away with murder—that offers a certain power.

Elif lowers the icon and places it in a niche that she herself carved in the rock wall two days ago. She folds her hands, bows to the goddess, and steps back. She must appear to the others as though she is dedicating herself to this warrior, but she knows well that she has already done that. A battle has begun, a full-scale war is coming, a conflict between ideology and the freedom of people, between men in power and the nation's citizens—and what's at stake is no less than the values and precepts upon which Ataturk built the nation.

She has not told the others to commit themselves, not even suggested it, but she watches as the first of them, a kindergarten teacher with black hair piled and pinned on her head, steps forward, bows deeply, and says, "I vow to use my skills on behalf of the Earth and the dear children that Ataturk loved."

Each of the other women comes forward and makes her own statement. The last is Tuğçe Iskan, the neophyte. She is sweating profusely, not enjoying this moment, not even understanding all of it, but feeling part of it. She has not often felt particularly good or bad in her life. She has rather measured herself in terms of utility, the amount of work she got done and the quality of that work. And in those terms, the operation she led has been a success. Her work since then has been worthwhile. But she has been waking in the darkness, feeling a suffocating heaviness about what has happened, especially to Mehmet's parents. She has been feeling responsible for the pain of the mother who lost her father and her son, the woman whose husband still lies broken in a secret Istanbul intensive care unit. She understands that much of what has happened is not her fault, but she is to blame both for the damage to that man and the immeasurable pain of his wife, who is not even allowed to know where he is hidden.

Iskan knows, too, that feeling guilt is in some way a first step, an important and necessary initial foray, into the world of deep emotion that she has so seldom ventured. She has been angry, of course, sometimes terribly, and proud of her abilities, her accomplishments—but now she feels *sorry*, which may ultimately be healthy but for her is currently *awful*. When Elif invited her to attend the group's meeting when the two of them talked again a week ago, she explained that there was no set ritual, no test to pass, no feat to perform. All Tuğçe had to do was commit herself wholeheartedly to the moment. To join the group, she must simply devote herself to the Earth—this sanctuary, the surrounding valley, the sea beyond, and the sky above.

But Elif also invited Iskan to speak with the others. And now, energy is pulsing through the crescent of women around the mouth of this cave. Their chanting rises and falls with an improvised rhythm not, as it has so often in the past, building to a crescendo. Their sweat glistens in the scant light. Elif waves, bidding Iskan to come into the center of the semicircle. She looks at each of the others who are again lowering their chants to a murmur that to her sounds like the turn of the planets and the wheel of the night.

Iskan is sweating even harder without knowing if it is the heat of the night or the anxiety of the moment—or both. Feeling her eyes welling, she bows her head and says, "I am sorry, Mother, for the wrong I have done in the name of right. For those I have hurt in my attempts to…." A tear runs down her left cheek. She has not wept openly since primary school when she hardened herself against those who did not understand her and would not try. She clears her throat and continues, "I will use my new position to right the wrongs being inflicted on our people." She does not know what that will entail, but she is beginning to understand the depth of the commitment she is making. "I ask you, all of you," she says to the others, "to accept me as I am…." There is more, much more, to say, but she is too choked up. She wants to tell them that she is *different*. That she has always been the bird without a flock, the wolf without a pack. That when she was a child, she was not allowed into the kitchen when her mother, her family, was cooking…and that she came to like that isolation. That at school, she won awards, but kept to herself, never joining any team. That in her work, she avoided cronyism and the corruption that went with it. That though she did her jobs well, she was shunned by and in turn avoided most of her colleagues. That it was not arrogance, as some of them would say, but rather a deep isolation. That she has always been the outsider who did not fit into any inner circle. There is so much more, but she does not now have the words. None at all.

Hyperventilating, Iskan turns toward the cave. Ducking, she enters the darkness that is both cramped and infinite. She drops to her knees, crawls forward seven meters, and begins feeling around on the rock with her right hand. She doesn't know what she is looking for, but she knows she will find it here in the pitch dark. She switches the Hadrian Aureus to her right hand and brushes the wall with her left as she crawls forward. She crouches and then rises to standing, her head still bowed, careful not to hit it on the rock.

Iskan squeezes her eyes shut until she sees stars. Finally, she finds a cleft less than the width of her forefinger. She transfers the coin again. Tangible but not visible, the coin holds no sheen here, its value no more or less than the rest of the rock. As she jams it, edge first, deep into the fissure, the weeping comes. No one except Özlem and Nihat knows that she has the coin—and *no one* knows she brought it with her. It is time to give it back, to return it to the Earth as Mehmet and his grandfather have been, as Hafize and Engin Suner will be. As she herself will be. Tears stream, her shoulders heave, and her breath comes in gasps.

# ORACLE

$W$*e accept another among us. Her auburn hair is tangled beneath her white scarf. Her eyes are downcast, her spirit quashed. She shuffles more slowly than the oldest of us. Her sadness sinks beyond despair. The woman has learned the actual cost, the deep cost, of your greed and your lust for power and your craving for violence which have been passed down from millennium to millennium to millennium back to Cybele's time and before. We can offer the woman companionship but not hope.*

*We need each other. We need society, but our societies clash. And time is an arrow as much as a ring. Gods rise and fall, taking states and caliphates, nations and empires with them. Sultans, sovereigns, czars, shahs, caliphs, moguls, premiers, and presidents come and go—inevitably. And you persist in worshipping mere idols, specious icons, apocryphal avatars. Current potentates, having learned nothing, annihilate the wisdom of the ages—culture, civility, civilization itself. Ambition threatens yet again. Evil stalks once more. The Aesklepion, the curing center where death was officially banned, is itself the site of another massacre. It and the Acropolis are scarred, as are we all.*

*And yet our need for society endures. We go on speaking through time: The earth will quake again, destroying your shrines and altars, your monuments and memorials, once more. And yet the Aesklepion's sacred fountain will still flow. The spring will pulse with light, despite the carnage. Worship no god. Breathe, instead, the flow of light, the sacred energy everywhere. Love the earth. Celebrate birth and rebirth. Respect life, yours and ours and others'. Listen to the springs, the wind, the valley, the hills, the sunlight and the darkness—the music that is within each of us and around all of us.*

*Stray, sacred dogs lie among us still. Even in the Aesklepion's damaged theater, dogs congregate as though they are on watch. And, perhaps, they are—waiting for the ancient Mothers to return. Or for new goddesses to rise from the devastation, the ashes, the ruins, the chaos.*

BOOKS BY JAY AMBERG

*The Healer's Daughters*
*Bone Box*
*Cycle*
*America's Fool*
*Whale Song*
*52 Poems for Men*
AMIKA PRESS

*Doubloon*
*Blackbird Singing*
FORGE BOOKS

*Deep Gold*
WARNER BOOKS

*School Smarts*
*The Study Skills Handbook*
*The Creative Writing Handbook*
GOOD YEAR BOOKS

*Verbal Review and Workbook for the SAT*
HARCOURT BRACE JOVANOVICH

$J$ay Amberg is the author of twelve books. He has taught high school and college students since 1972. Contact him at jayamberg.com.

Made in the USA
Lexington, KY
09 November 2019